For Lucy, my shining light.
With all my love.

Acknowledgements

The author is only the start of a book. So many other people are involved once the story has left my head. I'd like to thank, sincerely, Oli Munson, my agent extraordinaire, my brilliant and insightful and lovely editors Selina Walker and Georgina Hawtrey-Woore for believing and making things even better, Dan Balado for seeing things I couldn't, Richard Ogle for a beautiful cover, and the entire team at Century and Arrow from publicity to marketing to sales and beyond — I am so very grateful for all your hard work. Big thanks also to my publishers around the world for spreading the words.

Finally, my love to Terry, Ben, Polly and Lucy. Thanks for being a part of it. Couldn't do it without you!

Prologue

I've always wanted a baby, even when I was little and didn't know where they came from. It's been an ache deep in my soul for as long as I can remember — a sickness, a malignant desire creeping through my body, winding its way around my veins, twisting along the billions of nerve pathways, wrapping up my brain in a hormone-fogged desire. All I wanted was to be a mother.

A little baby girl. Is that too much to ask?

It's funny and makes me embarrassed to remember now. As a kid, I used to wish and wish with screwed-up eyes, summoning all the magic I could through clenched teeth and tight fists, concocting an imaginary magic powder from my mother's pink-smelling talc and a tube of silver glitter. I sprinkled it over Tiny Tears, holding my breath for the moment she would come to life — my pain-free, virgin labour lasting all of three minutes.

Yes, it makes me laugh now. Makes me want to smash things.

I remember the dusty halo of sparkly powder falling to the carpet in a disappointing drift when I gently poked the inanimate plastic doll. Why wasn't she breathing? Why wasn't she alive? Why hadn't the magic powder, or God, or my special powers — *anything* — made my dolly real? She was still cold plastic and as good as dead. How I sobbed when she just lay there, unmoving and rigid in my arms, swaddled in a knitted blanket. What about all the love I had given her over the years — the longest gestation on record? Didn't that count for anything? I wanted to snatch her from toy-box-land into real life so I could be her mummy. Didn't she want to be mine? Didn't she want to be loved and fed and rocked and played with and gazed at and cherished above anything else? Didn't she love me back?

I must have tried the magic powder a hundred times. Each time was a failure, like some kind of useless, waste-of-money IVF — not that I knew what that was back then. By the time I was twelve years old, I'd pulled Tiny Tears's head off and pushed it into the glowing coals of the living-room fire when no one was looking. She drizzled into the ash pan. Her eyes melted last, each one staring up at me in a different dizzy-blue direction.

Stupid molten baby.

'If anyone's going to give me grandchildren, it'll be you,' Mum always used to say as her right cheek twitched a feverish dance. I prayed I wouldn't let her down. Mum wasn't the kind of person who took kindly to disappointment. She'd had too much of it in her life to be lenient with it any more.

'Sissy' was what my older sister called me. The name had stuck when she couldn't pronounce my real one. There are only eighteen months between us in age, and being the only live babies our mother had, we were driven closer still by her smothering. Apart from us, there were eight miscarriages, three stillbirths and a little brother who died from meningitis aged two. I was the youngest — *lucky last.*

'We nearly lost you, too,' she reminded me regularly, as if losing children was what everyone did. She was sitting on the old bench, caught up in the dangling red creeper, crunching her tablets and chain smoking. She looked on fire.

Telling me how I survived against the odds should have made me feel special, as though I was her clever near-miss who had somehow broken the spell, like I shouldn't really be there at all but by good luck; by huge sprinklings of magic powder, here I was. Breathing and alive.

In contrast, Pa was a quiet, unassuming man, who ate his food leaning against the sink, watching the three women in his life, winking at me when the wretched guilty feeling about my existence squeezed tears from my virtually dry eyes. I felt sorry for all my dead brothers and sisters, as if I'd pushed in and taken their places. Pa forked up his mashed potato, a ciggie tucked behind his ear for afters, and always with those lines of coal dust circling his throat. Pa loved me. Pa stroked my hair when Mum wasn't looking. Pa had been dying for as long as I could remember.

The dirty circles were still round his neck when I peeked into his coffin as a virtually mute fifteen-year-old. The tattooed necklace from years down the mines (lung cancer and emphysema to boot, my mother proudly told everyone) was the only thing I recognised about him. At the wake, I overheard Mum talking to

Aunty Diane about the likelihood of Pa having gone to heaven and becoming a baby again. Mum was into all that crazy spiritual stuff and went to see a medium before Pa's body was even cold. Usually Aunty Diane would humour Mum during her 'less-than-normal times', as she called them, to make her feel better. But now, I think it was just to make me and my sister feel better, to make us believe that everything was all right when it wasn't. 'Your mother's as loopy as a box of weasels,' she told us once. After that, I wished Aunty Di was our real mother.

Later, in the bath, I scattered the remains of my old magic talc mixture all over my tummy, pretending it was my poor Pa's ashes, praying he would somehow be absorbed into my eggs, my womb, become a baby and not be dead at all. All I'd ever wanted was to take care of something. I figured it was the next best thing to being taken care of. Better than anything, though, I knew it would make Mum happy to have Pa alive again — even if he was born a little girl.

Having a baby, I decided, would be my life's mission.

1

'Someone's replied to our advert.' I peer over my laptop lid, making a semi-pained face. Part of me had been hoping no one would answer, that I could somehow manage alone. The heat of the computer is cooking my legs but I can't be bothered to move. It's work and a winter-warmer rolled into one.

'You shouldn't have that thing so close, you know.' James taps the screen as he walks past on his way to the cupboard. He pulls out the wok. 'Radiation and all that.' I love him for cooking, for caring.

'The scan says she's got all her arms and legs. Stop worrying.' I've shown him the ultrasound pictures a dozen times. He's missed all my scans so far. 'We have a healthy little baby girl on the way.' I shift uncomfortably and put the computer on the old saggy sofa beside me. 'Aren't you interested in who's replied to the advert?'

'Of course I am. Tell me.' James splashes oil in the pan. He's a messy cook. The ring of blue flames leaps into life as he turns the gas burner to high. He bites his lower lip and tosses pieces of chicken into the wok. The smoke gets sucked up into the extractor fan.

'Someone called Zoe Harper,' I say above the sizzling noise. I read the details in the email again. 'It says she's got loads of experience and has all the right qualifications.' I will phone her

5

later, get a feel for how she sounds. I must show willing even though the thought of a stranger in the house isn't a particularly pleasant one. I know how worried James is about me coping when he goes away again. He's right, of course. I am going to need help.

Our nanny chatter is suddenly interrupted by noise and fuss and screaming coming from the sitting room. I heave myself up from the sofa, legs apart and hands wedged in the small of my back to stop my spine giving way. I raise my hands to halt James's rescue dash. 'It's OK, I'll go.' He seems to think I'm incapable of anything since he's been home. Probably because last time he saw me I didn't resemble a house.

'Oscar, Noah, what's going on?' I stand in the sitting-room doorway. The boys look up at me. Forlorn, they have been sprung in the early stages of war. Oscar has something crusty and yellow stuck in the corner of his mouth. Noah is brandishing his brother's toy gun.

I only let them play with toys like that when James is home. He doesn't see the problem. Other times, they're locked away in a cupboard. Toy weapons were a hot topic at that dreadful dinner party, a few years ago now, not long after I'd met James. I'd wanted all his friends to like me, to not make comparisons, to trust that I had my own set of maternal instincts when it came to bringing up my newly-inherited sons.

'How do you handle things like that with the twins, Claudia?' she'd asked me, when I stated I didn't like to see children playing with swords and guns. God knows, in my job I see enough messed-up kids to know that there are better things they could be doing with their time. 'Must be hard being a mother ... but not *being* one,' she finished. I could have slapped her.

'Come here, Os,' I say, and do the unthinkable. I lick a tissue and wipe his mouth. He wriggles away. I eye the gun in Noah's hand. Taking it away from him would cause a major incident.

At the dinner party, I'd feebly explained that as step-mother to twin boys who'd lost their birth mum to cancer, I believed it pretty much gave me the right to call myself their mother — but no one really cared or was listening by then. The topic had moved on. 'James is in the Navy,' I heard myself saying, 'so of course they're fascinated by wars ... it's not taboo as such in our house but ... ' I was burning crimson by that point. I just wanted James to take me home.

'Give the gun back to your brother, Noah. Did you snatch it?'

Noah doesn't reply. He holds up the plastic weapon, aims it at my belly and pulls the trigger. There's a weak crack of plastic as it play-fires. 'Bang. Baby's dead,' he says with a toothy grin.

* * *

'They're asleep. Kind of,' James says. He's wearing his favourite sweater, the one he doesn't know I take to bed with me when he's away. And he's got a glass of wine. Lucky him on a Friday night. I've got peppermint tea and a pain in my

7

lower back. I'm convinced my ankles look swollen today.

He sits down beside me on the sofa. 'So, what did she sound like, this Mary Poppins woman?' An arm goes around my shoulders, fingers twirling the ends of my hair.

While he was tucking the boys into bed — drunkenly singing Aerosmith's 'Janie's Got a Gun' but putting the names Oscar and Noah in instead — I'd phoned Zoe Harper, the woman who replied to our advert.

'She sounded . . . fine.' I say it rather flippantly because I hadn't expected her to sound fine at all. 'Lovely, in fact. To be honest, I was hoping she'd sound like a witch and be slurring from booze.' The thing is, I've tried two nannies before and, one way or another, they weren't exactly what they claimed to be. Besides, the boys didn't take to having them around at all. So between understanding friends, day-care and, more recently, school breakfast and afternoon clubs, we've somehow managed to cope. James thoroughly advocates them being cared for in their own home while I'm at work and, now our own baby's nearly due, he wants things more settled.

'But she really didn't,' I say, watching his expression change to one of hope. 'Sound like a witch, that is.' What with James away at sea for weeks or even months at a time and me trying to cram a demanding job into hours that often aren't regular, I was tearing my hair out with guilt. I wanted to be the best mother I could but not give up my career. That was one thing I'd promised myself when I took on this ready-made family. I love my job, it's who I am. I guess I wanted it all, and now I'm paying the price.

'Yes, she sounded perfectly normal and down to earth.'

We sit in silence for a moment, both pondering the reality of what we've done — the advertisement took up several nights of deliberation. I don't think we ever considered the reality of what came after that: actually having someone live with us again.

'Oh God, but what if she's like the last two? It's not fair on the boys. Or the baby. Or me.' I shift my bump so I can curl my legs up on the sofa.

'Nanny-cam?' James says. He pours another glass of wine.

'Give me a sniff,' I say, leaning over, desperate for a sip.

'Fumes,' he says, holding the glass away from me and covering it with his other hand. I slap him on the shoulder and grin. It's only because he cares.

'But I need fumes. Nanny-cam? You're not serious, right?'

'Of course I am. Everyone does it.'

'Buggering hell, they do. It's a violation of . . . of their human nanny rights or something. Besides, what do you want me to do? Sit staring at my computer all day watching the boys play Lego while nanny feeds the baby? Kind of defeats the point of having her, doesn't it?'

'Give up work, then,' he says in his faint-but-serious voice.

'Oh, James,' I say, hardly believing he's trying that one again. 'Let's not go there.' A hand on his thigh is warning enough as he shrugs and turns the telly up. It's *Children's Hospital*. The last thing I want to watch is sick kids but there's nothing much else on.

I consider the nanny-cam idea. I suppose it could work.

Suddenly Oscar is standing frozen in the doorway for effect (he does it so well) — tiny boy in dramatic period setting with blood pouring from his nose. He doesn't even attempt to contain the flow. His Ben 10 pyjamas look theatrical.

'Oh, darling Ossy,' I say. No point me moving. James is up quickly with a handful of tissues plucked from the box on the table as he goes. 'Not again.'

James swipes our son up and plants him on the sofa next to me. He goes off to fetch ice, and Oscar leans on me for a cuddle. He rests his head on my bump and blood gets on my old T-shirt.

'Baby says she loves you, Ossy,' I tell him. He looks up at me with big blue eyes and a murderous bloody nose. James comes back with a pack of frozen peas. 'Tea towel?' I say, not wanting to put them on Oscar's skin directly. James nods and goes off to get one.

'How can she love me? She doesn't even know me.' He sounds all bunged up.

'Well . . . '

James returns again. I wrap the peas in the tea towel and hold it against the bridge of Oscar's

10

little nose while also pinching it gently. The GP says if it keeps happening it'll need to be cauterised. 'She loves you, I guarantee it. It's instinctive, built-in. Babies come with their own love and she already knows we love her.'

'Noah doesn't love her,' Oscar says from beneath the peas. 'He says he hates her and wants to shoot her off the planet.'

Even though it's just Noah, my little son-by-proxy, I flinch inside. 'He's perhaps a bit jealous, that's all. He'll be fine when she's born, you see.' I glance over Oscar's head and catch James's eye. We each pull a face, wondering what delights are in store with three under-fives, and then I'm fretting about getting them used to a new nanny again. Perhaps it would be easier if I did give up work.

'Now, let's see how things are going here.' I lift the bag of peas and peel away the red sodden tissue. The bleeding seems to have stopped.

'As I was saying,' I continue when Oscar's tucked up in bed, 'Zoe Harper sounded . . . lovely.' Other adjectives evade me. 'No, really.' I chuckle when James pulls a face. 'Oh God, I don't know.' I run my hands over my tummy. 'She's worked in Dubai and London apparently.'

'How old?' James's breath smells all winey. I want to kiss him.

'Thirty-something, I suppose. I didn't actually ask.'

'That was smart. She could be twelve.'

'Give me some bloody credit, James. I'm going to put her through the mangle, turn her hide inside out and then re-mangle her again. By the time I've finished with her I'll know more about her than she knows about herself.'

'I just don't understand why you're bothering to go back to work at all. It's not as though we need the money.'

This is the point at which I laugh. A good belly laugh. 'Oh, James.' I shift myself sideways and press up against him. I kiss his neck. 'You've known the deal from the start. We wanted a baby but I also love my work. Am I selfish to want everything?' I kiss him again and this time he turns his head and reciprocates, but it's so very hard for us. He knows the deal. Doctor's orders and I'm sticking to them this time. 'Anyway, everything would go to hell in a handcart in the department if I stopped working completely. We're understaffed as it is.'

'I thought Tina was running things while you're away?'

I shake my head, starting to feel stressed. 'Everyone's sharing out my caseload while I'm on maternity leave, but when the baby and the boys are settled, I'll want to go back. At least if I work up to my due date, I'll have more time at home with the baby after she's born.'

Sensing my anxiety, James cups my face and plants a smacker on my mouth. It's a warm kiss and says: I won't mention it again and, more importantly, I won't pressure you for sex.

'Anyway, Zoe Harper, nanny extraordinaire, is coming for coffee tomorrow morning at eleven.' I grin.

'Fine,' James says, switching the channel to

Sky News. He starts hoovering up all the stock market stuff and moans about his pension and investments. I can't really see that far ahead — being old, retiring, needing to draw off James's inherited pot. I can only see as far as the end of this pregnancy, having my baby, being a complete family. Becoming a real mother, finally.

2

I'm going to be late. I feel the frown chiselling into my face as the freezing air bites at my skin. I can't afford to be late. I need this job badly and it's not an option to fail. God, no one knows how much I need this position with James and Claudia Morgan-Brown. Get them — double-barrelled and all big-housed in Edgbaston. I pedal harder. I'm going to be a sweaty red mess when I arrive. Who decided cycling was a good idea? Was it to impress them with my love of the outdoors, my penchant for green transport, my love of exercise that I'll no doubt impart to their offspring? Or perhaps it'll just make them think I'm an idiot for arriving at an interview on a bike.

'St Hilda's Road,' I say over and over, squinting at road signs. I wobble as I stick out my arm to turn right. A car honks as I dither and waver in the middle of the road. 'Sorry!' I yell, although it doesn't look like the kind of neighbourhood where one yells. It's a far cry from my place . . . my *last* place.

I pull over to the kerb and take a bit of paper from my pocket. I check the address and cycle on. I pedal past two more streets and turn left into their street. The houses were big before but they're massive down St Hilda's Road. Imposing Georgian buildings sit squarely in their own grounds either side of the tree-lined street.

14

Gentlemen's residences, they'd be called by estate agents.

James and Claudia's house is, like all the others, a detached period property, the lower half of which is being strangled by a twiggy Virginia creeper. I'm no gardener but I recognise it from my childhood home, which incidentally would have fitted twenty times inside this place. The creeper still has a few scarlet leaves clinging on even though it's mid-November. I wheel my bicycle through a huge pair of open wrought-iron gates. Gravel crunches beneath my feet. I have never felt so conspicuous.

The Morgan-Brown residence is a symmetrical house built of red brick. The front door, surrounded by a stone portico, is painted shiny green. Either side of the impressive entrance are large stained-glass windows. I don't know what to do with my bike. Should I just lie it down on the gravel at the bottom of the front steps? It'll make the diamond-shaped rose beds and the neat squares of lawn set into the sweeping parking area look like a scrapyard. I glance around. There's a tree just outside the main gates. I quickly go back out onto the street. Its roots are pushing up and splitting the tarmac like a mini earthquake and the trunk is too big to get my security chain around. I walk along the pavement a bit further, wheeling my bike, and notice that there's another, smaller drive down the side of the house leading to a triple garage. I tentatively enter the property again, feeling as if dozens of eyes are staring out at me from the windows, watching my silly, incompetent arrival.

I still don't know what to do with my bike. It looks too shiny and new for someone who's meant to cycle everywhere. I decide that resting it against the side wall of the garage, out of view from the street and house, will have to do. I'm careful not to scrape the handlebars down the side of the massive four-wheel-drive or the BMW that sit side by side.

I take a deep breath and finger my hair into some kind of style again. I wipe the sweat from my face with my sleeve. I walk back to the front door and knock three times on the huge brass upside-down fish knocker. Its mouth gapes open at me.

I don't have to wait long. A small child pulls the door open as if it's taking all his strength. The little boy is almost see-through pale, about hip height, with shaggy mousey-blonde hair. One of my charges, I assume. They're twins apparently.

'What?' he says rudely.

'Hello.' I crouch down like nannies do. I smile. 'My name's Zoe and I've come to see your mummy. Is she here?'

'My mummy's in heaven,' he says, trying to close the door. I should have brought sweets or something.

Before I can decide whether to push against him and risk a tussle with the kid or revert to knocking with the fish again, a beautiful woman is looming over us. Her belly is enormous and pushes out from beneath a black stretchy top. It's right in front of my face. I can't take my eyes off it. 'You must be Zoe,' she says. Her voice is just

16

as lovely as the rest of her. It jolts me back to reality. The smile she gives me makes a fan of tiny lines on the outside of each eye as well as two dimples in her cheeks. She looks like the friendliest woman in the world.

I stand up and hold out my hand. 'Yes, and you must be Mrs Morgan-Brown.'

'Oh, call me Claudia, please. Come in.' She grins.

Claudia steps aside and I go into the house. It smells of flowers — there's a vase of lilies on the hall table — but mostly it smells of burnt toast.

'Let's go and get comfy in the kitchen. There's coffee.' Claudia beckons me on with her smile and her burgeoning belly. The kid that opened the door trots between us, glancing up at me as we walk along the black-and-white chequerboard tiled floor. He's got a toy gun tucked into the waist of his trousers.

We go into the kitchen. It's huge.

'Darling, Zoe's here.'

A man looks up from behind *The Times*. Good-looking, I suppose, as they all appear to be in this family.

'Hello,' I say, sounding as cheery as I can.

There is a moment's hesitation between us.

'Hi, I'm James. Good to meet you.' He stands briefly and offers me his hand.

Claudia gives me a coffee that's magically come from a shiny machine that looks impossible to use — a machine I'll no doubt have to operate if I get the job. I take a sip and look around, trying not to gawp. It's an impressive kitchen. Where I live . . . nearly *don't* live . . . has a kitchen the size of a cupboard. No room for a dishwasher or any fancy appliances, but then I remind myself it's just the two of us and it hardly takes any time at all to swill a couple of plates and a saucepan through.

This kitchen, though, it takes my breath away. Great big Georgian windows rise from behind the double Belfast sink affording a view down a garden that's far too huge to be in a city. There are cream-painted cupboards spanning three sides of the room with a red Aga as big as a car set into the old chimney breast. Wooden worktops the same honey colour as the old wooden floor give it a country feel. Up this end of the room, near the pine table, there's a saggy old sofa piled with cushions and a rucked-up rather grubby throw. It's littered with Lego pieces.

James folds his newspaper and shifts over. I sit down next to him. He smells of soap. There's no room for Claudia but she drags a chair over from the table. 'I'm better perched on this,' she remarks. 'It takes a crane to haul me out of that old thing.'

A moment's silence.

Then there are two little boys skittering at our feet. Both identical. They are squabbling over a plastic toy.

'Oscar,' James says wearily, 'give it up.'

I'm not sure why he should. He had it first.

'So,' I say when the din has subsided, 'you'll want to know all about my experience.' I have it all prepared, learnt off pat. Right down to the colour of my last employer's eyes and the engine size of their car. Greeny-brown and two point five litres. I am ready for anything.

'How many families have you worked for?' Claudia asks.

'Four in total,' I reply easily. 'The shortest term was three years. I only left because they went to live in Texas. I could have gone with them but preferred to stay in England.' Good. She's looking impressed.

'Why did you leave your last job?' James pipes up. First bit of interest he's shown. He's probably leaving the decision-making to his wife so he doesn't get it in the neck if they end up with a nanny fresh from hell.

'Ah,' I say with a confident smile. 'Nannies tend to get made redundant when the kids grow up.'

Claudia laughs but James doesn't.

I was careful to dress down for this morning — sensible tapered trousers for cycling, kind of rust colour, and a high-necked grey T-shirt with a pleasant primrose-yellow cardigan over it. Short and slightly mussed-up hair — trendy but not overly so. No rings. Just my silver heart necklace. It was a special gift. I look nice. Nanny-about-town nice.

'I was with the Kingsleys for five years. Beth and Tilly were ten and eight when I arrived. When the youngest went off to boarding school aged thirteen they didn't need me any more. Mrs Kingsley, *Maggie*, said I was worth having another baby for.' I put in her first name because that's obviously how Claudia likes things to be. First-name terms.

19

The way her hands rest gently on her swollen stomach . . . it's killing me.

'So how long have you been unemployed?' James asks rather bluntly.

'I don't see myself as unemployed exactly. I left the Kingsley house in the summer. They took me to their place in the south of France as a good-bye treat then I went on a short but intensive course in Italy at a Montessori centre.' I wait for the reaction.

'Oh, James. I've always said we should get the boys registered at a Montessori school.'

'It was an amazing experience,' I say. 'I can't wait to put into practice what I learnt.' I make a mental note to re-read the Montessori information.

'Does it help with four-year-old delinquent boys?' James asks with a smirk.

I can't help a little laugh. 'Definitely.' Then, right on cue, I'm showered with a bunch of wax crayons. I try not to flinch. 'Hey, are you trying to colour me in?' The twin from the front door — I only know this because of the green top he's wearing — hisses at me through gritted teeth. He grabs a couple of crayons from the floor and hurls them at me from point-blank range.

'Pack it in, Noah,' his father says, but the boy pays no attention.

'Have you got any paper?' I ask, ignoring the sting on my cheek.

'I'm so sorry,' Claudia says. 'I'd say they're feisty, not delinquent as such. And it's just Noah who's occasionally challenging.'

'Birth troubles,' James adds quietly as the boys

fight over who's going to fetch the pad of paper.

I look at Claudia and wait for her to tell me. I know it all anyway.

'Not *my* birth troubles,' she begins with a fond swipe of a hand across her belly. Then, in a whisper, 'The twins aren't mine. I mean, they are, of course, but I'm not their biological mother. Just so you know.'

'Oh. OK. That's fine.'

'My first wife died of cancer when the boys were two months old. Came out of nowhere and swept the life from her.' He raises his hands at my sudden pained expression. 'Nope. It's OK.'

I switch to a little sympathetic purse of my lips and a respectfully low flick of my gaze. It's all that's needed. 'Hey, well done, you,' I say as Noah races back to me flapping a pad of paper. 'Now, why don't you have a race to see who can collect the most crayons off the floor? Then it's a competition to see who can draw the best picture of me. Right?'

'Wight!' says Oscar. He jumps up and down with excitement. His cheeks turn pink.

Noah stands staring at me for a second — unnerving, I have to say — and then quite calmly he tears a piece of paper from the pad. 'For you, Oscar.' And he gives it to his brother.

'Good boy,' I say. 'Now, off you go and I want to see them both when you're finished!'

The twins shuffle off in their silly slippers — characters from some cartoon or other — and settle down at the table with the crayons. Oscar asks his brother for the blue. Noah hands it over.

'I'm impressed,' James says reluctantly.

21

'Pure distraction with a bit of healthy sibling competition thrown in for good measure.'

'We're looking for someone to live in Monday to Friday, Zoe. Would that be a problem?' Claudia's cheeks have turned coral, making me imagine I've touched my thumb to them, a little smudge of powder blush. The heat of pregnancy.

'That wouldn't be a problem at all.' I think of the flat, of everything contained in it. Then I think of living here. My heart flutters so I take a deep breath. 'I can totally understand why you'd need someone on hand all hours during the week.' If I'm honest, the timing of this job is perfect.

'But you could go home at weekends,' she says.

My heart sinks, though I don't show my disappointment. I must fit in with what they want. 'I could disappear on Friday evening and reappear magically on Monday morning. But I can stay weekends too if you need me.' An answer to satisfy for now, I hope. In reality, it won't work like this. I can't help believing in fate.

'Look!' Noah calls out. He flaps a piece of paper in my direction.

'Ooh, keep it a secret until you're finished,' I tell him, and turn back to his parents. 'When I take a job I like to become part of the family but to keep my distance too, if you know what I mean. I'm here if you need me, vanished if you don't.'

Claudia nods her approval.

'I'm away at sea much of the time,' James

22

informs me. He doesn't need to. 'I'm a Naval officer. A submariner. You'll mainly be dealing with Claudia.'

You'll mainly be dealing with . . . as if I already have the job in his mind.

'Do you want to look around the house? See what you'd be letting yourself in for?' Claudia is standing, hands on the back of her hips in that typical pregnant-woman pose. I make a point of not staring at her bump.

'Sure.'

We start downstairs and Claudia leads me from one room to another. They are all grand and some don't look like they're ever used. 'We don't use this one very often,' she says as we enter the dining room, echoing my thought. 'Just at Christmas, on special occasions. When friends come for supper we usually eat in the kitchen.' The room is cold and has a long shiny table with twelve carved dining chairs set around it. There's an ornate fireplace, intricate plaster cornices, and a chandelier in dusky hues of violet hangs centrally. It's a beautiful room but not at all cosy.

We cross the chequerboard hallway again.

'And the boys, well, they don't come in this room very often.' Not allowed to, she means. She shows me a large room with sumptuous cream sofas. No television, just lots of old paintings on the walls and antique tables with glass dishes and lamps set upon them. I imagine the twins wearing their muddiest shoes, leaping from sofa to sofa, brandishing large sticks, while the ornaments go flying and the paintings rip. I stifle the smile.

23

'And we watch telly in here,' she says as we move into the next room. 'It gets really warm and snug when the fire's lit.' Claudia holds the door open and I peek in. I see big purple sofas and a thick furry rug. One wall is lined with bookshelves, overflowing with paperbacks. I imagine reading with the boys in here, waiting for Claudia to get home, running her a bath, wondering about her due date. I will be the perfect nanny.

'And then there's the playroom.' She hesitates, hand on door knob. 'Sure you want to go in? It's usually a bit of a zoo.'

'Very nice,' I say, stepping past Claudia. This is where I must shine. 'Excellent. You have loads of Lego. I love it. And look at all their books. I insist on reading to my children at least three times a day.' I'd better be careful. Claudia is looking at me as if I'm almost too perfect.

Upstairs an array of bedrooms spans off the galleried landing. I peek into the guest suite, and then she shows me the boys' room. They share. The room is tidy. Two single beds with scarlet and blue duvets, a big rug printed with grey roads and flat houses, and, over in the corner, a couple of cages with, I suppose, hamsters or mice inside.

'We have a cleaner who comes in three times a week. You wouldn't need to do any of that.'

I nod. 'I don't mind doing bits and pieces around the house but I prefer to spend my time caring for the children.'

'Come up and see your rooms then.'

Your rooms.

Another flight of stairs takes us to the top floor. It's not an attic of the dusty-full-of-boxes kind but the sort with sloping ceilings, beams and old country-style furniture. A battered white-painted chest stands on the small landing. The floor is covered with sisal and patchwork hearts hang from the doors that lead off the area.

'There are three rooms up here. A small bedroom, a living room and a bathroom. You're welcome to eat with us in the kitchen. Use it as your own.'

Your own.

'It's beautiful,' I say. 'Very homely.' It's like something out of an interiors magazine and not really my style, if I'm honest.

'You'll get a bit of peace up here. I'll make it a no-fly zone for the boys.'

'Oh, that's not necessary. We could have fun up here.' I check out the rooms again, stepping into each like an excited kid. The bedroom has a sloping ceiling and a little window overlooking the garden, while the bathroom has a roll-top bath and an old-fashioned loo. 'I love it,' I say, desperate for her to know I like it without giving away my virtual homelessness.

Back in the kitchen, where James is behind the newspaper again, Claudia hands me a list. It spans two pages. 'Something for you to take away and consider,' she says. 'A list of duties and things we expect. Plus those we don't.'

'A great idea,' I say. 'There's no chance of confusion then,' I add, thinking that however many lists she writes, whatever ground-rules and job descriptions she dreams up, they'll all seem rather futile in the long run. 'I'm always open to suggestions from my families. I like to have a weekly meeting with parents to discuss how the children are doing, stuff like that.'

Then the twins are leaping about at my side like a pair of yapping terriers.

'See mine, see mine!'

'No, mine!'

'Look what you've started,' Claudia says with a laugh but then suddenly stretches her hands round her lower back. She leans against the worktop and grimaces.

'Are you OK, darling?' James makes to get up but Claudia wafts her hands at him, mouthing *I'm fine*.

'Let me see then. Hmm. In this picture I look like an alien with huge pink lips and no hair. And in this one I think I'm half human and half horse with a mane down to the ground.'

'Nooo!' the boys chant in unison. They giggle, and Noah shoves Oscar. He stands his ground. 'Which one, which one's the best?'

'I love them equally. You are brilliant artists and both winners. Can I keep them?'

The boys nod in awe and their mouths hang open, exposing tiny teeth. They run off happily and I hear a waterfall of Lego as an entire box is tipped out in the playroom.

'I think you're a hit,' Claudia says. 'Are there any questions you'd like to ask me?'

'Yes,' I reply, unable to help the glance at her bump. It's as if someone's revving the accelerator to my heart. 'When's the baby due?'

It's what I've been dying to ask all along.

3

Detective Inspector Lorraine Fisher had never thrown up on a job before. Leaning against the wall, she wiped her mouth across the back of her hand. She didn't have a tissue.

'Who are you?' she said to a man standing in the flat's tiny hallway. Her throat burned and her expression was sour.

'Will you give me an exclusive statement, Detective? Do you believe this is a murder inquiry?' he said.

'Get him the shit out of here, you idiots, this is a crime scene,' she barked at her colleagues.

A white-suited flurry of activity ensued and it was as if the journalist had never existed.

Lorraine felt another surge rising in the gurgling, disgusted pit of her belly but she knew there was nothing else left inside. She'd not had time for breakfast, skipped lunch, and dinner was looking unlikely. Even that bag of crisps wasn't inside her now.

'I've never seen anything like it,' she said, raising her hand to her forehead. She snapped it back down when she realised the gesture could give the wrong impression to those who didn't know her. Twenty years in the force and nothing this grim or pitifully sad had come her way. As a woman — as a *mother* — she was angered to the core. She pulled the white mask down over her face again and drew in a deep breath — partly

27

for courage and partly so she didn't have to suck in the decaying stench that filled the small bathroom.

It had all taken place in here, she could see that instantly. There was no blood anywhere else in the flat. The ceramic tiles, once white with mouldy grout stretching around the edge of the bath, were spattered and smeared with blood — some of it pinky-red and some of it dark burgundy, almost brown, as it crazed the tiles like some weird piece of congealed art at the Tate Modern.

Sweet Jesus . . . what had gone on in here?

In the basin there was a claw hammer and a kitchen knife. The knife was part of a set from the flat's kitchen. Both were bloodied. The bath tap was dripping every couple of seconds, making a clear river of white one end of the bloodstained plastic bath. The woman lying in it was half naked. The plug was in. The baby was blue and lifeless, its powdery skin mottled and delicate. Finger-shaped bruises decorated its shoulders from when, she supposed, it had been pulled from the womb.

Lorraine stopped herself. *It?* she thought. *It's a boy,* she chastised herself inwardly. *A little baby boy.*

She thought of her own children and glanced at her watch. Stella had a piano exam tomorrow morning and practice hadn't exactly been top of her agenda recently.

She had to think of these things — force her mind to focus on the normal, the everyday, the mundane.

28

Then there was Grace and her damned A levels. She had several exams after Christmas and Lorraine had no idea if she was on track with her work. She made a mental note to find out as she stared at the mess in the bath. Images of her girls as babies flashed through her mind. *It's OK*, she thought. *I'm fine . . . just grounding myself in this fucked-up world.* What didn't seem OK or fine was thinking about her family in the same headspace as whatever shit had done this.

The woman was young. Early to mid-twenties, Lorraine reckoned, though it wasn't easy to tell. Her once-pregnant abdomen had been cut open — quite cleanly, she had to admit — from sternum to pubic bone and was now puckered and deflated. There was still the slightly sweet smell of amniotic fluid swirled up with the metallic tang of blood, but mostly the nauseating stench was from decomposition. The plug was keeping safe whatever secrets the inch or so of viscous liquid contained. It would soon be on its way to the lab for careful analysis.

'He wouldn't have passed his medical exams,' Lorraine said through her mask and over her shoulder. She'd noticed DC Ainsley wobbling in the doorway, his hand clamped over his mouth. 'Wrong way, look.' She indicated with her finger, drawing a line in the air above the body. 'My scar's down low.' She felt compelled to touch it, the neat little opening through which both Stella and Grace had been pulled wriggling and screaming, but she didn't.

Lorraine stared at the woman's death face.

29

Twisted with agony, a bitten tongue lolling, fingers matted with her own hair as she'd torn it out in pain, claw marks down her cheek — this woman had left life in a fit of bloody terror and fear.

'What do we know about her?' Lorraine said, turning away. She had to get out. She felt claustrophobic in the tiny bathroom.

'Sally-Ann Frith,' DC Ainsley said. 'Single mum. Well, she was going to be a single mum,' he corrected. 'We don't know who the partner or father is. Neighbours say a couple of men visited occasionally. That sometimes there was shouting.'

'Keep talking to the neighbours. I want everyone in the building interviewed today,' Lorraine said, pulling on a pair of latex gloves. She walked slowly around the small living room, her eyes dancing over the contents. A patterned sofa, an old telly, a lamp, a fireplace with a few photo frames on the mantelpiece. Beige carpet with a few stains. All normal. There was a small desk in one corner with a laptop and a few papers and text books strewn over it. 'She was some kind of student, by the looks of it,' she said, casting an eye over the books. '*The Basics of Management Accounting*,' she read. 'Sounds like fun.'

'Ray . . . ' There was an urgent voice. 'I got here as soon as I could.'

Lorraine froze, but only for a second. She turned to greet him. 'Hello, Adam,' she said wearily. She'd secretly hoped someone else would have been assigned this one. Having her

30

husband lead a case never got any easier. 'Don't call me that, please.'

'Sorry. *Lorraine*,' he said, knowing full well she hated being called Ray on or off duty. 'Do we know what's happened?' He came right up to her, ignoring the way she tensed. He'd borrowed her new body wash. She could damn well smell it.

'There's a dead woman in the bath. She was pregnant.'

Adam went off to inspect the scene while she carefully lifted a few of the files on the desk. Most were typical student folders and paper files but one was different. It was bound with light grey plastic and had Willow Park Medical Centre printed in silver on the front. The words were topped by an image of a navy-blue willow tree — the surgery's logo. She heard Adam gag in the bathroom.

Lorraine opened the file. The first page contained general details about Sally-Ann. Date of birth, phone numbers, next of kin — someone called Russ Goodall, although she noted that a previous name had been scrubbed out in black pen so comprehensively that she couldn't read it. A previous partner, she wondered? The father?

The next few pages were charts and details of her pregnancy — weight, blood pressure, urine sample results. It all appeared perfectly normal. It was November now and the entries in the file had started in late April, apparently when she'd first visited the GP. Her due date was in two weeks.

Adam came back sweating and extremely pale. 'Jesus.'

'I know,' Lorraine said with heavy eyes. It didn't matter any more. None of it did. They had their girls, their home, their jobs. They were all right, weren't they?

'I'm sorry about earlier, Ray,' Adam said. She heard him forcibly swallow something down. He looked green.

'Yeah,' she said, and knew nothing more would be said about the outburst at breakfast. It had been a pointless tiff, fuelled by family logistics and petty jealousy. 'She was an accounting student,' she continued. She wouldn't even tell him off again for calling her Ray. 'Aged twenty-four. Next of kin is a chap called Russ Goodall. I'll get on to the medical centre.' She held up the file.

'Why would anyone do that to a pregnant woman?' Adam said, shaking his head and staring out of the window.

In the house opposite, a woman was folding sheets in an upstairs room, pretending not to stare across the road where half a dozen police cars were parked and the entire building was cordoned off with crime-scene tape. They needed to speak to her, Lorraine thought. She had a bird's-eye view.

'Someone had made an attempt to cut the umbilical cord. Did you notice?'

Adam nodded. He'd never had a good stomach for mess. She knew he'd need to run at least five miles to get this one out of his head.

'Maybe she went into labour, got into

difficulties and whoever was with her thought they'd be a hero and perform an emergency C-section,' she continued. He picked up one of three cards that were lined up on the window sill. 'It went wrong, they got scared and ran off.'

'Look at this.'

'Good luck! All my love, Russ.' Lorraine let out a sigh. 'No doubt the same Russ as in the medical file.'

'None of the cards actually says what she needs luck for,' he said, placing them back on the sill with gloved hands. 'One's from someone called Amanda and the other's from Sally-Ann's mum.'

'Do you really send good luck cards for giving birth? They could be for something else. A driving test or exams, perhaps.'

'Don't the cards usually come after you've had a baby?' Adam said.

'Are you asking me or telling me?' Lorraine said, feeling something inappropriate welling inside her. 'But then you're not great at sending cards for any reason, are you Adam, especially anniver — '

'Stop.' Adam held up a hand.

He was right. Lorraine was tempted to take hold of his rubber-clad hand but decided against it. In all the years they'd worked together — and God, she'd lost count of those — displays of physical contact or affection while on duty were their own personal no-no. It often came as a surprise to colleagues who didn't know them well that they were even married. Different surnames, regular bickering, and Lorraine

33

refusing to wear a wedding ring all pointed to them having nothing to do with each other outside of work. And inside it they often went out of their way to avoid each other. It was only the big cases — cases like Sally-Ann's — where they knew they'd be joining forces and combining decades of experience.

'They could be 'good luck for the operation' cards.' Lorraine was delving into the medical file again. She'd missed it first time round.

'What operation?' Adam said, joining her at the desk. He'd definitely been using her bloody Acqua di Parma body wash at nearly thirty quid a pop. He'd be shampooing the carpet with it next.

'This one,' she said, planning on hiding the stuff later. She'd only wanted a little treat, something to make her feel half an ounce special. Lorraine pointed to the neat handwriting in the top margin of the page. It was the same as the writing on the student folders — Sally-Ann's, they supposed.

Adam read out the jottings. 'Caesarean. Eighteenth November. Arrive before eight a.m. Dr Lamb. Bradley Ward. Pack bag.'

'That's tomorrow,' Lorraine said, staring at her husband. 'Except someone else got there first.'

4

Her bedroom's finally ready. I've made it as homely as I can. Oscar and Noah are fighting over whose teddy she will want on her bed. 'I think she might be too old for a teddy,' I tell them. They don't agree.

I'm exhausted. Even making up a bed does me in these days. At this rate, I wonder if I'll ever get my body back. James offered to help me, of course, but I told him it would be better if he entertained the boys. Clearly he didn't succeed as they've been snapping round my ankles the last hour, flopping onto the duvet with wafts of giggles as I wrestled it into the pretty pink-and-cream flowery cover. I'm pleased with how the room looks, and the living room. I want her to be comfortable, even though I'm a little nervous about her arrival. It's taken a lot to get my head round having a nanny again.

'How's it going, darling?' Just as I'm thinking about him and that awful, imminent date marked on the calendar when he goes away again, James comes up the top flight of stairs — two at a time by the sound of it — to see how I'm getting on. 'It looks super. She'll love it.' He's only been home for a fortnight this time.

'I hope so,' I say thoughtfully. He puts his arms round me and attempts a kiss but I'm too knackered even for cuddles. I flop down into the rocking chair. 'Ouch,' I say, grabbing my bump.

'Careful with her,' he says, giving me a tentative rub on the belly. He's been fussing over me from the minute I told him I was pregnant. Not surprising, really. He's not had the chance to grow with me and therefore get used to my new shape, the preciousness of it or even the resilience of it. I think it disorientates him, me being so huge, so incapable of doing all the things I used to, though he'd never say it. He's very respectful and we follow doctor's orders to the letter. My friend Pip says her husband adores her pregnant body and can't get enough of her. I guess, considering everything, James is being ultra-cautious and I appreciate that. I miss him though. I miss *us*.

'Counting the days 'til we can,' I say, and blow him a silent kiss over the boys' heads as they kick the teddy around the room. He knows what I mean. 'Oh, I forgot the towels,' I say, thinking of the trek down and up the stairs.

'Take a break now. I came up to tell you I've made supper.'

'You have?' Hence the boys not being entertained, I suppose, but I can't complain. When he's home, James is the perfect husband and father. He's a real Navy man but he also loves nothing more than pottering about at home. The two halves of his life couldn't be more dissimilar. 'Yes, Lieutenant Commander,' I say, snapping a quick salute. I can't stand to see him in his uniform, even though it's the sexiest thing he owns. It means only one thing — that he's off to sea again.

'Come on.' James hauls me out of the chair by

the hands. 'Let's get you two fed.' He grins and strokes his baby.

It's incredibly hard for him, too. I knew what I was letting myself in for when we married; knew what I was taking on. My friends said I was mad, that being mum to two baby boys who'd lost their birth mother just a few months before was crazy enough, let alone getting hitched to a Naval officer who was away from home two thirds of the year.

'Well, I really hope Zoe likes working here,' I say, flicking off the lights to her quarters. It was a joint decision to hire her although I feel utterly responsible for whether it works out or not.

'Time will tell,' James says, and he leads me down to the most glorious smell of chicken basking in a white wine and fresh thyme sauce.

★   ★   ★

I yawn. It's early and I didn't sleep well last night. I'm too huge and not used to having someone else beside me. Plus I was sweltering in my thick winter pyjamas. Poor James was woken with every toss and lumbering turn of my body as I tried to get comfortable so I quickly retreated to the spare room. After midnight, he tapped on the door, saying he couldn't sleep either. He was trying his luck, even though he knows it's hopeless and we can't.

'Just a cuddle then,' he complained through the door.

'Oh James,' I replied, and the ensuing silence sent him back to our bed alone.

When he returned from his last mission two weeks ago, I showed him once again the letter from my obstetrician spelling out the strict rules, 'no sex' included. 'It's serious,' I told him. 'You know my history. I won't do anything to put this baby at risk.' His expression nearly killed me. I hated lying to him. I'd not really told him everything about my previous losses because talking about them was so hard. 'Shore leave or not, we can't risk it,' I insisted. 'Not long now.'

$$\star \quad \star \quad \star$$

The doorbell rings exactly at eight o'clock and there's a mad scramble from the boys to answer it.

I follow them through to the hall. I am swamped by doubt and second thoughts. I'm still in two minds about having a stranger in the house, and also in doubt about my ability to cope alone when the baby arrives. The whole situation makes me feel a bit useless, to be honest.

James and I both agreed over the weekend that Zoe was pretty much perfect. We offered her the job at lunchtime on Monday once I'd had a chance to check out all her references and done an hour's worth of Googling to see if there were any Zoe Harper horrors lurking online. I found nothing. Her referees couldn't speak highly enough of her. When I phoned her, she was over the moon and said she could start Wednesday morning, which actually worked out perfectly because I have an antenatal appointment at ten-thirty today so I've taken the entire morning off work. First up, though, we will take the boys to school together. I want her to meet their teacher.

'Welcome, Zoe,' I say warmly. And there she is on the doorstep, a taxi pulling away and two old-fashioned suitcases at either side of her slim legs. I notice her bicycle leaning against the wall. 'How lovely to see you again.'

'Claudia, really good to see you too,' she says with a big grin. 'And Oscar, Noah . . . hmm.' Then she says it again but the other way round and points to the other twin with a big fake giggle. They love it.

Oscar heaves one of her cases over the doorstep. 'I got muscles,' he says.

'Mine are bigger,' Noah chips back, and drags the other suitcase inside. It instantly falls open and Zoe lunges for it as the contents spill across the tiles.

'Oh, Noah,' I say, 'look what you've done.' Slowly, I join the others in gathering up her belongings. T-shirts, leggings, undies, a couple of books — none of it's very well packed — and then I see it, poking out of a half-zipped-up toiletries bag. God knows I've seen enough of them in my time. A pregnancy testing kit.

Zoe whips it out of sight, cursing her stupid old suitcase and its dodgy catch.

My stomach lurches as I straighten up with the help of the door handle. Surely I must be wrong. I stare at Zoe but she's in deep banter with the boys. She grips a case firmly in each hand and has a canvas satchel slung across her body. She bends from the weight.

A pregnancy testing kit?

* * *

'No, really,' I tell James. 'I saw it clear as day. Unopened. Poking out of her wash bag.'

'Maybe she's just late and wants to make sure.'

He thinks I'm mad, I can tell. 'Or maybe it belongs to a friend . . . yeah, yeah, right.' Then I shut up as I hear her on the stairs.

The boys are like bits of litter in her wake as Zoe sweeps into the kitchen all pink-cheeked and happy. 'It's glorious up there, Claudia. Thank you for making it so nice. We've just been playing tag, hence the breathlessness.'

'And I won!' Noah yells.

'No you didn't, Zoe won.'

'From now on I think we should save tag for the park,' Zoe says. She points to the water filter jug on the counter which somehow never gets put back in the fridge. 'Do you mind?'

I wave my hand for her to carry on. 'Make yourself at home. There's a beautiful park not far away if you want space to charge about.' The boys know the garden is off limits for footballs and bikes. I don't pay the gardener for it to be churned up into a sports pitch.

'Canon Hill Park,' Zoe says between breathy gulps of water. 'I've been researching the neighbourhood.' She rinses her glass and dries it up.

'Wear 'em out as much as you can,' James chips in, moving towards the sink to wash his hands after bringing in the dustbins. I suspect James's casual attitude to having a stranger live with us comes from life on a cramped submarine with dozens of other crew members. Sharing our house is no big deal for him.

'Come on, we have a little bit of time for me to show you where things are, Zoe, then we must head off for school. I used to walk but I tend to drive now.' I resist the urge to pat my tummy. 'James is out later and I'll be off to my appointment and yoga class shortly. Then I'm back in the office for the afternoon. Will you be OK, do you think?' I instantly regret asking.

'Of *course*,' she says, and I almost think she's going to cry with joy. 'This is my *job* and I'm going to *love* it.'

★ ★ ★

I roll up my mat and push it into its bag. I'd never even considered yoga before I became pregnant. It totally focuses my mind, allowing me to forget all the troubles at work for a whole hour. It also takes my mind off my baby's imminent arrival. Can I see myself using meditation and the sun salutation during labour? No, of course not, is the honest answer. I know what it's like to give birth, although this time will be different. But for now it helps calm my mind and gives me something else to think about other than a particularly taxing case at work and the fact that I've left a virtual stranger in charge of my little boys.

'Stop worrying,' Pip says. 'You've done all the

right things and her references checked out, didn't they?'

'I spoke to her last employer myself. She couldn't rate Zoe highly enough. She said she was almost jealous of me having her as they'd become really good friends.'

'There you go then.'

Pip and I waddle towards the door where we wait for the others. It's become a bit of a ritual after the class — stuffing our faces with carrot cake and cappuccino at the coffee shop down the road. Even though I'm really busy at work, it delays going back for another half-hour and makes me feel a bit more like a proper mother.

'I'll have to bring Lilly round to yours for an after-school play-date and get the low-down on her,' Pip continues. 'I can be your spy.'

'You'll see her at school in the mornings, too. I can't tell you what a bonus it'll be having her drop the boys off. I can get to the office by eight now.'

Pip frowns. She began her maternity leave a month ago, and keeps suggesting I should give up work. I will, of course, but I'm not ready yet. 'And what will she do all day long before the baby comes?'

'I've left her a list. There are a hundred mending jobs for her if she's able to sew, then there's the shopping and the boys' washing and ironing. It's bound to be a bit quiet until D-Day but then she'll be rushed off her feet. I'm glad she has this time to settle in.' I hold my stomach as pretty much every pregnant woman does when they're talking about their baby.

'Have you decided on a name yet?'

Four of us are walking down the road towards Brewhaha, each carrying different weights of baby. Pip and I take first prize. We're about the same gestation, give or take a week or two, and we're both carrying girls.

'We're thinking Elsie or Eden at the moment. Going through an E phase.' We laugh. It's freezing today and I pull my cape-like coat around me. Usually I'm complaining I'm too hot.

'Such pretty names,' Pip says, holding open the door. The smell of coffee wafts out of the café.

'So, did we learn anything new in class today?' I ask our little group once we're all seated with too much cake and enough caffeine to induce labour all round.

'It's the breathing techniques that confuse me,' Bismah says. 'I don't know how to concentrate on that while pushing out my baby as well as sucking on gas and air and tearing off my husband's hand.'

'Don't forget screaming for an epidural either,' Fay says. She's probably the most terrified out of all of us. She's very young. At least I have a bit of life experience to suck on. And she's going to be a single mum. I feel sorry for her, hence inviting her along to our coffee meets. She didn't seem to know anyone at the group. I was happy to befriend her.

'So scary to think that within the next five months we'll all have had our babies,' I say.

'Reckon you'll be the first to pop, Claudia,'

43

Pip says. 'You're nearest to your due date. You definitely look as if you're carrying lower than last week.'

A good sign, I hope. I look at Pip's beautiful bump. She won't be far behind.

'I hope we can still all be friends when they're born,' Bismah says. 'I'd like to stay in touch.' Her long nails sink into a piece of moist cake as she picks it up. Her fingers are the same caramel colour as the icing.

Out of all the women at the childbirth classes, I reckon it's Pip I'm most likely to stay in touch with. She's a teacher and, coincidentally, her husband is also away from home a lot. Not nearly as much as James though. We had them round to dinner early on in my pregnancy, not long after I'd met her at the antenatal yoga class. We all had a good evening, but anything couples-based generally proves tricky. The reciprocal invitation arrives and I have to explain how James is half a kilometre under the Atlantic and won't be free for dinner for another two months.

'Do you know if your husband will be there?' Bismah asks me. 'For the birth.'

'I know for a fact he won't be,' I reply. 'Getting pregnant was hard enough so we didn't even bother to plan dates to ensure he'd be on shore leave when she arrives.'

'That's hard,' Bismah says, looking saddened for me.

I don't reply. Instead, I think about what she's said and tuck in to my cake.

★ ★ ★

44

They are pleased to see me at the office, yet slightly disappointed. 'Thought you'd gone and had it,' Mark says. He walks past my desk and drops a file onto it. 'Meantime, while we're all waiting for you to pop, Christine's gone and had another one. I think she's due for an unplanned visit.'

I stare at the file and wonder what is wrong with the woman who keeps bringing babies into the world only to have them removed within days of their birth. Apart from her first, Christine Lowe has not managed to keep one of her offspring in her own arms for much more than a week.

'This is number eight,' I say thoughtfully, scanning the file I know only too well. I try to help them, really I do, but she will never change. I know when I am beat. The best I can do is make sure her babies get the best start we can offer. 'Is she still with the same man?' I forget his name.

'She's confirmed him as the father but he's in prison again,' Mark says matter-of-factly.

'Do you think she stands a chance with him out of the picture?'

Mark lifts one eyebrow up and down a few times, a trick he likes to do if we all go to the pub on a Friday night. I get what he means.

'OK,' I say, and take a deep breath. We know it's hopeless. There are calls to make, paperwork to do, another child to remove from its mother. Sometimes being a social worker feels a little too much like playing God.

5

The house is quiet. The breakfast things are still on the table and the smell of coffee, children and love pervades. My stomach churns from it all. I gather the crockery and tentatively load the dishwasher. Is this my job, I wonder? Claudia said the cleaner comes when she feels like it but as long as she does her ten hours a week, no one cares how or when the house gets cleaned. Her name is Jan, apparently. I wonder if we will get on, if she will get in my way. I make a mental note to get chatty with her, find out when she's likely to be in the house. I don't want anything going wrong.

'I'm just off out then.'

I turn suddenly. I'd forgotten James was still here. He looks awkward in his own house. Earlier, Claudia told me he was in his study catching up on paperwork. I managed to poke my head round the door, take a sneaky peek when he stepped out for a moment. The room has a big leather-topped desk and bookshelves all around. It's decorated with nautical items — pictures of ships, photographs of uniformed men, certificates in frames on the wall, and a white porcelain head with phrenology markings on its skull. It made me smile when I saw the sunglasses balanced on its face. There's also a table made from a ship's wheel set between two armchairs. I imagined James and Claudia sitting there, sipping tea, discussing life. Claudia says he spends a lot of time in the study, which could make things tricky until he leaves.

'Bye,' I say, thinking I should have said something else. I smile and he waits, and then nods and leaves. I think he feels as awkward as I do.

I lean back, pressing my head against the wall. It's time to get on.

★ ★ ★

That afternoon, I set off for school early. Meeting Claudia's closest friends could be useful, and lingering in the school playground is the best way to do it. Besides, it's what a nanny would do. I go on foot, even though Claudia has given me use of a little Fiat tucked away in the garage or, for longer journeys, James's car after he's gone. Besides, it's a pleasant walk. The sun is glimmering through a skim of clouds and there's a nip in the air that will help numb my heart. It's the way it has to be for now.

Perhaps I'll take a detour through the park with the boys on the way home, see if there are any ducks, take a spin on the roundabout. Pretend I'm something resembling a nanny.

I thought I'd be the first to arrive at school, watch the others come into the playground oblivious of me lurking under the tree, figuring out who's who. It's not yet three and school doesn't finish until ten past but there are already several clusters of women gathered together in nattering groups. I hear PTA and plant sales mentioned, something about a boy called Hugh and his dreadful mother. Someone else is moaning about school dinners while another stands alone, clapping her gloved hands together and stamping her feet, self-conscious that she doesn't have anyone to talk to.

I'm pretending to read laminated notices on a board when a woman comes up to me.

'Let me guess,' she says. She has a vague Scottish accent. 'You must be Zoe.'

I turn and force a grin. My eyes flick downwards — I can't help it — and I replace the involuntary action with an even bigger smile. 'I certainly am. Word spreads fast.'

'I'm Pip,' she says. 'A good friend of your boss.' She holds out her hand. I shake it. Her fingers are icy cold.

'You're . . . ' Is it rude to mention it? I can't help it. 'You're pregnant too.'

'Must be something in the water round here,' she says with a lilting laugh. 'There's a whole group of us at the moment.'

The water. I have to hold myself back from slapping the side of my head and saying, *Oh, it's that simple is it? Take a few swigs from a Birmingham tap and you'll be up the duff in no time. Why the hell didn't I think of that one?*

But I don't. I laugh at her little joke and try desperately to think of something normal to say. 'How many children do you have at the school?'

'Just the one. Lilly. She's in the same class as Oscar and Noah. They often play together so if you're up for a bit of after-school chaos one day, we'll have to arrange a visit.'

'I'd like that,' I say. The playground, with its odd-shaped climbing frame and spongy tarmac beneath, its bricked-off area with several newly planted trees and chimes hanging from their twiggy branches, and a few big pots of dried-up rosemary and lavender (labelled, curiously, 'Sensory Garden'), is filling up with mothers. Some have pushchairs which they rock mindlessly back and forth while they chit-chat, some are on their own, and there's just the one dad with a group of women clustered around him as if he's a prize bull. 'I think the boys would love that. I want to keep everything as normal as possible for them.' *It's hardly their fault*, I think.

'She said you were good,' Pip says.

Her hand is on my arm. Gently, I pull away. 'I just want to be the most help I can. It's my job.'

'Where are you from?' Pip asks.

Here we go. 'Kent originally. Then my parents divorced and I ended up living with my mother in the back of beyond in Wales. Not many kids at my school went on to university, me included, but I knew from a very young age what I wanted to be. I've always loved kids. I went to college and studied childcare and it's landed me some amazing jobs. I've recently been in Italy where I took a course in the Montessori method. It was a brilliant experience.' I cringe inwardly. It sounds too rehearsed.

'No way,' Pip chimes. 'One of my other friends is crazy about the Montessori method. She's got her three little ones on a waiting list. I'll have to introduce you.'

Please don't, I think. Then that grin again. It's

49

as pre-programmed as my story and will remain that way until I leave.

Eventually the bell rings and, like a bunch of well-trained dogs, the waiting mothers and the father — who's now got several other dads around him — all turn to face the school door. A string of children files out with a weary-looking teacher leading the way. She makes them stand in a line and, one by one, they spot their mummies and their little feet itch to break away into the arms of home. Oscar and Noah are nowhere to be seen.

'Is this the reception class?' I ask Pip.

'It is,' she says, not taking her eyes off a little blonde girl at the end of the line. They are waving at each other. Lilly, I presume. With lopsided bunches and a cute turned-up nose, shiny shoes and a pink lunch box, she is clearly the class angel.

'I don't see the twins,' I say.

'Oh. No, you're right.' Pip glances up and down the line in case I've missed them. I don't think there'd be any mistaking those two livewires in this well-behaved line-up.

'I'll go and see the teacher,' I say. My heart kicks up a gear. Is it my fault if they've escaped from school or been kidnapped on my first day at work? Getting the sack this early would be no good. No good at all.

'Hi, Mrs Culver,' I say. 'The boys. The twins. Oscar and Noah.' Her expression tells me that she vaguely remembers me from this morning though her child-worn brain is probably yelling that it was a thousand years ago since we shook hands in the brightly-decorated classroom.

Mrs Culver scans the line-up. 'I counted them all,' she says. 'Lilly, do you know where the twins have gone?' Then she turns to me, ignoring what Lilly says. 'Probably making water bombs in the boys' loo.'

'I think that Lilly knows . . . ' I look at the little girl. She's trying to say something.

'Speak up, Lilly,' Mrs Culver snaps.

Lilly points inside the single-storey school building. I wink at her and grin. It will buy me points when we finally meet. I head off inside, leaving Mrs Culver to hand over the rest of the children to their parents.

Inside, it's dark and cool and smells of powder paint, school lunches and farts. The wooden floors kick up an evocative scent as I stalk the corridors. Through glass squares in the class-room doors I see older children still gathering their belongings. There'll be a stampede very soon. At the end of the corridor is a door with a sign on saying After School Club. A few kids have just gone in.

'Oh, boys, you scared me half to death,' I say, once inside.

The teacher, a man in his fifties, glances up from the work piled on his desk. 'Can I help you?'

'I've come to pick up Oscar and Noah. I'm their new nanny. Come on, lads,' I say. I need to get out of here. It's stifling and airless, the oxygen having been sucked up by three hundred greedy kids.

The teacher takes off his glasses. 'First I've

heard of it. The boys always come to after-school club. Their mother fetches them at six.'

'Not now she doesn't,' I say too brusquely and immediately turn him against me. 'Look, I'm Zoe Harper. Claudia Morgan-Brown introduced me to Mrs Culver this morning and let her know the new situation.'

'There are forms,' the man says unhelpfully. 'You'll need to see the secretary.'

'Where is she?'

'Gone home,' he says. 'But the forms need to be signed by the parent so you won't be able to take the boys today. Not without a form.'

'Oh for heaven's — ' *Keep calm*. 'Oscar, Noah, will you please tell your teacher who I am?'

The boys just stare at me. They are pulling apart dried-up Playdoh and scattering it on the floor. You'd think he'd want to be rid of them.

'Please?' I beg. 'You don't understand. If I can't pick up the boys, well, it just doesn't look good on my first day at work.' My arms dangle limply by my side. What they'd really like to do is hit the stupid old man.

'Sorry,' he says. 'Not my problem. I'll have to ask you to leave now.'

In a flash of desperation, I march up to the boys and grab each of them by the hand. Without a word, they obediently follow me as I tug on their arms. *Good lads!* I think, inwardly cheering them for not making a fuss as we run out. Behind me, the teacher's making one though.

Stop! Thief! Kidnap!

52

I hear him stumbling between chairs as he attempts a chase, but he's too old to catch us. He yells for his assistant and phones for help as I charge off with Noah and Oscar.

As we head for the park, I have to remind myself that it's not the done thing, stealing other people's children.

*   *   *

We're laughing about it later, of course, and she's totally on my side.

'Stupid secretary. I wrote her a letter. Sent her an email. Told her to circulate it to the staff. Even spoke to Mrs Culver before you started. And we met her this morning. God.' Claudia has just got home from work. Dumped her keys, bag and shoes in the hallway. 'Anyone would think you'd kidnapped them.'

I did.

'That's what some crusty old man said when I strode right out of there with them,' I said with a wry laugh.

'They phoned me immediately. I guess we can't blame them for doing their job.' And Claudia laughs — a beautiful laugh with white teeth and her head tipped back. Her neck is very pretty.

*   *   *

Later, in my bedroom, with the boys bathed and read to and tucked up in their own beds exhausted and happy with minty breath, I boot up my laptop. Speedily, I type an email and click send.

Then I set to unpacking the rest of my belongings. T-shirts and tops in one drawer, undies in another, all rather messily arranged. I think about the onerous task of packing it all up again every Friday evening. It seems ridiculous. Claudia wants me gone at weekends — I can understand they need their family time — but, in all honesty, I can't afford to do that. She is so close to her due date.

I grab my laptop and make some notes. When I write 'due date', my finger hits the wrong key and it comes out as 'die date'. I nibble on a broken nail. Eventually, with my computer balanced on my knee, I fall asleep fully dressed.

★ ★ ★

I wake later with a stiff neck. The clock beside the bed blinks two-twenty a.m. I stretch and straighten and slip out of my clothes. Completely naked, I stare at my body in the full-length mirror. I am all skin and bones. My empty hips jut out and my flat, almost concave tummy would be the envy of most women. I can't even begin to imagine myself pregnant.

6

Russ Goodall was a skinny, nervous man. If he were a dog, Lorraine thought, he'd be a greyhound. Just being in the same room as him made her nervous, and that didn't happen very often. She'd learnt, over the years — and especially recently — to emit a calmness and serenity that even Adam couldn't upset. Not even his early mornings and ten-mile runs or the way he counted out exactly the right number of prunes and weighed muesli for breakfast, his obsession with drinking exactly eight bottles of mineral water daily as well as the routine thirty minutes of meditation (he'd even been known to do this at crime scenes) wavered her solid centre of gravity. But Russ Goodall, for all his puny frame and wispy orange hair, had her teetering in his skittish aura.

'You sent her a good luck card.' Lorraine was hedging her bets. Russ wasn't such an uncommon name but unusual enough for it to be odd for Sally-Ann to have known two of them.

'I told you, I don't know anyone called Sally-Ann.'

'You were named as next of kin in her pregnancy notes. Willow Park Medical Centre confirmed that you are the Russ Goodall Sally-Ann wrote in her file. You are also a patient at the surgery.'

'They shouldn't have. That's a breach of confidentiality.'

'Not when I have a court order it's not.' Lorraine was trying to breathe in the shallowest way she could without actually fainting. The room stank — a nauseating mix of body odour, rancid fat from a dirty frying pan on a single gas burner stove, and cigarette smoke. Sally-Ann's parents must have been delighted when she brought him home for the first time. But oddly, the bedroom where Russ lived on the top floor of a large student-type house (even though he'd said he wasn't a student) was incredibly neat. Just a million miles from clean.

'Do you mind if I open a window?' she asked. Russ shrugged and watched the detective struggle with the sash opening. Eventually it gave in to her determined shovings and slid up. Lorraine leant out and sucked in a lungful of fresh air. 'So it's easier for all of us if you just admit to knowing Sally-Ann. Then you can help me with what I need to know.' She peered at the rubbish strewn on the flat roof below. Had Goodall chucked it there?

'Why?' he said. He lit a cigarette. He was sitting stiff and straight on the bed with his skinny and fragile-looking legs pinned together at the knees. His neck and shoulders shook, making his head tremble and bob like an ugly sweaty bloom. 'What's up?'

'I'm so sorry.' Lorraine turned towards him. She'd assumed he knew. 'Sally-Ann is dead.'

★ ★ ★

56

'That's when he started crying. Full on. The works.' Lorraine bit into a sausage roll and Adam picked bits out of his shop-bought lentil and bean salad as if it were radioactive. He usually made his own. 'How can you eat that shit?'

'Surely that's what I should be asking you?' he said.

They'd stopped at a bench. The morning's skim of ice had dissolved in the sun that had eventually broken through the clouds. It was freezing — too cold to be eating lunch outside — but they wanted the fresh air, the space, somewhere neutral to discuss the case. Twenty-four hours since the discovery and they were no further forward. Along with the team, each of them had been back to the scene several times, interviewed the neighbours, taken statements. And Lorraine could still smell the stink of Russ Goodall's disgusting room in the fibres of her coat. She made a mental note to pick up some Febreze on the way home.

'Anyway, after he'd calmed down, he agreed to help us. Thing is, no one could have faked the reaction he had when I told him the news. I genuinely believe he was clueless about her death.'

Adam raised his eyebrows with the plastic fork halfway to his mouth. 'I'll pretend you didn't make that assumption,' he said, and carried on eating.

'His reaction was very genuine. He said he was the father of Sally-Ann's baby and he agreed to give a DNA sample.'

'But they weren't living together.' A statement

rather than a question from Adam.

'No. Neighbours say he visited Sally-Ann often.' Lorraine brushed flakes of pastry off her trousers. 'Apparently Sally-Ann's parents were totally against their relationship and didn't know that Goodall was the father of their daughter's baby. Trust me, Adam, if one of our girls brought someone like him home, you'd have him taken out.'

'You're assuming too much again. Wait for the DNA test results before we label him as the father. Anyway, we don't know who the real target was yet. Mother or baby.'

'Or both,' Lorraine added, devouring the last of her lunch. 'And why wouldn't he be the father? Sally-Ann had put as much in her medical notes.'

'She'd crossed another name out before she wrote Goodall's name in the file.'

'Sally-Ann crossed it out?' Lorraine said. 'Now who's making assumptions?'

Adam tossed the plastic container of super-market salad into a nearby bin. He hadn't finished it.

7

'How was the antenatal class?' James asks. Annoyingly, he's sipping on a glass of wine.

'Fine. You should have come along.' I say it too snappily and instantly regret it. 'Sorry,' I say. 'Anyway, don't feel bad. There were only two other fathers there.'

With James having been at sea for most of my pregnancy, getting involved at this late stage would only highlight the fact that, unless I go into labour in the next few days, he's not going to be around to see the birth of our daughter. We agreed that — or rather *I* agreed that — going it alone in terms of appointments and classes would make it easier all round. But I can't say that I don't miss the thought of him stroking my head while I lie supine on my mat, cushion under the small of my back and another under my knees, or massaging my shoulders while I practise my breathing techniques.

'I came to your initial appointment. What more do you want?' He says it with a wry smile, one that lifts one side of his mouth and not the other; one that adds little wrinkles around his eyes and makes me chuckle back.

'That was big of you.' I remember marching into the doctor's office proudly clutching the plastic wand with the blue line that confirmed my newly discovered state — the beginning of the rest of our lives. 'Though nothing much happened, did it? It wasn't exactly hard for you to sit there.' I must stop now, before I get upset. I have to block out of my mind the thought of doing all this alone. I knew what I was taking on when I married James — a full-on Naval career and two little boys. Instant family, instant lifestyle change. 'You should try carrying this around.' Hand goes to bump.

'I carried your pregnancy folder when we left,' James suggests but realises he's taking the joke too far. 'Why don't you show me what strange yoga positions you learnt today, while the boys are busy?' He winks at me and I know what he's after.

'James!' I say, shocked. 'Zoe's upstairs and the twins could come in at any time.'

'Would it hurt so much if I, you know, just leant you over . . . ' He takes me ever so lightly by the waist — or rather where my waist used to be — and guides me to the kitchen worktop. He leans me forward so I have to support myself with my palms on the wood. From behind, he puts his hands lightly on my legs and works them a little way up my dress. It feels good.

'Stop it,' I giggle. I bat his hands away. 'Someone's bound to come in.'

'I could just . . . ' I hear him unzip. 'Just . . . like this. It'd be over so quick.'

I know he's right about that. It's been ages. I turn and kiss him deeply. My belly is pressed between us and it feels so odd to have it wedged between us at such an intimate moment. I turn round again, my bump hanging low as I lean forward.

60

'Quick then,' I say, praying everything will be all right, praying I'm not going to blow everything I've ever wanted with one foolish act.

★   ★   ★

Zoe is already in the kitchen when I come downstairs the next morning. I'm running late for work. The boys are in their school uniforms eating scrambled eggs on toast. They have orange juice and a banana set beside them. I feel oddly expendable at the sight of this simple scene. How will I feel when I hand over my baby each morning when my maternity leave runs out?

'I'm impressed,' I say.

Zoe turns from the sink. She is silhouetted by the morning sun streaming through the window.

'Looks chilly out,' I add, noticing the heavy frost.

There's a silence that I find awkward although Zoe doesn't seem to. She goes about her business, swilling dishes and drying them up. The boys chatter together and there's none of the usual shoving and bickering or refusing to eat unless it's brightly-coloured sugary cereal. Are they acting like this to show me up, because even though they love me, they know I'm not their *real* mother?

Let's be good for Zoe and horrid for her . . .

Their imaginary whispers make me shudder. Of course not, I think shamefully.

'What time will you be home tonight?' Zoe asks. She hangs the tea towel on the silver rail of the Aga.

'We have a dishwasher for all that, you know,' I say with a smile. She shrugs. 'About six-thirty.' And my paranoid mind is wondering why she wants to know. Is it so she can release the twins from their locked rooms? Evict the man she's been having sex with all afternoon? Know when to stop rifling through my belongings or wake up from a long nap?

Oh, for God's sake! I tell myself. It's hormonal havoc this morning.

'After I drop Oscar and Noah at school, I was going to go to the organic shop and buy some vegetables to make soup,' Zoe tells me. 'Would you and James like some for your supper as well?'

'Thank you,' I say, supposing it will be served with homemade bread, too. 'Sounds delicious, but I'm not sure the boys will . . . ' I glance at them. They're scraping their plates. 'Well, we can try, can't we?' I try to sound jovial. The thing is, I bet Oscar and Noah will go mad for Zoe's homemade soup. Before I know it, she'll have them growing their own veg and making it themselves.

The drive to work gives me time to think. Sitting in traffic, my selfishness hits me head on. It's what I wanted, isn't it? The perfect family life. Aren't I living my childhood dream? I have a husband who loves me, two sons who have accepted me as their mother, I have a good career and soon I'll have a little baby girl of my own. My house is straight from *Beautiful Homes* magazine and I even have a nanny who, after only one day, is proving invaluable. I'm certainly going to need her on my team if life is to resemble anything like the way it's been these last few years.

Who'd have thought, when I made that visit to two poor motherless boys, I'd end up marrying their father? I can't help believing it was all meant to be, as if someone had scripted my life.

Mark is the only one in the office when I arrive, even though I'm a bit late. As team leader I have five staff to manage as well as other agency workers and development and protection teams with which to liaise. As soon as I step into the building, any thoughts of self-doubt or self-pity are swept away by the torrents of need beckoning to me from dozens of at-risk children all neatly contained in stacks of files. I wonder how far they would go to become part of my life, to become my child, my loved one. It's something I think about most days. I dispel the guilt as I hang up my coat. It's an impossible thought. I couldn't take them all.

'Morning,' Mark says without looking up. It's all open plan here but we have our own areas — not cubes as such because I believe in seeing the faces of my co-workers as we bicker and banter back and forth about cases and reality TV and where we're going on holiday. I get a flutter in my belly as I imagine our next family trip. By summer, my little baby girl will be about eight months old.

'Morning,' I say. It comes out glumly. 'Where's Tina?'

'Her child-minder's sick. She's had to take a detour via her mother's house so she'll be late.'

Mark doesn't sound sympathetic. He has no children and isn't likely to have a family any time soon. He's been single as long as I've known him.

'That's annoying. She was going to come with me to the Lowes' place this morning.'

'You'll have to put up with me again then.' Mark drains his coffee mug. He drinks about ten cups a day. 'Can't have you going there alone. Not in your condition.' Now that Christine Lowe has come home from hospital with her baby, our visits to her will be daily. In the past, she's lashed out.

The first time I met her was soon after she'd had her second child. Within a week of her giving birth, we were rushing through the paperwork to take both children from her. Little boy, if I remember, and a two-year-old girl. Sweet baby with a mass of dark hair and purple welts across his legs. His sister was similarly decorated. That was about thirteen years ago. Since then she's had one every couple of years and we've taken them all away from her.

'Have you been following that awful story on the news?' Mark asks. I see him force down a swallow, wondering if he's overstepped the line. 'That poor pregnant woman?'

'Which pregnant woman?' I say, making him squirm on purpose. I smile a little, to let him know I'm kidding, that of course I've heard about it.

'It's just dreadful. How could anyone . . . ?' He doesn't know how far to go. Does he think I'll fall apart if we talk about it?

64

'Is that the murdered pregnant woman story?' Diane, ears pricked, comes in from the kitchen carrying a tray of coffee mugs. 'I couldn't believe it. And guess what? My mum actually knows the dead girl's mother. They went to school together years ago and keep in touch. When the photo of the dead woman came on telly, her mum was in the background and my mum recognised her. And the surname was a giveaway. Frith's not that common, is it?' Diane passes round the mugs — mine says 'Give me a gherkin NOW!' on it. No one really knows what to say about the murder. We see enough tragedy in the department without adding to it.

'You don't have to keep quiet about it for my benefit,' I tell them. 'It's no more awful for me to hear about it than for you. Just because I'm pregnant doesn't mean I can't hack real life.' I shrug and try not to think about what that woman must have gone through before she died. Two lives unnecessarily lost.

'Have the police arrested anyone yet?' Mark says, slurping coffee and returning to his computer.

'Don't think so,' Diane says. She tucks a strand of dark hair behind one ear and crunches into a biscuit. She swivels to face her desk. 'My mum's going to go round later. See if she can help.' She's tapping at her keyboard.

The first call of the day comes in. A local GP is worried about a young patient. There's a teenager in crisis and it's up to me to sort her out.

Christine Lowe hasn't changed much over the years. Despite multiple pregnancies, various abusive partners, having all her kids taken off her, and a drug habit that would impress even the hardest of addicts, these days she's a quiet, almost well-mannered woman who's resigned to her lot in life.

'Come in,' she says. A cigarette bobs between her lips as she speaks. Her house doesn't smell as bad as it usually does, and it looks as if she's even made an effort to tidy. Two German Shepherds are slumped in front of a gas fire. Beside them on the floor lies the baby in a very well-used Moses basket. Christine doesn't kick up much of a fuss when we come any more.

'Who have we got here?' I ask.

'Nathan,' she says resignedly. 'Any chance his grandma can see him before you take him? She's been in hospital.' She yanks a dog away by its collar as it moves lazily to sniff the baby's face. More a maternal action on the dog's part, I feel, and I doubt Christine would have intervened if we'd not been there.

'That depends,' Mark says. He gives me a glance.

'On what?' she snaps. She's never got on with the men in the department.

'On whether you manage to stick to the care plan we set out.' Mark is taking notes.

'How long is your mother going to be in hospital?' I ask, trying to rouse the baby. I don't like what I see. I want this baby out of here.

66

Christine puts a hand to her forehead and wobbles. She's very pale. 'Sit down,' I tell her. She dissolves into the sofa and a dog rests its chin on her knee. If only the dogs were in charge. 'Have you eaten today?' I ask. She shakes her head. 'Where's your partner?' Immediately I remember Mark telling me he's back in prison again. It's a wonder Christine gets pregnant at all.

'The nick,' she confirms.

'Is Nathan feeding properly?' He hasn't made a noise or moved since we arrived. I know the health visitor will visit every day but, until the paperwork is finalised, our hands are tied.

'Yeah,' she says. I can see she's thinking hard, trying to remember. Christine has learning difficulties. Part of me wonders if she even knows that it's not normal to have your baby taken away as soon as it's born. She stares at her son. 'He likes milk,' she adds, as if the notion's a revelation.

'When did he last have some?' I ask. Mark is stroking the baby's head now, trying to wake him. Slowly, he stirs. 'Turn off the fire,' I say, suddenly noticing how stifling the room is. There's no air.

'He had some in the night,' Christine replies, pleased with herself. She's very skinny for a woman who's recently had a baby. I've piled on the weight since being pregnant.

'You're having one too,' Christine says, beaming at me. She gets up and steps towards me, hands outstretched. She rests them on my belly. I'm so shocked that she's done this, I can't

67

move. 'It's a boy,' she says, beaming.

You're wrong, I think, already knowing I'm having a girl.

I lean over and whisper in Mark's ear, 'We need to get him out soon.' Mark nods. We both know that unless Christine agrees, we'll need an emergency court order.

'Would you like to have a break from looking after baby Nathan?' I ask. Even though I want nothing more than to scoop up the little mite, take him home, feed him, bathe him, cuddle him, things have to be done the right way. There are papers to be signed, and I know she could change her mind at any moment.

Eventually, Christine gives me the vaguest of nods and I say a silent prayer of thanks before we all leave for the office. I phone ahead to alert the team. I already have a nice foster home in mind.

8

'I'm off then,' Lorraine said, ducking into Adam's office on the way out. He looked up from his desk. 'To interview Sally-Ann's parents, remember?' She rolled her eyes. Adam raised a hand in a half-hearted wave as she left. He was immersed in something.

Lorraine took DC Patrick Ainsley with her, her favourite of the new blood that was flowing around CID. Between the pair of them, the GP who had just stopped by to administer more sedatives to the mother, as well as a rather traumatised family liaison officer, they managed to get Mrs Frith to string some coherent sentences together. Just a hunch, Lorraine thought as the woman gradually and painfully opened up, but she reckoned it would be the mother who would be the most help, rather than the stern, somewhat aloof father who had yet to react to the fact that his only daughter was dead.

'I just can't believe it,' Mrs Frith kept repeating over and over. Her voice was brittle, barely there. 'Pinch me, pinch me for God in heaven's sake. Make me wake up from this nightmare.' She rocked, clutching a bunch of tissues.

'I'm so sorry about your loss, Mrs Frith. It's incomprehensible how someone could do this. Please be assured we are doing everything in our power to find whoever's responsible.'

Responsible, Lorraine thought sourly. Whoever did this didn't have an ounce of responsibility in them. She'd only said that word to avoid using the word 'murderer'.

'Can you tell me when you last saw your daughter?' Lorraine was ready to take notes. DC Ainsley was in charge of the recording. They'd agreed to it this way — nothing formal, but important that they could listen to the Friths' comments later. It never ceased to amaze Lorraine what could be missed first time round. 'Mrs Frith?'

'Last Saturday,' Mr Frith interjected coldly. He'd hardly said a word. 'Daphne went round to see her, didn't you?' He stared at his wife. Lorraine supposed he was still in shock, grieving in his own way, even though his words were emotionless, as if it was all a bit of a nuisance.

Mrs Frith nodded in agreement.

'What time on Saturday would that have been?' Lorraine asked her. She leant close in the hope she would answer for herself this time.

'In the morning,' she replied quietly. She was shaking uncontrollably.

'Late morning,' Mr Frith added.

'And how did Sally-Ann seem to you?' Lorraine glanced at DC Ainsley.

'Fine. She was excited but nervous about having the baby.'

'She was having a planned Caesarean section, I understand.'

'Yes.'

There was no need to ask why. The hospital had already confirmed that Sally-Ann had a

70

placenta praevia — a condition where the placenta had grown to block the baby's natural exit route. The obstetrician had explained to Lorraine how a C-section was imperative, but then halted when she'd interrupted, explaining that both her daughters had been born this way for exactly the same reason. 'Unlucky,' was all he'd said, and Lorraine had to agree.

'So it was very important that Sally-Ann didn't go into natural labour,' Lorraine stated. Mrs Frith nodded. Lorraine remembered her obstetrician telling her all those years ago that if she did go into labour, she'd suffer life-threatening internal bleeding and the baby would be deprived of oxygen once the placenta detached. It wasn't exactly a win-win for either party and a pre-planned surgical delivery was the best option. Timing was everything.

'So awful,' Mrs Frith managed to say. 'That she died anyway.' She snatched a look at her husband as if she knew what was coming. Her eyes filled with tears.

'God wanted to take her and her bastard baby one way or another,' Mr Frith said. He crossed himself.

'I understand that's your grief talking, Mr Frith,' Lorraine said, trying to loosen the chill that had taken them all by the throats.

'No, it's not,' Mrs Frith said pitifully. 'He hated that Sally-Ann was going to have a baby.'

'Why was that?' It was for this very reason that Lorraine had decided to tape their meeting.

'She wasn't married,' Mrs Frith whispered, as if even saying the words was a sin.

71

'And no grandchild of mine was going to be born out of wedlock. It was shock enough knowing that Russell Goodall was the father.' Mr Frith's face was bursting red with hatred and anger. Blue-black veins wiggled across his cheeks and his strawberry-like nose, indicating a lifestyle that was most ungodly.

'Are you certain Russell Goodall was the baby's biological father?' DNA testing would soon tell them but she wanted their opinion.

'Sally-Ann told us he was,' Mr Frith said. He let out a half growl, half sigh.

'No, Sally-Ann wasn't sure, Bill,' Mrs Frith continued. 'She was a . . . a popular girl.'

'Slut, you mean.'

'Carry on,' Lorraine said to Mrs Frith.

'She had two boyfriends. She couldn't decide between them. When Liam found out about the baby, he didn't want anything more to do with her. He said it couldn't possibly be his,' Mrs Frith explained meekly.

'Fucking whore, that's what she was.'

'Bill!' Mrs Frith said as loudly as she could. 'Our daughter was not . . . she was not like that.'

'What's Liam's surname, Mrs Frith?'

'Rider. Liam Rider.'

'And married with a family of his own, I might add.' Mr Frith's hands were balled into tight fists. He sucked air in and out as if there was no oxygen left in the room. 'No wonder the dirty bastard went running when Sally-Ann got pregnant.'

'So you can't be sure who the baby's real father was?' What mattered more, Lorraine knew, was who each of the two men *believed* the father was.

'Sally-Ann got herself in a state over it. When Liam wanted nothing more to do with her, she tried to forget him,' Mrs Frith said. 'She wanted to scribble him out of her life, but it was hard. She loved him.'

Literally, thought Lorraine as she remembered the scratched-out name in the pregnancy file.

'Russell stepped up to the mark. He's a kind-hearted boy,' the mother continued.

'He's a loser, that's what.' Mr Frith's turn again.

'Where did Sally-Ann meet Liam Rider?' Lorraine asked. 'Who did she know first?'

'She's known Russ since she was at primary school. Liam, though, she didn't meet him until she enrolled on that college course. He was teaching her bookkeeping. Everything changed when she met Liam.'

'Teaching her how to be immoral, more like,' Mr Frith said. His face appeared to balloon at the cheeks and turn a deep shade of beetroot, then he broke down into dry, rasping sobs. He covered his face and dropped his head. The top of his scalp was swept across with strands of grey, greasy hair.

Lorraine glanced at Patrick. They gave the man a moment.

'Let it out, love,' Mrs Frith said, but he shrugged her hand off his back. He was going to have to do this his own way.

'One more question.' Lorraine drew in breath but then stopped. She'd been going to ask why

73

they thought Sally-Ann had put Russ Goodall as her next of kin on the pregnancy file and not either of them. But staring at them in turn, she kind of guessed.

★ ★ ★

Liam Rider wasn't home. A bemused woman of about thirty-five answered the door with a couple of kids peering on from down the hallway. It was a pleasant house, a Fifties semi with a neat front garden and a pot of pansies beside the front door. A waft of cooking food — baked potatoes or chips — spilled out as the woman stared at her ID. Lorraine felt her stomach rumble.

'Is everything OK?' the woman asked, paling a little. 'Is Liam all right?' She took hold of the doorframe as Lorraine convinced her that everything was fine, there were no accidents. She couldn't bring herself to say that no one was dead.

'It's Mr Rider I'd like to speak to,' Lorraine said. 'Do you know where I can find him?'

'At the college, I think,' she replied. Her eyes were flashing everywhere from beneath a neat blonde fringe. She didn't look like the kind of wife to be cheated on. Then again, Lorraine hadn't thought she was the type either until Adam, drunk on guilt, had decided to tell her that he'd had a brief — *oh so brief* — affair. Lorraine swallowed it away. Now wasn't the time.

'Craven Road Campus?' Lorraine asked.

The woman nodded. It was the place where her husband both worked and played away, except she didn't know it. *We have something in common, you and me*, Lorraine wanted to say, but didn't.

Brief . . . meaningless . . . over . . . Adam had gone on to tell her he'd been stupid, drunk, that he was having a crisis, that she'd pursued him and it wasn't his fault. What advice would she give the younger woman, Lorraine wondered? Get out while you can? Do the same back? Take him to the cleaners? While the house looked pleasant enough, it was clear Liam Rider wasn't exactly cleaning-out material. Neither was Adam, though that hadn't stopped her fantasising about it.

'If he comes home before I've spoken to him, will you ask him to call me?' Lorraine handed the woman a card. 'It's urgent.'

'He's not in any trouble, is he?' She shooed the children back as they approached the door.

'No. I just need him to help with some enquiries.' Lorraine smiled tersely before leaving for the college.

★　★　★

'You know the first thing he said?' Lorraine was perched on a bar stool in the kitchen. Once the girls were sorted for the evening, she was back to the office.

Adam shook his head.

'You won't tell my wife, will you?'

Adam pulled a face. He hadn't been present at

75

the interview. 'Natural.'

He'd just come in from his run and was dripping with sweat even though a frost had begun to creep across the pavements and railings. He wiped his face on the tea towel. Lorraine snatched it and tossed it through the door to the utility room. 'That's a disgusting thing to do,' she said. 'On both counts.'

She couldn't help the occasional comment. It hadn't quite been a year. Mostly, she was able to cope, to put it behind her, get on with life. Then there were the times she couldn't and all she wanted to do was make the rest of Adam's life as unbearable as possible.

'What else did Rider have to say?' Adam bit into an apple. 'Did he agree to a DNA test?'

'He'd heard about Sally-Ann on the news so he'd had a couple of days to absorb the shock. He was still very upset though. It wasn't a great way to find out. He said she was a promising student, trying to make something of herself by taking a course, blah blah.' She took a breath. Now wasn't the time. 'And yes, he agreed to give a swab straight away.'

Adam pulled off his luminous running top and tossed that onto the utility-room floor with the tea towel. 'Has the time of death come through yet?' he asked.

'I spoke to the pathologist. Best guess is she'd been dead a minimum of thirty-eight hours and a maximum of forty-one. Rider told me without being asked that he could prove his exact whereabouts for the last week. That's when he virtually begged me not to tell his wife. 'It would

76

kill her' I think were his words.'

Lorraine bit her cheek. Adam didn't look in the least bit uncomfortable.

'Rider had ended it with Sally-Ann several months ago, when she insisted the baby was his. She wanted money from him and he didn't have it to give. And of course he didn't want his wife to know about the affair or the baby. He took a risk, if you ask me, by dumping her, said that if it all came out, he was just going to deny it.' Lorraine stood up and leant against the worktop. She felt her heart kick up. 'Do you know what else he told me?' She paused. 'He told me that unless you actually get caught in the act, no one can prove a thing.' Lorraine had wanted to slap him at that point.

'I'll remember that then,' Adam said sourly, and went upstairs for a shower.

9

The worst thing about not being pregnant is that everything in life seems to suddenly involve babies. And the worst thing about having to make up so many stories, literally living in the centre of an ever-changing lie, is that the stories get deeper and deeper, more twisted and untrue, so that eventually I have trouble remembering who I really am.

But, all things considered, I decide that for the moment being someone else isn't so bad; that being the real me would be dangerous and unhelpful in my current predicament. I am here for one reason only and my time will soon come. The wait itself is a gestation.

'So . . . ' Pip says, trying to fill the gap. We're running out of conversation. Lilly and the twins are in the playroom. They seem to be getting along well enough. I can hear clattering and chattering and occasional whoops and at least they are not killing each other. Pip and I are sitting at Claudia's kitchen table (I think of everything in this house as belonging to Claudia) and exchanging banter about children and babies and pregnancy and giving birth. Then Pip strikes me full in the face: 'Haven't you ever wanted children of your own?'

It's one of those unanswerable questions. Well, it is if I am to remain in my newly-constructed bubble of lies and deceit as well as keeping my job, anyway. Mess up too soon and I'm out on my ear. Explanation is impossible.

To field it, I try a laugh. Then I try a long sip from my mug of tea. Next I try a shriek to the children to check they are still playing nicely. I glance at my watch and stare at the wall clock but Pip's only been here ten minutes. She won't be leaving yet. Besides, I haven't answered her question.

Haven't you ever wanted children of your own?

'I . . . ' I falter. I have no idea what to say. 'Well . . . '

Pip's interested smile has diminished and now she is also looking for ways to stop me having to reply. My body language has become awkward — pained face, crossed arms hugging my very un-pregnant body, both feet jiggling nervously on the tiles; I couldn't make it more obvious that I don't want to talk about this. But now I have to.

'It's complicated,' I say. The syllables are razors in my mouth.

Pip just stares at me, feeling wretched, wishing she'd never asked. *Look at her, sitting in Claudia's nice pine kitchen chair, all pregnant and wide and brimming with life and hope and love. Her breasts are big and heave together within her oversized sweater. It could be homemade — a hand-knitted effort to go with her home-grown baby. How lovely. How very not me.*

'I haven't really met the right person yet.'

I don't need to say any more. I should stop

right now. She would never understand. Pip would simply be relieved that her faux pas has passed and we could talk about baking or schools or how long she's known Claudia. Instead, for some unknown yet horrific reason, I continue. 'It's not for want of trying, I can assure you. I know what you're thinking, that I'm obviously in my thirties and no man in my life so I'd better get a move on, but how on earth am I going to do it without a partner?'

What am I saying?

I dig my nails into my palms to silence myself. I know only too well there are many ways to get a baby without a partner. It's just that none has worked yet.

'You're in your thirties?' Pip says in a lame, flattering attempt to change the subject. Her cheeks are crested scarlet. Pregnant women get hot easily.

'Thirty-three,' I tell her. 'Thirty-three, an old maid and no children.' I laugh, but it comes out slightly demented. I hear my mother's words from beyond the grave: *Fancy, she's not married, no children. Told you so* . . . Then another little laugh to lighten things up as, while I somehow want Pip — someone, *anyone* — to feel my pain, I mustn't let it ruin everything. The last thing I need is for her to tell Claudia I'm some baby-obsessed psycho. She'd kick me out in nothing flat. This is all so finely timed. I catch my breath. 'But it's OK. I'm lucky to be working with children.' Another laugh. More convincing this time.

'I'm glad to hear that,' Pip adds with a sigh,

80

which is clearly one of relief. A punctuation mark; a full stop.

'Mummy, Noah broke Barbie,' Lilly says, thrusting a contorted naked doll at her mother.

'Oh dear,' Pip says with a sideways glance at me as if it's somehow my fault. 'Let me see.'

'Noah,' I say with forced disdain, 'why did you do that?' Really, I'd quite like to pat him on the head and tell him well done.

'Cos Barbie's stupid and not real,' he says, echoing my thoughts.

'That's not a good reason to break someone else's doll,' I tell him. 'What do you say to Lilly?'

Noah shrugs. He bites his lip until it bleeds.

'Say sorry,' I tell him.

'She's not broken any more,' Pip says, handing back the mended doll to Lilly. 'Just bent a bit.'

I watch Noah's eyes track Lilly and slightly-bent-Barbie as they leave the room. He'll have another go for sure. I'm learning that he's quite like me: things that are perfect are just asking for it.

★   ★   ★

When Pip has finally left with a sullen Lilly in tow and a promise to make the play-date a weekly occurrence, I get started on the boys' supper. I promised homemade soup, didn't I?

I peek into the sitting room and see that the twins are glued to some cartoon or other. A double-take shows me that Oscar is actually asleep, lolling on the arm of the chair with a string of drool leaking onto the upholstery. Noah

81

glances at me idly, our new bond stretched silently between us, and turns back to the telly without a word.

I pull the door closed and grab my coat, purse and keys. On the top step, I scan the street left and right. There's no one about, no one paying me any attention. I can almost see it from here and, with a big breath, I launch myself down the steps and through the front gate. Without stopping, I dash to the corner shop, buy what I need — silently cursing the old woman in front of me counting out her change penny by hard-saved penny — and, before I know it, I am back in the hallway slipping out of my coat. Trying not to pant, I peek into the sitting room again. The boys are still safely in the same place, but then my vision goes blurry as adrenalin rushes through me. A hand on the doorframe steadies me.

'James,' I say automatically. I force the smile that's buried beneath the shock.

'Zoe,' he says, and I have less than a second to decide if he's angry, if he knows I left his sons alone. 'How was your day?'

'Fine,' I say, still unsure and cursing myself for having no idea how to make soup.

'You look chilly,' he says, standing up and stretching.

'I've just taken the recycling out to the bins,' I say with a silent prayer of thanks that I actually did this chore earlier in the afternoon and had the presence of mind to remember. Full bins in the kitchen would have given me away. I slide the plastic shopping bag across the floor with my foot, although I needn't have bothered because James flops back down into the sofa and shrugs an arm round each son.

'Great,' he says awkwardly, and now Oscar is awake and James is more interested in talking to his sleepy son than bothering with me.

'I'll get their supper started then,' I say, and leave for the kitchen.

★　★　★

'Something smells divine,' Claudia says. She looks tired and stressed but with the veneer of a brave face pasted over the top. I don't think she's entirely comfortable with me being here yet. What she needs to understand is that it's a necessity for both of us.

'It's the soup,' I say proudly. A great pot of it is simmering on the Aga's hotplate. A quick search on the internet told me how to use the damned thing before I started the job. Apparently my previous employers had one. 'Homemade, of course.' Ten empty cans — homemade soup only comes in big batches, I once learnt from my aunt — are now crushed and deposited right at the bottom of the recycling dustbin. Mix in a few fresh herbs and no one's going to question where it came from, not if they think I've been peeling and chopping vegetables all afternoon.

'Pip came round earlier,' I tell her to get her off the scent, but she's straight back on it with her nose hovering over the pan, belly pressing against the Aga rail, sucking in the smells of my faux home cooking.

'There's a secret ingredient, I'll bet,' she says, briefly closing her eyes.

Our faces are close. She's only a breath away. All that new life buzzing inside her.

'If I tell you that,' I say with a smile, 'I'll have to kill you.'

★　★　★

Later, when the boys have scraped their bowls and asked for not only seconds but thirds too, once they have sucked on peach quarters and licked their fingers, after a warm bubble bath shared with a dozen plastic dinosaurs and a story from me, and after I've said goodnight to James and Claudia (with a few questions to her privately about how she's feeling; if she thinks her time is close), I slump onto my bed as if my bones have dissolved from exhaustion and grief. When the tears come, I have to bury them in my pillow. When the anger comes, I bite into it, leaving little teeth marks of frustration in the crisp cotton.

Why did this have to happen now?

I pull my holdall from the bottom of the wardrobe. I unzip an inside compartment and pull out the little blue and white box. Clear Blue, it says on the front. Over ninety-nine per cent accurate. Two tests.

All it does is make me want to go home. All it does is make me feel empty and utterly useless inside.

10

'She's been smoking.' I'm waddling up and down the drawing room.

'Nonsense,' James says wearily. 'She doesn't do that. Have you forgotten we asked her at the interview?'

'I smelt it on her. No doubt.'

I think for a moment. He's right. She definitely told us that she didn't smoke. But I don't want the boys watching her have a sneaky cigarette outside the back door or even smelling it on her. Before you know it, they'll think it's OK to do it themselves. It's not the way I want them brought up.

'Ask her if you're that bothered by it,' James says.

'How can I?' I reply. I'm pacing back and forth between him and the fireplace. 'It's no good if she thinks we don't trust her.'

'You're being so silly,' James says. For some reason, he's pointing at the empty grate. It's always chilly in this room but James insisted we come in here to talk as it's furthest away from the boys' room and Zoe's staircase. 'Don't you remember that she lit the sitting-room stove earlier and was complaining how hard it was to get going? She said the room filled with smoke and she was apologising. That's all it was, Claudia. Wood smoke on her clothes.'

Surely James knows as well as I do that there's

a difference between the two. I may be pregnant, but I haven't lost my sense of smell.

'No, no, you're wrong. It was cigarette smoke on her breath.'

We are suddenly silent as the door clicks open at the same time as we hear a quiet knock. 'It's just me,' Zoe says. 'I'm sorry to interrupt your evening.' She looks anxious.

Did she hear us talking about her?

'Come in,' James says.

I pray she didn't hear me.

'It's nothing really,' she says, perhaps sensing our embarrassment. 'We can talk tomorrow if you're busy.'

She's waiting nervously in the doorway looking at each of us in turn. Her face is both pleading and apologetic. There's something on her mind and she's not sure how to say it. She looks as if she's already been in bed, maybe unable to get to sleep. Her hair is slightly mussed on one side and the light eye make-up she was wearing earlier has been removed. The pale skin of her cheeks and forehead has the soft sheen of night-cream still absorbing, while her back-to-front T-shirt and woolly bed socks are another give-away of the intention of an early night.

What led her downstairs again, I wonder?

'We're not at all busy,' I say, feeling slightly sorry for her. I pat the empty space on the sofa, and when she tentatively sits, I glance at James with a slight widening of my eyes that only he would notice.

No smoke without fire, something my mother always used to say, flashes through my mind.

'What's bothering you?' I'm suddenly struck by the thought that, after only two days, she's going to hand in her notice. I hadn't considered that she might leave us.

'Nothing's bothering me, exactly. It's just . . . '

'Would you like me to leave you two to talk?' James suggests.

'Good idea,' I say. 'Why don't you put the kettle on?'

James nods and marches out, grateful for the reprieve.

'Just what?' I ask Zoe, picking up her tentative thread again.

'I'm not sure how to put this. I guess asking you outright is the best way.'

Zoe picks at her clipped nails. Her hair scratches around her neck in thin tufts. If I were her mother right now I'd tuck it behind her ears and gently push a finger under her chin to lift her head. I'd stare into her milky grey eyes and fathom what was wrong before she even knew it herself. I'd pull her close, hug her, make her realise that I'm there for her, whatever she was going to ask.

'It's about the weekends.' Her words are gossamer thin.

'Yes?'

'Well, I don't know how you feel about . . . it's just that it would be really useful if . . . ' She bows her head further.

'Zoe, I don't bite.'

Finally, she lifts her head and stares at me square on. Her jawline is neat and petite, as if sculpted with fine fingers. Her cheekbones echo

87

the precision of her face; they in turn give way to those misty eyes. She looks as if she has permanent tears just waiting to drop.

'I don't really have anywhere to go at the weekends.'

I try to figure out what it means, but before I can, I've already answered. 'Then you must stay here.' It was the gush of relief that she wasn't handing in her notice, despite my suspicions, that made me say it.

'Really?' Her chin lifts higher and her eyes brighten. There's a glimmer of a smile.

'Yes,' I say, more hesitantly now, realising I should probably have asked James first, especially after what I just accused her of. But I'm certain he won't mind. Besides, he's away again very soon and it was him who was keen for me to have home help in the first place. 'Is everything OK, Zoe?' I feel I have to check. Despite the interview, her CV and references, it strikes me that I actually know very little about her home life.

'That's so kind of you.' She nods gratefully. 'And everything is fine. It's just that . . . ' Again, she looks so sad, so pained, so unsure of me.

'What, Zoe?'

'I have some issues with the person I'm living with.' She pauses and thinks. 'Was living with, I should say. We've had some problems and it's not working out. I don't want you to think I'm taking advantage of you.'

'A break-up?'

Zoe shrugs, and I realise that by hiring domestic staff I also take on their personal lives.

88

'Kind of,' she says. 'Some things are impossible to work out.'

And for some reason, she stares longingly at my pregnant stomach.

★ ★ ★

I'm lying on our bed, exhausted. I'll disappear to the spare room soon enough, but for now, I know I'll never sleep. James is lying beside me, almost asleep, and I need to talk. He's barely listening.

'I can't say it was creepy exactly,' I tell him. 'But almost.' I prod his shoulder a little.

I'm lying on top of the covers in my tent-like flowery nightie and a thick robe that only just reaches round my middle. James often jokes that the last time he saw me naked was when my waist was a neat twenty-seven inches. I hope I'm back to that size again next time he comes home. The women in our antenatal yoga group are always comparing stretch marks and girth measurements. I prefer not to think about my body. Too much thought and I go into a flat spin of terror. I've had too many disappointments.

'James, did you hear me? I said I can't say it was creepy exactly — '

'Then don't,' he mumbles. His eyes are closed. He's lying on his side, facing away from me.

'It was just the way she looked at me. It was . . . ' I don't want to sound smug. 'It was almost as if she was jealous of me or something.'

James opens his eyes and rolls onto his back. He stares up at me. I'm propped on one elbow and not very comfortable. 'It's late, Claud.' The eyes close again. 'Don't be weird.'

'And then the cigarette smoke too . . . Did she lie to me?'

James's eyes are open again now. 'Your hormones are getting the better of you, Claud. Zoe isn't creepy or jealous and she doesn't smoke. End of. She just wanted to stay weekends. It could work out well for you both.'

'I'm not sure, James,' I say quietly, but his eyes are shut again.

I flop back onto the pillow and play the scene through my mind again. It was the moment she said 'Some things are impossible to work out'. How much sadness did those words contain? 'Sounds complicated,' I'd replied, but she didn't divulge anything else.

'That's when she reached out and touched my tummy, James,' I say to my dozing husband. 'James,' I say louder. 'I said she put her hands on the baby.'

James rolls over and groans. 'So?' he grumbles. 'It's what women do, isn't it?' He pulls a pillow over his head.

He's right, of course. Since I've been showing — and that wasn't for about five months — I've attracted way more attention than I'd like. Initially, I chose not to tell many people I was even expecting, excluding family and close friends, although I was wary with them, too. Given my history, disappointing everyone with yet another miscarriage was another burden of grief I could do without. I'd learnt my lesson. Plus, in my line of work, people are all too willing to criticise me about becoming a mother as retaliation to me simply doing my job.

'It was the *way* she touched me, James. As if . . . ' I pause and shift positions. I'm tired. I'm probably not making sense. 'Oh, I don't know. But she put both palms right here,' and I touch my bump even though he's not looking. 'She left them there for way longer than was necessary. She stared right at me, right into my eyes. I didn't like it.'

'She was probably waiting for a kick,' James mumbles.

'Maybe,' I agree with a sigh. 'I'm tired. I'm going to bed.' I kiss the side of James's head and leave for the spare room. We'll both get a better night's sleep this way.

Once I've cleaned my teeth, when I'm lying in the spare bed, hot as anything even with the window open an inch, I mull over the part that I didn't tell James; the part that, just for a second, made my heart miss a beat.

'You're so lucky,' she'd said with her hands pressed against me. Her eyes were full of tears, brimming with that profound greyness. 'You're so lucky to be pregnant.'

11

I let out a huge sigh of relief as I go back up to my bedroom. Securing regular weekend accommodation with Claudia wasn't as hard as I'd thought and it's saved a whole load of hassle and heartache. I feel as though I can breathe again. Besides, I don't want anything happening while I'm not here. She decided all by herself, before I could say otherwise, that I must be a mess when it comes to relationships; assumed I was a walking man-disaster zone. In the end, she judged it best not to ask. Very wise of her. I'm pretty certain she won't probe further. By the look on her face, she thought I was going to quit my job. No chance of that. Not yet, anyway.

I unplug my mobile phone from its charger and stare at the screen. No texts since I last checked. I tap one out but then save it as a draft, thinking I probably shouldn't send it; that it would be reckless and cause more trouble. I go to the holdall in the bottom of the wardrobe and pull out a half bottle of Scotch. Not the done thing for a nanny but I'm tuckered out and my back hurts from carrying those boys upstairs. They're good kids, spunky and interested in things, although from my limited experience with children, I'd say girls are easier.

The thought of that alone makes me take a sip from the bottle — just a small one — and pick up my phone again. I toggle through all the draft messages I've written in the past to let off steam. Then I re-read the message I've just typed. It gives me butterflies and makes me feel a little sick to imagine the recipient reading it. I put the bottle to my lips again and this time I take a big swig. With the line of whisky still searing down my throat, I hit send. I couldn't help myself.

You know I'll always love you flies out into the ether.

★ ★ ★

When I come down in the morning, a little twin hand inserted in each of mine, Claudia has already left for work. James strides into the kitchen wearing his Naval uniform and the boys make a fuss as they eat their Weetabix. 'Don't worry, I'm not going away just yet, lads,' he says as they abandon their breakfast and lunge at his legs. How heart-breaking for them to have their father away at sea so often, especially after their mum died. How convenient he married Claudia. How lucky she hired me. Children passed down the line. When will it stop?

'I have a business meeting,' he says to me after a cursory good morning. My ears prick up. I'm not convinced he likes me. I'm going to be with his wife and boys when he can't be; look after them while he's away. I'm the new man of the house. 'I'll be back by six and Claudia will be home around then, too. She left early to deal with a tricky case.'

'Oh?' I say, trying not to sound nosy, but really I am. There's so much I have to find out about them and so little time. I desperately want to ask about James's business meeting.

Plus, I admit Claudia's job intrigues me. I know she's a social worker and works in the child protection unit, that she heads up a team. But what her daily routine involves, I don't have much of an idea. I suppose she tries to make people's lives better, gets them to live the way she believes is right. Don't neglect your children; don't get pregnant when you're fifteen; don't hit your girlfriend; don't take drugs.

Then it occurs to me that she must work with the police quite regularly. The thought of it sends a burst of adrenalin through me just at the same moment Noah knocks over his glass of orange juice. My first thought is to yell at him but I manage to keep calm. James hasn't yet left. I heard him go into his study.

'Oopsie,' I say with a laugh. 'Fetch the dishcloth, would you, Noah?' He does as he's told while Oscar teases him for being clumsy. He drags his finger through the spillage instead of sopping up the mess. 'Here, let me do it,' I say. I don't need a trail of sticky juice all the way to the sink. Mopping the floor is the last thing I want to do. There are other, more important jobs to be taken care of.

* * *

'Would you and the twins like to come to the indoor play centre with Lilly and me after school today?' Pip is stamping her feet and clapping her gloveless hands together. It's freezing.

The thought of it fills me with dread but I find myself saying yes anyway. No doubt I'll be surrounded by more pregnant women than I can cope with, each corralling an under-two-year-old while nursing the obligatory huge belly, wondering why they signed up for the lark that is motherhood. They're everywhere at the moment, pregnant women. It makes everything that much harder — makes me feel emptier than empty; lonelier, more useless and unable to do anything than I ever have done before. I tell myself it's not for long; it won't be this way for ever. Things will work out.

My phone vibrates in my pocket. I can't possibly get it out here. My heart skips a beat.

'It'll wear the twins out good and proper for bedtime,' Pip continues. She's wearing a faux fur coat with massive cuffs. She's got a hat to match. 'Lilly loves it there. They have this gigantic ball pit that she literally gets lost in . . . ' She goes on and on about the play centre and I smile and nod and laugh out shots of icy breath as I try to think of an excuse to leave. My gloved fingers caress the phone in my pocket.

'Oh look, they're going in to school,' I say as the lined-up classes of children snake off to their respective classrooms. I wave frantically as the twins go off without a backward glance. I'm not their mother, after all.

'So shall we meet up when school finishes?' Pip asks as we leave through the school gates.

'Sure,' I say, wondering how I can get out of it.

Finally, I veer away, leaving Pip to chat with another group of mothers. I wait until I'm

95

around the corner before checking the text on my phone.

I love u 2 sets me right up for what I have to do next.

★   ★   ★

When I open the door, Claudia and James's bedroom smells faintly of deodorant, hairspray and perfume. The mix of all three combined with a faint whiff of sleep makes me think that someone's actually in the room with me. The curtains are still closed, which is probably a good thing in case any curtain-twitching neighbours opposite catch sight of me. I flick on the light and go right in. This room's as good a place to start as any. Despite my paranoia, I'm certain I'm the only one in the house. I even checked the garage to make sure James's car had actually gone. In order to leave with what I came for, I have to find out as much about them as I possibly can. I daren't go through his study until he's left the country. I can't blow this. I only have one chance.

I go into the ensuite bathroom. The smell of Claudia is even more pungent in here, with the steam of her early morning shower still hanging in the air like sweet pollution. There's a towel on the floor and the shelf above the basin is a mess — littered with uncapped bottles and lotions for face and body. A line of floss dangles down while a toothbrush lies discarded in the basin. The bristles are touching a globule of toothpaste that's stuck to the porcelain, as if someone left in a hurry.

I gaze around. What am I supposed to glean from the inner sanctum of Claudia and James's existence? There's little point me being in here but I couldn't resist a snoop. Every bit of information I can get will help me build a picture.

I imagine Claudia at work in a haze of perfume and neglectful parents, making life-changing decisions about broken families that she doesn't really know enough about, not if she's honest with herself. Then, in my mind, I see her sitting in her office, chewing on her pen, changing people's lives for ever, but before she knows it she's suffocating beneath an avalanche of baby powder and a mountain of soiled nappies, and being deafened by a thousand screaming infants. She's choking, sucking it all up into her pregnant body. She instinctively grabs her stomach, wincing from the pain as she goes into labour. She falls to the floor, legs apart . . . and then I am there to help her . . .

'Stop it!'

I stare at myself in the mirror. What's wrong with me? My cheeks are sunken and I have grey rings beneath my eyes. I must take control. Taking a deep breath, I switch off the bathroom light.

Back in the bedroom, Claudia's wardrobe is more organised than her messy bathroom. On the left side she hangs her tops and dresses, and on the right she has a selection of stretchy skirts and large-waisted trousers. Most of these are dark in colour to contrast with the voluminous and brightly-coloured tunics she's stocked up on. I imagine her wearing each of these outfits, all perfectly chosen and coordinated from expensive boutiques. Me, if I were pregnant (the very thought makes me morning-sick with envy) I'd wear tight-fitting T-shirts in shades of brown or grey and have them stretch and ruche over my bump. I'd sling on a man's cardigan with big deep pockets in which to stuff my tissues. There'd be a lot of tissues. I'd be very emotional, all those hormones racing through me, controlling me, making me feel crazy and sad one minute then ecstatic the next. But, as things stand, I am stuck on the even keel of not being pregnant; no wacky rush of hormones for me today. I'm pretty numb to it now.

I touch one of the maternity dresses and it slides off its hanger. I stare at it on the floor of the wardrobe. I pick it up and hold it against me. Claudia is taller than me. Un-pregnant, I imagine she's a size twelve or fourteen against my size eight. The dress is a pink and orange Pucci-style print and it makes me look barely there behind its gregariousness. It comes down to mid-calf on me whereas I reckon it would be a more fashionable knee-length on Claudia. Plus, her colouring — those swathes of dark hair and her rosy complexion — would handle the clash of hues on this bright dress. On me, it would simply confirm my invisibility.

I throw it onto the floor and stamp on it in my socked feet. Sobs well up in my throat, as if someone has their hands round my neck, squeezing ever more tightly. When will this choking feeling end?

I grab the wardrobe for support and still myself, head bowing between my arms. What was I thinking? Momentary loss of control is not part of my agenda. I pick up the dress and shake it out. It mustn't look creased. I hang it back in the wardrobe and am about to shut the doors when I notice something on the floor of the cupboard. It's a pretty white and green floral box with 'Keepsakes' printed on the lid.

I've seen this sort of thing before. Oh yes, many times on numerous trips to the baby department of John Lewis or Debenhams or stacked up among Baby's First Albums and soft rag books in that fashionable little baby boutique near my place. My *old* place.

I stop and tilt my head to the ceiling, trying to make the tears go back in.

I take a breath. This is a box for keeping safe newborn photos, first bootees and locks of hair tied with cotton. This is the kind of place you stash wobbled-out milk teeth — tiny and jagged — and snapshots straight after the birth that Mum doesn't want in the family album. It's where you find baby's first birthday cards and a christening order of service, or the first wavy marks ever made on paper by a clumsily-held crayon. This box holds the deepest memories, the most special mementos, the very beginnings of life. It gets opened once every few years and added to less and less as time goes by.

I lift it out. It's heavier than I'd expected. I give it a little shake. There's stuff in there. Has Claudia already been collecting keepsakes from her pregnancy? Or perhaps the contents are for the twins, collected by James and his first wife. The lid is veneered with a skim of dust, indicating it's not been looked at in a while.

I blow hard at the top of the box, place it on the carpet, and kneel down beside it. I stop. Listen. Did I hear something, someone? My heart thumps in my throat like a second, guilty beat. What would I do now if Claudia came home, burst into her bedroom to find me rummaging through her wardrobe? *Sorry, Claudia. I just wanted to know what it feels like to be pregnant; to have pregnant things; to wear pregnant clothes.* Would she accept that? Would she understand that I probably want — no, *need* her baby more than she does?

I lift the lid. I stare at the contents.

I feel as if I've taken a peek inside a womb, the very inner sanctum where life is held so precious. My fingers itch to rifle through this box of . . . of . . . what are they? Keepsakes? Treasures? My vision goes a little blurry at the sight of them.

Oh my God.

My heart pounds faster, if that's possible. I hold my breath and crouch over the box. On top of all the items in the box is a photograph. It's not particularly in focus but it's of a baby — a tiny, naked, baggy-skinned baby — lying in a clear plastic hospital cot. The baby is blue-grey-purple and has no nappy wrapped round its frog-like legs. A white plastic bracelet dwarfs its twiggy arm.

Someone has written in blue marker: *Charles Edward. Born prem at 22 wks.*

I lift the photo with freezing fingers. I'm shivering. Beneath it I find a tiny woollen hat, knitted in the finest and palest blue yarn. A bloodied yellow umbilical cord clip is nestled within the woolly folds. Then I see a strip of printed-out ultrasound scan photographs, already yellowing around the edges with age. I've seen these type of things on the telly and admit to taking a look at some on the internet, wondering what it would be like to have the doctor explain to me where each limb was, if it was a boy or a girl, showing me the flappy heartbeat as it lub-dubbed what little blood had so far formed around tiny veins.

The small digital print on the dark image reads *Claudia Brown.* They are her scan pictures then, but the date — 19/4/2003 — tells me they are not from this pregnancy. The womb is identifiable — a dark oval area — and within this space is a fuzzy white-grey blob. If it's a foetus, it doesn't look very big. I am staring inside Claudia's womb. The thought makes me shake more. On the back, someone has written: *Baby Ella. 18 weeks. Stillborn.*

Saliva pools in my mouth as if I'm about to be sick.

I continue my trawl of tragedy. The box is brimming with many similar mementos, each one a reminder of a baby lost. There are three further scan pictures, each from a different pregnancy taken around fourteen weeks' gestation and all with the date of miscarriage written on the reverse. There are poems penned by a bereft mind — *My empty arms ache to hold you . . . The smallest fingers, the cutest nose . . . No woman as barren as me* — and a crumpled piece of paper bearing two footprints: *James Michael, passed 7/10/2008.*

'These are the prints of a doll,' I whisper, marvelling at the ten tiny perfect toes.

Claudia's misery, her emptiness and self-loathing are apparent from the heartfelt poems. I'm assuming it was she who wrote them as my eyes drag over the grief they contain. How can one woman suffer such loss and yet still continue to try for a baby? I drop my hands to my lap. It makes me feel even more wretched about what I am going to do to this family. 'But all this has made her strong,' I say to myself, stroking the side of the keepsakes box, trying to lessen the guilt.

I stop dead still. Did I hear someone? There it is again.

I replace the lid on the box and shove it back inside the wardrobe. I dash out of the bedroom and run down the stairs. Someone is hammering on the door. When I get there, a delivery man is standing on the top step tapping his fingers on a large package leaning against his thigh. 'Sign here, please,' he says impatiently, handing me an electronic gadget and a stylus. I do this, and he passes over the box. He leaves without another word and I lug the delivery inside.

It's addressed to Claudia, and one end is caved in and damaged. Through the open bit I can see something straw-like but wrapped in plastic. Don't they say you should check

102

delivered items immediately? Or is that just my inquisitiveness getting the better of me? Either way, I don't want to get into trouble.

I drag the box through to the kitchen and snip the remaining tape. I peel back the cardboard and inside I find a straw Moses basket wrapped up in polythene. I slide it out of its wrapping and find a crisp set of white sheets and drapery to go on it. I arrange the bedding and set the crib on the white metal stand it came with.

Standing back, admiring my work, I try to imagine Claudia's newborn baby sleeping in this cot. For some reason, I can't.

★ ★ ★

'What are you doing in my room?'

I turn. My hands are shaking. She's caught me even though I was doing something nice for her. I'm not rummaging through her private belongings.

'This was delivered earlier,' I say. 'Isn't it lovely? I thought I'd surprise you and set it up. The packaging was badly damaged and I wanted to make sure that whatever was inside was OK. Thought I might as well bring it upstairs for you.' I step aside from the Moses basket. Claudia's curtains are still closed and it's dark outside now. 'Isn't it lovely?' I say again as she silently walks up to the basket. I've put it beside her bed.

'Yes,' she says vaguely, squinting at me as if she doesn't trust me. She's still wearing her coat

103

and leather driving gloves. Her handbag is slung over her shoulder and she smells of winter. She gives the basket a little wobble then stares straight at me, straight into my eyes. I see the tiniest muscle twitch on her cheek.

12

Liam Rider sat in the waiting area with his legs spread and an elbow resting on each knee. His head was dropped forward and his black and grey hair was mussed and unwashed and thinning at the crown. At first glance, he appeared nothing more than a Saturday-night haul, albeit on a weekday, a drunken misfit who was teetering on the edge of either vomiting or passing out. It took several moments for him to look up when Lorraine called his name. The others in the waiting room glared at him. The pierced woman with the irate toddler, the man in a suit, the couple of lads in tracksuits — they'd all happily queue-jump and take his place.

'Mr Rider,' she repeated. 'I can see you now.'

Lorraine held the security door wide open until Rider got his act together and realised he was needed. He stood slowly with all the effort required by a man whose life was about to fall apart. Lorraine couldn't help the little inward smile. He'd come here of his own accord, after all, so she'd made herself promise to be . . . to be *nice* to him, see what he'd got to say. He walked through the door and Lorraine caught the faint whiff of a man on the brink, a man whose bathroom habits had been bumped down the list of priorities. And all for what? A few shags with one of his students. She wondered if he thought it was worth it now.

'Take a seat,' she said once they were inside the interview room. It was a grey and dull space with not very much natural light. She didn't bother flicking on the fluorescent strips. 'What is it you want to see me about?' she asked, perched on the corner of the second, smaller table in the room. Sitting down opposite him would have somehow signalled her approval of his presence and, in turn, his behaviour. She couldn't condone that. If he'd come to say something helpful to the investigation, fine. If not, she would make this quick.

'I am Sally-Ann's baby's father,' Rider said quietly, shaking Lorraine from her thoughts. His hands were clasped together — fingers entwining like hopeless lovers — as they poked out from the ends of tweed sleeves. 'She wasn't sleeping with anyone else.'

What a total caricature, Lorraine thought as she absorbed the smugness of what he'd just said. How did he know Sally-Ann hadn't been sleeping with anyone else? The same way his wife no doubt believed in her husband's fidelity, Lorraine supposed. She imagined him mixing with university professors and getting up to endless scholarly antics and jolly japes. Then she remembered he was just a teacher at the local community college — hardly an Oxford professor — and the leather elbow patches, untamed hair and thin-rimmed glasses suddenly lost their intellectual appeal. She wondered what on earth Sally-Ann, a pretty young woman, had ever seen in him.

'I already know that,' she said. The results had

just come back from the lab.

'But I swear I didn't kill Sally-Ann.' He bowed his head.

I know that too, Lorraine thought, but didn't say it. His alibis had checked out. Rider was teaching at the college on the day in question and there was CCTV footage to prove it. Russell Goodall's movements, however, hadn't been quite so easy to map. 'Why should I believe you? You have a strong motive.'

'I might have fucked things up with my wife and Sally-Ann but I'm not a murderer, for Christ's sake.' Rider gripped the table and, for a second, Lorraine thought he was going to cry. 'I'd have done the right thing by her and the baby somehow. Taken a second job or something. Just don't tell my wife.' He hung his head again. 'Please.'

'Is that the only reason you wanted to see me in person?' Lorraine suddenly felt powerful. He'd come to beg.

'No.' A glance up again. He swallowed. 'I have the name of someone who might be able to help you.'

'Oh?' *Bastard*, she thought. 'So you want me to promise not to tell your wife about your misdemeanour in return for this little gem of information?'

Rider nodded.

'You realise I could arrest you right now for that?'

Rider swallowed. 'I . . . I'm not withholding anything. I just want it to be fair. Sally-Ann and I — '

'You were cheating on your wife, Mr Rider. Why should any of this be fair?' Lorraine felt her heart quicken. It was like a drug she couldn't shift from her system; a drug she wished she'd never heard about.

'Fair for my wife,' he clarified. 'I know what I did was a shitty thing to do. But it's over now.'

'Obviously,' Lorraine stated.

'So there's no reason for Lesley to find out or get hurt then?' He leant back in the plastic stacking chair.

'You'd better ask the journalists,' Lorraine said. She glanced at her watch. 'They'll print what they want.'

'Look, Sally-Ann went to these childbirth classes. She'd seen them advertised in the local paper. Once or twice she asked if I'd go along with her but, obviously, I refused. It wouldn't have been right. I think she saw some kind of future for us, hoped I would leave Lesley and my kids. There was no way I was going to do that. Anyway, Sally-Ann made some new friends at the class and got close to one woman in particular. Amanda Simkins. They hit it off right away.'

'And?' Lorraine was lost. 'Did you ever meet her?'

'Several times,' Rider said. 'But I didn't like her from the start.'

Lorraine didn't quite see the relevance of all this but she allowed him to continue.

'They used to do breathing and yoga, learn how to spot the signs of labour and change nappies.' Rider paused. 'That kind of stuff.' He

108

made a face that indicated he'd never understand.

'All sounds very normal to me,' Lorraine said, sliding off the edge of the table. She folded her arms. 'Pregnant women going to childbirth classes and making friends. Don't tell me, I bet they went for coffee afterwards, too.' She added a little chuckle.

'They did indeed,' he said. 'But want to know something odd about that woman?' Rider added, also rising.

He was a good deal taller than Lorraine so she stared up at his unshaven face. 'Go on then.' Her hand was on the door handle. She could hardly wait.

'Amanda Simkins isn't even pregnant.'

* * *

They didn't tell the class instructor they were coming. Instead, they waited in the hallway of the old Baptist Church Hall, peering in through the glass square in the door at a dozen or so women in various stages of pregnancy writhing around on yoga mats.

'You didn't do anything like that when you were pregnant,' Adam said through a sour smile.

'No,' Lorraine replied. 'I was too busy catching criminals to have time for such luxuries.'

The woman taking the class, Mary Knowles, kept glancing at them through the foot-wide aperture with an increasing frown spreading across her brow. In the end, curiosity got the better of her and, once the women were lying down with blankets covering them and the blinds drawn and the lights dimmed, she came to the door and yanked it open.

'Can I help you?' she said in a fierce whisper.

'I'm DI Lorraine Fisher and this is DI Adam Scott.' They showed her their IDs. 'We're from the Major Investigations Unit.' Lorraine paused to allow the introduction to sink in. 'We were going to wait until your class was finished but . . . ' She trailed off and raised her eyebrows.

'It's about poor Sally-Ann, isn't it?'

Lorraine nodded. 'We're interested in what you know about her. In particular, the women she got friendly with at your classes, like Amanda Simkins.'

'Oh, I see,' Mary Knowles said, almost apologetically. 'That would have been at my Bordesley Green class. I run several in different areas of Birmingham. They're very popular.'

'We can wait until you're finished, if you prefer,' Adam said, peering back through the door at the women on their backs. 'And talk properly after your class.' Several of them were shifting uncomfortably.

'It'll be over in five minutes,' Mary said. 'They're just relaxing now. It's important.'

Lorraine and Adam retreated to a wooden bench and waited. Lorraine wished she could relax. She let out a huge sigh and turned round. Notices of several events taking place at the hall were pinned on a cork board above them. An indoor car boot sale, a brownie cake sale, a youth disco. One or two had already passed and the

110

leaflets were outdated. There was one advertising Mary Knowles's antenatal classes. Apparently she hired out water-birth pools as a side-line.

'Does it take you back?' Adam asked as they waited.

'Not really,' Lorraine replied, but then wished she'd said yes as the door opened and a stream of chattering women waddled out, some having to open both of the double doors to get through. Their daughters were fourteen and seventeen now, young adults, and it made Lorraine sad to think about the relentless passing of time. These women were just starting out, with sleepless nights, endless nappies and guilty feelings of inadequacy stretching ahead of them. But then she felt suddenly relieved to have got to this point in her life without too much maternal trauma. She'd been a good mother, hadn't she? And now that the girls were older and more independent, as well as beautiful, loving, popular and hard-working, she was technically more able to do what she wanted in the little free time she had. It was just that she never had any. *Although everybody else bloody well does*, she thought, glaring at Adam.

'Do come in now,' Mary said from within the hall after the last woman had left. She'd opened the curtains at the tall windows and a low winter sun grazed in across the dusty wooden floor. She wriggled her arms into a grey tracksuit top, snuggling her pert breasts within as she zipped it up. Lorraine didn't fail to notice Adam watching her as she did this. It was pathetic.

Or was she the pathetic one for noticing him

noticing, she wondered? Or perhaps he wasn't even noticing them at all and she just thought he was? Paranoia, then. Perhaps they should try another counsellor after all.

'So,' Mary said rather authoritatively, as if she was the one in search of information, 'Sally-Ann Frith.'

She broke the words down into precise syllables. It made the poor lass seem still alive, somehow, Lorraine thought. She remembered the girl's mother, Daphne, how strangely in control she'd seemed despite the terrible death of her daughter. If it had been one of her girls . . . she shuddered, shaking the thought from her mind. Golden rule: don't personalise cases. Ever.

'She was due any time, if I remember correctly. Let me recall . . . yes, I think she was having a C-sec, wasn't she?' Mary Knowles stared at Lorraine and Adam down a long nose. Her whole face was long, like a horse, Lorraine thought.

'Yes. Someone beat the hospital to it, I'm afraid, as you've no doubt heard,' Lorraine said.

'My ladies are a bit twitchy about it, you know,' Mary replied, as if admonishing them for not having caught the killer yet.

'Twitchy?' Adam said stupidly. He probably thought it was a side-effect of being pregnant.

A slim finger with an unfeasibly long scarlet nail tucked back a strand of hair. 'What if he strikes again? What if he's a serial killer targeting pregnant women?' Her voice was virtually begging Adam to save her, Lorraine thought.

'It's not *women*,' she said, in order to stress

112

that this was an isolated case. Of course, to pad out the short statement they'd so far fed the press, several of the national papers had delved into similar stories in the States where babies had been ripped from their mothers' wombs in jealous fits of foetal abduction. It was enough to stir speculation. 'We have no reason to believe Sally-Ann was targeted because she was pregnant. What would be really helpful is if you could tell me something we don't know about Miss Frith.'

Mary thought for a moment. 'She was lovely and a popular member of my class.' Her voice quivered a bit. 'And she was taking care of herself and the baby. You know, keeping healthy and eating all the right things. I don't think it was a planned pregnancy, but she'd resigned herself to being a mother.'

Lorraine nodded. 'What about Amanda Simkins? Do you know her? Did she come to your classes?'

'What about her?' Mary said with a laugh, without actually answering any of Lorraine's questions. 'She's a one, that's for sure.'

'What do you mean, 'a one'?' Adam said.

'You know, a *one*. Someone who stands out but not necessarily for the right reasons.'

'In what way did she stand out?' Adam asked.

Mary glanced out of the window as if that might help the words come. She wrinkled up her nose. 'She's what I call a wormer-inner,' she said finally. 'Always trying to get in on the act, never wanting to miss a trick, desperate to be the centre of attention. You know.'

'I see,' said Adam, although Lorraine could tell that he didn't.

'To sum her up, I'd say she's needy.' Mary appeared pleased with her description.

'When's her baby due?' Lorraine asked, recalling Liam Rider's strange comment earlier. She glanced at Adam.

'That's what I mean,' Mary said. 'She's not even pregnant. She comes to my classes because she thinks it will help her *get* pregnant.' Then she said in a whisper, 'I think they're having a hard time, she and her partner. You know . . . '

'Isn't that a bit odd, coming to an antenatal class without actually being pregnant?' Lorraine thought it was, anyway.

'A little, perhaps, but not unheard of. I've had one or two ladies in the past who simply wanted the relaxation. I'm not going to turn them away.'

'Pregnancy by proxy,' Adam said insensitively.

'Absolutely,' was Mary's reply. 'That's just the kind of woman she is. A wormer-inner. But it's another fiver a week to have her in the class and her money's as good as anyone else's.'

'Can you give us her address, please?' Lorraine asked.

'Certainly not,' Mary replied. She gathered up the paper file on the table and stuffed it into an oversized shoulder bag. 'My ladies' details are confidential.'

'Mary,' Adam said, beating Lorraine to it, 'we are the police. This is a murder inquiry.'

They both stared at her. Lorraine suddenly remembered that Grace had a driving lesson during her lunch break and she'd forgotten to

114

give her a cheque that morning. Adam cleared his throat loudly, impatiently.

'OK,' Mary said as a slight look of fear swept over her face. 'But don't tell her I told you. I can't afford to lose another lady.'

'Another?' Lorraine blurted out without thinking.

Mary pulled the folder from her bag. She flipped it open and scribbled an address on a notepad. She ripped out the page. 'Well, Sally-Ann won't be coming to class any more, will she?'

13

'She was *in our room*, James. Are you not hearing me correctly?' I'm shaking. Is it anger or fear? I need a stiff drink but can't have one.

'So?' James doesn't see the problem. 'She works for us, Claudia. She lives here now. You'll have to get used to her popping up in weird places at weird times. Wait until I walk in on her when she's in the bath or we find her snogging some chap on the doorstep.' He is pan-frying lambs' livers. They look and smell disgusting.

'I sincerely hope she's past *that* phase,' I say, calming down a bit. 'That's why I went for someone a bit older and therefore, hopefully, more sensible.'

'Exactly. Did you ask her what she was doing in our room?'

'She was setting up the new Moses basket. It was delivered today.'

'Oh no!' James mocks. 'Surely that's worth an immediate sacking.' He waves the wooden spatula at me and I poke out my tongue. He's already made a caramelised red onion sauce, which smells delicious, and there's a pot of creamy mash keeping warm, and some sprouting broccoli in the steamer. But those little slices of liver, they don't look so good, all coated with flour and crisping at the edges as he slides them around in the butter.

'Both boys out like lights!' Zoe startles us by

singing out her success. 'They're exhausted from that play session earlier.' Her hands are shoved tightly in the front pockets of her grey skinny jeans. On top she's wearing a faded green T-shirt with a zip-up fleece over the top. She looks a lot younger than her thirty-three years. Her skin is clear and smooth and still wrinkle-free, making me feel about twenty years older than her, not the six I actually am. I smooth down the creased grey jumper dress that I've stretched over my bump today. Along with thick tights and ankle boots, I didn't look too bad early this morning. But a day of dragging-on-for-ever meetings and a particularly unsavoury home visit hasn't helped my appearance, or mood. I feel tired and tetchy.

'We went to Tumblz Play Zone with Pip and Lilly,' she says proudly, as if she's just taken a walk on the moon. 'It was crazy fun. I ended up in the ball pit, completely buried.' She laughs and swaggers into the kitchen. 'Listen, I'm sorry if I upset you earlier, Claudia. I didn't think it through. I shouldn't have gone in your bedroom.'

James looks at me expectantly. I hold up my hands. 'Hey, no problem,' I say. 'It was kind of you to carry the Moses basket up for me. It's so pretty, James. I can hardly believe we're going to have a daughter in just a couple of weeks.' I swallow down the lump in my throat. I hate saying things like that, tempting fate. What if something goes wrong? With my history, I won't breathe easy until I'm actually holding a healthy baby girl.

'You could be late going into labour,' Zoe says,

as if she's an expert on such things. 'So it could be up to a month from now, couldn't it? They'll induce you if you go past forty-two weeks.'

'You're right,' I say.

'There's increased danger of infant mortality both post-and antenatal in babies delivered following an extra-long gestation. Then there's the risk of other complications, too, such as placental failure or hypertension.'

'My midwife's taking good care of me,' I assure her, impressed with her knowledge of late pregnancy, although I can't help wondering how she knows so much.

★ ★ ★

By the weekend, I've become a little more accustomed to Zoe's presence. It's a good job because from Monday onwards it's just me, her and the boys. James suggests a day out for all of us, and immediately one of those corporate team-building places comes to mind where we have to build a raft together or make a bridge out of lollipop sticks strong enough to hold a man. I know he's doing it for peace of mind before he leaves. One final check he's not abandoning me to Psycho-Nanny.

'But it's bucketing down,' I say. Bed is warm and cosy, and even though we haven't opened the curtains yet, I can hear the drumming of the rain on the roof, the cars, the already sodden ground.

'But quite mild, though.'

James rolls over and tries to sling an arm over

my bump. I gently push him away. It's just not comfortable like that. Or, I admit to myself, it's not comfortable knowing we can't finish what we start, and definitely not comfortable that he's leaving so soon. I snuggle into the crook of his shoulder. He smells of sleep and deodorant and it pretty much kills me cold inside that we're going to be apart for so long.

'It was a nice surprise to find you here when I woke,' he mumbles.

He's referring to me crawling into bed beside him at four this morning. I'd been awake since three. My mind was racing with everything that lies ahead.

'Do we have to go anywhere today? It's so cold and miserable out.' I just want to stay here for ever with James nestled at my side. I feel bigger than ever, bundled up against the sub-zero temperatures in my thick winter pyjamas and towelling robe. James always makes fun of me. One minute I'm complaining I'm too hot, the next I'm moaning that it's freezing.

He lowers his voice even though there's no way Zoe can hear. 'I think we should all go out together. It'll give me one final chance to make certain about her before I leave. I'm doing it to put your mind at rest.'

'And what do we do if we're not convinced?' James doesn't answer but I can almost hear him telling me that I'll have to give up my job. 'Look, I'll be honest. Do you know why I really came in here so early?'

James emits a deep, resonant laugh. 'To share your insomnia?'

'I heard noises coming from the top floor.' My turn to whisper.

'That'll be because we have our nanny living up there, Claud.'

'She was banging about all over the place. I should know. The spare room's directly below her.'

'Perhaps she went to the loo. Or was hungry. Or perhaps, actually, she still feels a little unsettled having moved in with a new family and she couldn't sleep either.'

'No. It wasn't any of those things.'

'Rather certain, aren't you?' James rolls over and props himself up on his elbow.

'I didn't hear the toilet flushing. You know how loud the old pipes are. If she was hungry, she'd have come downstairs, and she didn't. I know every sound in this house. And she's certainly not fretting about living here. Far from it. She asked to stay here at the weekends, didn't she?' I'm already regretting agreeing to that. A couple of days alone with my children each weekend was what I'd envisaged.

'You're right, of course.' He tries to grab me. 'She's undoubtedly a psychotic insomniac murderer who's going to do away with all of us in the middle of the night.'

'James, don't.' I roll away from him and slide my legs out of bed. I heave the rest of my body up before he can grab me again. Suddenly I'm not in the mood for cuddling.

I pull back the curtains and groan. The weather is not good for a day out. Straight shafts of rain pelt from a low, greeny-grey sky that seems to merge with the rooftops like a smudged painting. I glance up and down our street. Despite the weather, people are still going about their usual Saturday-morning business. Mr Ford, the old man who lives opposite, wanders down his front path with Ned, his terrier, on a long leash. He once told me he was born in that house; that everything in his whole life had happened there — deaths, marriages, divorces, fights, love stories, laughter and tears, he said with a sad glance at his feet. 'This house was once so full of people, Claudia my dear.' He'd made a point of introducing himself as soon as I moved in with James. 'It was always so busy and vibrant and stuffed with noise and chatter — the scrape of a violin being practised or a piano being hammered to within an inch of its life.' He'd laughed a toothless laugh, and I'd noticed a fat tear in each eye. He'd sniffed them back. 'Now it's just me and Ned.'

I imagine him rattling around the six-bedroom Victorian home with its brown-painted banisters, creaky doors and Fifties-style kitchen in which he prepares microwave meals for one.

'All empty,' he'd finished, banging his heart, and I knew exactly what he meant.

James is beside me, peering down the street. 'Curtain twitcher,' he says fondly. His arms are around me, hugging around my chest like a tight empire line. I can't breathe so I ease him off.

'Poor chap, he's all alone,' I say as the stooped body of Mr Ford wrapped in a brightly coloured sou'wester progresses slowly down the street in a yellow blur.

121

'He's all right. Off to get his paper, give Ned a bit of a walk. It's all about routine at his age.'

'I guess,' I say, turning and kissing James. His mouth feels warm and deep and I feel so utterly lucky and grateful to be a part of this family.

★　★　★

Two hours later and I'm face to face with a hammerhead shark. I can't help but be impressed and also a little scared of the two beady-eyed creatures that swim up close to the glass, making Oscar and Noah catch their breath at the absurdity of their faces and the proximity of danger. The sharks are ugly yet beautiful and have absolutely no idea that they are in the centre of Birmingham. They seem happy enough despite being far from home.

'Can they see us?' Oscar asks. He pushes two fingers inside a tiny box of raisins.

'I don't know. What do you think?' Zoe is crouching beside the twins, alternating her look between them and the sharks. She pulls back slightly as one of them approaches the glass at speed then veers off at the last second.

'Yeah, and they think we're in a zoo,' Noah replies quite intuitively. I slip my arm through James's as our son giggles at the thought of us all being in captivity.

'But what if they break out?' Oscar asks.

'Then we run!' Zoe says with a silly face.

'But why?' Noah says, crushing his empty box of raisins. 'They can't chase us. They don't have legs. I'd actually help them.'

'That's very kind of you, darling,' James says. 'Shall I take a photograph of you with the sharks?'

'Yeah!' both boys chant together. They huddle up against the glass.

'Go on, Zoe, you get in too,' James says. 'One for the family album.'

'Family Flickr now, isn't it?' I say. James has been scanning lots of old photos and putting them online so that the rest of the family can see the boys growing up.

'Oh no, you don't want me in it,' Zoe says bashfully. Her cheeks go pink and she steps away.

'Of course we want you in it,' James reiterates. 'Go on, get between the boys.'

'No, really,' she says. 'I won't.'

She's pretty red-faced now, I notice, and breaking out in a sweat. 'Don't force her, James.'

'I need the Ladies,' she says, and scuttles off.

'It was only a bloody photo, for Christ's sake.' James is feeling a bit embarrassed at having upset her. He snaps a couple more shots of Oscar and Noah.

'Don't be too harsh,' I say. For some reason I want to defend Zoe, although her behaviour was rather odd.

'You've changed your tune, haven't you?' James glances at me and then toggles through the photos with Oscar and Noah straining to see the camera's screen. They jump about at his side.

'Look, that's us!' Noah says excitedly.

'But no sharks,' Oscar notes. It's true. There's one blurry lump in the blue fuzzy background but nothing that could be identified as a hammerhead.

'Take another one, Daddy,' Noah demands, but Zoe returns and James silences him.

'Well,' I say. 'Shall we go and find the squid?'

'Is that cally-mary?' Oscar asks, as if it might be a friend from school.

I'm still thinking what he means when Zoe realises. 'You mean calamari?' she says with a laugh. She seems fine now.

'You have them with mayonnaise,' Noah says, licking his lips.

'The boys discovered them on holiday last year,' I explain to Zoe. 'They thought they were onion rings at first,' I whisper, holding on to my bump as we make our way through the displays and tanks. The array of colours and water through the glass makes me dizzy so I take James's arm.

'Are you OK?' he says, quietly concerned. I nod in reply.

'Oh wow, look!' Zoe grabs each of the boys by their hands and drags them off at top speed down the darkened walkway. I hear their gasps of shock as she points into a large glass tank. We amble up and arrive just as the largest crab I have ever seen pokes out a long skinny leg in our direction.

Oscar cries and covers his face.

'You're a baby,' Noah says. 'It's just a stupid old crab.' Despite his bravado, I notice his dimpled hand grip tighter around Zoe's fingers. Her nails are short and practical and she wears a single ring.

'Am not,' Oscar replies. He clings to James's leg.

'Look at his eyes,' Noah says in awe. 'Are they made of big caviar?'

We all laugh, but Oscar whimpers. 'It's like a horrid spider,' he says. He turns his back on the tank, which is teeming with other fish and crustaceans.

As we carry on and walk through the tunnel with fish swimming overhead like birds, with coral as bright as jewels and unidentifiable creatures flapping and sculling all around us, Oscar begins to cry.

'What's up, sweetie?' I ask, doing my best to get down to his level. James will have to help me stand up again.

Oscar buries his face in James's overcoat, twisting the tweed wool between his fingers, covering the dark fabric in snot. 'There are shadows everywhere in here,' he says through hiccupy sobs. He peeks out and glances around the tunnel. It's true. Crazy colours and swathes of darkness wash around us as if we really are in the unknown depths of the ocean. It's beautiful, but frightening to a sensitive four-and-a-half-year-old.

'They can't hurt you,' I say, and Zoe is right beside me offering tissues and reassurance and whatever hugs little Oscar will take. 'It's just the weird lights making us look funny colours. And those are just reflections.' He jumps as another family walks past, their faces big as ghouls in the glass. 'Nothing to worry about.'

'I'm scared, Mummy,' he says, transferring his

grip from James's coat to my hand. 'That shadow looks just like the bad person in my room last night.'

I glance up at James at exactly the same time Oscar's eyes widen to saucers. I'm not sure if it's amazing that he called me 'Mummy' or utterly disturbing that he's claiming someone was in his room last night.

14

They're probably going to sack me now they think I've been creeping around their kids' bedroom scaring them witless. They no doubt think I'm a freak because I rather vehemently avoided having my photograph taken in their fit of family nostalgia. As we walked back to the car, I overheard Claudia talking about noises coming from my bedroom during the night. James told her, in a terse whisper, that she was being silly, paranoid, hormonal.

Of course she is, I feel I should say as we drive home in silence.

Between us, James and I scoop Oscar and Noah from the cocoon of their car seats, but by the time we've lugged them inside and prised the dead weight of their bodies from within the thick padding of their coats and scarves, they've woken up. They're grumpy, and Oscar has wet himself.

'I'll sort him out,' I say as Claudia's face crumples at the thought of dealing with her son's accident. She looks exhausted. I bet she's thinking that it's my fault he's been sitting in his own pee, that his car seat cover will need washing and his brother is meanly laughing at him for being a baby. She believes it was me lurking in his room last night like a shadowy underwater creature, scaring him to the point of wetting himself in his sleep, giving him nightmares. 'It's no problem,' I say when she asks if I'm sure. It goes some way to stamping out the flicker of guilt.

'I'll make some macaroni cheese then,' Claudia says with relief. She waddles off into the kitchen while James hangs up coats and dumps shoes on the rack in the porch. He catches my glance as I lead the boys, both now whining, upstairs. I notice a twitch on the soft grey skin beneath one eye.

Half an hour later and the twins and I go back downstairs in much better spirits. The bath has warmed and woken them while clean pyjamas, their favourite cartoon slippers and the smell of cheesy macaroni sends them scampering to the table. 'Just in time,' Claudia says, spooning dollops of creamy pasta onto five plates. The table is already set — apple juice in a jug, an open bottle of white wine, glasses, knives and forks spread out with gingham paper napkins in between.

'None for me,' I say just before she serves the last plate. She stops, looks at me. 'I'm . . . I'm going out tonight. If that's OK.' I bow my head. It's last-minute. It's crazy and dangerous, I know, but I can't help myself. I feel my cheeks redden.

'No supper before you go?' she asks sweetly. 'There's plenty.' She waves the serving spoon and a clump of macaroni plops back into the dish.

'I'll get something while I'm out.' That's a lie. I don't feel at all like eating, in or out.

'No problem,' she says. I can't help noticing

128

the slight note of relief in her voice. Now they can eat without me, a family of four, just as they used to do before I came along. 'Pass these to the boys, James,' Claudia continues, and her husband silently puts food in front of the children. Together they watch me leave the room.

When I have fetched my coat and bag from upstairs, I call out the cheeriest good-bye I can manage. The front door is closed before I hear their reply.

★ ★ ★

The pub is crowded but I'm certain she's not here yet. My nerves aren't firing or aching as if they've been stripped raw, and my pupils aren't stretching to saucers at the sight of her. The hair on the back of my neck isn't prickling with anticipation and I can't detect the musky notes of her sad perfume.

'Gin and tonic, please,' I say to the lad behind the bar when I finally inch my way to the front. His hair is long and messy and he's wearing a T-shirt with 'God Save the Queen' printed on it. He turns round to fetch a glass from the shelf. I don't usually drink gin but tonight it feels as if I should. It somehow seems fitting. He puts my drink on a white paper mat and I give him the money.

I turn, sipping the bitter fizziness, and look for an empty table. What we need is a quiet corner for two, a hidden alcove where no one will see us. I don't want anyone spying. But all I can see is a pub full of bodies — mostly men, mostly roaring out hilarious stories to one another before they finally head home to their families. There are several clusters of women standing about wearing impossibly high heels and dresses that are more like tops. I squeeze between a group of businessmen and stand on tip-toe to see if I can spot a table. I can't. It wasn't the best meeting place to choose.

My text was spur of the moment yet I'd spent all of last night thinking about it, pacing about, unable to sleep for worry. *I want to see you. 8pm The Old Bull, cnr Church and Brent Rd. X*

I didn't receive a reply until we'd come out of the aquarium, blinking in the low winter sun that had finally made an appearance after the morning's rain. The world was suddenly mirrored, fresh, dangerous — seemingly reflecting everything I was trying to ignore. The feelings I had wouldn't stay hidden for ever.

She'd agreed to meet me. *OK* was the briefest of replies, and without the usual *X* at the end. That alone instantly sent me into a flat spin of worry about her.

There is a small gap near the door so I go and stand in it, hoping to spot her if she comes in. I barely have room to breathe. People are all around me, jostling and shoving as they make their way outside for a smoke or to the loo.

It's her hair, as ever, that I spot first. It's as if the pub's caught fire and we're all burning up.

I shake my head. I'm being ridiculous.

'Cecelia!' I call out, way too loud. I put my hand above my head and wave frantically. Everyone stares at me. I lower it the second she sees me, and then the blush comes.

I watch her walk towards me, pushing through the crowd with ease. The world lurches into slow motion as she drags our entire history behind her.

'Heather,' she says. Her voice, low and sweet as if she drank syrup, catches me unaware even though it hasn't been that long since I last heard it. She raises a nearly full glass at me, and I wonder how long she's been here, how I could have missed her.

There is a biting moment when neither of us knows whether or not to draw close and peck a kiss, but then some jerk seals our indecision by jostling me and making me slosh my drink over my hand. It dribbles down to my elbow. I glare at him, and in a second Cecelia is mopping me with a tissue. I laugh nervously. It's so unlike her to do that.

'I'm glad you came,' I tell her. The words tumble over each other. She must think I'm drunk.

'You sounded . . . urgent,' she says. 'I thought something was wrong.' How she gleaned that from a plain and simple text I don't know, but then that's the thing between us. I'm suddenly reminded of the twins and the way they seem to know what the other's thinking. It's happened several times already since I've been working for Claudia, as if their connection is way more than common growing space in a womb.

Oh God, *Claudia*.

My stomach rolls and knots as if I'm stricken

with disease. I don't want to think of her right now, yet here I am, squashing back the feeling of guilt that I'm about to shatter the Morgan-Brown household into a million pieces. It's not a matter of if. It's a matter of when.

'I've been on the lookout for a table, but there aren't any.' It doesn't seem right, telling her standing up. That's the thing with Cecelia — and don't I know it: everything has to be perfect. Even with her own brand of just-picked-it-up-off-the-floor meets vintage-shop-finds, Cecelia's image is carefully crafted right down to the mismatched shades of nail polish she wears on each finger, and the quivering strands of red hair that appear not to have been brushed for a week but have, in fact, taken half an hour or more to place into mussed clumps.

'My feet are killing me,' she comments, and I glance down between us. Ridiculously high chunky grey and yellow wedges still don't bring her up to my height.

'Poor you,' I say, although, in truth, I don't really mean it. I feel annoyed with her.

Distracted, I stand on tip-toe again and spot it, littered with empty glasses. 'Quick,' I say, right up close to her ear. She smells of cinnamon. 'There's a table free.' I make no apologies for legging it across the pub and lunge down into one of the three chairs just as another couple are about to settle in. I can't help noticing that the woman is pregnant. I look away, pretending not to have seen.

132

'Well done,' Cecelia says. She's wearing fuchsia tights and a short patchwork skirt. She wiggles it down as she sits, legs primly folded away from me.

I don't know how to begin so I sip my drink instead. I wish I'd ordered a double. Triple. The whole bottle. A distillery. 'How's the work going?' I ask, and she immediately tips her head at me and pulls back her hair. 'Oh, wow,' I say. 'They're stunning.'

'It's Diana. She's a fertility goddess.'

I feel the lump that's sitting deep in my neck pulse. Did she wear them to make a point? I lean towards the earrings and take a closer look. Anything to distract myself. 'She's half tree.' I sound inane.

'I morphed her legs into an oak tree. Diana was a hunter, too. She's kind of my heroine.' She says this with a slow laugh from over the rim of her glass as she takes a sip.

I already know this. She's told me a million times. I suddenly feel very inadequate. Cecelia is very talented. I uncross my ankle and bump her leg with my boot. 'Sorry.'

'How's the new job going?'

I can't believe she's asked. My nose wrinkles and my lips part but nothing much comes out. What am I supposed to tell her? 'We were talking about *your* work,' I say.

Cecelia seems happy enough to veer back to her jewellery. It's part of her, intrinsic to every day of her life. 'I got a new order today.'

I nod. 'Good.' I imagine the client choosing from her bizarre pieces. She once designed a controversial range of jewellery that she called 'Rape'. She was even featured in a couple of Sunday papers. The next day, there were loads of complaints about the accompanying photographs. What did she expect? The model was semi-naked, draped in what appeared to be used condoms, and blood, and was bound up by handcuffs and had a masked man, also semi-naked, looming menacingly over her while the designs glittered somewhere in the mess. She was accused of glamorising sex crimes. I can't say the jewellery was particularly pretty or wearable although it certainly got her noticed as a designer. A couple of stores in London regularly order as a result, although what she supplies to them isn't quite as eye-widening as the phallic necklaces with removable female body parts. That was Cecelia on drugs or something.

'So. How's it going?' I ask lamely, simply to postpone the inevitable.

'Yeah, like I said, I'm OK,' she says, peering at me over the top of her glass as she takes a sip of wine.

'Cecelia . . . ' I put out my hand but she halts it with her look.

'No need,' she sings. She tilts her head. 'What did you want to see me about, anyway?' She knocks back the rest of her drink. A sure sign that she's becoming angry. A sure sign that I did the right thing by moving out.

This is it then. The proper end. No going back. I'd better get it over with. 'I thought you should know, after everything' — *after all your hopes, your plans, your dreams* — 'that I'm not pregnant.'

She stares at me a long while before getting up and leaving.

15

Lorraine left Adam at work. While the Frith case was currently eating up most of their time, he'd told her that he had some other matters to take care of. She'd stood there winding her scarf around her neck, pulling on her leather driving gloves before slinging her bag over her shoulder. She'd hoped he'd come home with her. 'Sorry,' he'd said, glancing up from behind stacks of files. She'd walked out of his office feeling empty, slightly bereft, and sad. It was the first time she'd felt like that about him for ages. Since he'd told her, actually.

'Grace?' Lorraine called out when she got home. 'Stella? Anyone home?'

In the kitchen, Lorraine found her eldest daughter sitting at the kitchen table with several files of work and a text book spread out in front of her. There was a plate of uneaten burnt toast and a glass of water sitting beside her. Lorraine wondered how she could see well enough to study. The main lights were off with only the under-cupboard lights casting a vague glow across the room.

'Hello, love. That looks nourishing. Didn't you see my note?' She waved the morning's quickly-scribbled instructions under Grace's nose. 'Stew in fridge. Microwave for five mins. Too hard?' She was about to ask where Stella was but then remembered she'd gone to her friend Kate's for the evening. No doubt she'd get a phone call at about ten to come and fetch her.

Grace said nothing. She looked worried, Lorraine thought, sitting there like a lost waif, twiddling her pencil and clearly not paying a scrap of attention to her books. She was determined to apply for university but this didn't look like the studious daughter she knew.

'Don't you feel well, love?' Lorraine stood behind Grace's chair and stroked back her long hair. It felt a little greasy. Grace pulled away, so Lorraine went round and sat down opposite her daughter. 'What's wrong, Gracie? Bad day?' Lorraine blew out in a big sigh to signal that she too had had a taxing one and perhaps they could compare notes, have a giggle like they usually did. 'Gracie?'

Grace definitely wasn't looking at her books. She was staring at the table. The old pine surface was stained with years of spilled wine, rings from hot coffee mugs, bored kids scratching grooves with pencils, compasses, fingernails, and what looked like some of last night's dinner still stuck to a placemat. Surely the history this bit of furniture contained wasn't that captivating. No, Grace's eyes were focused on somewhere a long way off and, sitting there in her crumpled school uniform — she hated that the sixth-formers at her school still had to wear it when other local schools did away with it in the A-level years — she could have passed for a miserable fourteen-year-old rather than the burgeoning, happy young woman Lorraine knew her to be.

'Better get a clean one ironed for tomorrow,'

Lorraine said, leaning forward and swiping a finger down the front of Grace's white shirt. 'Bit grubby.' She tapped her on the nose but Grace flinched away again. 'Fancy a cuppa?'

Nothing. No response.

Lorraine had had enough. She stood up. 'If you won't tell me what's wrong, I can't possibly help you, so I'll say no more about it.'

'Is this how you interrogate criminals?' Grace suddenly said. Her voice quivered over the words.

'No, I go much easier on them.' She tried to sound light as she sat the kettle on its base and flicked it on. She leant back against the worktop staring at Grace's back, noticing how her spine was rolled forward a little, having the effect of drawing her shoulders protectively up round her ears. Her shirt had come untucked from the grey pleated skirt that she insisted on wearing ridiculously short. Her black woolly tights ended with pink velour slippers with red check bows on the front. They were old and worn at the toes.

She's still just a kid, Lorraine thought.

'Aren't you hungry, or is there something wrong with my cooking?'

'There's nothing wrong with the food,' was Grace's lean reply.

'Shall I warm some up? I might join you. Dad's going to be late back.' She was careful not to allow any bitterness into her voice. They'd kept his confession from the girls, and both intended to leave it that way. But sometimes, just sometimes, she wished she could pour it all out to Grace, have her stroke her head for a change,

138

bring her tissues and a hot water bottle, watch a rubbish movie and scoff a pile of chocolate together. The times she'd done that for her girls over the years, she thought, as the moppings-up of countless best-friend fallouts, bad grades at school (in Stella's case) and boyfriend woes (Grace) tumbled through her mind. Each, in its own way, was as immense to her girls as the crap she was stuck with in her head about Adam. The stupid thing was, she still loved him.

'What?' Grace shifted in her seat, turning round to see her mother staring at her.

Oh God, had she just said all that out loud, Lorraine wondered? 'You look pale and tired. I'm not taking no for an answer. I'm going to heat up the stew and — '

'I'm leaving,' Grace said matter-of-factly. She turned back to her books, reanimated by something.

Lorraine frowned. She began warming up the food. 'Surely you've got time to eat before you go.' Her mind tracked through her daughter's schedule. Leaving? What did she have on tonight? Drama club? Was Matt picking her up? Were they off out — cinema, bowling? As the food warmed, a comforting smell of onions, garlic and red wine permeated the room. She poured a glass of Merlot for herself.

'I mean I'm *leaving*, Mum.'

'It's not drama tonight, is it?' Lorraine said, puzzled. Grace didn't respond. She must be seeing Matt then. 'Where are you two lovebirds going? Try to be home by half ten.' More than once she'd had to stop Adam charging down the stairs and out into the street to prise Matt's mouth off his daughter's as they said a prolonged goodnight. The lad was nice enough, but being older than Grace and owning his own car meant that he had a lot of freedom. And he expected to enjoy a lot of it with their daughter.

'Not leaving as in going out for the evening,' Grace said impatiently. 'I'm leaving *home*. For good.'

Lorraine dropped the wooden spoon into the pot and watched it sink. She took a large swig of wine and paced over to the light switch. With a forceful click, she illuminated the room.

'What on earth do you mean?'

'I can't say it clearer than that, Mum.' Her eyes stared into nowhere again. 'I'm just sick of it here.'

Lorraine stared at her daughter, trying to read the resentment behind her tired eyes. She looked exhausted. Had she been eating properly? Lorraine couldn't be sure, and with all the pressure of looming exams and the extracurricular stuff she took on, no wonder she was having a blow-out and cooking up crazy plans. It would probably all be over by morning.

'I understand exactly how you feel,' Lorraine said. A stock reply, straight out of a parenting book. She knew it meant nothing really; meant nothing because, if she was honest with herself, she hadn't a clue how Grace felt.

'Mum, don't bother. I'm moving in with Matt. It's all arranged. I'm leaving school, and we're getting married soon.'

No! Lorraine forced the explosion to stay

140

inside. It was all so sudden, sounded so final. What the hell had got into Grace? She sloshed more wine into her glass and turned to find her daughter standing, packing up her books.

'What are you doing?' Lorraine took another mouthful, the Merlot searing down her throat.

'Putting my stuff away. And don't bother trying to change my mind.'

'And just how do you think you're going to support yourself?' She trembled at the thought. Her daughter, her precious Gracie, was leaving home, quitting school, and *getting married*. A bad day had turned into the shittiest one of her life.

Grace glanced at her watch. 'Matt and I are going to get jobs, of course. I've already applied for some.' She smiled tersely, which made Lorraine feel as if it was all her fault. Of *course* it was her bloody fault! 'Don't worry, we've got it all worked out.'

'And what do you think your father will have to say about this hare-brained plan? What about your exams, university, the rest of your life? Do Matt's parents know?' Lorraine felt her face redden and prickles of sweat break out. At the other end of the hormonal spectrum, this was no time to be getting a hot flush.

'Mum,' Grace said with a laugh — a *laugh!* — 'you're overreacting, as usual. You can't stop me doing what I want. And yes, of course Matt's parents know. They're giving us our own room until we get a place of our own.'

Lorraine suddenly felt about ten years older than when she'd arrived home. 'I didn't even know you and Matt were . . . ' She trailed off, trying to block the thoughts of her daughter and Matt in bed together. 'I hadn't realised . . . ' — *it was that serious*, but she couldn't finish. 'What's wrong with living here, with us, your family? What about Stella?'

'Mum, just drop it.' Grace swished back her hair. 'We love each other. We're engaged.' She thrust out her left hand to show off the slim band of gold with a small, faintly glittering stone. 'He's going to get me a better one when he can aff — '

'You stupid, stupid little girl!' Lorraine shouted. 'Do you honestly think I've got time for this?' She was visibly shaking. 'Get this ridiculous idea out of your head right now and go and finish your studies or do something useful like ironing a shirt.'

'You've forgotten already, haven't you, Mum?' Grace was standing with her hands on her hips, her chin jutting forward, the crests of her prominent cheekbones flushed rose. Her eyes still appeared sunken with grey circles beneath, and Lorraine couldn't help noticing again how thin she looked. Hadn't she been wearing that same school skirt for aeons? 'You once promised me that whatever happened, whatever I did, whoever I became, you'd love me and support me and respect me.'

The words were bullets and sank directly into Lorraine's heart. She had indeed once said those words, probably when Grace was about six or seven.

'So show me you actually meant it,' Grace

said, walking out of the kitchen and closing the door quietly behind her.

★ ★ ★

She'd finished most of the bottle by the time Adam got home.

An hour earlier, she had taken some food upstairs. 'Love?' She'd knocked on Grace's bedroom door and put the tray on the floor outside. 'There's some dinner here.' She'd then gone directly back downstairs knowing that her daughter would, fox-like, be more tempted to open the door and take it if she weren't there watching, ready to pounce. She'd poured herself more wine.

God, she could do with a cigarette. Then she remembered the emergency packet tucked away at the back of the booze cupboard, mainly for when their friends Sal and Dave came round for supper. Perched on the back-door step, they would inhale the smoke and blow it all out again through drunken giggles as Adam, who didn't smoke, sat alone at the table chucking insults and health statistics at them. 'Poor Adam, he's fuming in his own way,' Sal had once noted through a bubbling laugh. It had seemed hilarious at the time.

She pushed aside sticky bottles of Southern Comfort and Baileys that only ever got drunk at Christmas. There. At the back. The red and white beacon of a pack of Marlboro. She reached in and shook it. Not full by any means, but there were some left.

143

A few moments later she was standing in the back garden, hidden by the shadow of the shed, shivering, freezing, wishing she'd put on gloves as well as her coat and scarf, sucking as deep and hard as she could on the first cigarette she'd had in ages. It felt bloody glorious.

Stamping her feet to keep warm, she allowed Grace's shocking news to gradually sink in. *Leaving home? Getting married?* Her daughter was serious. Adam still had the sickening swell of realisation to go through; at least she was one step ahead of him there, although she felt regret at her outburst. She knew she'd overreacted, but Grace's announcement had pressed a button. Was her daughter's life so intolerable that she wanted to move in with another family? If she was honest, it was this which stung the most.

There was a noise. A shaft of light fell across the darkened lawn as the back door opened. 'Ray?' *Damn it, don't call me that!* 'Are you out here?' Then she heard low murmurings followed by 'you were supposed to fetch Stella'. The door slammed.

Shit.

Lorraine dropped the half-finished cigarette, knocked back the rest of her wine and left the glass on the low wall beside the shed. She dashed back to the kitchen door, feeling wobbly and unsteady. She made it inside just as Adam was leaving the kitchen with his arm round Stella.

He turned and glared at her. 'You forgot her. She's been phoning you but you didn't answer.'

'Stel, I'm so sorry, love. Time got away and . . . ' She ran the tap, poured herself a glass

144

of water, and downed it in one. Her fingers smelt disgusting.

'What's the matter, Mum? Are you mad at Dad?'

'No, love, I'm not.' *More mad at myself*, she thought.

Lorraine glanced at the clock. Ten-thirty. She needed to be at work at six. 'I need sleep, and so do you. Plus I want to have a word with your father.'

It usually meant trouble when she said 'Your father' instead of 'Adam' or 'Dad'. Adam pulled a face and yawned.

'Night then, Mum. And don't worry about not fetching me. Kate's mum didn't mind. She said you were probably working. Catching criminals and stuff.' Stella pecked a kiss on each of her parents' cheeks and went upstairs.

Only when Lorraine heard her bedroom door close did she speak. 'You're not going to like this,' she began. 'Sit down.'

Adam frowned but remained standing. 'The case?'

Lorraine shook her head. 'It's Grace.' Then she held up her hands at the sight of Adam's concerned face. 'She's upstairs. She's fine.' She paused. 'Fine-ish.'

'What is it?' He folded his arms. Strong forearms, Lorraine noted, somehow feeling slightly saved now that he was home to share the burden. 'Tell me.'

'She's dropping out of school and fucking getting married, that's what.' There was no easy way to say it.

145

Adam walked over to the drinks cupboard, fished out a bottle of Scotch, and poured himself a glass. They both sat down and looked at each other across the table. The house was silent apart from the large kitchen clock, which suddenly sounded ridiculously loud.

He wiped his hands over his face. 'Christ. Surely not?' was all he said.

Tired doesn't sum up how he looks right now, Lorraine thought with a stab of sympathy. She felt as if her family was crumbling around her.

'Oh, and she's moving in with Matt's parents until she and Matt find jobs and a place of their own.'

'She's winding you up. It's just a strop.'

'I think she's pretty serious about this, actually.' Lorraine knew when her daughter was dishing out empty threats. This was different.

'But why?'

'Because she obviously loathes us. Or rather, she loathes me. And from what she said, I know she's sleeping with Matt.'

'Fucking hell,' he said. 'Have you tried to talk sense into her?'

The kitchen door suddenly opened and Grace came in carrying the tray. She had eaten her meal. 'Thanks, Mum,' she said brightly as if nothing had happened. She put the plate into the dishwasher.

Adam stared at Grace, apparently unable to speak.

'I know what you're talking about,' she said, standing straight and tall. Lorraine could tell

146

she'd been crying though she'd done a good job of disguising it.

'Love . . . ' Lorraine trailed off. *Love, what? Love, we wish you were being more sensible? Love, we wish you could be more like your sister? Love, we wish you were eleven again?*

'What, Mum?'

'Dad and I, we were just discussing . . . talking about, you know, about you getting married. About you leaving home.'

'I'm really serious,' she said, 'in case you were thinking it would all blow over.' She flashed the engagement ring at her father. 'It won't.'

Adam and Lorraine each recoiled in their own way. Lorraine internally, her heart shifting and shrinking within its maternal cage, and Adam with his shoulders hunched, his fists clenching and unclenching. None of this was what they'd planned for their daughter.

Finally, Adam slammed a hand down on the table, making his glass jump. He rose, towering above his daughter. Grace stepped back.

'Like *hell* it won't!' he roared.

Grace fled the room.

With a sigh and a resentful last look at Adam, who had just made things worse, Lorraine followed her.

Upstairs, she sat beside Grace, who had climbed into bed fully clothed. She stroked her back, her hair, her shoulders, wondering how she could even contemplate chucking away her life like this. It took immense willpower to whisper stuff about everything being OK, that they'd make it work somehow, that she wasn't really angry. And while doing that she must have fallen asleep, because when she woke, when she prised one eye open and then the other, she was curled into the question mark of her daughter's body and it was already light outside.

16

Today's the day I lose my husband.

I roll over, hoping that by not opening my eyes, by not fully waking up, it might not actually happen. I don't want him to go. I love him. I want us to be a whole family. Soon we will be five. Adrenalin churns my stomach at the thought of it happening while he's away.

It's one of the most important Naval exercises of the year, my darling.

But it's the Mediterranean.

He wasn't even allowed to tell me the operation's codename. Just that it was in the Med. Somewhere. For up to two months. A pang of envy had torn through me. To me, the Med was a place of sun, bikinis, romantic dinners and dancing until after midnight. For James, it was many long weeks of being locked aboard a sub with a hundred crew, six-hour watches and a bunk shared with missiles, breathing machine-made air.

I hoist myself upright. My feet feel around for my slippers. Finally, tying my robe around my bulk, I pad through to our room to find the bed empty. He's already up and has to leave at ten sharp. He couldn't tell me how long he'd be away exactly, but it'd be in the region of six to eight weeks. I knew he saw the pain set deep inside my eyes.

'When you come back, she'll be here.' I'm

standing in the kitchen doorway, rubbing my tummy, trying to sound upbeat. He's biting into toast, glancing at *The Times* spread out on the worktop, coffee in one hand. He looks up. 'I told work I'd be in late. I want to see you off.'

'Darling,' he says, and comes over to greet me. His body feels warm and strong as if it's somehow preparing for the long days and nights at sea. He won't see the sun or the moon. He won't know the moment when I first hold our daughter or when she snuffles into my neck, hungry for a feed. He won't hear her first cry. 'I did try to warn you,' he says tenderly but also half joking. 'About marrying a sailor.' He senses my despair.

Sometimes I wish he'd give it all up, retire, abandon ship. It's not as if we're hard up. Not in the least. Even without his Naval career, James already has money. 'Too much to even talk about,' he once said in a silly hushed voice when I asked just how wealthy he was. 'I leave such matters to my accountant.' So why does he spend so many hours of shore leave holed up in his study poring over paperwork? When I suggested he get a better accountant, he was defensive. 'The Jersey firm has taken care of the family's affairs for decades. It's old money. Things like that don't change.'

When he refers to 'family affairs' and 'old money', he means the Sheehans. He inherited the lot from his first wife, Elizabeth, when she died. Early on in our relationship, I remember her brothers coming to see James, having lengthy meetings behind closed doors. Once, there was

150

shouting. I didn't want to pry but that's part of the reason I've kept working, so I'm not spending a dead woman's money. It wouldn't feel right. I think James feels the same about his Navy career.

'Coffee?' he asks while pouring me one anyway. He hands it to me and I perch on a stool. 'I want you to name her without me,' James says solemnly. 'I trust you. Get the boys to help you decide.'

Even though we've discussed suitable names many times, we've not settled on anything. I said we'd need to see her before we could choose, but then James broke the news that he would be away for the birth.

I smile at the thought of the boys naming their sister. Already I can hear rumblings upstairs as Zoe prepares them for school. I love them dearly and will treat them all the same but can't help thinking that this new baby, *my* baby, will feel slightly different. She'll really belong to James and me; truly be a sign of our love, our commitment to each other. I can't wait to bring her into our family. I just hope the twins will love her as much as I already do.

I stand up and go to the fridge but trip on the way. I grab the wall. 'Oh, she's kicking!' I think my stumble must have woken her. 'Quick, feel.' James comes over and I guide his hand to the spot. 'There.'

'Yes, yes, I felt her. Perhaps she's saying good-bye to me.' James grins, delighted with whatever it is he feels against his palm.

The twins come bowling into the kitchen

looking clean and fresh in their white shirts and grey pullovers. If I'm honest, Zoe has been an absolute boon to the running of the household and I almost feel ashamed at my early wariness of her. I admit that I'm actually looking forward to having a female companion while James is away.

'Lads!' James says, bending at the knees and curling an arm round each son. 'You know what day it is today?'

'Yup,' Noah says morosely. 'It's Daddy-going-away day. It's pooey.'

Oscar hangs his head and emits hiccupy sobs. James tightens his hug and I'm simultaneously jealous and proud of the male three-way bond.

'Who'd have thought,' he once told me — New Year's Eve, in fact, when we'd both had too much to drink — 'who'd have ever thought that my boys would be mostly cared for by someone who isn't me or Elizabeth?' He regaled me with tales of him and his first wife, how they'd had the big dream — the house in the country, four kids, dogs, ponies — and how it had been stripped from them in six short months from diagnosis to death. James told me that Elizabeth had made him promise to choose a new mother for the boys carefully. It was some consolation to me, I suppose, as I tried to swan happily around the cocktail party in my new red dress. James apologised in the morning.

'Hey, silly billies, I'll be back before you know it, and guess what?'

'What?' they chant in unison.

'You're going to have a very special surprise to

show me, aren't you?'

At this, the boys straighten and seem happy. They glance up at me, and Noah says, 'A new baby sister.'

They've had it all explained to them. I think they have a pretty good understanding of the situation. They don't remember Elizabeth, though James and I make a point of including her in conversation when appropriate. It's hard but necessary. She is their mother. I am trying to be.

'But I want the baby now,' Oscar says in a whiny voice.

All this time, Zoe has been clattering plates and toast and cereal and fruit onto the table. She deposits Marmite and strawberry jam, milk and a carton of juice in the centre and then fishes out a mug and helps herself to coffee. I suddenly feel very lucky, and the anticipation of holding my baby makes me quiver with excitement, although I try not to think about the pain and angst of getting to that point, of coming back home, settling her in, and, eventually, going back to work. After everything I've been through, it all seems so impossible, so far-fetched.

'Come on, Oscar and Noah,' Zoe chimes. 'Hurry up and eat your breakfast or we'll be late.'

The morning rush continues in much the same way as usual, except that when the boys have brushed their teeth, collected up the packed lunches Zoe has made and slipped on their shoes and coats, it all gets rather sad again.

'Bye, Daddy,' Oscar sobs. 'Be careful under

the water.' I'm reminded of his aquarium fears and realise that they probably stem from what he knows of his father's Naval antics. I doubt there was anyone really lurking in his room.

'Bye, Dad,' Noah chants. He likes to use 'Dad' against Oscar's 'Daddy'. It makes him feel more grown-up. 'Have fun with the fishies.' He grins and pulls a half-eaten packet of fruit pastilles from his coat pocket. His face lights up.

'No way, José,' I say, and take the sweets from him. He pulls a face.

'You keep this place ship-shape until I come home, understand, boys? Look after . . . look after Mummy.'

He doesn't know how wonderful it makes me feel to be called Mummy.

'I'll be back before you know it.' James gives a sharp salute and pulls each of the boys' hoods up. 'It's cold out. Can't be too careful,' he says with a laugh. 'Now off you go or you'll be late.' I know how hard this is for him. His little boys stare up at him, pale-faced and expectant. James leans down and plants a kiss on each of their cheeks. 'Love you both,' he says, and I breathe out a sigh of relief.

'Love you too, Daddy,' they sing back, then they leave the house, one each side of Zoe as she calls out a friendly good-bye and good luck to James. The door shuts.

'That was awful,' I say.

James wipes his hands down his face. 'I'm so sorry,' he says. 'So sorry I'm not going to be here for the most important day of our lives. I hate myself for it.'

He told me he'd been there at the twins' birth. He'd watched the surgeon slice into his wife's belly and remove them — Oscar first, who came out wriggling, lavender-coloured, and screaming. Noah followed minutes later but was initially lifeless and a dull grey colour. He was given oxygen and rubbed vigorously but had to be taken to the Special Care Unit. Elizabeth blamed herself — a Caesarean had been the only option due to her health. The poor woman knew she would never see her babies grow up. But by the next morning she was allowed to hold them both. Healthy, but small. Perfect, and theirs.

'Look, James, I won't hear any more about this. I honestly think I'll go mad if you don't stop feeling so guilty. I'm a grown woman. I can cope. And I have Zoe.' I smile. I want him to know that everything will be fine while he's away. 'When you come back, your new daughter and I will be waiting at the window for you. I'll keep the home fires burning.' I laugh. It's a nervous laugh that smacks of fear.

James nods and heads for his study. 'A few things to clear up. I'm all packed. I'll give you a shout when I'm leaving.'

My cue, I think, to give him space before he leaves. He's already told me he's going to lock the study while he's away. It's something he's never done before, but he's told me where he'll hide the key. I don't imagine Zoe will be very interested in what's in there, but I go along with James's need for security.

I go back upstairs and lock myself in the shower room. This precaution is automatic, not a conscious thought, as with James and his study. I'd be mortified if anyone walked in on me while I was naked and saw me like this. I can't say I currently like the look of my body. I strip everything off and stare at myself in the mirror. I turn on the shower as hot as I can tolerate, and let it drench me. I stare down at the ceramic tray and convince myself that everything is fine, there is no blood, I am not miscarrying. I've promised myself that will never happen again. Nervous, fearful of the past, I breathe a sigh of relief as the water continues to run clear. When I shampoo my hair, it turns milky and frothy between my toes.

An hour and a half later, dressed in a navy tunic top with a black roll-neck sweater underneath, stretch-waisted work trousers and sensible loafers, my hair blow-dried, a little make-up, and I'm ready to face the looming separation.

It's a comfort knowing that Zoe will be fetching the boys from school, allowing me to throw myself into an afternoon of work and distraction. There'll be a lot to catch up on. I make myself promise not to think about my husband until I'm tucked up in bed later. Then I will imagine him preparing the submarine, catching up with his associates, swapping family stories and photographs, focusing on his tasks, setting out to sea, sinking deeper and deeper until no one knows where they are. HMS *Advance* will be nothing but a ripple on the surface.

We kiss. We hold each other. James bobs down

and allows his lips to linger on my belly.

'Did you feel?' I say.

'No,' he says sadly.

'It was a deep kick,' I tell him. 'She wants to get out.'

Another kiss, a hug, and he is gone. It's the way we've always done it.

I hear Zoe clattering about in the kitchen.

'That's that then,' I say, allowing my hands to flop at my sides. 'James has gone.'

'Tea?' she says. She tilts her head and her lips roll inwards in sympathy. She puts the kettle on.

'A quick one.' I must get off soon. I have so much to do.

'How come you haven't gone on maternity leave already?' she asks.

I laugh, glad to be distracted from the hole in my heart. 'The department's always over-stretched. I'm healthy, coping fine, so there's no reason not to work up until my due date.' I've already sketched out my job as a social worker to her, but I'm not sure she entirely understands. 'Besides, it'll give me more time to get to know my baby after she arrives. I don't want to rush back.'

'I understand,' Zoe says. She stares at my tummy but looks away when she sees me notice.

'I know. I'm a house, right? Not even semi-detached any more. I'm a full-blown stately home.' I laugh, and we sit down together at the kitchen table. I have to pull out a chair whereas Zoe can slip easily between the table and the bench that's against the wall. 'I can vaguely recall being your size once.' She's wearing jeans and a black T-shirt, which rides up as she sits down. She wraps her fingers around her mug. 'Aren't you freezing?' I ask, suddenly feeling like her mother even though our ages wouldn't allow that.

It's her turn to laugh now, making her look like a mischievous pixie. Her eyes sparkle. 'No, I'm fine. And don't worry, the boys took their coats to school.'

'Sorry, I didn't mean to sound — '

'I like it that you care.' Zoe's head lowers. The crown of her head radiates with darker hair showing through the blonde.

'Still finding things hard?' I'm referring to the break-up she mentioned.

Silence.

'Sorry, I didn't mean to pry.'

'It's complicated,' she confesses.

'At least there aren't any kids involved.'

Her head whips up and her eyes harden to cold steel. Her knuckles whiten as she grips the mug. 'No,' she says slowly, painfully. 'At least there aren't any children.'

'Zoe,' I say rather pathetically. I lean across and give her a hug, feeling the little leap of her ribs as a sob leaves her body. 'I'm so sorry. I didn't realise . . . '

I know that look — the look of an empty woman. The look of need, desire, and the craving to nurture. The look of an unfulfilled mother. God knows I've seen it in the mirror enough times.

'I'm just really glad you're here,' I tell her honestly. It's the best I can do for now. I squeeze her hand.

'I have to go out,' she says finally, and dashes to the hall.

A moment later the front door bangs and I am all alone in the house.

17

Lorraine watched as the forensic photographer straddled a patch of blood shaped something like Australia. She snapped on the plastic shoe covers and stepped reluctantly into the room. Adam followed her. He hadn't said a word yet. He didn't need to. His face showed enough disgust and despair for him to remain silent.

They'd received the call and immediately left what they were doing, arriving at the scene moments after the pregnant girl, barely alive, had been taken to hospital. She was clinging on to life, they'd been told, and it was touch and go. Her abdomen had been cut open but they'd not had news of the baby.

Lorraine glanced around. The ghost of the woman seemed to hang in the air, screaming out the fear and panic that was evident from the grotesque mess left behind. If it hadn't been for her friend arriving, making the emergency call, she'd be dead by now. Adam and Lorraine cautiously assessed the scene as if even the tiniest breath would destroy a key piece of evidence. Like last time, it just made no sense.

'Someone she knew?' Lorraine suggested, closing her eyes to prevent another gag. The air reeked of fresh blood.

'Possibly. There's no sign of a break-in,' Adam noted, glancing at the door.

'Who'd want to?'

They looked around the grim flat. There wasn't much to see. A tiny kitchenette with an old gas cooker took up a cupboard-like amount of space at one end of the council accommodation, while a dingy living room — the only window was shadowed by an evergreen tree outside — contained a single sofa, now bloodied, and an old portable television. The bedroom was filled with a double bed and a wooden cot, which was piled high with what appeared to be clean laundry. Lorraine assumed it was clean, anyway.

'The victim's friend found her on the sofa here.' Adam was stalking around the living area. He was getting in the photographer's way.

Lorraine peered at it. Mushroom-coloured velour had largely been transformed into rust-red. Congealed and already cracking around the edges, the blood had made a remarkable pattern. If viewed through a squint the sofa's new style could almost be mistaken for something deliberate, something macabre.

'She was due any day.'

They stared at each other, everything else in their lives on hold temporarily.

'The friend is waiting next door with the neighbour,' Adam said, and then took a call on his phone.

Lorraine went back out into the communal hallway. The dark, cold space stank of urine and weed. A cluster of youths had gathered at the top of the concrete staircase. 'Get off with you,' Lorraine said to them as she peeled off her shoe covers. She bagged them and gave them to the guarding officer to dispose of. The kids just

161

stared at her. One belched. She felt ancient again.

The door to flat number seventy-three was ajar so Lorraine went straight in. She could hear the soft weeping of a female overlaid with the cajoling tones of a trained officer. As she went through to the living room — the flat had the same layout as next door but in reverse — Lorraine heard the rasping voice of an old man trying to help. Cups were clattering.

'Hello?' she said, and rapped on the living-room door. 'Detective Inspector Fisher here,' she added, going straight in.

A young woman sat in a puddle of grief in a green wing-back chair. The gas fire belted out a fierce, dry heat. The window was dripping with condensation and the sill was crusted with years of black mould, oddly mimicking the young girl's face with her tears and streaked mascara. She couldn't have been more than twenty.

'I'm so sorry about what's happened to your friend. Is there any news from the hospital?' It wasn't a murder inquiry yet, unless the unborn baby had died.

When the girl didn't manage an answer, the WPC turned and shrugged. 'All we know, ma'am, is that she was still alive when she was taken away. Emma here is very upset. She wants to visit her friend in hospital — Carla,' the WPC added in case the DI didn't already know the victim's name.

'Thanks, love,' Lorraine said, feeling doubly maternal as she noted the similarly young age of the constable. She sat down on the edge of a

162

small matching sofa.

The old man, presumably the occupant of the flat, came in with a tray of tea. 'Now we need another one,' he grumbled, staring at the detective. 'Sugar?'

'Not for me, thanks,' Lorraine said. The hygiene of the place was dubious. 'It's good of you to have us here. We'll be gone soon, once Emma recovers.'

'No problem,' the old man said. He scratched his balding scalp. White flakes floated to his shoulders. His brown cardigan was covered in bits of skin. 'She came a-hammering on my door something urgent,' he continued. His voice was caked with phlegm and he struggled to clear it. He gripped his crotch briefly. 'When I let her in she was screaming to use the phone. Thought they all had them mobile things these days.'

'Thank you, Mr . . . ?' Lorraine wanted to talk to Emma. The old man would have to wait.

'Mr Duggan,' he stated.

'I need to speak with Emma now. We can talk about what you heard shortly.'

The old man muttered something and went back into the kitchen. There was more clattering.

'Emma,' Lorraine said, 'I want you to tell me everything that's happened to you this morning.'

The WPC passed Emma her tea. Emma's hands shook as she took it, spilling some on the grey marl track pants she was wearing. They were grubby anyway, Lorraine noted. But the pink and blue sweat top she had on appeared clean and was printed with the fading name of a band, perhaps someone she'd seen years ago. It

163

was far too small for her. Emma's streaky blonde and mousey-brown hair was pulled back into a high and tight ponytail. Her life, her looks, her past, her prospects couldn't be further from that of her own daughters.

And then she remembered that her eldest child was giving up her comfortable home and loving family and most likely heading for a life of single motherhood on benefits. Perhaps they weren't that different after all.

'I was coming to see Carla, yeah?' she began. It was all mixed up with sniffs and sobs and quick bursts of breath. 'We were going to get a shake or something.' Something was 'sumfing'. Lorraine was patient. 'I knocked but there was no reply. I heard something, like an animal in pain and that, yeah? So I just went in. The door was unlocked.'

'Go on.'

'My eyes didn't believe what they was seeing. As soon as I went into her living room, even before that, there was this smell. This stink of blood and shit.' Emma let out a small retch as she recalled. 'Then I saw Carla lying on the sofa and I thought she were dead, yeah?' She stared directly at Lorraine. Her eyes were velvet brown, her pupils indistinguishable through the tears and sadness. 'She was naked apart from her bra. She had blood all over her. On her face, her arms, her legs. Oh God!' Emma dived into her hands and sobbed. The constable produced some tissues. 'There was this big gash on her belly and it was like she was heaving or pushing, like her body didn't know what it was doing.'

'And there was no one else in Carla's flat, apart from her?'

Emma shook her head. 'She opened her eyes and looked at me. For a second, she knew I was there.'

'Did she say anything?'

Emma paused and thought. 'All she said was 'Help me' before she passed out again. I was screaming and I ran round here to use the phone.' She was panting again, blowing her nose, rubbing her eyes with the snotty tissues. 'I called for an ambulance and the police. They came really quickly and took her away. I stayed with her until they came and when I tried to follow them, they wouldn't let me. They said I had to stay here to talk to you. Is she going to die?'

Lorraine sat up straight. 'Honestly, I don't know the answer to that. We'll get an update from the hospital soon. Tell me about the baby's father, Emma. Do you know him?'

'No,' Emma replied, as if it was a silly question. 'Not even Carla knows that.'

★ ★ ★

Carla Davis was in theatre when Lorraine and Adam arrived at Queen Elizabeth Hospital. They were met by the ward sister who told them that Carla would be brought to the critical care ward within the hour. 'Don't expect much from her,' she added. About the same age as Lorraine, the sister was a stocky red-haired woman with green-framed glasses, the lenses of which made her eyes appear twice their normal size. 'She'll be groggy from the anaesthetic and pumped full of drugs. My guess is she won't be fit to interview until at least the morning.' She nodded a firm full stop. 'You can wait in here if you've nothing better to do.' She eyed the pair suspiciously.

When the ward sister left them to it, Lorraine went off to find a drinks machine. When she came back, Adam was talking into his phone. He hung up as soon as he saw her return. Lorraine's stomach knotted. She bit the inside of her mouth and handed Adam a bottle of water.

'How long do we wait?' she said.

She could see Adam was about to give a considered reply when they heard a scuffle and noise coming from the nurses' station. 'I want to see her now . . . I'm her fucking father . . . let me see her . . . I have rights, you know . . . ' They went to find out what was going on. The young girl from the flat, Emma, was attempting to calm down a man dressed in black jeans and a leather biker's jacket. He had a helmet under one arm and wore long buckled boots that reached his knees. He reeked of cigarette smoke. The ward sister had been joined by a male nurse, and between them they weren't doing a particularly good job of silencing him.

'This is a hospital. You need to keep the noise down and respect what the sister is telling you.' Adam's attempt at discipline wasn't much more successful.

The man swung round. 'Who the fuck are you?' His face was a mix of anger and fear.

'The police, so you might want to pack it in,' Lorraine replied wearily.

'Don't tell me what to fucking do.' He took a step forward. Lorraine and Adam stepped closer, ready to restrain him. 'My daughter's been fucking stabbed so don't you — '

'Mr Davis?' Lorraine interrupted. The man nodded, his face crumpling. Lorraine thought he was going to break down. 'We're here about your daughter's case. She's in theatre right now.'

'See, Paul? I told you they was going to make her better, didn't I?' Emma's hopefulness was, well, hopeless, Lorraine thought. From what she'd heard so far about Carla's injuries, it was less than fifty-fifty at best.

'Can we speak to you, Mr Davis, while we're waiting for news of Carla?' Lorraine asked. 'We can talk in here.' She led the way to the visitors' room when Paul Davis showed a flicker of compliance.

They sat in plastic stacking chairs that were set out around an old wooden coffee table strewn with magazines. Paul Davis's leg was jiggling up and down while his hands pulled tirelessly at the wisps of hair hanging around his ears. Emma sat silently, and the fluorescent lights buzzed overhead, making everything seem rather surreal. Occasionally there was the beep of a machine in a side ward and a nurse would dash past. The telephone rang, porters clattered along the corridors with beds — some empty, some filled with patients hooked up to drips and monitors.

Lorraine asked questions as carefully and tactfully as she could.

'Carla's all I got,' Paul said. 'She's so independent. Likes to manage alone.' His voice

167

was croaky, as if he was a heavy smoker.

'Is her mother around?' Lorraine asked.

'She died a couple of years back.' He paused a moment. 'I never expected nothing like this to happen to Carla. They said she's been stabbed. Who would do that to a pregnant lass?' The man writhed in his chair. His face was torn with pain and he swept his hands down his face. 'I couldn't stand to lose her too.'

Lorraine glanced at Adam. Like her, she knew he would be feeling dreadfully sorry for this man. She also knew that the shock of Grace's news was still sitting just as heavily in his chest as it was in hers.

'Does she have a boyfriend?' Adam asked, mirroring Lorraine's train of thought.

'She's had a few. Don't they all, these young girls?' He glanced across at Emma. That single, questioning look told Lorraine that he hadn't really got a clue about his daughter's life. She'd moved out, lived off benefits and probably, truth be known, hadn't seen her dad in months. Was this how things would be between them and Grace?

'Carla had a few one-night stands. She were dead pleased about the baby when she found out,' said Emma, who, Lorraine thought, would probably be the best source of information until they could speak with Carla herself. 'She hasn't had much luck with boyfriends and that. When she were in care — '

Emma received a sharp kick in the leg from Paul Davis.

'Foster care?' Adam asked.

'It wasn't nothing,' Paul replied quickly. The nervous leg-jiggling started up again. 'Sandy and me, well, we found it hard sometimes. We thought it best if Carla were looked after. She could be a difficult girl.'

Adam and Lorraine each made a mental note to contact Social Services. There'd be a case file, the usual miserable story of a family gone to the wreckers through lack of money, drugs, alcohol, laziness, violence, or a combination of those things. It might throw something up.

The ward sister came into the visitors' room. Her face was expectant, her tone reserved. Everyone looked at her. 'Carla's on her way back from theatre. She's stable. Things went as well as they could.' She took a breath that seemed to suck all the air from the miserable room.

'Things?' Lorraine said, standing. Carla's father also stood, and approached the nurse in a slightly aggressive way. Adam was immediately beside him, watching his every move.

'It's the baby, I'm afraid,' she went on. 'There was nothing they could do to save it.'

'But Carla's going to be OK?' Paul said, grappling with his emotions.

'There's a good chance, yes,' she replied.

Paul sobbed, stumbling back to the chair with Emma's help. Lorraine beckoned to Adam and they left the visitors' room together. They waited in the corridor and within ten minutes a pale young woman was trundled through to a side ward on a high-sided bed. The porters nodded at them as they watched the girl go past. She didn't look much older than Grace. Unconscious,

169

waif-like, hooked up to a drip and portable monitor, it was obvious there would be no talking to her that day.

'I'll wait,' Adam said, glancing at his watch. 'You go home. Grace will be back from school soon and she needs her mum.' He squeezed her arm. Lorraine stared at his hand on her jacket before shrugging it off. 'See if you can talk her round.'

On the drive back, she rang the unit for an update. DC Barrett told her that aside from a three-month suspended sentence for theft, Carla Davis was a heroin addict and her baby was already on Child Protection's at-risk register. It would probably have been taken into care as soon as it was born.

Lorraine pulled up outside her house. She locked her car and went inside. 'I'm home,' she called out. As usual, there was no reply. She heard the faint thud of music coming from upstairs. Then louder giggles as a door opened and someone scampered across the landing, banging the bathroom door. Moments later there was more girlish laughter.

My beautiful daughters, Lorraine thought proudly. A soft smile crept across her face as she draped her coat over the banister rail. Then her stomach knotted once more at the thought of it all.

18

The door is locked. I rattle it again to make sure I'm not mistaken.

Damn.

I want to kick it, punch it, get a crowbar, shove it between the brass knob and the frame and wrench until the wood splinters and cracks and falls away, allowing me in.

I glance at my watch. I don't have much time. I need to find out about the family and how much money they have, how they function, who's in control of what, who deals with the finances. Any snippets going will do. I want to build a picture of their past, their present, but not their future. I can guess what that holds. For now, I want a snapshot of their lives — the big picture as well as the minuscule one.

I crouch down and peer through the keyhole. I can see the front of James's desk but that's all. Last time I was in his study was to extract Noah from the green-leather captain's chair behind the desk. He was begging Oscar to spin him round but his brother was standing in the doorway shaking his head and biting his bottom lip, crying that they weren't allowed in there. 'Come on, Noah,' I said from behind Oscar, my arms spanning the doorway. It felt as if there was an invisible force-field protecting the entrance, but, while Oscar and I knew not to cross it, Noah didn't care a hoot. What was it James had said, not long after I'd moved in?

It's private in here.

There must be a key somewhere. I glance around the hallway. There are several tables — a battered pine one on the way to the kitchen and an antique demi-lune piece set against the long wall leading to the staircase. A vase of fresh lilies adorns its semi-circular top, and there's a drawer in the mahogany front. I open it. There are some receipts, some batteries rolling around, a lone glove and a couple of biros. There are also two keys on unlabelled plastic fobs. They don't look like the sort that would fit the big old door to the study, and I'm right. When I try, they're a hopeless match.

I fumble my way through all the pockets of the coats hanging in the porch, and suddenly it all feels very underhand, as if I'm betraying their trust in me. My mouth goes dry, which is frankly ridiculous, and I'm reminded of being a kid desperately in need of money for the cinema or some sweets and scrounging off my parents by secretly checking their clothes for loose change. I always found a quid or two, always managed to just fit in with my mates somehow, appear like one of the gang even though I wasn't. Considering everything, I was the lucky one.

I don't find any keys. Just an assortment of tissues, half a packet of mints, a hair band, and a set of ear phones.

I think carefully as I rearrange all the coats. James would have been the one to lock the door before he left. It's his study. But it would be impractical for him to take the key with him.

Claudia is bound to need to go in there at some point while he's away. What if there is a financial crisis, or a passport or birth certificate or other important document is required? I'm certain he keeps that sort of thing in there. He has filing cabinets. I've seen him poring over papers when the door's not quite been shut late at night. He'd glance up from his desk, eyeing me as I walked past with piles of laundry or a sleepy boy in my arms. Only important things get kept in fireproof metal filing cabinets.

I conclude that the key will either be somewhere in this house or in Claudia's possession. Earlier, after I returned to the house following my unexpected trip out this morning — what was I supposed to do after she hit a nerve so raw it took all my willpower not to cry out in pain? — Claudia had left for work. There was a note on the kitchen table.

I'm so sorry. I didn't mean to upset you. We can talk tonight. Love C.

No throw-away kiss like Cecelia would have used. Straight, neat handwriting slightly sloping to the left. What is it they say about that, those profilers who reckon they can tell everything about you by your scrawl? That it's a sign of repression, of hidden emotions, of fear and withdrawal? I let out a little laugh and stuff the note in my pocket, thinking that kind of person sounds more like me than Claudia.

Upstairs in Claudia and James's bedroom, I resume my search, listening for echoing remnants of words. *Here, darling, I'll leave the key in my cufflink box . . . When you need it, the*

173

study key is in my bedside drawer . . . Remember, I'm hiding the key under my socks . . .

I hear none.

I stare at the bed made up with white linen. It's huge. I'm reminded of Cecelia, of her lean body selfishly slicing up the bed. Marble-cold skin on crisp cotton sheets, her hair like a murder in the anaemic scene; me standing in the doorway, watching her, not knowing what to do with her misery.

I turn suddenly, catching my breath. There's no one there. I close my eyes, take a moment to compose myself.

Everything is fine.

I think carefully, slowly scanning the large bedroom. Vibrant peacock-print wallpaper adorns the chimney-breast wall, while the rest of the room is painted in a pale ochre that probably has a pretentious name. The massive bed, the centrepiece of the room, is carved mahogany with four shoulder-height posts. The bedding is perfectly arranged with vintage lace cushions that would, if I slept in here, get tossed on the floor.

I imagine James packing his holdall. I was surprised at how small it was but I suppose he has to travel light for life on a submarine. I think of him carefully placing starched shirts into the bag on top of crisp pressed trousers, all folded with military precision. They'll be stowed in the most unlikely of compartments on board the vessel, while the men go about their work in cramped conditions. I see Claudia watching on as her husband prepares to leave, holding her beautiful burgeoning belly, a tear in her eye as

174

she imagines giving birth alone. Does she even remember what he told her about the key's whereabouts, or was she too upset about his looming departure?

Will I even find anything useful in the study anyway?

Quick as a fox, I'm rifling through every drawer in the room, trying not to mess up the contents. Wafts of sweet-smelling fabric softener fan off the clean clothes and underwear, but there's no key. Without disturbing a thing, I look on the white-painted dressing table. I carefully lift the lids of a couple of china pots that contain earrings, safety pins, buttons and a couple of baby teeth. No key.

I hold my breath as I lift up each corner of the heavy king-size mattress, praying I'll see a fob labelled 'Study'. All I find is a magazine with Japanese writing on the cover and a tiny, virtually nude girl peering over the top of pink sunglasses. It looks old. It looks well used. James must have bought it on one of his overseas missions. I drop the mattress down, betting it's not the only dirty thing he's picked up in a foreign port.

Suddenly my heart aches for Claudia and I have a ridiculous desire to warn her about what I'm going to do.

I take a moment, a breather, although it feels a little like lingering in the lions' den. Claudia could come home from work — perhaps in early labour, needing to fetch her hospital bag. Maybe James's mission has been cancelled or rescheduled, or he's had a change of heart about leaving

Claudia alone for the birth of their baby. What if he has left the Navy in a fit of regret and is already home? Perhaps he's silently taking the stairs two at a time and if I turned, if I twisted my head round just a little bit, I'd see the dark shadow of him in the doorway, watching me, reaching for the vase on the landing table, raising it high to bring down on my head.

I see pieces of china shattering around me as I slump to the carpet.

'The gilet,' I say, as if the imaginary blow has made me remember. When James locked his study last night, he was wearing beige chinos and a navy body warmer.

I go to his wardrobe. In the foxed mirrors I see myself looking eager, scared, as I swing both doors wide. Inside everything's arranged neatly, as I would have expected. The scent of old wood and male cologne wafts around me as I bat my hands between the garments. Shirts to the left, then sweaters, and jackets to the right. Among the tweed and pinstripes, the cardigans and sweat tops, I see the gilet. It's squashed in tight, and when I pull it out a brown zip-up cardigan falls off its hanger. I imagine James wearing it, sipping a brandy beside the fire, a newspaper spread out on his lap.

There are so many pockets. I shove my hand in each of them and am about to give up hope when my fingers stumble upon something cold, something metal, something that makes me think I'm a tiny step further forward.

Downstairs I slip the key into the lock. It slides in beautifully and the brass knob turns and gives.

My heart bruises in my chest. Someone is ringing the doorbell.

★ ★ ★

'I thought we could walk to school together, to fetch the children,' she says. Her face tells me she thinks it's the idea of the century.

I stand there, dumb, wringing my hands.

I locked the study and pressed the key deep into my jeans pocket in immediate response to the bell. I made out her shape through the stained glass before I even opened the door — she was standing sideways so her massive bump wasn't hard to miss — and my first thought was not to answer it, to let her ring again and again before she tramped sullenly off down the path. But that would raise suspicion with Claudia when they gossiped. *Where was she? What was she doing?* I can't risk getting fired yet.

'That would be lovely,' I lie. I don't like the way Pip has latched on to me, as if I'm a newer, younger version of her bump-buddy, available whenever suits her. Except I don't have a bump. 'I hadn't realised it was that time already.'

Pip glances at her watch. 'Quarter to three,' she sings, but then leans forward with her hands on the outside wall. She blows out through pursed lips.

'Oh, Pip. Do come in. I'm sorry. Are you OK?'

'I'm fine,' she says, straightening at my invitation. A pregnant woman can get anything she wants — a seat on the bus, a foot rub, supper

177

in bed, or worm her way into my business when she's not wanted.

'Time for tea?' I offer when we are in the kitchen. She's timed her arrival perfectly.

'Thanks,' she says, and then I'm clattering mugs and getting the milk from the fridge and not doing what I need to do in the study at all.

'Look,' Pip says eventually. I turn. The kettle judders on the Aga. 'I actually came to talk to you about Claudia.'

I fight to keep from blushing, from twitching or breaking out in a sweat. 'Oh?' I take the kettle off the hotplate and close the lid. I slosh boiling water into the mugs. 'Milk, sugar?' I ask with my back to Pip.

'Two, please,' she replies. 'Truth is, I'm a bit worried about her.'

I give her a mug of tea and sit beside her at the kitchen table when all I really want to do is run away. 'Why?'

Pip sighs and thinks. 'She seems different, unusually stressed. That's hard for you to gauge, I suppose, given that you've not known her long and have nothing to compare it to.'

I pull a thoughtful face, as if I'm really trying to help. 'It's no wonder she's stressed, though, is it? She's probably got one of the most demanding jobs going, and I know for a fact there are a couple of really troublesome families in her caseload at the moment. And, of course, she's eight and a half months pregnant.' I take a sip of tea. 'Plus James has just gone away. I know she has me to help, but having a virtual stranger move into your home must be quite . . . unsettling.' I leave it at that, hoping that describing my presence as unsettling doesn't make her suspicious.

'She's really lucky to have found you,' Pip says, and I believe she means it. She stares unwaveringly at me with an almost longing smile, as if she wants one of me too.

'I hope to make her life a lot easier.' I take another sip of tea but almost choke. I hate lying, but it has to be done.

'I'm very fond of Claudia, although she's one stubborn woman. I don't think she realises just how much stress she's under. I've tried to tell her.'

'My mum was a bit like that. Everything had to be perfect. She expected everyone else to be, too. I was a huge disappointment.'

Pip laughs. 'Nonsense. I'm sure your mum is very proud of you.'

'Was,' I correct. 'And she wasn't.'

'I'm sorry to hear that.'

I shrug, inwardly kicking myself for talking about my personal life. 'I'm over it.' I imagine my mother examining my scrawny, un-pregnant body, tut-tutting at my love life, narrowing her eyes with disdain every time I mentioned my work. *No grandchildren for me then*. I still hear her mocking laugh reverberating through my dreams.

Pip takes my hand. She's being very nice to me. In fact, that's Pip all over. Plain nice. She cares about Claudia and she cares about me. I bet she hand-knits scarves and hats for everyone at Christmas and makes oodles of homemade jam for the school fête. As a teacher herself, she's done the sensible thing and taken a full year's maternity leave. She's the kind of woman to get things right in life, the type to follow 'Ten Ways To Please Your Man' magazine articles to the letter, the sort who sends hand-stamped thank-you notes following dinner parties; and I'd bet anything that she digs a small veggie patch in the spring, is saving up for a hybrid car, and washes on thirty degrees just to show she fucking *cares*.

'Parents, eh?' Pip says as a tactful closer to the subject. She rubs her bump. 'What am I letting you in for?' she says sweetly to her unborn baby.

'They have a knack of screwing you up,' I say, harsher than I'd intended.

'Just promise me one thing,' Pip says. She rummages in her bag and pulls out a pen and notebook. 'If you get worried about Claudia at all, day or night, promise me you'll call me. I always have my phone with me. You know, in case.' She taps her bump again. She jots down her number and rips out the page. 'I was hoping perhaps you could have a word with her, maybe persuade her to finish work now.'

'Me?' I doubt she'd listen to anything I have to say. I glance at the note and stuff it in my jeans pocket. I feel the key against my fingers. 'Sure,' I say. 'Of course.'

We finish our tea and walk to the primary school. The playground is humming with wrapped-up mothers, grizzling toddlers in pushchairs and pre-schoolers hanging from the ice-glazed climbing frame. Pip introduces me to some of her friends, but there's no point in me remembering their names or getting to know them. It won't be long before I'm gone, just a nasty memory, a bad taste, rumours flying. *How shocking! How did she get away with it?*

Back home, I settle the boys in front of a DVD. I give them a glass of milk and a slice of cake each. That should keep them quiet for half an hour at least. I click the sitting-room door shut and, across the hall, insert the key into the study door.

Once inside, I begin my meticulous, methodical work. I soon discover this could take a very long time. Dozens of files need to be inspected, pored over, read. At every stage, photographs need to be taken and everything logged. How else am I going to build up a clear picture? How else will I get what I want from them?

The telephone rings. The extension on James's desk emits a shrill echo of the main bell in the hall. The caller ID tells me it's Claudia. 'Hello,' I say brightly even though my hand is shaking and my banging heart is making my throat close up. The timing of her call — it makes me wonder if she knows exactly what I'm doing.

19

Amanda Simkins lived in a brand-new house on an estate where roads ended in gravel tracks with juddering JCBs and half-built houses. Flags drooped in front of corner-plot show homes as Adam and Lorraine drove in what seemed like an interminable loop before finally locating the correct cul-de-sac within the warren-like development.

'Number thirteen,' Lorraine said, changing down into second gear as they peered at the house numbers. In truth, neither of them believed that speaking to Amanda would prove particularly fruitful, but they had to go through the motions.

Adam was sipping on a Starbucks coffee. He'd been late back the previous night, by which time his entire family was asleep. He'd only had about four hours in bed, Lorraine worked out as he readily accepted the strong coffee she'd made him at breakfast. She grinned inwardly at his resignation to caffeine, to the crash he would no doubt suffer by lunchtime now that he was on his second — a large Americano with an extra shot. So much for healthy living.

Lorraine wrenched on the handbrake and they got out of the car. Adam slugged back the remaining coffee and chucked the empty cup into the footwell.

'A well-cared-for front garden,' Lorraine noted

as they approached the door. Even in winter, the small area was spotted with colour from pansies perfectly arranged either side of the gritted path. A basket of trailing ivy and bright red cyclamen hung to the left of the door; still dusted with the night's frost, it reminded Lorraine of Christmas. Her stomach lurched. Would everything be normal again by then?

She rang the bell.

A woman in a pink dressing gown answered the door. Her long dark hair was pulled back into a messy ponytail, and she had yesterday's mascara smudged under her cheeks. There were red marks — *bruises*, Lorraine wondered? — on one side of her neck. She appeared the antithesis of her tidy front garden. 'I'm not religious, sorry.'

She made to close the door, but Lorraine already had her ID out. 'CID,' she said. Door-stopping words. 'Amanda Simkins? I'm Detective Inspector Lorraine Fisher and this is Detective Inspector Adam Scott.'

The woman stared at them. Her eyes became as frosty as the garden. She swallowed.

'Could we have a word?'

Suddenly, she reanimated. 'Yes, yes, I'm Amanda. Sorry, please come in. You must be freezing.' She held the door wide and wrapped her gown further around her. 'Sorry I'm not dressed. I'm not feeling well.'

'I'm sorry to hear that,' Lorraine said. They were shown into a living room with two cream sofas. The floor was wooden, shiny and immaculate. Lorraine was conscious that her thick-soled shoes might leave marks. 'We'll try not to keep you long.'

'Would you like a cup of coffee?' Amanda asked.

Lorraine accepted on behalf of them both before Adam could protest. He twitched at the thought but didn't say anything. It would give them a moment alone at least.

They studied the framed photographs set out on the white mantelpiece. A large group of children stood in an awkward arrangement, a couple of the older ones, teenagers, holding a baby each. There were toddlers, school-age kids and young adults. Some were grinning, some looked fed up, and one clearly needed a wee. Judging by the smart clothing they were all wearing, it was a wedding or christening or similar gathering.

'Happy families,' Adam commented sourly. He picked up another photograph and turned it over. It was a baby in a lilac dress lying on a sheepskin rug with a cloudy blue background. 'Bit cheesy.' Once their girls had left primary school, they'd given up on the annual guilt purchase of the school portrait. 'Nothing we couldn't do better ourselves,' Adam had griped, though he'd never followed it up with the digital SLR Lorraine had bought him for his next birthday.

'Here you go,' Amanda said, returning with a tray of mugs. 'Sugar and milk here if you want it.' Lorraine added both, while Adam took neither. He eyed the mug suspiciously.

'Well,' Amanda continued, 'I never thought I'd be entertaining two detectives this morning.'

184

She'd let down her hair, which covered the marks on her neck. Lorraine also noticed she'd wiped under her eyes while in the kitchen because the old make-up wasn't as obvious now. 'I hope it's nothing too serious.'

Most people, Lorraine thought, would want to know what was wrong *before* they bothered making drinks.

'We've come to chat with you about Sally-Ann Frith,' Adam began. Lorraine wanted to scowl at him but didn't. His voice was choppy, accusing, not right for Amanda. Already Lorraine could see that she was the type of woman who liked to be in control, to have her thoughts and ideas accepted without question. It was obvious from her perfect house — the neatly tied-back curtains, the combed fringe of the small rug beside the fake fireplace, the dust-free surfaces — that she didn't accept chaos well. Apart from her own appearance this morning, it would seem.

'Oh yes, Sally-Ann.' Amanda smiled fondly. 'Is she OK?' Her face gradually crinkled into a worried expression. 'She's going to have a baby soon.'

'No, she's not OK at all, I'm afraid.' Lorraine got in before Adam could deliver a coffee-fuelled blow. 'There's bad news.' She paused. Had Amanda really not seen the newspapers, the television? 'Sally-Ann was discovered dead several days ago. I'm so sorry. We assumed someone would have told you, or that perhaps you'd have seen it on the telly.'

Amanda immediately turned a very pale

colour. Lorraine watched her intently, almost convinced her white-grey pallor meant she would faint. 'Oh . . . my . . . God,' she whispered. Her cheeks suddenly burned scarlet and then she broke down into fits of sobs. Any remaining clumps of mascara on her eyelashes coursed down her cheeks again.

'I know it's shocking. Just take a moment if you need it,' Adam said, surprisingly sympathetically.

'She was in your antenatal yoga group, I believe,' Lorraine added. 'Were you very good friends?'

Amanda broke off from weeping. She wiped her face on her gown sleeve. 'Yes, kind of,' she whimpered. 'We used to spend time together, usually after the class. She is . . . was . . . lovely. Such a good person. How did it happen? Was she ill?'

'That's what we were hoping you could help us find out,' Lorraine said. 'Had you known her long?'

'Since the first time she came to Mary's classes about five or six months ago. I'd already been going for eighteen months. We really hit it off.'

Adam cleared his throat. 'I hope you don't mind me saying, but why would you attend antenatal classes when you're not actually pregnant?'

'You don't know I'm not pregnant,' Amanda snapped in defence. 'You don't know that at all.'

'Sorry,' Lorraine added on Adam's behalf. 'It's just that we understand you've been attending the classes for some time now and haven't actually ever been preg — '

'You've been checking up on me? A woman's been murdered and you've been finding out about *me*?' Amanda began to shake. She splayed her fingers out over her conspicuously flat stomach.

'It's just routine. We need to talk to as many people as possible who knew Sally-Ann. I'm sure you under — '

'What do you want me to say?' she spat out. 'That I killed her? Yeah, well that's about as likely as me being preggers, I'd say.' More tears followed.

Adam put down his cup. They'd both noticed Amanda's accent had dropped several notches as if suddenly she didn't belong on this pleasant middle-class estate but rather the council one a mile away.

'I'm sorry,' she said, pulling a tissue from her pocket. 'It's just really upsetting news.'

'You've had difficulty conceiving then?' Lorraine asked. Or was it a statement? It didn't come out with much empathy, either way.

'Yes.' Amanda blew her nose. She balled the tissue and looked up. 'You got kids?'

Lorraine's stomach swam, as it had the last couple of mornings when she woke up, remembering Grace and her ridiculous plans. 'I have two.'

'You?' Amanda directed the same question at Adam.

'Two also,' he replied.

'You're lucky then. You don't know what it

187

feels like to want a baby so badly it's an actual pain in your soul, a gaping hole in your very existence. It's the true meaning of heartache.' There was a pause as Amanda Simkins seemed to draw on a reserve of resignation and strength. She was evidently used to feeling this way; used to never giving up hope.

'Did Sally-Ann ever mention anyone who might want to hurt her? Did she have any enemies that you know of?'

Amanda took time to think. Her eyes rolled upwards to stare at the ceiling then dragged down the pastel walls to the fireplace, over the polished coffee table, across the shiny floor and then back onto her lap where her fingers were nervously knitting an invisible garment. 'If anyone was going to kill anyone then it'd be Liam taking a swing at Russ, or even . . . ' She trailed off. 'Do you know about them?' she asked, suddenly excited, as if she was the keeper of a great secret. 'Sally-Ann confided in me.'

'Go on,' Lorraine coaxed. She was taking notes.

'Russ has always loved Sally-Ann. He's a weird one, all right, but his heart is in the right place. He and Sally-Ann went to school together, did the teen romance thing, and have been on and off ever since. She's tried to get rid of him loads of times. Shit to a blanket, was what she told me.'

'And Liam?' Adam asked, trying to move things on. It was becoming clear that Amanda was the type to swathe herself in other people's misfortunes to blanket her own. What was it

Mary Knowles had said about her? *A wormer-inner.*

'He was her teacher at the college,' she said. 'They had this really passionate affair. Clandestine meets late at night in the park, dirty weekends with Liam pretending to his wife that he was away on work conferences, secret gifts, everything. Sally-Ann phoned me once from the bed-and-breakfast place they were staying in. She said it was all fish, chips and shagging. No wonder she got preggers.'

Amanda said it as if 'preggers' was something you bought at a seaside shop. Lorraine thought it bore little relation to the serious business of creating another life.

'Anyway, apparently Russ was crazy jealous. But then he found out some big secret about Liam and all hell broke loose.'

'Secret?' Lorraine said, feeling as if she was suddenly in a soap opera.

'Apparently,' Amanda said, drawing out the word, 'Liam was having an affair with someone else as well as Sally-Ann. Russ told her about it, and she got really upset. She threatened to tell Liam's wife.'

'Do you know who the other-other woman was?' Lorraine asked incredulously.

'I know that she ran a class one evening a week at the college. Some jewellery design course or something.' Amanda blew her nose. 'Sally-Ann was grateful to Russ for warning her what Liam was like. Although you'd think she'd have realised.'

Lorraine made notes. 'A right royal mess

189

then,' she said with a sigh that only Adam knew the meaning of.

Amanda suddenly hunched into a bolus of shaking shoulders and snotty nose. Tears dropped from her face onto her lap and her arms cradled her head. The news about her friend hadn't sunk in yet.

'Is there someone we can call for you, to come and sit with you for a bit?' Lorraine offered. 'A friend, perhaps?'

Amanda's head whipped up, and her expression was one of scorn rather than sadness. Her eyebrows had pulled together in a knotted V and her mouth had crinkled into a sharp sphincter of red. But it was her eyes that unsettled Lorraine the most. She had never seen such a venomous stare. 'My only friend is dead.'

20

It's all still there — a ton of work piled up and waiting to distract me from James getting further and further away. When I finally make it into the office, much later than I'd intended, I feel as if someone has scooped out the contents of my huge middle and all that's left is a vacuous womb full of sorrow. I hang up my coat, exhausted and bereft, and go straight to the toilet.

'Hi,' Tina says, without looking up from her computer, when I come back in. She's typing madly, updating case files no doubt. 'Thought you weren't coming in today. Everything OK?' I know she means it sympathetically, but she's so immersed in the email she's typing, it comes out rather cold.

'Yeah . . . ' Mark replies absent-mindedly, not having even noticed my arrival. 'Did you just hear my stomach rumbling? Seems like lunch was hours ago.' His words are slowed by concentration as he leafs through a file. 'I'm starving again.'

'Claudia's here, dumbo,' Tina says to him. 'I was talking to her, not you.'

Mark looks up. 'Oh, hello,' he says, realising he's not been making much sense. 'How are you?'

I nod. 'Sorry I'm so late in. It's not been the best day.' I pick at my fingernails and manage a smile.

191

They've been through this with me many times before. Later, if there's time, we'll have Krispy Kreme doughnuts and make silly jokes about mermaids and secret beach holidays and what a great time James is having without me. They'll ask why I don't just retire and become a kept Navy wife, which I could be with some degree of style. I could lunch several times a week with friends from the tennis club I'd no doubt join, and sip freshly squeezed juice at the gym following a session with my personal trainer. I'd take classes in flower-arranging and watercolour painting, and host dinner parties that would be talked about for months afterwards. Plus the walls in my home would be a shrine to the latest up-and-coming artists because I'd be invited to all the best London gallery previews.

'James went this morning,' I say with a shrug, and they offer faces of sympathy and a cup of tea.

I settle at my desk, but instead of concentrating on work I wonder what Zoe and I will talk about when I get home. I'm certain I upset her earlier, the way she dashed out and banged the front door. I have no idea where she went. Will we sit silently in front of the television, perhaps each asking tentatively what the other wants to watch; are you warm enough, will it snow tomorrow, would you like a drink? Or will we chat incessantly about men, about her so-far-mysterious past, her recently failed relationship, our favourite movies and books, and all our hopes and dreams? What I need most tonight is company, human warmth, and consolation. It makes me wonder if I hired Zoe to look after the boys or me.

I groan as my computer jumps to life. Time away from my desk has resulted in a crammed inbox. The last email to come in is marked urgent and says I have to attend court in ten days' time as a witness. I skim-read the details. I feel nauseous. It's the day of my antenatal class, if indeed I'm still pregnant then. I really don't want to miss it.

I click on to the next message. 'Oh Christ,' I say out loud. 'Mark, did you see the link to the story about the Fletcher case?' It's been copied to him too.

'I've not checked for ten minutes.' He clicks his mouse, reads and goes pale. We know it's part of the job but when it happens, we take it personally. It's a strike against our department, against us, narrowed down to whoever was responsible for another one slipping through the net we cast out as broadly, yet as precisely, as we can over our community.

'That's a dose of horrendous then,' I say. One failed case cancels out a thousand success stories once the newspapers get hold of it.

'It wasn't our fault,' Mark says. 'There were no grounds to remove him at the time.' He then tells me that he already knew this was going to break, that he hadn't wanted to burden me with it. Does he think it will be easier when I finally have my baby?

'So, they're saying we allowed him to starve to death,' I say, in a way that implies I'm hardened to these things. The reality is quite different. I think back. Other members of the department were dealing with this case. He wasn't on my load, although I did see him once when I was asked for a second opinion. I reported that there was no cause for concern. I remember seeing the baby's food-stained clothing, his ruddy chapped cheeks — he was plump and putting on weight, goddammit. The teenage mother seemed in control and had a good support network — her own mother, an aunty, a partner all wanting to be involved. 'We let him down,' I whisper.

It never gets any easier.

There is silence as we all get on with our work, as we consign the child's demise to the box in our minds reserved for such tragedies. What happens when it fills up, I wonder? What happens when there's no more room for starving children, self-harming teenagers and alcoholic parents? An image of a white-tiled mental institute, endless therapy and a cocktail of medication to make it all better swoops through my mind. I'm being selfish — *ridiculous* — and that's not what this job's about. I screw up my eyes, but the person I see locked up, slamming her palms on the toughened glass windows, being wrapped up in a straitjacket begging them to let her out is me.

'I have a meeting with Miranda,' I say, reining in my thoughts. 'Anyone else need to see her?' My unrelated and frankly far too chipper question hovers limply in the dank atmosphere of our stuffy office. A small electric heater in the corner belts out crackling dry heat. We're too cold without it yet all energy seems to evaporate

194

when it's switched on. The central heating thermostat's broken, Mark discovered a month ago, and I daren't put in a request for a repair when we get turned down for so many necessary items.

'I'll come with you,' Tina says. She thinks I don't see the glance she gives Mark, but I do. In return, he offers the tiniest of nods. Inwardly, I smile. I like it that they're watching out for me.

'Great,' I say, glad of the company. 'We'll leave in twenty minutes. If there's time, we can bring an obscene number of doughnuts back with us.' I am enormously grateful for their concern, for the carbs we will sink our teeth into, for the countless cups of tea they put on my desk, for the way Mark helps me out to the car on these dark, icy afternoons, and for being ready to take over my work at a moment's notice. It's hard to admit, but I know it's going to be the toughest time of my life.

★   ★   ★

'So how's it going with Mary Poppins?' Tina asks.

We're in her car. Even though I already know, I can instantly tell she doesn't have kids: the footwells are devoid of sweet wrappers, comics and broken plastic toys, and the upholstery doesn't have any chocolate smears or wee stains on it. It's certainly nothing like the vomit-stained interior of my family car. And it suddenly seems such a foreign notion that I even drive a family car, a safe vehicle for the kids who aren't mine, a space waiting for the baby seat, and I feel a little bit apprehensive again when I think of what it all really means, the responsibility I now have.

'She seems fine,' I tell Tina. *Fine*, I think shamefully. *Is that all you can say about the woman who's come to live in your house?* 'Though when I say fine,' I add, so aware of my own fears they spill into speech, 'I mean, you know, it's a bit early to tell.' I swallow.

'Must be a bit weird, having some student type living with you.' Tina brakes hard as the lights turn red. I lurch forward. The seatbelt pulls tight around me. 'You OK?'

'Yeah, fine,' I say, releasing the strap from my stomach. 'Actually, she's not a student. She's thirty-three and has loads of experience. She's even done a Montessori course. Reckon that'll sort Noah out.' I laugh. Little Noah, my naughty one.

'I'm so happy for you, Claudia,' Tina says as we pull up at Willow Park Medical Centre. Some kids have scrubbed out the 'ow' and put a 'y' in its place. Tina chuckles.

'Kids today haven't got anything better to do,' I say as we walk past the sign.

The waiting room is empty apart from one woman and a grizzling toddler. The whole place reeks of illness and despair. We go straight into Miranda's office.

'It's all awful, isn't it? Ghastly. Can't believe it.' For a moment I think Miranda's talking about the defaced sign outside, but then I spot the spread-out newspaper with the face of a smiling woman under the headline 'Police Still

196

Baffled by Pregnant Woman Murder'. She folds up the newspaper when she sees me. I shudder and gently, inconspicuously, wrap my arms around my tummy. I try not to show it, but seeing this story upsets me greatly.

'I *know*,' Tina replies. 'Diane's mum actually knows her mum and . . . ' Tina trails off.

'Do they know what happened yet?' I ask.

Miranda shakes her head and sighs. 'I don't think so. The police were here the other day interviewing Sally-Ann's doctor. They took her medical file.' She sighs. 'Did either of you hear the latest news on the radio?' she asks tentatively. We frown, shake our heads. We didn't have it on in the car. 'It sounds as if it's happened again.' Miranda pulls a face and taps the newspaper.

'Another death?' I say, aghast.

Miranda nods. 'Sounds as if it could be another pregnant woman. They didn't release a name or many details. It was breaking news.' She flicks the switch on the kettle and drops teabags in mugs. 'Ghastly business.'

I feel the heat of both Miranda and Tina's stares, as if it's going to be me next and there's nothing they can do to save me. 'That's just awful,' I say, making no attempt to hide the quiver in my voice.

Miranda rubs my shoulder as she goes to get milk from the tiny counter-top fridge. Her starched navy outfit seems to scuttle around her office all by itself, as if there's no body inside controlling it. If a sparrow were human, it would look like Miranda.

'I heard that it was Sally-Ann's lover that did

it,' Tina says with tabloid authority. She bites into a pink wafer biscuit. 'Maybe this latest one was his lover too, and he did the same to her.'

'The news bulletin said she'd been taken to hospital, so perhaps she's still alive.'

Miranda passes round the mugs of tea.

'Well I won't be going out alone at night,' Tina says pointlessly. 'And neither should you.' She directs this at me.

'I certainly won't,' I say quietly, wishing James was at home.

We soon get down to business, poring over the medical file of a six-year-old whose teacher noticed bruising on her arms and back. Then there's the Jimmy and Annie case, twins whose care barely falls inside the minimum standards we set out for them. My vision goes a little blurry and the first throb of a headache pulses inside my temple. I hear Tina and Miranda discussing neglect, nutrition and nurture as if they are everyday things you can buy from the market. What about me, I wonder, as my ears close off to their life-changing conversations? What about my parenting skills? How do they know I will be a good mother? Will I feed and adore my baby girl enough? Will I give her everything she needs? What if love just isn't sufficient? I start to panic.

'Claudia?' I hear Tina saying, as if her voice is coming back into focus. 'Your thoughts on this?'

'Sorry,' I say. I wipe my hands over my face. I'm sweating. I suddenly feel exhausted. 'Sorry.' I hang my head. I haven't heard a word they were saying.

'You shouldn't be here,' Miranda says intuitively. 'What are you now, thirty-eight, thirty-nine weeks?'

'She really shouldn't,' Tina echoes.

'I'm fine. Just a bit . . . ' I don't know what I am, exactly, so I don't try to say it. All I know for sure is that I want to be home, safe within my own walls, with James and the boys; and then I'm thinking of Zoe and her tinkering in the kitchen in her long, baggy cardigan and I'm wondering what it is about her that unnerves me so, even though she's shown our family nothing but kindness. 'I think I need to take the rest of the day off.'

When I stand up, I feel dizzy. Tina rises with me and cups her arm beneath my elbow. I appreciate her concern. 'We can do this tomorrow, can't we, Miranda? I'll drive you home, Claudia.'

By the look on Miranda's face, I know that's not possible. We can hardly ask the parents to wait until I feel better before they neglect their children. 'Don't worry. I'll call someone.' I take my phone from my bag. 'Honestly, I'll be fine. Tina can brief me first thing tomorrow.' I walk out of Miranda's oppressive office before her little sparrow talons can pull me back.

In the car park, sitting on a low wall beneath the tampered-with sign in the semi-darkness, I scroll through my address book. My heart quickens when I tap 'Home' and bangs fervently in my chest when she answers. Thankfully, she's back from the school run.

Will you put me to bed, stroke my head,

199

whisper that everything's going to be fine?

'Zoe,' I say as brightly as I can manage, 'it's me. I was wondering if you could do me a little favour.'

21

Quick as a flash, I put everything in the study back exactly as I found it. I lock the door and coax the twins into coats and shoes. I bundle them into James's great big car and reverse out of the drive into the street-lit murk. Another car flashes me frantically and, as I change through the gears, I realise that I've forgotten to put on the headlights.

'I want Daddy,' Oscar says, probably because the car smells of his father's cologne, and his hat and scarf are discarded on the seat between his sons.

'Well, he's underwater,' I say. It comes out rather cruel-sounding, even though I didn't mean it that way. 'In his submarine,' I add. I need them to like me for as long as this takes. Once I've got what I came for, it doesn't matter what they think of me, although I'd like to think that my brief presence in their lives won't scar them too much. It's hardly their fault their father has inherited so much money — although finding out exact details is proving tricky — and not their fault at all their mother just happens to be heavily pregnant. It's a perfect, if not rather cruel, storm.

'He's at work, silly,' Noah says meanly, and then follows it with a yelp when Oscar pokes him.

My eyes dance between their emerging fight

and the brightly lit road ahead. Straight on at the first three roundabouts, she said, then left at the lights. I'm good with directions and have no problem locating the medical centre she said she was waiting outside. She didn't sound well. I'm sincerely praying that she's not going into labour early. That would be a disaster. Timing is everything, and I reckon I only have one shot left.

At first, I don't see her. It's as if her grey coat and pallid face have pulled her into winter itself. Had I not recognised her pregnant body, I would have missed her completely. I drive easily into a parking space and turn off the engine. Claudia doesn't move off the wall.

'Wait here,' I tell the boys. Noah has found a packet of sweets in his pocket and is revving up an argument by not giving any to Oscar. 'Share,' I say, without taking my eyes off their mother.

I close the door and walk over to where she is. 'Claudia, are you OK? Is the baby all right?'

Slowly, she glances up at me. Her eyes are filled with tears. 'Thanks for coming,' she says.

'Just tell me the baby's OK.'

'She's fine,' she confirms, and I let out the breath I hadn't realised I'd been holding. 'I just came over a bit tired all of a sudden. How very useless of me.'

'Let's get you home,' I say, and hook my arm through hers. I lead her to the car. Oscar and Noah's sweet fight is peaking and I see the pain on Claudia's face as she hoists herself up into the passenger seat. 'Shush, lads,' I say, as pleasantly as I can. 'No need to fall out over wine gums. How about we go down to the corner shop when we get home and you can both choose some treats? Maybe a comic each, too?' As I start the car, I notice Claudia's face soften.

'Then Mummy can have a lie-down. Your little sister's making her feel tired.' I resist the urge to reach out and stroke her bump, and grip the wheel tightly instead as I set off on the drive back.

The cyclist comes out of nowhere. It all happens so quickly — the flash of his bright jacket, the look of horror on his face as he sees me heading straight at him, the panic as he swerves out of my way. I jam on the brakes and manage to miss him. Claudia lets out a gasp.

Then the deafening smash, the sudden jolt, as we're hit from behind.

Claudia lurches forward in slow motion, even though I know it's over in a split second.

'Oh my God!'

The boys are screaming and crying but Claudia is silent. Her head is lolling sideways, having bounced back from the dashboard. She isn't wearing her seatbelt.

'Christ, Claudia, are you OK? Speak to me!' I undo my seatbelt and lean over her.

Someone is hammering on my side window. *Stupid fucking woman . . .*

Slowly, Claudia's hands reach around her baby. 'I'm fine,' she says weakly. She looks deathly pale. 'I'm OK. Really, I'm OK.'

'Oh I'm so sorry, Claudia.' My very first thought isn't her baby's safety but that she's sure to sack me now. Who would let such a bad driver ferry her children around? 'I don't believe that happened. The bicycle . . . he just appeared from nowhere and I couldn't . . . ' The twins are still crying in the back.

Someone opens my door. 'What the hell do you think you were doing, idiot?' He shouts. He stares around the car. 'Is everyone OK?' he asks, noticing Claudia's pregnant body and the young boys.

'No, we're not OK!' I snap back. 'And you're the idiot for rear-ending me! There was a cyclist.' Then I see the blood. 'Oh, Claudia, you're hurt.' Instinctively, I touch my finger to the small cut on the side of her forehead. The blood colours up my skin like a squashed berry.

She flinches. 'It's nothing,' she says. 'I should have put my belt on but it's so uncomfortable to wear these days.'

'I must take you to the hospital,' I say, suddenly panicking that I've probably brought on labour. But then the repercussions of taking her to hospital are dreadful. What if they keep her in, induce her, notify the police of my careless driving?

She turns round to face me, giving the driver standing outside the car a quick glance before settling her gaze back on me. Her expression is full of forgiveness. 'Don't be silly. I'm absolutely fine.'

'I have to take you to be checked out and that's final,' I say, because it's what any normal person would insist on. I turn back to the man. He's jotting something down in a notepad.

'Look, I'm sorry,' he says. 'I didn't expect you to stop so suddenly. Your car's hardly marked.' He beckons me out to take a look. We're causing a traffic jam as other cars struggle to get past the blocked junction.

'Shall I call the police?' someone yells out of another car. My heart pounds inside my chest.

'No need,' the man calls back. 'Here are my details just in case,' he says to me, ripping out the page. 'See? Only a tiny mark on the bumper. These things are built like tanks.' He grins, trying to sweeten everything now he knows there's an injured pregnant woman in the car and two small children. The front bumper on his car is crumpled and both headlights are smashed, but he clearly doesn't want a fuss.

'Thanks,' I say, and watch as he takes a note of James's registration number.

'What's your name?' he asks. I see he's wearing a wedding ring. His hands are brown and strong — worker's hands.

'My . . . name?' My heart kicks up again. 'Zoe Harper,' I say hesitantly, already imagining the police searching through hundreds of Zoe Harpers, none of them me. 'Are you going to report the accident to the police or your insurance company?'

'I don't think that's necessary, do you?' He peers inside the car again, satisfied.

'No, I don't think it is,' I say, calming a little. 'I have to go.'

I get back into the car. Claudia still looks ashen. 'I really should take you to get checked out,' I say tentatively. 'You might need a stitch in

205

that.' Her head has stopped bleeding, leaving a crescent-shaped crust of blood on her skin. The boys are now quiet in the back. Thank heavens I strapped them in to their seats.

'Just take me home, Zoe,' she whispers, imploring me with her eyes. 'I'm so tired.'

'It could be concussion,' I warn her.

'I am *not* going to the hospital. Understand?' She is determined. 'I'm in no mood to be waiting in A&E for hours and giving statements when the doctor feels obliged to notify the police. I just want to go home and rest. *Please.*' Her shaky voice and heart-wrenching plea make me start the car.

'OK, OK,' I say, relieved. 'But I want you to promise that you'll tell me if you don't feel right.' If she goes into labour, then I'll have to act fast.

'I promise,' she says, and her hand rests on mine for a moment as I shove the gearstick into first.

22

'You need to talk to her,' Adam said. 'Woman to woman.'

He's actually serious, Lorraine thought, stifling a laugh. 'You honestly think the way through this tangle of teenage angst is that easy?' If he really expected everything could be resolved by mother and daughter sitting down at the kitchen table with a pot of tea, hell, they might even solve the murder cases between them while they were at it.

Adam shrugged, showing he knew how simplistic and evasive his suggestion was.

Lorraine watched her husband sort through the mess on his desk. It seemed everyone had used it as a dumping ground, a barrage of interview reports for both cases having come in at once.

'What do you think about Amanda Simkins' statement that Liam Rider was having another affair?' she asked, needing to move on from contemplating a heart-to-heart with Grace. 'Is it worth following up?'

'Of course,' Adam said coldly. He ruffled his hair. 'Why don't you do it?' He was unnecessarily casual with her.

Lorraine nodded. 'Adam, look, you're right about having a talk with Grace.' He stared at her, unnervingly. 'But it needs to be both of us.'

He sighed and unrolled his shirt sleeves. Lorraine knew that the jacket would go on next — the old battered leather one he'd bought aeons ago — and then he'd reach for his keys and make up some story about following up with an interview or being late for a meeting. Anything to avoid dealing with his wayward teenage daughter. Anything to avoid dealing with personal issues full stop.

Lorraine took a deep breath. 'You know how I said I didn't want details?' She couldn't believe she'd just said that. She felt faint.

Adam stopped, jacket half slung over broad shoulders. He didn't turn, as if he already knew what was coming.

'Well, I've changed my mind. I want to know everything. Who she is. What she does. Where you met. How it happened.' Lorraine swallowed. '*Where* it happened. How often.' She didn't even know how serious it had been. Was it really just one night or something more deep and meaningful?

There was silence. A static hiatus that crackled with unspoken resentment. It could, Lorraine thought, turn into one hell of a scene. Did she really want that right now?

She sighed. 'If not now, we're going to have to face this some time, Adam.'

At this, he reanimated. He shrugged on the remainder of his jacket, grabbed his car keys, then halted again.

'We need to speak to Carla Davis's social worker,' Lorraine continued, trying to act as if nothing had just happened.

'Get Barrett or Ainsley on to it,' was his flat reply.

'It's OK,' she replied quietly. 'I'll do it myself.'

Adam glanced at his watch and frowned. She knew what he was thinking. He'd already said she should be the one at home when Grace came back from school — *if* she came back from school — and was hoping they'd have all this getting-married nonsense sorted out by the time he came in. They both knew it had to be talked about soon, it's just that Adam didn't seem to want to be a part of it.

'Grace texted me earlier,' Lorraine said, waiting for a reaction. 'She has a netball match and won't be back until seven.'

'At least it sounds as if she's actually coming home,' he said, pulling a face that reflected his annoyance with the whole situation. To Lorraine it screamed that she should have done a better job with their daughter, as if it was all her fault.

A moment later he was gone, flicking off the lights while she was still in the room.

★ ★ ★

Thankfully, she caught two of them before they locked up for the evening. A reluctant security guard had buzzed her into the building, watching her walk all the way down the corridor into the grey bowels of the dull council offices. The social care department had its own key-coded door but someone had wedged it open with a waste bin, leaving the way clear for Lorraine. She found herself in another reception area — though it

209

didn't appear as if the general public were ever greeted there — and when she heard voices from one of the other rooms, she went straight through.

'Hello, the door was open,' she said, to get their attention. A man and a woman, both probably in their mid-thirties, were chattering while shifting boxes of files. It looked as if either a hurricane had whipped through the open-plan space, or they were moving offices. 'Hope you don't mind.' Lorraine briefly showed them her ID and told them her name.

'Excuse the mess. It's not normally like this.' The woman had a biscuit in her mouth but removed it to speak. She had a giant hand-knitted scarf around her neck and they both wore coats, hers dark purple and his grey tweed. Between them they looked exhausted but determined. If they were planning on moving all the boxes stacked around the desks, they'd be here a couple of hours yet. 'We're up and down between here and archives. That's why the door was open. And why we're wearing coats,' she added. 'It's freezing down there.'

'We're having our annual housekeeping session,' the man said. 'And we're short-staffed to boot.' He cleared his throat. He was pale, clean-shaven and appeared rather delicate. Lorraine imagined the woman would be doing the bulk of the lifting. 'How can we help?'

'I'm here about Carla Davis. I believe she's on your case list.' Lorraine added a smile. It couldn't hurt.

The pair looked at each other. 'I'm Mark

Dunn,' the man said in a professional tone. 'Social worker, Children's Services.' He paused, weighing up any confidentiality breaches against Lorraine's introduction as a detective inspector.

'Is she OK?' the woman said, confirming to Lorraine that at least she was in the right place. 'I'm Tina Kent, by the way. Social worker-cum-removals girl.' She grinned.

'She was attacked this morning, I'm afraid. That's why I'm here.' Lorraine mirrored the sudden anguished expressions of the pair and gestured to a couple of office chairs. They immediately sat, while Lorraine perched on the edge of a desk.

'Is she . . . ?' Tina asked tentatively.

'Carla's alive but in a bad way. Sadly, her baby didn't make it.'

'Oh my goodness.' Tina's hand went to her mouth in shock. Mark sighed and dropped his head into his hands.

'The attack happened in her flat. Her friend raised the alarm. She saved her life, actually.'

'Jesus,' Mark said. 'We've not seen her recently because she turned eighteen a while back.' Lorraine sensed it was a sensitive washing of hands. 'She used to be one of ours. In and out of care and foster homes, that kind of thing.'

'Actually, she flagged up again, Mark. A few months back.' Tina spoke softly as if trying to exclude Lorraine from the confidential information. 'When she fell pregnant,' she almost mouthed directly at him.

'I'm assuming her unborn baby would have been a priority for you, knowing Carla's background,' Lorraine said.

Tina nodded, still absorbing the shock. 'Yes, her lifestyle wasn't exactly conducive to raising a child. We were working with her to get her on track ready for the baby's birth. If she didn't manage it then we'd have had to step in.' Tina was sweating now. She unwound the thick scarf from her neck. Her cheeks were tinged red and she pushed her fingers through her hair as she thought. 'We all had dealings with her over the years.' Her voice was wavering.

'I think her most recent contact was either you or Claudia, wasn't it, Tina?' Mark said.

'It was me. I was assigned to her when we learnt she was pregnant from her GP,' Tina blurted out, as if it was entirely her fault. She was on the brink of tears. 'But I first met her when she was about eight years old. I'd recently qualified and she was one of my very first cases. Her home life wasn't good at all. Excuse me a moment. Sorry.' Tina pulled a bunch of tissues from the box on the desk and a few steps' walk suddenly broke into an emotional stride out of the room. Her footsteps echoed down the desolate corridor although her sobs were even louder as she dashed to the toilets.

'It's been a tough week,' Mark said.

Tell me about it, Lorraine thought.

'You mentioned that someone called Claudia had worked on Carla's case. I'll need to speak to everyone involved. It's important to have as clear a picture as possible who Carla knew, who her friends were, what she did with her time. That kind of stuff. We don't want to miss anything.'

212

'No problem,' Mark confirmed. 'Is Carla going to be OK?'

'It's a bit early to tell. We've tried to interview her but she's not made much sense yet. Her injuries were very serious.'

Mark pulled a face. 'I've been a social worker for nearly thirteen years. Nothing surprises me any more.'

Tina came back into the office. 'I'm sorry about that,' she said crisply, over-emphasising her return to self-control. 'I was on annual leave when Carla was originally signed off our care. She was allocated housing and seemed to be doing OK. Then a few months ago, Carla's GP notified us of her pregnancy and that she was still taking drugs. He told us about her unstable mental state, too. She's not one for coping, put it that way.' Tina was obviously ready to talk now. 'So she's back on our radar again — or rather her unborn baby was.'

'I'd like you to make me a list of everyone you think she knew, places she often visited, where she got her drugs from, anything to do with her life. Even if you're not sure it's relevant, please include everything you know. I can't be certain if or when Carla will be in a fit state to help.'

Mark and Tina nodded.

'I'd also like access to her case file,' Lorraine stated.

'I can try to find it,' Mark said. 'Though it's going to be hard at the moment.' He indicated the mess in the office.

'I think Claudia has the file,' Tina said to

Mark, looking worried. 'She was doing supervision on it with me and I'm pretty certain it was in her possession. She wasn't feeling very well earlier. She went home from a meeting. I doubt she'll be in tomorrow either.'

'Can you let me have her address? I'll visit her at home,' Lorraine said.

The pair nodded and Tina suddenly rallied, fumbling for a pen and paper. Lorraine knew they worked closely with the police on a regular basis — just not usually with her department or about such serious crimes.

Lorraine turned to leave. She paused. 'I don't suppose the name Sally-Ann Frith means anything to you, does it?'

Mark and Tina glanced at each other and took a moment to think. 'Only because she's been on the news,' Tina said. Then her eyes widened as if her thoughts weren't far behind those of the detective.

'Thank you,' Lorraine said, leaving before they had a chance to ask questions. 'I'll see myself out.'

* * *

When she got home, the house was full of teenage girls. There were four splayed out in the living room, feet up on the sofa — shoes on — bowls of crisps balanced on bellies and cans of Coke lined up on the carpet within arms' reach. A movie was blaring from the television. Two girls Lorraine didn't recognise greeted her lazily from their perch on the stairs as they giggled at the screen of an iPhone, while a further cluster congregated in the kitchen. They were crowded round the cooker, deliberating over a big pot of something that actually smelt quite good.

Lorraine dumped her bag and keys loudly on the kitchen table. She was taking off her coat when Grace turned round with a wooden spoon halfway to her mouth.

'Mum,' she said brightly. 'Fancy some curry? We made it.'

It's as if nothing's bloody well happened between us, Lorraine thought angrily. Grace's apparent cheerfulness was clearly just for the benefit of her friends.

'But what about . . . ' Lorraine trailed off. She could hardly say *But what about your plans to move out, leave school, get married, the bloody talk we need to have?* 'Smells good,' she said instead. 'I'll have some if there's enough.' She glanced out into the hallway. 'There are a lot of mouths to feed.'

'Oh, that. Yeah. You don't mind, do you, Mum? I said you'd be cool about it. We won, you see. Twelve-four. It was an amazing match.'

'Yeah, we slaughtered them!' The girl had a mouthful of braces and, even though she'd changed out of her sports kit, her skin still glistened with sweat. Strands of dark hair stuck to her forehead.

'Fab,' Lorraine said, trying to sound vaguely cool. She didn't understand how Grace could behave so normally: surely she understood she was about to throw her life away. 'As long as you get it all cleared up by nine-thirty.' They both knew that meant get rid of everyone by that time or there'll be trouble, but, judging by Grace's defiant expression, she wasn't sure that was very likely.

Lorraine swiftly pulled the cork on a bottle of wine. She'd promised herself a detox week soon, much to Adam's amusement when she'd mentioned it to him earlier. She took the bottle and a glass upstairs to escape the mess of girls. She would eat later, perhaps with Adam if he got home in time and they were still actually speaking.

On the way to the bathroom, she stopped at Stella's bedroom door. She heard her youngest daughter talking on the phone.

'I know, right . . . I'm gonna move into her bedroom as soon as she's gone. She's asked me to be her bridesmaid!'

Lorraine shuddered. Apart from anything, she was painfully aware that she'd been ignoring Stella these last few days due to the trouble Grace had slung at them, not to mention the two investigations. But sometimes life was like that. In another few weeks there might be more time to spend together as a family. She hoped so, anyway.

Lorraine took a sip of wine before tapping on Stella's door.

'Shit. I gotta go.'

Since when did Stella use language like that? 'Hi, love. Just checking in. All OK?' *Jesus,* Lorraine thought, *I sound like a text message.*

'Yep,' Stella said, lolling about on her bed.

'When are that lot downstairs going?' She pulled a disapproving face.

'Nine-thirty, with any luck. Have you got homework?'

'Done it. I'm bored.' She lay spread-eagled with her head hanging off the end of the bed. Her hair draped nearly to the floor.

'I was going to have a bath but I can stay and chat if you like?' Suddenly the idea of curling up on Stella's beanbag, discussing make-up, magazines and boys, seemed utterly idyllic to Lorraine, taking her mind as far away from Carla Davis and Sally-Ann Frith as it could possibly be. Right now, she didn't want to do anything else in the world. She stepped inside the messy room and took another sip of wine.

'Sorry, Ma,' Stella said. 'But, you know. I'll just go on Facebook or something.'

Lorraine felt a pang of disappointment, and then her phone rang. It was Adam. Stella had opened her laptop and was already tapping away at the keys as if she didn't exist. Lorraine stepped back out onto the landing, feeling somewhat bereft.

'What?' she snapped too hastily.

'Carla Davis has woken up. She's given a description.'

'Oh?' said Lorraine keenly. This was a big development. 'That's sooner than they expected.' Adam had waited as long as he could at the hospital after Carla had been brought back from theatre, but he'd eventually had to assign another officer to continue the vigil.

'Can you come to the office? I've called a

217

meeting in half an hour.'

Lorraine peered down the stairs. The two girls she'd climbed over on the way up had gone but there was a steady stream of kids carrying plates of curry and rice into her living room. She sighed. 'OK. But tell me some good news. Tell me you're bringing the suspect in as we speak.'

'I wish I could,' Adam said.

23

'Taking a baby or child away from its mother isn't as easy as you'd think.' I'm telling this to Zoe as she sits there, watching me, shivering, her mouth slightly open and her cheeks developing a summery shade of rose pink even though it's freezing in the house. Her expression gradually gives way to shock as I tell her about my work. To add to a bad day, the boiler has packed up so we've pulled our chairs close to the Aga and layered on an extra sweater each. Zoe did the same for the boys then lit the fire in the sitting room, snuggling them under a blanket with their favourite cartoon to watch.

We finger mugs of tea. I've been holding a bag of frozen peas to my head but they've melted now. Zoe reaches over and takes the dripping pack from me.

'I mean, how can you do that? Legally take someone else's child?' She emphasises 'legally' as if there's another way to do it.

'It's not easy. Children are referred to our team by a number of people — the police, GPs, hospital doctors, health visitors, midwives, teachers, friends, relatives, neighbours, you name it.'

Zoe pulls an interested face. She sips from her mug like a timid bird, watching all around her constantly.

'Then we do an assessment. Basically that's

lots of meetings with and without the parent or parents, as well as making surprise and planned visits to their home. We have to decide if the child or children or babies, even unborn ones, are safe to stay in their environment. If not, we apply to the courts to have them removed to a safe place, usually temporary foster care, until a permanent home can be found.'

'So the baby's taken away from its mother,' Zoe says in a vapid voice. I'm not sure if it's a question.

'It happens,' I say, trying not to crush her with the reality. 'But what you have to understand is that it's always done with the child's best interests in mind. Why let a kid grow up in a violent, abusive, dirty or neglectful household when he or she could live in a contented, loving one?' My head is still throbbing.

'But what about the mothers? What happens to them?' She seems upset and distressed, as if it might one day happen to her.

'Well,' I say carefully, feeling as if I'm trying to explain something horrific to a small child, 'some of them are hopeless cases from the start. Even with support, they don't try to change their lives. Sometimes they're actually relieved if their children are removed.'

'More money to spend on drugs and booze.'

I nod. 'But some of them turn their lives around and get their children back.' I gently rub my stomach. The thought of anyone taking my little girl away from me when she finally arrives is unthinkable after all the years of longing and disappointment and trying and loss. I shiver again, unsure if it's from what I'm thinking or the cold.

'Is she kicking?'

I nod and smile. 'Feel.' I take her hand and place it on the spot. Zoe frowns a little and moves her hand to another spot. I notice the tremor. 'I think she's gone back to sleep,' I say when Zoe's face registers nothing.

'You don't think . . . well, you don't think the accident . . . upset her, do you?'

I laugh. 'Oh no, not at all. She's been kicking loads since we got home. Don't worry.'

'I really think I should have taken you to hospital. I couldn't bear it if anything happened — '

'She's fine. I'm fine. Trust me.' I pat Zoe's hand. She feels very cold. 'I'll call the plumber again.' I dial the number and this time he answers. He promises to be round within half an hour.

Zoe makes the boys a late supper and I decide to read through some case files to take my mind off everything that's happened. The last twenty-four hours have been a torrent of emotions and occurrences beyond my control. It's not been the best day, that's for sure, I decide, settling at James's desk with my battered leather messenger bag. James bought the bag for me last Christmas. It's perfect for hauling chunky files between meetings.

'It's second hand,' I'd said to him curiously after pulling off the wrapping paper and running my fingers across its worn surface.

'It's vintage,' he'd corrected with a laugh. 'It's

an old mail satchel. I thought you'd like the idea of all the good news it's delivered.' He'd wrapped his arms around me, as if I was his Christmas present.

All I could think of was all the bad news the bag would now be conveying.

'What's that?' I say out loud, shoving James's spare study key back in my bag. There's something on the floor. I bend down and pick up a button. It's unusual — a dark green toggle with a purple swirl running through it. It's certainly not from anything James wears and I don't recognise it as my own. Shrugging, I stuff it in my pocket and get on with the pile of reading I need to do before tomorrow. Though I have no idea if I will go in to work after my antenatal class. I'm taking it one day at a time when it comes to this baby's arrival. No one can blame me for that.

Twenty minutes into a shocking read — the handover of a teenage girl from another area — the doorbell rings. I listen as Zoe answers it. She deals with the plumber courteously, showing him to the utility room.

I go back to the tragic life of the fifteen-year-old, pregnant by her step-father. She refuses to name and shame him when every professional who has been dealing with her knows he is the one delivering the assortment of bruises and broken bones. Emergency foster care has been found for her two brothers but not the pregnant girl. She is due to give birth any day and her baby is on my priority list. I stop and imagine her young body bulging with new life

— a life created from hate and fear. How will she ever be able to love that baby? I doubt she's capable of loving herself, let alone anyone else. The psychologist's report confirms a long history of self-harm, starvation, cutting, head-banging, substance abuse — it all swims off the page. There is a photograph of her clipped to the inside of the file. She is slight and pale with shoulder-length mousey hair. She's wearing a red and blue striped top and her eyes are huge and brown, filled with utter despair.

But, nestled in the corner of each eye like tears she can't let go, I see glimmers of hope. I desperately want to help her.

There's a knock at the door. 'Come in,' I say, and before I know it, Zoe is standing in front of James's desk with the plumber at her side. Her eyes flick all around James's study.

'Hello, Mrs M-B.' He's been calling me that ever since he refitted the bathroom a year ago. 'Good to see you.' He notices my stomach. 'Heavens, Mr M-B's been busy!' He roars with laughter and wipes his hands down his boiler suit.

'Thanks so much for coming out, Bob. We're all freezing.' I'm still shivering, despite the extra sweater.

'Not good news about the boiler, I'm afraid. I need a part that I won't be able to get until mid-morning tomorrow. Will you survive the night?'

My heart sinks. 'Do we have hot water?'

'I've made sure the immersion heater is on, so yes, you do. But you'll have to keep the home fires burning for the night, I'm afraid. I'll be back about eleven. Will someone be home?'

I nod and make arrangements with Zoe. I have no idea what tomorrow will bring for me yet.

There's a yelp from the kitchen where the boys are eating supper. Zoe dashes off while I see Bob out.

'Thanks again.' I click the door closed and gather up an armful of the numerous coats, jackets and woollies hanging in the hall, deciding we all need another layer. 'Here,' I say, dumping them on the kitchen sofa. 'Let's all look like Michelin men.' I burst out laughing at the same time as Zoe. Her look says it all: *you already do* . . .

'That's *my* coat,' Oscar complains when Noah snatches the padded jacket from him.

'No, here's yours, Oscar,' I say. 'The one with the badge, remember?' I nip the battle in the bud. I pull out an oversized chunky-knit cardigan I don't recognise from the pile. 'This is nice,' I say, examining it, wondering if it's a long-forgotten garment or something Pip left behind.

'Oh, that's mine,' Zoe says gratefully with a histrionic shiver.

As I hand it over, I notice the row of green and purple toggles stitched down the front. One is missing.

* * *

Pip gives me a little wave from the floor. I want to talk to her but I'm late and the class is already under way. Compared to my house, it feels so warm in the usually freezing church hall. I struggle down onto my yoga mat and ease myself onto my side. It's an effort. Mary is telling us about centring and aligning our chi and how it's all linked to breathing. It's a bit too New Age for my liking. When I think about bringing my baby into the world, all I can imagine is screaming and pain. There's nothing peaceful and balanced about childbirth as Mary is suggesting.

I begin the low leg raises that she's demonstrating. Even these gentle exercises begin to pull my useless abdominal muscles after only a few seconds.

'Breathe through the movement: in and out . . . in and out . . . ' Mary's voice is rhythmic and soothing. 'You're strengthening your core ready for the big day . . . in and out . . . that's right. Claudia, make sure you keep your knee straight and don't lift too high.'

I glance over at Pip. She winks. She can hardly lift her leg. I swear she's bigger than me now.

Are you OK? I mouth at her.

She nods. *You?*

I wrinkle my nose. She frowns and taps her watch. I nod. I've missed seeing her since Zoe took over the school runs.

'On your feet now, ladies, and we'll continue with our core exercises. It's important to keep your balance on this one. Foot down if you feel a topple coming.' Mary laughs in her automaton voice and begins a forward lunge that looks impossible with the great weight at my middle. She eyes us all individually. I wonder if she actually has any children of her own. She doesn't look the type.

Ten minutes later, as we're lying on our mats relaxing, tears fill my eyes. Any moment, one of them is going to drip down my cheek and onto the floor. I clench my fists to fight the emotion but I can't help it. I'm imagining James God knows how deep in the sea, practising drills and procedure in a submarine crammed full of husbands, brothers, sons. *Come home safely, my love*, I say in my mind, even though I know it's just a routine mission. I focus on the baby I will have waiting for him upon his return, how we will be a family of five, how he will be so very proud of me. *Me*, the woman who has suffered countless miscarriages and stillbirths; *me*, the woman who was told she'd never be able to carry a live baby full term; *me*, the woman who only ever wanted the chance to be a mother.

★ ★ ★

'Are you sure it's hers?' Pip says.

We are both stuffing our faces with carrot cake. We can't help it.

'She admitted it was.' My mouth is full and I wipe crumbs from my lips.

'Look at us greedy pigs,' Pip says, laughing. 'I'm always losing buttons. It probably just fell off when she was in there chatting with James or something.'

'Maybe,' I say. 'Though I found it by the window, near where James sits. I don't understand what she was doing over there. James is very protective of his study.'

'Oh Claud, stop it! Maybe it fell off in the doorway and got kicked.' She crams in more cake and hungrily eyes the delicious display of pastries on Brew-haha's counter.

'Kicked?' Bismah says, eavesdropping. She was talking to Fay, who's been feeling sick all morning even though she's five months now. 'Who's kicking? Let me feel.' Her dark shiny hair is ponytailed down her back and I'm convinced her huge eyes are going to burst at the thought of feeling a baby's foot or hand.

'No baby kicks, I'm afraid,' I say, wondering what Zoe would make of that. She's been paranoid about me since the car accident.

'And how is that nanny of yours, Claudia?' Bismah continues. 'I wish Raheem would agree to get me a nanny, then I could go back to teaching.' Her laugh is gentle and tells me she has no real intention of going back to work, nanny or not. She's just saying it for my benefit.

'Zoe,' I say thoughtfully, almost as if I've forgotten her name.

'Yes, Zoe,' Bismah says, amused. All three are waiting eagerly to hear what I have to say.

'I'm in two minds about her, really,' I say, shocking myself with the open admission.

'Ouch,' Pip says slowly. 'Bit late to be thinking of a change now.'

'I know, I know.' I pull a pained face. If I can't tell my girlfriends, best friend included, then who can I tell? 'It's fine, really. I mean, she cares

227

greatly for the boys and keeps the house nice and — '

'But you don't like her,' Pip says brutally.

'No, it's not that either. Truth be known, I really like her. She's a little reserved and keeps herself to herself, but that's understandable. I think she's had boyfriend troubles.'

'There you go then.' Bismah always sees the best in everyone.

'There's just something about her. I can't put my finger on it, but if I was forced, I'd say . . . ' I stare at the ceiling. 'I'd say that . . . oh, you'll think I'm being stupid.'

'No, go on,' Bismah says. Everyone's listening.

'I'd say that she's got other reasons for being in our house.'

As soon as I say it, I regret it. I remember all the nice things she's done for the boys since she's been with us, not to mention how she's really made an effort with me. 'I've not been mean to her or anything,' I add when I see the shocked faces of my friends. 'I'm sure it'll all work out fine.'

'Hor-mon-al!' Pip sings in a silly falsetto.

'I am not,' I say sternly, and we all laugh. 'Well, yeah, maybe I am a little bit.'

'Give her another few weeks. Once the baby's born, once James is home again, everything will fall into place, you'll see. Zoe will get stuck into a routine with the children, you can enjoy your maternity leave, and life will be pretty much perfect.' An overstated smile punctuates Pip's reassurance. The stretchy tunic top she is wearing clings to her bump, showing off just how

228

close to giving birth she is. I love the sight of her. I love the sight of all of us.

'You're right of course,' I tell Pip. But I still can't help feeling the way I do.

24

Carla Davis looked dead even though she wasn't. There were needles and tubes stuck in the back of her hand and sticky monitor pads on various parts of her body, exposing patches of pale flesh beneath the anaemic hospital gown they'd put her in.

'It could have been a load of bollocks, of course,' Lorraine said, staring down at the poor girl in the hospital bed. 'The drugs talking.'

'Barrett did say she was drifting in and out of sleep.' Adam picked up the clipboard attached to the end of her bed. He soon replaced it, the scrawled notes and dots on the charts not meaning much to him. 'But she kept mentioning the woman.'

'Which potentially changes everything,' Lorraine said. Possibilities rattled through her mind and none of them fitted with the meagre profile they'd so far built up. And they still couldn't be certain that the two attacks were linked, even though they were gruesomely similar. Lorraine had hoped more leads would be forthcoming from Carla's injuries, but the first priority was to save her life, get her fixed up in theatre, not have forensic pathologists probe around the mess on her body.

'Tell me again what else Barrett reported,' she said. He was one of their best DCs and had never let them down in an interview situation.

He was thorough and thought on his feet.

'We've been over this a thousand times already.'

It was true. They had discussed the investigations in depth at the meeting last night, with most of the team present. It had run on late into the evening. Then Adam and Lorraine had talked further at home while they cleaned up the mess Grace and her friends had left.

'The ward sister only allowed Barrett to speak to Carla for a couple of minutes. He didn't think that she had much idea of where she was or what had happened to her. She was very confused. She knew stuff like her name and where she lived but she had no recollection of the actual attack, only the moments leading up to it. But she kept saying that there was someone at the door, that she had to answer it. She got quite distressed about this, apparently.'

'This mystery woman,' Lorraine said, knowing the story anyway.

'Correct,' Adam said. 'Barrett asked for a description and she just kept saying 'thin' over and over. Doesn't really help us much.'

Adam was suddenly leaning over Carla as she stirred. 'Carla, can you hear me?'

Lorraine thought he was going to shake her. 'Stop it, Adam, you'll scare her.' She also approached the young woman's bedside. The sheets were draped over what she could only assume had been a very large abdomen until a short time ago. Did she even remember she'd been pregnant, Lorraine wondered? 'Hello, love, can you hear me?' she said softly. 'I'm a detective. I just want to ask you a couple of questions.'

Lorraine ran a finger up and down the inside of the girl's wrist. There was a plastic cannula taped to the back of her hand with a thin tube snaking up to a drip stand. Lorraine studied the skin on the inside of her elbow. The veins were bruised purplish-red with tell-tale dots of older scars contrasting starkly with her milky skin. This was not the work of doctors.

'Love, can you hear me?'

Carla made a brief moaning sound and twisted her head left then right. Her eyes were closed although they opened momentarily. Lorraine could tell she wasn't focusing on anything.

'I want to find who did this to you, love. Can you remember anything about the attack or your attacker? What did they look like?'

Carla didn't say anything. The machine behind the bed beeped, showing her blood pressure, oxygen saturation and breathing rate. Lorraine didn't understand the numbers, but the machine was making a steady sound, somehow reassuring them that Carla was at least maintaining a hold on life.

'I'm going to have to ask you to leave now.' A nurse had come in. 'I have to check her wound drain.'

'We'll come back later,' Adam said.

'Thank you,' the nurse said, gently removing the bed covers from Carla.

She moaned again and the hand with the

232

cannula flapped by her side.

'Steady, now,' a second nurse said in a lilting Irish accent. 'Don't want you ripping all this out.'

'If only she'd speak again,' Lorraine said as they left the room. They exchanged brief nods with the young PC on guard duty and then swapped glances with each other, remembering their own early days in the force. Lorraine swiped away the inevitable memories of how she'd met Adam, how she'd idolised him — no, *worshipped* him — back in those days. Here she was now completely unable to understand how the twenty-foot-high brick wall had grown between them. She refused to believe it was entirely her fault.

They were standing beside Adam's car, Lorraine squinting into the burst of sun which had forced through the clouds, no doubt before the forecast sleet arrived later. 'Fancy a coffee?' she asked, pointing to the parked-up trailer serving drinks and snacks. The smell of bacon was irresistible.

'Do you think they have green tea?' Adam asked with a smirk.

'Let's find out,' Lorraine said, surprising herself by briefly touching Adam's arm as they wandered over to the kiosk. 'Then you can come with me to visit Russ Goodall again. I have a few questions for him. With any luck he'll have done a spot of housework.'

*   *   *

233

There was no reply when Lorraine knocked. She peeked through the grimy plastic letterbox. A putrid smell billowed out in a waft of warm air. 'Jesus Christ,' she said, recoiling. 'Did someone die in there?' She and Adam looked at each other, both sincerely hoping that wasn't the case.

Adam stuck his nose close to the flap. 'Not death,' he said matter-of-factly. 'The rubbish needs taking out.'

'Disgusting bugger,' Lorraine said, banging her fist on the door then stepping back to peer up the tall building when they heard a window above them open. 'Hello?' she called out. 'Police. Will you come down, please?'

There was a brief expletive and then moments later they heard thumping behind the door as someone came down the stairs. The door was unlocked and opened and they were faced with Russ Goodall in a vest and boxer shorts, shivering as if he'd been out in the snow for three days.

'I was in bed,' he said apologetically.

'May we come in and talk to you?' Lorraine asked. She could almost feel Adam's disgust.

'Yeah, s'pose,' Russ replied, standing aside. He stumbled on a bag of rubbish that had been left by the door.

'Couldn't we have brought him in to the station?' Adam whispered as they went up the stairs. Lorraine strode past him into the tiny bedsit and nudged him on the shoulder for being stupid. She often wondered if it was a good idea for them to work together any more. More so at work than anywhere, their behaviour was likely to deteriorate into that of squabbling children. God knows what would happen if she went for divorce. A transfer for one of them would be inevitable, but why should she be the one to move?

'Sit down if you like,' Russ offered in a voice whose high pitch betrayed fear and surprise.

There were only two options: a dirty plastic stacking chair beside a small table or the messed-up bed that appeared to double as a sofa. Adam darted for the chair, leaving Lorraine no option but to sink onto the mattress and release a fug of warm, stale body odour. She would thank him for that later.

'I just wanted to run over a few things about your relationship with Sally-Ann, Russell. It's nothing to be worried about, we just have to be clear in our minds about everything. Why don't you pop some trousers on, eh?'

The cotton of his boxers was so thin that Lorraine was convinced she'd see more than she wanted to if her eyes strayed any further down than his chest. As it was, she could make out most of his skinny, undernourished torso through the worn, greying material of his baggy vest. He nodded and pulled on some ripped jeans. A nasty smell exuded from them as he battled them up his legs, hopping around the worn rug as he did so. Finally, he sat on the bed next to Lorraine. She moved to her left.

'Did you and Sally-Ann ever argue, Russell?' It was Adam who spoke first. Lorraine had been about to ask the same question. They just wanted to warm him up a little, have him almost relieved to spill the truth about anything he might now regret.

She took the interview baton that Adam hadn't exactly held out. 'And by that, we don't simply mean the usual bickering that all couples do.' She looked at Adam. He didn't reciprocate but she noticed his jaw clench. 'We're more interested in knowing if things ever got, well, a bit hot under the collar, if you know what I mean.'

'I never hit her, if that's what you're implying.' Russell was fidgeting.

'We understand how these things go: petty little disagreements escalating beyond all proportion . . . ' Adam said, offering a quick glance back at Lorraine.

'And we also understand that sometimes these little disagreements aren't quite so little; that maybe one of you might have had a very good reason to get upset.' Lorraine emphasised the words 'very good reason'.

'Although sometimes these *very good reasons* can be misunderstood by one party entirely,' Adam added, glaring at Lorraine.

'But assuming they weren't *misunderstood* at all,' Lorraine continued, talking directly at Adam, 'assuming one party was completely certain they were in the right, then we'd understand if you felt as if you might become *violent* towards that other person.' Lorraine felt a sweat break out on her forehead. She steeled herself against the ridiculous emotions brewing and turned back to Russell.

'Although I must stress that we'd never

condone violence.' Adam jutted out his jaw, and Lorraine could almost see the pressure building up inside him.

'I'll remember that, Detective,' Lorraine said tersely through a forced smile. *Before I thump you*, she added in her head.

'I never hit her, I swear,' Russ said, completely oblivious to the subtext passing right under his nose. 'She got into these awful moods.'

'Go on,' Lorraine said.

'I reckon being pregnant made it worse.' Russ hung his head and picked at a rip on the thigh of his jeans. A patch of white, hairy skin showed through. 'One minute she was happy — I mean, like, *really* happy. The next she wanted to end it all.'

'Was she depressed?' Adam asked.

'Maybe. I dunno. She used to go to the GP a lot.' Russ looked utterly miserable. 'It all started when *he* came on the scene.'

'Liam?'

Russ nodded. 'He ruined everything between us. I reckon we'd have got married if it weren't for him sticking his nose in. He used Sally-Ann, he did. Used her for casual sex, like he did that other poor woman.'

'We know for certain that he was the baby's biological father,' Adam said, causing Lorraine to sigh. She'd been going to wait before telling Russ this news, but it was said now.

Russ's face took a moment to react, but when it did, it was clear that he'd been convinced he was the father. 'Oh, no,' he said flatly. 'That's really sad.'

'Is it true that all the uncertainty caused a lot of friction between you and Sally-Ann?'

Floored by the truth, Russ nodded. 'Yeah. But I was going to do the right thing. I'd have stood by her. I wanted that baby.'

'Did Sally-Ann?' Lorraine asked.

Russ dragged his head up. After a few seconds he said, 'No. No, I don't think she ever really did.'

'So why didn't she have a termination?' Adam said. 'Women have choices.'

'There was this one time I really thought she was going to, to actually get rid of it, but she changed her mind.'

'And when was that?'

'She'd only just found out she was pregnant. After the initial shock had worn off, she got really excited. We were in the Bullring looking at baby stuff in a department store. All these little soft pink and blue things. But then she suddenly got really stressed about coping, about being a good mother, about the cost of everything. It was as if someone had flicked a switch.'

'In the department store?' Adam said.

'Yeah. One minute she was fondling Babygros and the next she was swiping at displays and pulling tiny clothes off racks. She was yelling and everything. Making a right spectacle of herself. She nearly destroyed the shop.' Russ was clearly troubled by the memory.

'That sounds terrible. What happened?' Lorraine said.

'I tried to calm her down. Her arms were swiping and flailing and she was kicking stuff.

238

She was screaming that she didn't want the baby, that she wanted to get rid of it right there and then, that she'd do it herself if she had to. She yelled that she hated it, that it would ruin her life.' Russ was whispering now, clearly traumatised by the memory. 'People were staring, gathering round. One lady came to help her, said she understood, that she needed to calm down. Sally-Ann slumped to the floor and then the manager came and took her round the back for a cup of tea. Then we went home.'

'Powerful things, those hormones.'

Lorraine glared at Adam. He was a prize idiot sometimes. 'That must have been very distressing for you, Russell,' she said. 'Did anything like that ever happen again?'

'She still got moody, but she never said she wanted an abortion after that. I asked her to marry me.' Russ managed a small smile at the thought.

'I'm so sorry for you, Russ.' Lorraine meant it. 'Can you give me the name of the other woman Liam Rider was apparently seeing?'

Russ scratched his head. 'I only found out by accident,' he said. 'I went to the college to have it out with him, to warn him off my Sal. I found him . . . well, you know, doing stuff with this other woman. It was disgusting.'

'Her name?' Adam reminded him.

Russ thought hard. 'She ran an evening course at the college. Jewellery-making or something. She was a right weird-looking woman, I remember thinking.'

'Name?' Adam persisted.

Russ shrugged. 'She had an odd name, too. Like Delia or Celia. I dunno. Ask the college. She had this frizzy red hair, all tangled up.'

25

I nearly don't bother to answer the door but if it gets back to Claudia that I missed a delivery or failed to greet a friend then that'll make her wonder what I was up to. I promised her I'd sort out the linen cupboard and finish the pile of sewing that looks as if it's built up over a lifetime. Various items have been bagged up in the utility room with a sticky note saying 'needs mending' attached.

It's jobs like these, Claudia told me when I started, that will make all the difference around the house. She smiled as if it — as if *I* — was the most important thing in the world.

How very trivial, I remember thinking when I told her that I liked sewing, that I had an eye for detail. Perhaps I have, I think as I reluctantly approach the front door. Maybe I got it from Cecelia as I watched her work through the long winter evenings. She'd hunch over the table in our tiny flat, an angled light shining above her as if she had a private mini sun in her own little world. Sometimes she'd work peering through a giant magnifying glass on a stand. I once looked at her through it. Her body morphed as if she were in the hall of mirrors at the fairground. She was huge and distorted like a great pregnant animal. I didn't say anything. It would have killed her, especially as she wasn't pregnant.

Whoever it is has rung the bell three times now.

I unlock the door and open it wide.

'Is Claudia Morgan-Brown at home?' a woman in a suit asks.

'Sorry,' I say. 'Not until tonight.' I try to remember what time she said she'd be back.

'I'm Detective Inspector Lorraine Fisher,' she says.

I stare at her. I feel faint. The floor falls away from my feet.

Shit.

'Are you OK, love? You look a bit pale.' She takes a step forward.

'I'm fine,' I say, steadying myself on the doorframe.

'Any idea what time tonight exactly?' she continues, stamping her feet as if she's both cold and impatient. She shoves her hands into her coat pockets.

'I . . . I'm not sure.' I pray she's only come about the accident yesterday.

'And you are?' she asks.

My mouth won't work. What should I tell her? I wasn't expecting this. 'I'm Zoe,' I manage to say pleasantly. 'Claudia's nanny.' Why would they send a detective for a road traffic incident? I can hardly stand to think of the answer to this.

'Ah,' she says, clearly believing me. 'But you have no idea what time Mrs Morgan-Brown will be back?'

'I suppose it'll be about six or seven,' I say vaguely, glancing at my watch. I force my mind back to earlier. Claudia said she felt better, that she wanted to go to her antenatal class and then on to the office.

The detective looks exasperated by my imprecise answer.

'Look,' I say, 'if it's about the accident, she's fine. It was all sorted at the scene. I decided not to take it any further.'

'Accident?' she says.

'Someone rammed the back of our car yesterday. What with Claudia being pregnant and . . . well, there was thankfully no harm done.' I even manage a little laugh.

'That's not why I'm here,' she continues. 'Give this to Mrs Morgan-Brown, will you? Tell her to get in touch if I haven't located her in the meantime.'

I take the card from her gloved hand and watch her leave. When I've shut the door, locked and bolted it, I lean back against the wall. It takes all my willpower not to slide down to the floor. I stare at the card. The words Major Investigations Unit are printed across the middle. I rush to the toilet and throw up.

★ ★ ★

It's no good. I need to see her again. I tap out a text but can't bring myself to hit send. Instead, I walk around the garden in bare feet, allowing the cold wet grass to poke between my toes and the mud to slip beneath my nails. Back inside, I turn on my computer and log into one of my email accounts — the one reserved for communicating with her — and

243

swiftly type a message she can't ignore.

I want to tell her that I will always love and care for her. I don't know what else I can do.

Dear Cecelia . . . I scrub that. It sounds too formal.

> Hi Cecelia,
>
> *I know things didn't go the way you'd hoped in the pub the other night, but that doesn't mean I don't still love you. You know I always will. I made a promise to you and I will keep it. I just need a little more time.*
>
> *With love, H.*
>
> X

Anything to keep her going, to keep the hope alive.

I laugh to myself and delete the email. I can't send this. It could be viewed or intercepted by anyone. It's all too traceable. I'm not stupid. I might well be breaking all the rules by communicating with Cecelia but leaving an electronic trail, pretty much stating my intentions, is not how things should be done. I delete the draft text also.

I glance at my watch. There's still time. The boys are playing at Pip's house until six. Impulsively, I pull on my coat, my boots, my scarf, and grab the keys to the car. If I go to the flat, no one can ever prove what was said between us.

★ ★ ★

I park and march up to the door. I still know the code and, as usual, no one has bothered to turn the main lock so I'm straight inside the building. Kim's bike is propped against the wall. Has she not gone to work today? The hall table is strewn with mail, most of it junk by the look of it, and there's a bag of bottles ready to take to the recycling. It's been there for ages.

None of this had to happen, I think sadly. She could have got help, done things differently, listened to me. *It's still not too late*, I try to convince myself, while also blaming myself for being too weak. Over the years, she's forced me to do things I would never have dreamt of. It's always been the way between us — her unfathomable need fuelling my time-starved guilt. It's some consolation, I think, as I tramp up the creaky stairs, to know that it's not entirely my fault. Away from her clutches, I see things more clearly. Cecelia is a powerful, persuasive woman; she always has been — a desperate woman with magic powers that work only on me. That was why I tried — *tried!* — to get away from her, but she and I both know that's not as easy as it sounds. She preys on my weakness for her, knowing I'll do anything she asks.

I head up another flight of stairs towards the top-floor flat. I knock on the door. I press my ear to the wood but I can't hear anything. Usually when she's working she has the radio on and sings along to any old rubbish. It used to drive me mad. Mad in a good way; a madness that made me love her all the more. She knew I'd do anything for her.

'Heather!' she says, shocked to see me. She's wearing a floaty kaftan. She made it herself from an old sari. If Cecelia isn't creating something, she isn't being Cecelia. 'What are you doing here?'

'I kind of live here,' I tell her.

'No you don't,' she says immediately. 'You left. You left me and this flat. And you left most of your stuff here. Is that why you've come? To collect it?' She's twitching and shaking beneath the fabric. Her hair is cast around her shoulders in glorious bonfire waves.

'No. Actually I've come to see you.'

'Oh.' She sounds disappointed, even though I know this is Cecelia's way of being pleased to see me. 'I was going to make tea.' She leaves the door wide open and retreats.

Cecelia and tea is a love affair in itself. No teabag thrown into a mug for her. Instead, she sets the dining table (an oval gate-leg table we bought for thirty quid at an auction when we first moved in) as if she's serving a three-course meal. She begins by putting the kettle on. Then she clatters a huge dented teapot that I swear is made from aluminium and has been doing us no good at all down from a high shelf and onto the messy work surface. When the slow old kettle's boiled, she warms the pot, but in the meantime she's been laying out bone-handled cake forks, chipped and mismatched floral tea plates, cups and saucers, and the cake stand she bought from Harrods last January sale. 'Every kitchen should have something from Harrods in it,' she once said, unwrapping the delicate floral structure

246

from its tissue paper. It just made me love her more.

Or perhaps I just felt sorry for her.

'Baked fresh this morning,' she says, spreading out an array of bright purple and orange iced cupcakes on the bottom layer of the stand. On the top tier she piles French fancies with edible silver baubles pressed into the fondant icing that I know she will also have made. They are all slightly misshapen, each one carefully crafted to be different from the others. Cecelia sees baking the same as her jewellery making. It should be lavish yet somehow quaint, demure but still tantalising, and, most importantly, apart from being handmade, no two pieces should ever be the same. She roared herself pink when she told me this.

Cecelia.

'Help me cut off the crusts.' She passes me the bread knife and a stack of brown bread. I know exactly how she likes them. The ritual is strangely comforting, a far cry from what I am faced with in my job. The job Cecelia knows nothing about, the job that keeps me from tumbling into the same place where she now resides — an insane landscape I've only dared to glimpse. It's all for her own good.

'Prawns?' I ask. It's what she usually has.

'Smoked salmon today,' she says, popping a strip of the fish between her lips and giving me a guilty grin over her shoulder as if I've never known her.

I press the salmon between the slices of bread after adding a bunch of clipped cress. I cut the

247

sandwiches into diagonal quarters and line them up on the middle tier of the cake stand. I place the whole lot on the table. Cecelia spoons Lapsang Souchong tea leaves into the pot and re-boils the kettle. Soon we are sitting opposite each other, me hunched over my violet- and forget-me-not-rimmed plate and Cecelia with the sun flaring through her hair as light streams into the flat. It only lasts for about twenty minutes at this time of year but goes on for nearly an hour in the summer.

'This is more lunch than afternoon tea,' Cecelia confesses. 'You know what I'm like when I'm immersed in work. Days go by without me thinking about food.'

That's not entirely true. Cecelia is obsessed with the stuff but still manages to be pencil thin.

'Eat up,' she says, noting my empty plate. 'If you were pregnant, you'd be ravenous.'

She might as well have slapped me in the face. 'I'm sorry to be such a failure.' I take a sandwich and bite into it. It tastes of nothing and goes some way towards quelling the tears.

I stare at Cecelia. She is still there but somehow changed. I've done everything I can for her, everything I promised, but it's as if we're on different sides of a very tall mountain. I don't see a way around.

'You're not a failure.' She slides her hand past the cake stand and takes hold of mine. Her strong fingers knead deep against my knuckles. She's hurting me. 'As such. We'll just have to think of another plan.'

I nod. If I was watching this scene in a movie,

I'd be screaming, 'Get out! Run!' I wouldn't foretell a happy ending. Why, I ask myself as my fingers mesh into a net with hers, do I always let her do this to me? If I'm honest, I know the answer to that but I'm just too stupid to face up to it.

'It wasn't meant to be this time,' I tell her, as if I'm ready to try again, as if all my resolve is a blown-away dandelion head. I wipe my mouth on a napkin. 'I'm working on a plan.'

Her eyebrows raise into two curious peaks. She makes me sigh. 'And just what are you proposing?' she asks. 'An immaculate conception?' She giggles and takes a cupcake from the stand. She places it on her china plate and licks her finger and thumb. She pours more tea, watching me from beneath the frizz of her hair. Her eyes are bright green, sparkling provocatively like forgotten emeralds from within the charity-shop décor of the flat. I'm certain she's accumulated a ton more stuff since I left.

'I can't really say,' I tell her, knowing immediately it's like pouring petrol on a fire. 'You'll just have to trust me.'

'You know I don't,' she says, biting into the cake while reading me with heavy eyes.

'It's complicated. But there will be a baby.'

If I analysed rationally what I was saying, what I was planning *again*, and so soon after last time, then I might as well have myself locked up now. *What am I thinking?* But then I look at Cecelia and remember how happy we once were, and if there's a slim chance we could get that back then I'm willing to take the risk, however it might end. It's only right.

'How's your *job*,' she asks. I feel the bitterness as she chucks out the word.

'I . . .'

'Oh yes. Silly me. I forgot that you don't like discussing it.'

I bow my head. Telling her about Claudia and James, involving her in the twins' lives . . . she wouldn't understand. *Couldn't* understand. It would begin with mild curiosity, a gentle interest, until she boiled with furious jealousy and rage. With everything that's going on, it's imperative she knows nothing about them. It would be too cruel. 'Yes, you know I don't want to talk about that,' I tell her, as I always do. There's a lump forming in my throat and it's got nothing to do with the sandwich I'm cramming in to stifle what I really want to say. I'm adept at biting my tongue.

'Oh la-di-dah to your precious jobs,' Cecelia sings rudely. 'Truth is, you can't hold one down long enough to have anything interesting to tell me. How many have you had in the last year alone? Five, six? I reckon it's more.' She's right. I have had many jobs. And she's right, too, that none of them has gone particularly well.

She stands up and picks up her empty plate, turning it round and round in her hands. 'I think you've had dozens of stupid jobs and you've been fired from them all.' She raises the plate above her head. 'Tell me what I should do with you, Heather. You won't give me a baby and you have no career.' The plate spins across the room in slow motion, smashing against the wall above her work table. The shards shower around her latest piece.

I try to swallow the sandwich but it won't go down so I let it drop out of my mouth onto the table. I stand up. My legs are shaking. 'You know I want you to be happy, Cecelia,' I whisper, crumbs falling from my lips. I grip her narrow shoulders and she flinches. 'It's just that . . . '

The look on her face halts me — that look of trust, of need, of hope.

Don't let me down, her expression implores.

'You will have a baby,' I say, and I leave, feeling sick with the thought of what I must do.

26

I've got the heating turned up full blast now that the boiler's fixed. It's wonderful, walking around the house with bare feet and a huge baggy T-shirt over my tracksuit pants. Last night's frost has lasted right through into the afternoon, high-lighting our street silver. I called work after antenatal class and told them I wouldn't be in. I'm too tired. There's stuff I can do from home and I'm much more comfortable working here. Zoe has gone out, perhaps to run some errands, and I'm enjoying the peace. But as soon as I've settled down with a pile of folders and a list of phone calls to make, the doorbell rings. I heave myself from the sofa and waddle to the door. A man and a woman are standing there looking so serious I swear my heart stops for a second.

It's the moment every military wife dreads.

'Is it about James?' I ask in a panic. They look just as I've always imagined. The woman is wearing a dark trouser suit and has sunglasses forked on her head and the man is standing stiffly in a long black coat. 'Oh God, tell me he's OK.' Whether James is working in a war zone or not, his job is often dangerous. He told me once what would happen, that they come in pairs, that the boys and I would receive support. My mouth is dry and I think my heart has raced so far ahead of itself it's given up completely.

'I'm Detective Inspector Scott and this is DI

Fisher,' the man says, as if he's said it thousands of times in his life.

'Who's James, love? Your husband?' the woman asks with a pleasant smile. I nod. 'Don't worry, it's not him we're here about. Are you Claudia Morgan-Brown?'

I nod again, and take a deep breath. 'How can I help you?'

'I called round earlier. I spoke to your nanny,' she says.

I feel instinctively guilty, as if they think I've done something wrong. 'Oh, I see. She didn't tell me.'

'Can we come in?' the woman says.

'Yes, of course,' I reply, stepping aside. 'Come on through to the sitting room. I'm working from home today.' I gather up the files and move them onto the coffee table to make room. 'Please, sit down.' I lower myself into the space beside the woman. The man sits opposite.

I wish James was here.

'We're here about your work, as it happens,' the man says. 'We won't keep you long.'

I let out the breath I hadn't realised I'd been holding. 'I'll help however I can,' I say. We deal with the police all the time in the department but only once have I ever encountered detectives. It's not unheard of though. I begin to relax.

'You probably saw in the news that there's been another attack on a pregnant woman,' DI Fisher begins. She glances at my tummy and I know what she's thinking, that she shouldn't really mention it for fear of upsetting me.

'Miraculously, the lass survived,' she adds sympathetically.

'Her baby wasn't so lucky, though.' The male detective's concern is more businesslike. 'So we're dealing with another murder case.'

'Oh, that's just so terrible.' I don't know what to say.

'We hope this won't upset you ... ' The woman takes another quick glance at my bump.

'I see bad things happen to children all the time in my work,' I tell them honestly. 'I wouldn't say you get hardened to it, but my personal life is separate.' I want them to understand. 'Social workers wouldn't ever have children if they couldn't draw a line between the two.' I try to make a joke of it but it falls flat. The detectives remain serious.

'The latest attack was on someone you've been dealing with, I'm afraid. We're sorry to be the bearers of bad news.' There's a pause, and I brace myself. 'The pregnant woman was Carla Davis. We're so sorry.'

And instantly my resolve to keep work out of my home life is broken to pieces. It's almost as if Carla is in my sitting room, yelling at me for letting her down, for allowing such a thing to happen to her. How could I have done things differently?

I bury my face in my hands and stifle a sob. For Carla's sake, I can't let myself go. I have to stay strong and help them. 'Oh good grief,' I say. 'I had no idea. I heard about the story briefly but didn't realise it was Carla. I don't believe it.'

Even sitting down, I feel faint and dizzy. This is terrible news.

'I'm so sorry,' DI Fisher says. 'It was a shock for your colleagues too.'

'We work so closely with these people,' I say quietly, hardly able to take it all in. 'We get to know them, become part of their lives, monitoring them and checking their progress, trying to give their children a better start in life. I know I said I don't become emotionally involved, but it's so hard.'

'I understand that, love.' She sounds as if she means it. 'Unfortunately, Carla's baby has just been denied that right to life. We need to ask you some questions about her. She's in hospital and so far hasn't been able to tell us much.'

I hide my face again at the thought. My body aches in sympathy. 'Please . . . ' I hold up my hand. 'I'll tell you everything I know, but I'm not good with the specific details . . . you know, about what happened to her.' I want to help them. 'Just tell me, is she going to be all right?'

'It's too early to tell,' the man says. 'But the doctors are hopeful.'

I nod solemnly. 'I first encountered her when she was about twelve although I know she's been under the watch of our department for longer. I think her school alerted us. It was the usual stuff — bad home life, unemployed drug-addict mother, and her father in and out of prison. Her mum died not so long ago.'

'We're keen to find out who her friends are, especially who the father of her baby might be.'

I take a moment to think. I want to get it right.

255

'I remember she had one very good friend. Emily, I think her name was.'

'Could that be Emma?'

'Yes, yes, Emma. That was it. She was quite a help to Carla. Emma came from a more stable background and actually worked with us in Carla's rehabilitation. Like her mother, Carla also had a heroin addiction.'

The woman detective is taking notes. 'Tell us more about the drugs.'

'She'd always been into something or other — cannabis, any type of pills she could get her hands on, crack, and finally the heroin. She was usually hooked on something, pretty much from when we first got her, right up until she was eighteen and set up in her own flat. I think she was clean for a couple of months then. Getting pregnant actually helped her on a practical level and almost gave her the momentum she needed to get her life straight.' I sigh, remembering the first time we went to visit Carla in her own place. I prayed she'd sort herself out. 'It wasn't her we were interested in any more — she was over eighteen — but rather her unborn baby. No child should have to be raised in the conditions Carla was offering.' Then I'm thinking of her dead baby and I feel sick and the room is swimming in and out of focus. I just can't take in what's happened.

'So any ideas about the father?' the man asks.

I think long and hard. 'She did have a few boyfriends,' I tell them. 'But as far as I recall, none were long term. A young woman like her living alone is so vulnerable.' Then I'm thinking about myself. At the opposite end of the social spectrum, my life is worlds apart from Carla's, but when it comes down to it, it could just as easily have been me who was attacked. When James is away, I'm as good as a single mother. 'You'd best ask Tina Kent, my colleague, to be sure. She's been dealing with her recently. I was providing supervision on the case. Tina would likely know more about the baby's father.'

'We spoke with Tina earlier. We've taken some of the case files, although Tina did comment there was one missing, the most recent, signed out to you apparently.'

'Ah yes,' I say. I should have taken it back days ago, but it's quite safe locked in James's study. No one can get to it there. 'I can fetch it if you want to take a look. As head of department, it's my job to regularly review cases that the other social workers are dealing with. We think of it as quality control.' I'm already on my feet, puffing as I speak, in order to fetch the file.

'Thanks,' DI Fisher says, 'that would be helpful.' Then she adds, 'How long have you got to go?' She points at my bump.

'Too long,' I say with a laugh. 'A couple of weeks, but if she came now I'd be very happy.'

'She?'

'The scan showed it was a girl. I already have twin boys — I'm their step-mum — so I'll be glad of the female company.'

'I have two girls. Teenagers. Nothing but trouble.' DI Fisher says all this through a grin.

I waddle off to the study and open the filing cabinet James allows me to use for work. If the files are taken out of the office, I'm not allowed to leave them in the car or unattended, but they're fine temporarily in fireproof storage in a locked study. I locate the papers and go back to the sitting room. The detectives have been talking but stop when I come in.

'Here,' I say, handing it over. 'You should really sign a receipt at the office for this.'

DI Fisher produces a copy of the form Tina has already filled out for the other documents. I add this file's details and initial it alongside the detective's signature. I'm satisfied I've done the right thing. It's not as if I can withhold information from the police.

'I really hope it helps.'

For the next fifteen minutes, they ask me more about my dealings with Carla, her drugs habit, her mental state the last time I saw her, her family, and even about her aspirations. I should probably have offered them a cup of tea, but I just want them to go. The shock of all this is making me feel ill.

Finally, they make a move.

'If there's anything else I can do,' I say, leading them through the hall, 'please do get in touch.'

They both nod and shake my hand, grateful for my help. As they turn to leave, Zoe is coming up the drive with a twin attached to each hand. She is tugging them up the front path. She slows and stares at the detectives, suddenly dropping her gaze and turning away. The detectives barely notice her, talking intently to each other, and now the man is on his phone as they stride off down the street.

258

As Zoe brushes past me, muttering and grumbling, I'm trying to figure out why she looks so ghostly thin and pale.

★ ★ ★

Later, there's an email waiting from James. I wasn't expecting one so soon. My heart flutters at the thought of savouring the couple of lines he will have sent. I settle onto my bed with a cup of tea and gaze at the laptop screen as it balances on my legs. I want to absorb the message-sender's name and subject line as it sits unread and full of promise in my inbox. I miss him so much.

What will he have to say this time? Perhaps he'll tell me the sub's turned around and is on its way back to port. Maybe he's driving along the motorway right now to our land-locked home, ready to chuck in his Navy career. It's not as if we need the money. I'm certain the inherited family wealth would be enough to keep us comfortable into old age and beyond, but James says the money can't be touched yet, that it doesn't even feel like his. I don't understand, but he gets irate if I pry.

I sip my tea and click on the message. As I suspected, it's short. It will have been vetted by the military before it reached my inbox.

Dearest Claudie, Missing you all desperately. Are the boys well? Now in Med and operation going to plan. I can't help wondering if you've had our baby. As ever not much time, but my

259

heart is with you all. Is Z behaving? I hope she's proving her worth. Email when you can with news. Will check often. All my love, as ever, James.

It's always pretty much the same, except this time he's mentioned Zoe. It must be some comfort to him that I'm not entirely alone. Neither of our families lives nearby, with James's parents in Scotland and my mother having emigrated to Australia years ago. Elizabeth's family is based in the Channel Islands so the twins and my baby will have no doting grandparents at close call. But James looks on the positive side and says we have ready-made holiday homes.

The first time James left me to go away was only two weeks after I'd moved in with him. Friends were worried that he'd rushed things after Elizabeth's death, that I was simply ready-made childcare for the boys, but I didn't mind. I loved him from the start and knew I wanted to be with him for the long haul, military career or not. He came as a package deal and that was fine by me. Even then, I wanted to give him a baby and he was entirely agreeable to that idea. He told me it might be difficult to conceive, what with him being away so much. I wanted to tell him that if we didn't conceive, that wouldn't be the reason.

I rest my head back against the pillow and listen for noise. All is quiet. Zoe bathed and put the boys to bed an hour ago, and I read to them and kissed them on their mops of hair. They clung on to me, asking when Daddy would be home.

'I'm going out later,' Zoe then told me in the kitchen. To be honest, I was glad of the time alone. The detectives' visit had unsettled me. I'd just intended to watch some television to take my mind off it but then decided to email James instead, which was when I saw that he'd beaten me to it.

'Zoe, Zoe, Zoe,' I say, putting the laptop beside me on the bed. I'm still concerned that she's been snooping in James's office. I hate to think of her prying into our affairs.

I pick up my book and settle down to read, but I just can't concentrate. I want another cup of tea. Out on the landing, I hear one of the boys stirring so I poke my head round their door. Oscar has thrown off his duvet and his hand is feeling around for it in his sleep. I rearrange his bed, plant another kiss on each twin and leave the room, pulling the door closed.

Back out on the landing, the house is still and quiet. Has Zoe gone out already? I'm not sure. I wonder if she'd like a cup of tea, too, but don't want to call out up the stairs to the top floor in case I wake the boys. I brace myself for the strenuous climb, trying to convince myself it's just because I want to be friendly, to offer her tea, not because I want to take a look at her stuff. I haven't been up there since she moved in.

When I'm near the top, I whisper her name as loudly as I dare. There's no response. Peering through the banisters, I see the small landing area of her quarters. The light has been left on. A pair of trainers has been discarded haphazardly on the carpet and a towel is draped over a chair. A strange scent hangs in the air — slightly floral, a little musky, but strangely sad and old-fashioned. It draws me up.

'Zoe?' I say again as I step up onto the landing. I clutch my lower back. 'Are you up here?'

Nothing, so I peek into the room she uses as a living room. We put a TV in there for her and there's an old sofa as well as a beanbag. We assumed she'd want guests round occasionally, although she hasn't had any yet. If she's just split up with her boyfriend, she's probably not feeling very sociable yet. She didn't mention where she was going tonight.

I knock gently on her bedroom door but there's no reply. I glance towards the stairs. I can hear one of the boys snoring softly. I know every sound in this house — every floorboard creak, each door's peculiar noise, the pathways of the old clanking plumbing — and, after checking up here, listening carefully again, I'm now positive Zoe's not home.

'Are you in there, Zoe?' I try once more, my obsessive nature getting the better of me. I would hate her to think I was spying, though if I'm honest with myself, I'm desperate to take a quick look in her bedroom. It's our house, after all.

I ease the door open a little and look inside. It's dark and I can't see much, even with the landing light seeping in. My eyes widen. At first glance it appears there's a figure lying on the bed, but when I swing the door fully open I see it's only a heap of clothes and a suitcase. It almost looks as if she'd been packing up her stuff and thought better of it.

What if she comes back? I stop and listen for noises but can only hear the sound of my breath and the whoosh of fear in my ears. If Zoe returns, I won't be able to escape quickly.

'Oh stop it,' I whisper out loud. 'You're overreacting.' It's my house, I can come up here if I wish. I might simply be looking for something — there's a bookcase on the landing, after all, with some of my old university text books in it. I'll tell her I'm searching for a title.

I lift some of the clothes that are strewn about — there's a whole tangle of stuff I've seen her wearing recently. T-shirts, jeans, cotton shirts and a couple of cardigans have been thrown onto the bed, which is unmade and just as much of a mess. Perhaps this is her dirty washing. Maybe she was going to bring the whole lot down to the laundry room in the suitcase, although it's rather large to transport just a few items.

The sight of blood makes me catch my breath. I recoil and gasp but then lean closer to inspect the rust-brown stain smeared on the inside of a sweatshirt. It's turned the wrong way round and part of the woolly fleece lining is encrusted with something that certainly looks like blood. I run my forefinger over the stain. It feels dry and congealed. I lift the garment to my nose. There is a stale metallic tang. I feel slightly nauseous, but then stop myself from being ridiculous, from becoming even more paranoid about Zoe. She probably just cut herself, I decide, though it must have been a bad gash if this was the result. As I lay the sweatshirt back down, I notice the small tear on the shoulder and the dark ring of blood around that.

I pick it up again and dangle it between finger and thumb. I try to swallow but my mouth is dry. *Oh God, what if she hurt one of the boys.* My mind races but I soon realise I'm being irrational. If she'd done that then their clothes would have been bloody too and I'd have surely noticed. *Unless she washed it off before I spotted it . . .*

'Oscar and Noah would have told me,' I say out loud, forgetting that Zoe could come up at any moment. Noah's not exactly the passive type.

Nevertheless, I can't help feeling concerned. I've become so paranoid recently and I don't like it one bit. James would say it's my hormones getting the better of me, that my body is awash with ungovernable feelings. I would say it's me being protective of my family — overprotective, I realise, but I can't help it. Once my baby's here, our unit will be complete and I'll be the fiercest mother around. How can I trust Zoe now I've seen this?

I turn away from the bed, feeling dizzy, and Zoe's room becomes a blur as if I'm on a speeding merry-go-round. There are tears in my eyes and I know they're there for no good reason but I just can't help it. What is she hiding from me? I'm certain there's something.

In a fit of recklessness, I fling open her wardrobe doors. It's apparent that my nanny doesn't have good organisational skills when it comes to her own possessions. It's as much of a mess as the rest of the room. And then I see the pregnancy testing kit — the same one that fell out of her bag when she first arrived. The box is lying beside a pair of boots on the floor of the cupboard as if it's been chucked down there. I pick it up. The cellophane wrapper has been removed. I open it to find one of the two white plastic wands is missing and the remaining one is snapped in half. It appears to be unused. Why would Zoe take this job if she thought she was pregnant?

'I wonder if this is to do with her breaking up with her boyfriend,' I say quietly, although it's really none of my business. But I suppose it is my business if the result was positive.

I put the pieces of wand back in the box. Why did she break it? Was she angry at the result? Perhaps she *wanted* to be pregnant — or not. It's no good second-guessing Zoe's personal life. The only way to find out for certain is to ask her. But then she'll know I've been snooping.

My heart flutters with curiosity when I see the camera — a small digital one that looks as if it's either been dumped on the floor of the wardrobe or it fell from a jacket. It's compact enough to fit in a pocket. My mouth salivates at the thought of flicking through her photos while my heart protests with guilty palpitations. It's only because I feel there's more to Zoe than I know about. That's what I tell myself anyway.

I creep towards the door and listen again. The snoring has stopped and the house is completely silent apart from the tick-tick of a radiator as the central heating kicks back into action. I know I have to do this, even though James would say I was mad. 'Oh Claudia, let it rest. Come and sit with me beside the fire.' I can almost hear his exasperated voice.

I pick up the camera and remove it from its slim case. It's expensive-looking and a newer model of the one James and I use. I turn it on, thankful that it works in the same way. I move closer to the door, one ear straining for sounds. Would I hear the front door from up here?

I toggle through Zoe's pictures and smile at the first few. She has snapped Oscar and Noah at Tumblz Play Zone and Lilly is in some of them. The next dozen or so are of Pip from across the room. It doesn't look as if Pip knows she's being photographed. Then there are a few from our aquarium visit, though they're dark and out of focus. Then there are pictures of our street. It's as if she's photographed it from each end as well as focusing on our house in some of the shots. No doubt to send to family or friends, I assume, to show them where she works. That's normal, I tell myself. We're lucky to live in such a lovely neighbourhood.

My brain doesn't assimilate the next few pictures immediately, so I flip back and forth through them. They appear to be photographs of documents. I can't make them out exactly, but there are loads, and each one is the same . . . yet subtly different. My fingers hover over the camera buttons, momentarily unsure which one is for zooming in, but then I remember. I enlarge an image at random and my mouth goes dry and my heart races so much I think it might fly up my throat. I put a hand on the wall to steady myself.

'Oh my God,' I say as the photographed text resolves. 'What on earth . . . '

I strain my eyes to read the writing, even though I don't need to. The name at the top of the page tells me exactly what she's been taking pictures of.

Then I hear it — the familiar sound of the heavy front door banging shut. The noise funnels up the stairwells, reverberating through the silent house.

Shit, shit, shit.

My hands fumble with the camera, desperate to turn it off and get it back in its case. I try to fasten it but the zip gets stuck. I drop it back in the bottom of the wardrobe and waddle as fast as my body will allow towards the stairs, closing her door behind me. I can hear Zoe's footsteps approaching. She's humming a soft tune, as if she's happy. I'm too slow. I'll never make it down even to the first-floor landing without being caught along the way so I lower myself onto my knees in front of the bookshelves. I try to stifle my breathlessness.

'Zoe, don't jump,' I call out as normally as I can without actually yelling. I don't want to wake the boys. 'I'm up here looking for a book.'

'Oh,' Zoe sings back, sounding intrigued. Her head appears behind the banister spindles. We are close, and it's as if one of us is in a cage. I have a feeling it's me.

'Sorry,' I say. 'It's called *Social Work and the Law* and I can't find it anywhere.' I run my finger along all the spines of my old textbooks. I know exactly where it is but pretend not to see it.

Zoe comes up and crouches down beside me. She turns her head sideways. 'Here it is.' I can feel her stare burning my cheek.

I pull the book out. 'Thanks,' I say, turning to her. Our faces are inches apart. 'Couldn't see it for looking.' It breaks the crackle of tension between us as I attempt to stand up.

Zoe holds out her hands and laughs. 'Good job I came back,' she says, 'or you might have been stuck down there all night.' There's something about the way she says it that makes me think she knows what I've been doing.

'You saved me,' I say with a return laugh and head down the stairs.

'Goodnight,' she says quietly when I am out of sight.

'Goodnight,' I reply, and go into my bedroom.

Immediately, I boot up my computer. Within seconds, I am searching for the name Zoe Harper on the internet, as if all my previous reference checking and research has been a waste of time. Top of the searches are the usual Facebook entries and other social networking sites. I click them all but none is her. There are various videos of people called Zoe Harper and entries in address databases and businesses run by people of the same name as well as a plethora of random pages containing my search words. My eyes scan down the results and I review the bulk of them. There are too many to check. Half an hour later, I am none the wiser.

I call James's phone just for the comfort of hearing his voice. There's no point me leaving a message as he won't pick it up until he returns. 'Honey, I need you. I'm scared,' I whisper after hanging up. I consider sending him an email but that would only worry him witless and there's nothing he can do.

I lie back on my bed fully clothed. I stare at the ceiling. I have no idea what I should do. Why, oh *why*, has my nanny been photographing Carla Davis's social work file?

27

Lorraine was beside herself with worry for Grace. Not because she wasn't answering her phone — she often didn't pick up, and was sometimes late replying to texts — and it wasn't because she'd forgotten to take her packed lunch with her this morning or because she missed her driving lesson (the irate instructor had called mid-meeting). Rather, Lorraine was developing a deep, troubled feeling that one day very soon she simply wouldn't come home at all.

She toyed with the bottle of Cabernet. It was definitely too early in the day for a glass, however small. Drinking wine wouldn't fix anything, let alone change her daughter's mind. She placed the bottle on its side again in the wine rack.

'Oh Grace, Grace, Grace . . . '

Leaning on the sink, she stared out of the window and thought. She wondered how long it would be before the gossip started once Grace left school, moved out, got married. Stories would be rife: the parents couldn't cope, the poor girl ran away, she was being abused, she got pregnant, they kicked her out . . . Lorraine shuddered. Whatever they believed to be the truth, she, as the mother, would get the blame. And maybe she deserved it. If Grace wasn't happy, if she wanted to be with Matt's family, then it *must* be her fault. She'd hardly been a regular stay-at-home mum lately, having been on call virtually twenty-four hours a day. She couldn't remember the last time she'd watched Grace play a netball match or made it to a parents' evening at school. As for going out to the cinema or shopping and lunch on a Saturday, that hadn't happened in ages. And what about just a simple, honest mother-and-daughter chat at the kitchen table?

Lorraine covered her face then reached for the wine again. This time she opened it. 'I'd like to see how stay-at-home mums would bloody cope with a job like mine, a husband who thinks he can . . . can . . . ' She closed her eyes in despair. 'And a daughter who's intent on doing everything to ruin her life.' She poured herself a glass and took a sip, sitting half slumped at the kitchen table, muttering to no one.

'Whassup, Mum?'

Stella was already nosing in the fridge by the time Lorraine realised her youngest daughter had come in. Had she heard her ramblings? Whatever happened, she didn't want the girls to suffer for what Adam had done. No, it would be kept private between the two of them, although she wasn't sure why she protected him. Perhaps it was because broadcasting her husband's weaknesses would mean that she had some too; that she wasn't able to keep him. The question was, how long could she maintain the charade?

Oh . . . she chased the thought from her mind and gave Stella a hug instead. 'Missed you, little one,' she said.

'You haven't called me that in ages.'

Lorraine felt her daughter's arms reciprocate,

271

and for a few seconds everything seemed fine. 'Well I'm calling you it now. Little one.'

There was a mutual grin, Lorraine's accompanied by the thought that at least one member of her family hadn't gone completely mad.

Stella pulled away gently and returned to the fridge. 'What's for dinner? I'm starving.'

'When's Grace home, love?' It occurred to Lorraine that, as her mother, she should probably know this. She felt ashamed having to ask Stella. It also occurred to her that she should have bought some food.

'She said she wouldn't be . . . ' Stella trailed off, turning scarlet. A mop of blonde curls fell over her face as she bowed her head in thought. 'Gosh, actually, I can't remember when she said she'd be back.'

'Stella . . . ' Lorraine warned.

'Maybe later?'

Lorraine took Stella gently by the shoulders despite her swell of panic. 'Where is your sister?'

'At Matt's? With a suitcase?' Again, questions rather than a statement, but it told Lorraine all she needed to know. Had Grace told Stella of her plans? She knew her girls were close.

'Thank you, sweetheart. Dinner will be a take-away.' She dashed to the stairs. 'Once I've got your sister back.'

Upstairs, she poked her head round Grace's bedroom door. She hadn't been in there for ages. It was a mess and hard to tell if Grace was in the process of moving out or there'd been a burglary. But her dressing table told a story. Most of her make-up was gone along with the various photos

272

of Matt she'd stuck to the mirror.

'Fuck.'

Lorraine ran back downstairs, grabbed her coat, bag and keys — thankful she hadn't drunk more than a mouthful of wine — and prepared for a confrontation.

* * *

It had been Adam's idea to make a note of Grace's boyfriend's car registration number. At the time, Lorraine had called him a helicopter parent. Now, she stifled a half-angry, half-hysterical laugh as she drove, remembering Adam flapping his way around their bedroom dressed only in stripey boxer shorts pretending to be a helicopter. But before that he'd been peeking out of their bedroom window, spying on Grace and Matt saying goodnight in the red Mazda Matt drove. It was hard to see much through the steamed-up windscreen, but that alone told Adam they were getting up to no good.

'No good?' Lorraine had said. 'I don't think many teenagers in love would say that a snog in a car was 'no good'.'

At the time, Adam hadn't yet dropped his bombshell on her. They were still happy, or so she thought.

'I don't like it, that's all,' had been his reply as he watched them through a gap in the curtains.

'Leave them be,' Lorraine had said, patting his side of the bed. 'At least he's brought her back at a reasonable hour. It could be a lot worse.'

Adam had grunted and begun hunting around the bedroom.

'What are you looking for?'

'A pen and paper.'

'Why?'

'To write down his registration number.'

'Oh for God's sake,' Lorraine had said, flicking off her bedside lamp. 'Just get into bed, Adam.' But he'd continued fumbling around the bedroom in the dark. 'Put it in your Blackberry if you can't find a pen.'

'It's in the kitchen charging.'

'Bloody hell.' Lorraine had put the light back on and tossed her phone at him. 'Here, use mine.'

Now, driving towards Selly Oak, where Grace had once said Matt lived, she was grateful for Adam's obsessions. It had been a two-minute call to get the car's registered address. During the short time Grace had been going out with Matt, they'd never once met his parents or found out exactly where he lived. It hadn't seemed necessary. They'd assumed the relationship would burn itself out soon enough, like all the others had. They simply didn't have time to play at meeting the in-laws.

Lorraine blew out a tight sigh as she drove down Matt's road. Grace had once mentioned something about Matt's dad working at the hospital and Lorraine hadn't given it much reflection; she'd thought briefly porter, security guard, male nurse. Judging by the large houses around here, he was clearly a consultant. Under normal circumstances, that would have pleased her no end. Now all she could think of was that he'd have the money to spend on a slap-up wedding, and to help them get a place of their own.

Cranley Lodge was a large mock-Tudor house with a wide front garden and sweeping in-and-out drive. Three cars were parked on the block-paving — a Range Rover, a Mercedes, and Matt's Mazda, a sleek MX something-or-other that Adam had complained about bitterly. *Who'd buy a new driver something like that?* A rich parent, Lorraine now knew, although at the time she'd stuck up for Matt, suggesting perhaps he had a Saturday job and had saved up. Ironically, she recalled defending the lad as being nothing less than utterly sensible.

Lorraine's phone rang as she got out of the car. It was Adam. She listened intently to what he had to say, barely commented, told him that she'd be home in half an hour and they would discuss it later. Even what he'd found out about Carla Davis didn't put Lorraine off her stride. She pressed the doorbell hard while simultaneously rapping on the letterbox.

She wanted her daughter back.

'Hello.' A petite woman in her early fifties answered quickly. She was elegant and well groomed. *Typical doctor's wife*, Lorraine thought bitterly as she tucked her unstyled hair behind her ears.

'I'm Detective Inspector Fisher,' she said gravely. It was no doubt the only score-settling moment she'd have, she thought as she watched the woman's made-up, probably Botoxed face

275

attempt a concerned frown.

'Is everything OK?' she asked.

'Is your son here?' Lorraine said, still with her business voice on. She wanted the woman to have a moment of anxiety at least a tenth of the level hers was at.

'Matt? Yes. Why?'

Lorraine waited a beat, as long as she dared, before forcing a smile. 'Good, then that must mean my daughter's here too.' It was then that Lorraine noticed the suitcases dumped on the hall floor — suitcases she recognised from home. Seeing actual evidence of Grace moving out made her feel sick.

'Ahh,' the woman said graciously. 'You must be . . . please, do come in.' She stepped aside. 'I think they're watching a movie. I'm just cooking — '

'I'm sorry, she won't be staying for dinner. I've come to collect her.'

Matt's mother seemed perplexed but, despite Lorraine's brusque manner, she kept annoyingly calm and pleasant. 'I'll get Grace. You probably want to talk.' She went off down the corridor before Lorraine could protest that there wasn't any talking to be done, that Grace was coming home now, and that was that.

Moments later Grace emerged into the hall, looking sullen. Lorraine suddenly felt intimidated by her own daughter. 'What are you doing here?' She had her slippers on and her arms were folded. She leant against the wall.

'I've come to get you, love,' Lorraine said as calmly as she could. Her mouth was dry.

276

'No, Mum,' Grace said. 'I told you. I'm living with Matt now.' Matt had appeared at her side and was leaning against her, his arm loosely slung around her hips. Matt's mother completed the line-up — a wall of players on the opposing team. 'We're watching a film and Nancy's cooking a curry.' Grace looked fondly at Matt's mother.

Nancy, Lorraine thought sourly, half wanting to burst into tears.

'Well, you're not watching a film or eating curry any more. You're coming home with me.'

'No way. I've moved out and I'm living here now. You can't stop me.' Grace sighed, as if she didn't quite believe what she was saying herself, but she stood her ground nonetheless. Matt moved in closer.

'I think your mum's just worried about you, Gracie,' Nancy suggested.

Gracie! Lorraine pressed down on the lid of her anger.

'This is not like her, I'm afraid,' she said to Nancy. 'I'm so sorry to be disturbing you like this.'

'Not at all,' Nancy said kindly. 'Grace is very welcome here.'

'That's most kind of you, but Grace, really, you have to come with me. Now.' One final glare, one more purse of her lips, one more imploring look that she prayed her daughter would take to be the final word — but no. Grace simply smiled, turned her back, and walked off down the hall.

'Sorry, Mum,' she said over her shoulder.

'Matt and I are engaged. We're living together now. That's just the way it is. Bye.' And she disappeared into the sitting room with Matt following her.

After a brief exchange with Nancy, Lorraine finally left without her daughter. She couldn't believe what had just happened. Why had she given in so easily? Why hadn't she done something? Dragged Grace off by the arm, yelled at her, handcuffed her! She felt bereft, angry as hell, a failure, and more frustrated than she'd ever been in her life. She drove home in a daze, utterly incredulous at what had just happened.

'I've lost her,' Lorraine said quietly, pulling up outside her house. 'I've lost her to someone else.'

In comparison to the Barnes's big detached place, their home looked shabby and slightly depressing. Before she went inside she pulled her phone from her bag and tapped out a text message to Grace: *We've got to talk. Please. X.*

When she got inside, she found Adam in the living room hunched over his laptop.

'What's up?' he said in response to Lorraine slamming the front door and hurling her coat on the stairs. 'Where's Grace?'

'She's left home.'

Adam stood and reached out an arm to Lorraine. She flinched and went through to the kitchen. This time she had no guilty feelings about picking up her half-finished glass of wine.

'She's at Matt's. I went round to get her. She barely spoke to me and refuses to come home. I could have physically manhandled her but there would have been an almighty scene. I just don't know . . . ' Lorraine felt the tears building up. 'I just don't know what to do. She's gone. She's bloody gone!'

'Oh, Ray,' Adam said, stepping towards her. She didn't back away.

'She's ruining her life. What about her exams, university, all her dreams of a career?'

Adam sighed. 'If Grace is determined to leave school and live with Matt, I'm afraid there's not much we can do except support her. Before you know it, she'll be eighteen and will do it anyway.'

She couldn't believe what he was saying. It wasn't long ago that he'd been in this very room roaring 'Like hell it won't!' at his daughter. Looking back over the years, being a parent had been easier for him. A whole lot easier. Sure, Adam had done his share of nappy-changing and night feeds, but when it came to taking time off work — for maternity leave or illness — chasing a promotion or being delegated a major operation, it was she who had lost out. Even now, Adam was the detective in charge of the Frith/Davis investigations, the one considered first and foremost the best man — *man!* — for the job. Lorraine had never exactly burned her bra over such issues, her life was what it was and she was content enough, but she still felt sometimes the unfairness of their situations, and never more so than now.

'Look,' she said, realising she'd forgotten to stop off at the Chinese take-away, 'I'm just saying that she's acting rashly. We need to step in and avert a disaster that she'll regret for the rest of her life.'

'She thinks she's in love. And maybe she is. Give her time and see what happens.'

'She hasn't *got* time. What about her exams? She needs good grades to get into university . . . ' Lorraine trailed off. It was pointless arguing with him. Besides, Stella had padded into the kitchen. She was wearing thick socks and one of Adam's oversized cardigans.

'I'm starving, Mum. And freezing cold.'

Adam plucked a menu off the notice board and picked up the phone. Stella automatically yelled the news that they were getting a Chinese upstairs to Grace, and then Lorraine had to take her by the shoulders and gently explain that her sister wasn't at home and wasn't likely to be any time soon, either.

★   ★   ★

'You'd better tell me what it was you wanted to talk to me about earlier,' Lorraine said to Adam later.

They'd both made a pact that they wouldn't leave the house again that night, not unless something major broke. If the development he had mentioned on the phone earlier was case-changing, he'd have already said.

'It was something I read in Carla Davis's file.'

'The one we picked up from the social worker's house?' Lorraine said.

Adam nodded. He stretched out on the old sofa. His shirt came untucked at the front, but Lorraine made a point of not looking. She knew he was fit, annoyingly so. Where her stomach had harboured two children and since been rather neglected, Adam's was finely honed, exercised and healthily fed. She never usually felt self-conscious about how she looked but there was some kind of competition between them these days; it seemed that way to her, anyway. Fitness-wise, they were poles apart.

'What about it?'

'There was a note made that she'd been booked in for a termination when she was sixteen weeks pregnant. It was going to be done under general anaesthetic.'

'I see.' Lorraine wrapped her arms around her body.

'But obviously Carla didn't go through with it,' Adam continued.

'Do we know why she didn't have the termination?'

'Carla's case worker wrote a note in the file simply stating that she'd changed her mind.' Adam shrugged.

'Either way, it ended the same,' Lorraine said coldly.

'Yes, but it's really the only link we have between the two cases, apart from the similarities of the actual crimes, of course.'

Lorraine thought for a moment. 'Both women had wanted terminations but didn't go through with them.' The only sound was the hiss of the living-flame gas fire. The connection was a start, she supposed, albeit a tenuous one. 'What about the results of the second DNA sample they got from Carla's flat?' A hair — a different colour to Carla's or her friend's — had been found on a piece of Carla's clothing and sent to the lab for analysis.

'There's a chance we could have a result as soon as tomorrow. The results from Sally-Ann's bathroom should have been back by now but there was some kind of delay.' Adam pulled a face. There was nothing new about lab results taking too long. He sat up and flicked on the ten o'clock news. 'And we're also waiting on Carla's fingernail scrapings, though the quality was debatable. Watch this space, basically.'

Lorraine already knew this. She curled her feet beneath her and stared at her husband watching the news. She tried to understand him, to make sense of his attitude to Grace's decision to leave home, and failed. And she convinced herself that if she allowed any more thoughts of Sally-Ann or Carla Davis or pregnancies or wayward teenagers to fill her head that night, she wouldn't be able to sleep a wink. She stood up and said goodnight to Adam, praying that tomorrow would bring some different kind of news.

28

It was funny how James and I met. It was the most unlikely of circumstances, though such meetings happen to me every week of my working life. Except that James wasn't your typical father-under-investigation and I hadn't expected to fall in love with the man whose sons I'd been sent to assess.

Had I known the full circumstances, I'd probably never have bothered visiting the suburban property in the first place. The babies were being cared for perfectly adequately. And I'd certainly never have felt the tingle of envy as I'd driven down the tree-lined road searching for the correct house. It was pretty much the street of my dreams — beautiful homes stuffed full of comfort and love and parents who doted on each other and, most of all, brimming with happy children.

Any one of the grand period properties would have done — Victorian red-brick detached places with huge sash windows and monkey puzzle trees in curved front gardens, or white rendered Georgian residences with multi-paned windows reflecting the serene street scene as I drove past. It was the complete opposite to my modest flat. I appreciated my home, even in all its magnolia loneliness, but it wasn't like this.

Someone's minted, I remember thinking as I pulled into the in-and-out drive of the property

I'd been sent to. The homes I usually visited to do my assessments possessed nothing like the grandeur of this home. Of course, I wasn't naive enough to think that money equals well-cared-for children. Rich parents are just as able to neglect their offspring. You just don't see it as much. Or perhaps no one dares report them.

I walked up to the front door, with no clue that three months later I would be moving in to this very home. I stood in the grand portico, clutching a thin, pristine file for twin baby boys named Oscar and Noah because their mother had died. It had been a whole week and their father was unreachable. Since we'd been informed the father was in the military, it was a routine visit to check on the family's plan to care for the babies. Back then I didn't understand why the father had gone away and left a sick wife. Now I realise he had no choice.

'Please, come in,' the woman who opened the door said resignedly. She was thoroughly elegant and stick-thin with not-quite-grey hair pulled back into a loose chignon. A pink cardigan hung off her bony shoulders. She told me her name was Margot and encouraged me further inside. The place reeked of grief but she fought it off with a dignity that made her seem cold yet utterly brave. The facts were heart-breaking. Her daughter had just died of pancreatic cancer. There was no one else to care for the baby twins except her. Her son-in-law was in the Navy and on a top-secret mission. The Navy refused to jeopardise national security by informing him of the news or anyone else of his whereabouts. He would simply have to wait until he got home to learn of his wife's death. 'It's not as if Elizabeth and James weren't prepared for the inevitable,' Margot told me. 'They just didn't realise it would be this soon. The pregnancy finished her off, if you ask me.'

That rang a few alarm bells with me. As their main carer now, did she resent the babies?

We were in the kitchen and she was at the back door, wedging it open with a black patent pump. She lit a slim cigar. 'I don't do this near them, if that's what you're wondering.'

'Smoking's always a concern,' I said as compassionately as I could. She'd just lost her daughter. I thought a cigar — I'd never seen a woman smoke one before — was forgivable.

'They didn't find out about the cancer until she was pregnant. She refused to terminate. After they were born, she began chemotherapy. They said she'd have a year, maybe two, with the boys.' Margot blew out in a grey sigh that swirled right back into the kitchen on a warm breeze. Sheets were snapping on the line outside. It was one of those rare summer days that refused to be spoilt even by talk of death. 'But they were wrong. I suppose now a part of her lives on.'

'How old was she?' I asked. I didn't know what else to say.

'Thirty-two,' she replied. 'You'll want to see the twins.' Margot held the half-finished cigar under the cold tap then tossed it in the bin. 'They're taking a nap but we can stir them. It's time for their bottles soon.'

'I'd love to meet them,' I told her.

285

I left the file and my handbag on the kitchen table and followed Margot up the stairs. The house was grand but retained a homely, slightly shabby feel. I remember noticing the heavily patterned carpet on the stairs — a crimson and navy Axminster, I later learnt — and it was well worn at the front of the treads from decades of use. The brass stair rods were tarnished and a couple were missing. I soon had them replaced and polished, but the carpet remains. I changed a few other things after I moved in, mostly the colour of a wall here or a pair of curtains there, but I didn't want to erase the feel of the place completely. That would have been hard on James.

'This is their room,' Margot said, and gently pushed the door open. There were two cots side by side against the far wall, protruding at a right angle. In the dim light, I could see that one of the babies was already awake and wriggling gently, silently, beneath a fleece blanket. There was a vague whiff of dirty nappies in the room and Margot noticed immediately.

'Which one of you little lambs needs changing?' she asked, switching on a bedside lamp shaped like a hot air balloon.

'Probably both,' I said with a laugh.

Standing between the two cots, I leant over each one in turn, eager to get my fill of new babies. It was a joy to actually do an assessment where the children were clearly not at any risk. I didn't know which one to give my attention to first. The second baby had also begun stirring so I lowered a hand into each cot and swept my palm across their virtually hairless heads. 'Oh, aren't you both adorable.' But, despite their contentment, I was filled with instant sadness — perhaps more so than if I'd had to put them into foster care. This unexpected feeling bored deep into my heart. These little boys had been born with everything — a loving family, a beautiful home, plenty of money, lives full of prospects. But they had no mother. Who would they grow up loving, I thought? Who would they call for in the middle of the night? Who would come to their school concerts, make their nativity costumes, run for them in the mothers' race on sports day? Their eyes appeared almost black in the half-light, as big as pebbles, staring up at me. I sighed so heavily my throat felt sore.

Their grandmother lifted each boy up in turn and sniffed at their nappies. 'It's you, Noah, isn't it?' Whisking him off across the room to the changing table, she muttered something about it *always* being him.

'And who are you?' I said in the high voice that everyone reserves for talking to babies. I reached into the cot and scooped up the little bundle. He was heavier than I'd imagined and his head was last to leave the towelling sheet. I quickly supported it with my fingers splayed beneath his neck and brought his face to my lips. The soft down of his skin felt tender and warm as I kissed him.

I was suddenly drowning in love, desire, emptiness.

I caught Margot's eye and snapped out of the ridiculous reverie. It was the first and last time I thought I felt — even *smelt* — Elizabeth's presence. Was she pleased I was there to take charge of her babies? Did she know, even though I didn't, that I would become their mother? All I knew was that when I had my own baby, no one would ever take it from me.

Then there was a noise out on the landing. A throaty, soul-destroying moan accompanied by the heavy thumping of footsteps. I looked at Margot. She froze, mid-nappy change, and her face crumpled into a map of lines as a man appeared in the doorway. 'Oh James, my darling,' she said, and dashed across the room to him. She allowed herself to be engulfed in his arms as they sobbed together in what should have been a private moment of grief.

I felt awkward and embarrassed. I knew nothing about these people yet here I was immersed in their lives. I turned to Noah, alone on the changing mat. Too young to roll off, but I didn't like seeing the little mite so vulnerable so I went to him, still holding Oscar, with my back facing the doorway. It seemed right.

I heard low mumblings, sobs that resonated deep in hearts, and crashing swearwords that cut through lives. The sound of a man crying is a piteous noise, almost worse than an infant's cry. Babies are either hungry, sick or bored, or need changing. This man was none of these things. He was wrapped in grief as deep as the ocean, and no one could do anything to help him.

'I'm so sorry, Miss . . . ' Margot trailed off.

I turned round to see mother and son-in-law still in tight embrace. I was holding both babies,

288

one in the crook of each arm. No mean feat. I jiggled up and down. 'Miss Brown,' I said. There seemed little point in telling her to call me Claudia. I would never see them again. This was merely a visit to tick boxes.

'I'm so sorry you had to witness this. James has only just found out.'

I was nodding profusely so she didn't have to repeat exactly what it was James had just found out. But the man still had strength enough to approach me with an outstretched hand. His Naval training, I supposed.

I kept on nodding. I couldn't offer up my hand with a baby in each arm.

'James Morgan,' he said in a voice constricted by grief. 'Thank you for coming.'

In their low whisperings of a moment ago, Margot must have informed him I was a social worker. No one had ever thanked me for coming before. The people I visit usually hate me, want me to leave, throw things at me, accuse me of ruining their lives, of stealing their children or trying to cut off their benefits. If the parents I'm trying to help don't destroy me with their vitriol, then the department itself or even the press will take a shot when things don't go according to plan. The majority of cases, the children whose lives we change for the better, for ever, well, no one hears about them and all the good work we do.

'It's just a routine visit,' I replied. 'We work closely with the hospitals.' I hoped that explaining how I had come to be there wouldn't conjure too strong an image of his wife's last days. Last days that he'd had no part of.

James came close to me and we made the transfer of babies from me to him. It was somehow symbolic, and also about that moment when I fell in love with him. Seeing him holding his babies and being in his house and watching him in the midst of the most terrible day of his life, seeing it all play out in his unfathomable eyes (oh how the boys inherited those!), falling for him came as naturally as breathing.

Two days later I was back in his kitchen. I'd left him my card in case he needed help. My love for him was firmly nailed in place at this meeting. He wanted to ask me what his options were, for the boys.

'Options?' I'd said.

Under normal circumstances I'd have thought it a particularly lame excuse for asking me on a date. It was why I'd left my card after all, although I'd not expected to hear from him, at least not this soon. But James was swallowed up in misery. His wife had recently died. He wasn't asking me out at all, rather he was genuinely wanting my professional advice regarding his sons. I'd already admired his stoicism for bearing up against the news of Elizabeth's death; now my admiration lay in his realising he couldn't do this alone.

'I must tell you,' he said as we stared into our coffees. His eyes were rimmed red. 'Margot doesn't want a piece of it.' He waved his arms around. He meant his home, the boys, his family. 'She lives in Jersey. With the rest of the Sheehans,' he added with what I thought could be a twist of bitterness. 'If I'm honest, Margot and Elizabeth never really got on.' He managed a small laugh.

'How come?' I couldn't help prying into the mother-daughter relationship.

'Elizabeth was a free spirit, somewhat bohemian,' he added with a tight laugh. 'She didn't live like the rest of the Sheehans, and she certainly didn't believe in their lifestyle or morals. The whole lot of them are wrapped up in their trust companies and offshore finances and socialite goings-on. She was nothing like her three brothers. They all work in the family business. They are the family business.'

'It sounds as if Elizabeth was quite a woman,' I said. I admire anyone who stands up for what they believe. But James was being realistic, practical, frank. And I admire honesty in a man above anything. 'Are you going to leave the Navy to look after the boys?' With hindsight, that was a particularly stupid question. But I didn't know.

'I won't be leaving my job,' he said matter-of-factly. 'I need to arrange childcare for the times I'm away. It's going to be hard.'

'But you want to keep the boys, surely?' All kinds of thoughts were racing through my mind. Did he want to have them adopted? Was he going to look for a live-in nanny? Perhaps get them signed up for boarding school as soon as they were old enough?

'Of course I want to keep them,' was his reply. 'I just don't know how to do it.' It was apparent that James had no idea how to go about hiring nannies or au pairs or any kind of domestic help.

'Elizabeth was marvellous,' was all he said. 'She did everything.'

The man definitely needed help, just not the kind I was able to provide professionally.

'I can put you in touch with some reputable agencies,' I said. 'You can interview live-in nannies. It won't be easy, but you'll find someone, I feel sure of it.'

'I do hope so,' he said, and I forgave him that his hand crept across the table onto mine because he didn't know what he was doing.

Within three months, I had moved in. And within a year, we had married.

29

I've been here for little more than a week, and the cleaner is coming again this morning. An old house like this seems to sigh out dust, and every few days Jan comes to make it right again. This is the first time we've really chatted; the first time she's set down her vacuum cleaner and bucket of sprays.

'I knew Elizabeth well.' She buttons up her cardigan. 'She was nothing like Claudia,' she confesses from over the froth of her cappuccino. I've finally learnt how to use the coffee machine. 'You wouldn't think the same man chose them both as his wife.'

My ears prick up. I don't know much about Elizabeth outside the information learnt during my snooping session in James's study — although none of that proved exactly what I needed. All I really know is that she was James's first wife and the twins' birth mother.

'Elizabeth was different to the rest of her family, that's for sure.' Jan lets out an approving chuckle. 'She absolutely adored James. She was madly in love with him and wilted for at least a fortnight after he left on a mission. She distracted herself with her work and would catch the bus to her office completely barefoot. She was a lawyer,' Jan added almost proudly, as if Elizabeth had been her own daughter. 'Fought for the rights of parents whose children had been abducted by family members, she did. Fancy that. One man stole his daughters and took them to Oman. His English wife would never have seen them again if it wasn't for Elizabeth. She had lovely clothes,' Jan went on. 'Bright and dreamy, like her.' She drained her cup.

I'm shocked that Jan is telling me this. I suddenly feel protective towards Claudia, as if she needs all the help she can get competing with the colourful memory of Elizabeth.

'And then there was the money,' Jan continued. I can tell by the way she's standing now that she thinks she ought to be working but can't resist telling me just another snippet or two of gossip. 'Elizabeth's family is extremely wealthy. More money than the likes of you or I could ever imagine. *Ever*,' she stressed. 'Thing is, she didn't seem to want any of it. Elizabeth didn't agree with all their banking deals and trusts and all the kind of stuff that goes on in those tax heaven places.'

'Haven,' I correct. 'You mean tax haven.'

'Whatever it is, she was . . . ' She paused and thought, leaning on the hose of the vacuum cleaner. 'Elizabeth was purer than that. She'd hate to live off money that wasn't fairly earned or ethically gained. Sometimes she did her work for free, for mothers who couldn't afford her services.' Jan gives a succinct nod. 'Between you and me, I think James had pound signs in his eyes when he married Elizabeth. He spent a lot of time trying to build bridges between her and her family — her brothers especially. They liked James, approved of his Navy career and his politics. But ooh, listen to me. Can't stand here nattering all day.' She picked up the vacuum cleaner. 'It's a different world with them lot though, but you didn't hear it from me.'

'No,' I say pensively.

'Worlds apart,' she almost sings, and is about to leave but thinks better of it. 'Elizabeth always gave me a Christmas bonus, mind.' Jan leans forward on the vacuum. 'Two hundred pounds cash,' she whispers with a sly nod. 'Nothing like that from Claudia, you know. Just a box of Quality Street and a cheap card.'

I have no intention of being around at Christmas to find out what kind of gift, if any, Claudia will bestow upon me. I'll be long gone by then. I try to block out the destruction that will follow in my wake, the aftermath of my presence in the Morgan-Brown household.

'She'll be giving birth soon, won't she,' I say, wanting to find out exactly how much Jan knows about Claudia's dates.

'You say that,' Jan says, taking a biscuit, still stalling her work, 'but I thought she'd got another month to go, from what I'd worked out anyway.'

My heart flip-flops in my chest. This could change everything. More time is a blessing but could also be a curse. The longer I'm here, the more likely I am to get caught out. I need to know exactly when she's due.

'I could be wrong,' Jan says dismissively. 'Maths was never my strong point. But watch out, she's going to be one of those possessive, overprotective mothers who likes to be in control of everything. Reckon you'll have your work cut out with her more than you will the baby.'

'How come?' I notice the shake in my voice, but I don't think Jan does.

'Don't get me wrong. I like Claudia. She just ain't no Elizabeth. Put it this way, she's had a lot of bad luck in her life when it comes to having babies. I think it's made her bitter.'

'I don't understand,' I pretend. 'She seems so happy.' I try not to think of Cecelia but can't stop the fire of her hair, the depth of her wrath, the size of her disappointment and subsequent anger seeping into my mind.

'She's lost so many in the past, I think she'd just about given up conceiving.' Jan nods knowingly and crosses her arms across her chest. 'Miscarriages and stillbirths one after the other. Bang, bang, bang, all gone. She told me so.' Her arms explode outwards as if to symbolise babies getting lost in the ether.

'They've had a turbulent first few years of married life then.'

'Oh no,' Jan says. 'She hasn't lost any pregnancies with James. This was all before they were married.'

I can't quite imagine Claudia pouring out her heart to the cleaner, but then perhaps the joy of finally carrying a baby to term made her want to shout it from the rooftops. I remember the box in the wardrobe and its heart-breaking contents. I feel even worse about what I'm going to do. I tell myself to remain detached and cold, or I'll never follow through. Later, when Jan calls out that she's leaving, singing out that she'll be back tomorrow, I tap out a text to Cecelia. As ever, I delete it before I send.

★   ★   ★

Later still, in the school playground, I sidle up to Pip. The frozen yard is gradually filling up with gossip and hearsay as the mothers, and a few dads, gather to collect their children. Pip is chatting with several mums I don't recognise. I want to ask her something about Claudia. It could make a difference.

'Oh my goodness. Is she OK?' Pip says, looking concerned after I explain briefly about the accident the other day. 'You should have told me. Shall I come round later?'

'She's fine. She's at work.' I see the shock on Pip's face. She clutches her bump in sympathy.

'And you didn't take her to hospital?' Pip is incredulous.

'It wasn't as bad as it sounds. Claudia refused to get checked out anyway.' I don't tell Pip that it was really my fear of the police becoming involved that prevented me from insisting she go to A&E. 'I half expected it to induce labour, but it didn't.' I keep my tone light, as if it's all nothing.

Pip doesn't share my light-heartedness. 'I'll call her this evening,' she says seriously, clearly annoyed with me.

'She'd appreciate that, I'm sure.' My mind's been racing all day, since I found Claudia up in the attic last night. Ever since, I've had a nagging feeling that she wasn't looking for a book as she

297

said. And things had been moved in my room, I'm convinced of that. It's second nature for me to notice such things. It makes me wonder if she suspects something. I'm desperate to find out from Pip if Claudia's said anything about me, but I don't know how to bring it up.

'Here's Lilly,' I tell Pip as her little girl comes trotting out of school with a sopping painting rubbing against her leg.

'I wish they'd let them dry first,' Pip moans as Lilly flaps it about. The twins follow shortly after but neither of them is carrying a painting.

'Don't you guys have a picture to bring home?' I wink at Pip, secretly thankful they don't.

'We did one together but got told off and had to sit in the corner all lesson,' Noah says, almost proudly.

'How come?'

'He made me do it. I didn't want to.' Oscar is bordering on tears.

'Did not!' Noah snaps back.

'Did too! Mummy, tell him to — ' Oscar looks mortified when he realises his mistake. I smile warmly, although him calling me Mummy only adds to my growing guilt.

Noah continues with the tale. 'We did a painting of the bad man that cut out the lady's baby.'

The cold prickles my eyes as they widen in shock. What do they mean? What do they know? They are only children. 'That's horrible,' I say, trying to keep calm.

'That's boys for you,' Pip says, ruffling Oscar's

hair. She turns to me and says quietly, 'They could have overheard Claudia and me talking the other day. You know, about those poor women. And it's been all over the news. You take notice of things like that in our condition.' She takes Lilly's hand and waves at me with the other. 'Tell Claudia I'll phone later.'

I nod, quite unable to speak. Everything is pressing down on me.

★ ★ ★

The boys are doing another painting. I told them to do a self-portrait as a present for their mum. Atonement, I figured, for their ghastly subject matter at school. I leave them in the kitchen, two hunched figures on an island of newspaper, while I dash up to my room. It hadn't occurred to me before now to check my camera. I berate myself as I climb the stairs — for being distracted by Cecelia, for letting her interfere. How could I have been so stupid? From now on, the camera either lives on me or is hidden somewhere less obvious than the wardrobe.

Moments later I'm relieved to see that all the pictures are still on the camera's storage card. I have no way of knowing if Claudia has been flicking through them. If she saw them, she'll be trying to work out how I got into James's study. She'll be wondering when exactly I took them, and more importantly, *why*.

I select a photograph at random and zoom in closely. My mouth goes dry and my heart beats a crazy rhythm. What would Claudia have thought if she'd seen them — close-up snaps of that pregnant girl's file? Carla Davis's name is clearly printed at the top of the page. I imagine her confronting me, screaming at me for spying on their affairs, for delving into business that's just not mine, demanding to know what I've done, what I'm *going* to do. I imagine myself running away. I imagine that poor girl mutilated, slashed, bleeding to death.

It's more than I can stand. I tear down the stairs to the kitchen to find Claudia sitting between the boys. She's admiring their portraits.

'Zoe said we mustn't paint murderers, Mummy,' Noah says spitefully, glaring at me.

I'm standing in the doorway, panting as if I've just run for my life. The camera strap is still twisted around my knuckles.

'And Zoe's right, darling,' Claudia says without taking her eyes off me. Her gaze switches between my camera and my face as if she's looking for clues.

I have no idea if she knows.

30

Lorraine wondered if this was what it felt like to drown. Her senses tingled, reaching for earth, for air, trying to ground her in the familiar. It didn't work. All she felt was a patchwork cacophony of riotous overload that made her want to end the interview before it had begun.

'Would it be possible to turn off . . . ' Lorraine glanced around for the source of the din — or rather dins, as she heard not one or two but at least three layers of noise.

'Sorry,' the woman said. Her hands exploded into the air to accompany the theatrical grin. 'But I do need my daily dose of the news and can't live without Chopin while I'm working.' She went deeper into the room — if that was possible, stuffed as full as it was — and removed an iPod from its dock. She chucked it onto the sofa and Lorraine felt as if it might never be seen again as it sank like a stone in quicksand beneath the cushions. Then the woman turned off a transistor radio. There was still a din. 'I forgot I'd even put that on. Do you like death metal?'

'I can't say I'm a fan,' Lorraine confessed. She thought she'd overheard Stella talking about it once, rather scornfully she was glad to recall. Finally, there was silence. 'Can we sit down?'

'Oh, oh!' the woman said, apparently mortified she hadn't already offered. She swept her eyes frantically around the room and, when they settled on a cluttered oval table, her arms went into action. In two deft arcs she'd cleared it, unperturbed by the mess now on the floor. 'We can sit here. I'll brew coffee.' The woman virtually skipped and clapped her hands with excitement.

Lorraine refused the drink. She felt slightly sorry for the poor creature but also a tiny bit wary. There was a link between her and Sally-Ann Frith although she wasn't particularly hopeful that the interview would buy her any useful leads. Still, it had to be done.

'No, really, I'm fine,' she reiterated, but the woman had already disappeared into the kitchen alcove of the bedsit and was rummaging among the detritus for cups. Lorraine leant against the wall, now loath to sit down if she didn't have to. The woman clearly wasn't going to be still any time soon so she'd just have to ask her questions while she busied about. 'What's your last name, Cecelia?'

She turned and stared at Lorraine as if she'd asked her to undress. Her wayward hair danced in the shaft of sunlight that strained in through the stained-glass circular window above the sink. 'Paige,' she said quietly. 'I am Cecelia Paige.' A nod confirmed this, and then she stuck her head in a tiny refrigerator, muttering about the milk being off.

'And how long have you known Liam Rider?'

Again, another turn and pause. Her stillness suggested she was incapable of making coffee and talking at the same time. 'Liam,' she said, almost as if she'd never heard of him. 'I know

302

him through my college work.'

'Yes, I'm aware of that. But I'd like to know how long you've been acquainted with him.'

'*Acquainted* acquainted or just . . . acquainted?'

'Either,' Lorraine replied.

'I've been teaching my course at the college for a little over a year. You get to know faces, see people around . . . staff room, canteen, library, in the car park. That kind of thing.' Cecelia removed the top from the milk and sniffed. Her nose wrinkled. 'I first saw Liam in the photocopying room. It was jammed.' She put the lid on the milk and shook it vigorously. 'I unjammed it for him.' She held the plastic bottle up to the light and nodded approval. 'By kicking it,' she whispered. 'You know how it is. We got chatting. Got friendly.'

'You knew . . . know that Liam Rider is married.'

'Of course. I wouldn't want a single one.'

Lorraine's heart instinctively pushed harder than normal against her chest. 'And why would that be?' Was that Adam's floozy's reasoning, she wondered?

'Because all I wanted was a little bit of sperm, not a whole man.'

She prayed that hadn't been the floozy's line of thought. The idea of Grace and Stella having half brothers and sisters was . . . well, she didn't know what it was as she'd only just considered the idea but it wasn't feeling good so far.

'Couldn't you have gone to a sperm bank for that?'

'I could have,' Cecelia replied. 'Although that

303

gets very expensive after a while.' Tarry black coffee dripped from a machine into a glass jug. Lorraine willed it to drip slowly so she didn't have to drink any. 'But this is — was — more personal. And it was fun while it lasted. Don't worry, we didn't have sex exactly.'

Lorraine didn't reply to that. She certainly wasn't worried whether they'd had sex or not, although Russ Goodall's allegation suggested they'd been up to something. 'Do you know anyone called Sally-Ann Frith?'

'Of course,' Cecelia said, as if everyone did. 'Bitch,' she added.

'Oh?' Lorraine's heart quickened again.

'Well, of course she was a bitch. She was Liam's other bit on the side. And, to make matters worse, the stupid cow was actually pregnant.' She took a moment to calm herself, Lorraine noted, as if things were getting too intense for her liking. Her self-control was impressive. 'Anyway, my involvement with Liam was emotional as much as anything,' Cecelia added. 'The feelings for a physical relationship just weren't there for me, even though he's sort of attractive. And he's a good deal older than me. But when he told me he'd read maths at Cambridge, I knew he was the one. It was a long time ago, admittedly, but it shows he must be clever. And I wanted good-looking, clever sperm.' She sighed.

'He didn't study at Cambridge, love,' Lorraine said, entirely unable to help the air-punch that took place inside her head. And she hadn't thought him that attractive, either. 'Because of

. . . of everything, we've been over him thoroughly. He got his accountancy qualifications at Uxbridge Polytechnic in nineteen eighty-three. He's been divorced twice. I'm not sure he's very clever at all.'

Cecelia shrugged. 'His sperm must have died anyway because it didn't work.'

'Work?'

'Well she didn't get pregnant, did she?'

Lorraine watched as Cecelia swilled out two mugs and set them on the table with the coffee jug and the bottle of sour milk. She put a packet of sugar on the table with an encrusted spoon sticking out.

'Let's sit. I'm more of an afternoon tea person myself.' Cecelia smoothed down her jade dress before lowering herself carefully into a pink-painted wooden chair. Lorraine found herself doing as she was told while Cecelia poured the coffee. 'Milk?' she said, bottle poised.

'Black for me,' Lorraine insisted, swiping the cup away. She was damn well going to have to drink this and wanted to keep as much extra bacteria out of it as possible. 'Who didn't get pregnant with Liam's sperm?' she asked. This was not the conversation she'd imagined having this morning. And, while all indications pointed to Cecelia being slightly unhinged, Lorraine couldn't decide if it was simply long-amassed quirks of creativity at play in her psyche, or something more sinister.

'Heather, silly. She must have done it wrong. I showed her what to do.'

'Who's Heather?'

At this, Cecelia wilted into the chair. Her body seemed to deflate beneath her dress. 'Heather moved out,' she said sullenly. 'She left me.'

'She was living here?' Lorraine wondered how even a mouse could live alongside Cecelia. If the clutter didn't squeeze out the other person then Cecelia's personality would.

'Obviously . . . if she moved out.'

Lorraine was certain there were tears in Cecelia's eyes although she did seem to have a general misty aura about her, as if she was glistening with dew or had been rubbed with exotic balm. She let her continue.

'I can barely live without her. Do you know what it's like to lose the person you love most in the world?'

Lorraine wanted to say she'd actually just found out, but kept quiet. If she was going to confide in anyone, it certainly wouldn't be Cecelia.

'The thing is,' Cecelia continued, 'I saw it coming a long time ago, even before Heather did, if I'm honest. Things were getting . . . strained between us. Being honest again, I think my desire for a baby wore her down. Out of the two of us, she's never really wanted children, you see. Me, I was virtually born wanting one. Now I'm alone, I'll never get one, will I?'

Lorraine took a moment to assess what she'd just said but was left with a bizarre image of an infant caring for an infant and, like Cecelia herself, it just didn't add up.

'It's hard when there isn't a man, if you see

306

what I mean,' Cecelia said. Lorraine nodded that she understood. It wasn't all that unusual these days. 'You have to think of other ways to have a baby. Families aren't all mum, dad and two point four children any more, you know.'

'Quite,' Lorraine replied.

'Anyway, Heather is utterly selfless and wanted to help me all she could after my operation last year.' Cecelia paused and sipped her coffee. Lorraine noticed her cheeks flush briefly with a shade of crimson that clashed with her hair. 'I'd always had terrible women's troubles, which eventually led to a full hysterectomy. I thought I was going to die. It explained why I'd never got pregnant. No chance now.' She'd whispered the words *women's troubles*.

'I'm sorry to hear that, Cecelia,' Lorraine said genuinely. She wasn't sure her medical history was crucial or appropriate but pressed on all the same. 'So Heather volunteered to carry your baby for you?'

'Yes. She said we could use her womb. I'd already spent so much money on sperm samples for myself but, after my operation, I had to give up. Heather was so kind. We couldn't afford to keep paying for the expensive and select sperm of doctors and professors so Heather decided to . . . ' Cecelia hesitated, uneasy with what she was about to say. 'Well, Heather decided to go it alone to get a baby, if you see what I mean. She told me she'd do what she had to.'

'I see,' Lorraine replied, when she didn't at all. 'What did she have in mind exactly?'

'Look, it went against everything she believes

in, everything she stands for, but she was doing it for me, right?' A small sob left Cecelia's throat as if it had been caught there for months. '*Is* doing it for me,' she added.

'She's still trying to get pregnant on your behalf? I thought you said she'd moved out?'

'That's how selfless she is,' Cecelia added. 'Her last attempt failed again. She's almost as desperate as I am now.'

'How desperate?' Lorraine asked, feeling more uneasy by the minute.

Cecelia stood up and went to the mess of objects that she'd swept off the table. She towered over them before crunching a green stiletto heel into something resembling a finely beaded brooch. 'I hate this. It's shameful to my reputation.'

Lorraine stared at the glittering fragments. 'Did you make it?' she asked gently, sensing the woman's precarious state of mind.

'Yes, of course.' She turned to face Lorraine with shining eyes. 'No one will buy it now though, will they?' She picked up the pieces and allowed them to fall from her fingers in a mini shower of peacock blue and bronze. 'Business is going well. I get orders from shops in London. They'd have paid five hundred for this. That's another vial of sperm, you know.'

'Your work is lovely.' Lorraine meant it. She couldn't help bending down and gathering up a couple of pieces that would no doubt end up crunched underfoot too. 'This is so unusual.' She dangled a heavy pendant on a silver rope chain. 'Very mystical-looking.' Lorraine liked it. It was different. She wished Adam would surprise her once in a while with something like this for a birthday or anniversary. Sometimes, she thought he didn't know her at all.

'The stone she's sitting on is cut gaspeite. Don't you love the green colour? It's like the inside of a minty chocolate bar.' Then Cecelia was on the floor again, sifting through the mess. 'This butterfly brooch goes with it.' She held it up and pressed the two pieces together. Lorraine had to agree they were both breathtaking. The nude fairy-like creature sat twisted on the gemstone while her arms reached up the silver rope. Lorraine imagined her staring up imploringly at the wearer's face. 'She's a fairy without wings and needs the butterfly to travel.'

'I see,' Lorraine said, certain she could hear Adam's voice booming at her for being so fanciful. She watched Cecelia grovelling on her hands and knees, suddenly seeming remorseful for trashing her work table.

'Do you know the last thing Heather said to me?' Cecelia said, pressing a scarlet ring to her lips. Lorraine thought it looked like a drop of blood. 'She said, 'You will have a baby.' I have to believe in that, Detective.'

* * *

'It was the most surreal experience,' Lorraine told Adam. She had half a mind to mention how much she'd liked the jewellery but didn't want to stir things up. Before she'd left Cecelia's flat the woman had tried to give her the fairy and

309

butterfly set, but Lorraine had refused, telling her it wouldn't be ethical. Anyway, she was always grateful for the book tokens, the perfume or whatever else Adam usually got for her.

'But did you learn anything interesting, apart from having morning coffee with a baby-crazed eccentric?'

'I did,' Lorraine said. 'And you're right. She's exactly that — desperate for a baby and a very odd character. Apparently, her recently-separated partner, Heather, is still trying to 'get her a baby', whatever that entails.'

'Then we need to speak to Heather. Did Cecelia give you her new address?' Adam was texting as he spoke.

'Well, when I asked, she went vague and silent. She said she didn't even know where she worked any more. Apart from the baby thing, their split seems comprehensive.'

'You came away without follow-up details?' Adam put down his phone.

'Yes, Adam. That's exactly what I did.'

Piqued, Lorraine launched herself at the bowl of seeds Adam had on his desk. He smacked her hand away before she could grab a handful.

'You won't like them,' he said.

'Cecelia confessed to following her ex after she last visited,' Lorraine continued. Adam sat up and frowned. 'You'd have to meet the woman to understand,' she added, recalling the look of delight on Cecelia's face when she was able to provide an address for Heather.

'It's posh,' Cecelia had said, proudly or with a

tinge of jealousy, Lorraine hadn't been sure. 'A really big place down a lovely street. She had no idea I was following her.' Cecelia had tapped the side of her nose and let out a childish giggle. 'I still have Ernie, you see. Heather bought him for me a year ago, after my operation.'

'Ernie?' Lorraine had asked incredulously.

'My car, silly. A little Fiat.'

Lorraine had nodded slowly, wondering what might come out next.

'I kept a good distance, slowed down and pulled over when I had to. Heather wobbled once or twice on her bike at junctions but I managed to track her back to this place.' Cecelia had written down the address and handed it to Lorraine. 'She's going up in the world, look.'

Lorraine had done a double-take when she read the house number and street and pocketed the paper. She wasn't sure what it meant yet.

'Anyway,' she said to Adam, 'Cecelia couldn't really be certain that Heather actually *lived* at this address. She'd made a whopping assumption, that's all. Her full name's Heather Paige. Same surname as Cecelia.'

'They did the whole civil partnership thing, then?'

Lorraine nodded, wondering who Adam had been texting. 'Must have. Aren't you going to ask me then?' She couldn't believe he hadn't picked up on it yet.

'Ask you what? Why you're dancing about like a cat on a barbecue? Why your cheeks are flushed? Why you have a twinkle in your eye the size of Venus?'

Lorraine produced the scrap of paper from her pocket and handed it to Adam. He scanned the address, thought for a moment, and when he looked up, he too had a light the size of a planet in his eye. 'What are we waiting for?' he said, sliding the bowl of seeds towards her.

31

There was once a point when I thought I wouldn't be able to continue with my work. Looking back, it was a bleak, cold and lonely time, but something I truly believe I had to go through. I wouldn't be the woman I am today otherwise. It was part of life's great journey and not unique to me. I really believe that we're all here for a reason, a higher purpose, and it's our mission to stay on the right path, or even find it in the first place. Pip, it seems, has other ideas.

'Piffle,' she says. 'God, I could use a glass of wine.'

I glance at my watch. 'I hope they won't keep us waiting. I have so much to do back at the office.' I try to catch the waiter's attention but he's doing a good job of ignoring us so far. He clearly thinks two heavily pregnant women are incapable of rushing. Pip may not have anything on this afternoon other than a nap, but I have two home visits, a department meeting and three reports to write up before I can go back to the boys.

'And it's not piffle. It's what I believe. Anyway, what are you having?' I'd only agreed to the lunch because she'd sounded . . . well, sad, I suppose. It's because I understand and know what she must be feeling that I made time to slip down the road to Orlando's for a quick bite with her. By the end of our brief phone chat earlier I was convinced she had something serious to talk about. 'And you're not having any wine. I won't allow it.' I give her a playful kick beneath the table.

Pip pouts, and the waiter finally hands out menus and takes our drinks order. The young lad looks shocked by our sizes, perhaps petrified he'll have to deliver us both simultaneously. We both burst out laughing when he retreats behind the bar.

'Did you see his face?' I say.

'Priceless,' Pip says with a smile, although I know she's feeling pensive.

'I'm sorry, Pip. I didn't mean to get on my high horse before. I just feel passionately about it.'

'No need to apologise. I'm worried about you, that's all.'

'Worried? About me?' It comes out even more incredulous than it feels.

She was the one to bring up my job as we wandered down the high street together. She asked how I deal with the emotional side of things as well as the physical issues that I witness each and every week. After we were seated, I got talking about some sensitive issues I'd had within the first year or two of qualifying. I hadn't really meant to bring it up, but it followed on naturally from what we'd been discussing. Then that got me started on everyone in life having a path, whether they realise it or not. I think I might have sounded a little too New Age or religious for Pip's liking, even though I'm not. I was trying to be vague, so I didn't have to explain everything. It still rubs a few raw nerves.

'So what about your miscarriages and the stillbirths?' she asks quietly as we are offered bread rolls. 'Are they a 'path' in life too?'

I'm shocked that she's even brought this up, but she deserves a thoughtful reply. 'It's not as if I would have chosen that path if I'd been asked,' I try to explain. 'But if losing my babies was *their* path in life, then I feel honoured to have been part of it.'

She almost agrees. I can see her mind ticking over as she scans the menu, wondering whether to have the wild mushroom and scallop linguine or her usual chicken Caesar salad.

'And do you feel honoured to be part of the lives of the children you work with? How does it fit into both your and their paths when you take them away from their parents?'

I feel it's an attack, but she's entitled to her opinion. 'Pip, it's not exactly like that,' I begin, but quickly realise that is exactly how it is going to sound whichever way I tell it. I love our lunches together — since we met at the antenatal class, Pip's become my best friend — but we've never really chatted much about the ethics of my work before now. When you get down to the nuts and bolts of it, the rights and wrongs, people generally have very strong views about what I do.

'I would imagine they don't include your presence in their lives as part of their life's plan, that's all I'm saying.' Pip unfolds her napkin and places it on her lap.

I don't know why she's being so sensitive about issues over which I have no control.

I sigh and dive right in. 'About eighteen months after the start of my first placement, when I was living in Manchester, I had to take extended sick leave,' I tell her. Her face softens, encouraging me to continue. 'I'd just found out I was pregnant. I was overjoyed. It was my first time and we'd been trying for months to conceive.' Pip begins a smile but it quickly falls away. She knows what's coming. 'Anyway, the stress of my work had been really getting me down. I was depressed. I wasn't coping on a day-to-day level. To begin with the tablets helped but, being pregnant, I was reluctant to take them for long.'

I wait for Pip's reaction but she shrugs casually and comments, 'Everyone I know is on happy pills, or has been at some point.'

'Things began to get worse,' I tell her. 'I wasn't functioning at all well because of all the stress. I certainly wasn't in much of a fit state to make sound decisions at work.'

Whenever I get this close to telling anybody, I always stop here. But in my head, the dreadful horror of what I did rattles through me with the same force as when my supervisor broke the news. Maybe if I'd ticked another box, written one sentence differently in my final report, alerted someone to the depth of neglect that I suspected but failed to prove, then maybe she'd still be alive today. As it was, I'm convinced the pressure of the case, the little girl's death, the subsequent investigation, the newspapers latching on to me as if I was some sort of criminal — all of it contributed to my miscarriage.

'But you know,' I say flippantly, 'I had the therapy, got the T-shirt. And here I am.' I've been pressing my hands together so hard my fingertips have turned white.

The water and breadsticks arrive. I crunch into one immediately to stop myself from blurting out more. Pip, it seems, is a good listener despite her apparent prejudices. I try to change the subject but it doesn't really work. 'As a teacher, you have a similar responsibility to the children. We often get school staff ringing up with a child they think might be suffering at home.'

'Thankfully I've never had to do that,' Pip is quick to say.

'But would you, if you suspected something?' I pour the water.

'Of course.'

'Even if you knew the child would be taken from its parents?'

'Still of course.' Pip reaches out and takes my hand. 'What you do, Claudia, is a remarkable thing. No one realises that you go into a family home with a clear head and a heart full of hope and very often leave with a bucketload of despair and a ton of paperwork.'

I laugh. 'You're so right.' I marvel at how she's just managed to sum up each and every day of my life. 'They put me in hospital,' I say quietly. It comes from nowhere and sounds like someone else speaking. I've not even told James what happened. My hand rises to my mouth as if I've just vomited all over the table. 'But it's private,' I add, as if that will erase my even telling her.

317

'A mental facility?' Pip says in a fake American voice that I think is meant to sound like a crazy person. 'Straitjackets and all?'

'Yes, it was a psychiatric ward. But it was fine. It did me good.' In reality, I didn't get out of bed for three weeks, and it didn't do me any good at all. The nurses allowed me to just lie there, dissolving in my own grief. When the doctor came, he tut-tutted that I should be up and about, participating in the occupational therapies on offer, socialising with the other patients, attending group therapy sessions and generally being normal. I told him that if I could do all that then I wouldn't need to be there. 'Look, it's not as sinister as it sounds. Work got the better of me, I had a miscarriage, and had a bit of a breakdown.' I tap my head.

'Then I admire you greatly,' Pip says. I think she means it. 'And that makes me probably not worried about you at all right now.' She smiles broadly.

'Good,' I say. The last thing I want is for her to fuss over me.

I offer her a smile as our food arrives. My mozzarella and vegetable panini is steaming hot and served on a bed of greenery and dressing. I don't feel in the least bit hungry, even though I left the office famished. Pip tucks in to her linguine, wrapping the pale ribbons of pasta around her fork. The whole lot slides off just as she's about to put it in her mouth. She sighs and puts down her cutlery.

'It's just that I thought you seemed a bit down or distracted the last couple of times I've seen you,' she says. 'But it's probably because James has gone and you're getting used to Zoe.'

My heart thunders in my chest when she mentions Zoe. I should be spending the limited time we have together telling her about what I found in her room, asking her opinion about the photographs, the pregnancy testing kit, the blood on her top. Pouring out my heart about times long gone and done with, harping on about my grand path in life and my woes at work, should not have been a priority.

But talking about Zoe now somehow seems wrong, and Pip would only say I was jumping to conclusions, reading too much into very little. She'll think I'm making it up, being paranoid and irrational. Besides, I know she really likes Zoe.

'Anyway,' I say, 'you don't get off that lightly, Mrs Pearce.' I force myself to pick up my sandwich. 'When you rang this morning, I thought *you* sounded horribly down in the dumps.' I gauge her reaction. 'Us beached whales need to stick together, you know.'

At this she laughs. 'I'm fine. Just a bit apprehensive about the birth, but nothing I haven't done before.'

'How was it with Lilly?' I'm keen to know her story. 'Easy, quick, caught on the hop, or a long, drawn-out affair lasting days?'

Pip forks up another mouthful and ends up with creamy sauce on her chin. She wipes it away with a grin. 'Awful,' she says. 'Nearly died.'

'Oh that's terrible, Pip.' She has previously

mentioned that her labour wasn't straightforward, but I had no idea she nearly died.

'I was alone when it happened. Being my first time, I was absolutely terrified. The pain was unbearable.' Pip pours more water. 'I couldn't get hold of anyone.'

'When *what* happened?' What I really need is to hear about an easy pregnancy, a gentle breeze of a labour and a dream of a baby born with a smile on her face.

'*It*,' Pip says, breaking apart a bread roll. She has a fierce appetite today. 'You know, labour. The pain. The terrible, crippling, back-biting, madness-inducing pain that never ends.'

'Oh,' I say, slightly disappointed. 'So nothing actually went wrong?'

'No. My labour was text book. It was just plain awful, and Clive wasn't answering his phone. He was in Edinburgh at the time. I swore I'd never have another baby but . . . here I am.'

'Here we are,' I say, feeling more scared than ever.

32

However hard I scrub, the blood won't come out. It's embedded, the keeper of guilty secrets. The water is tinged pink beneath the suds so I sprinkle more soap powder onto the stain, rubbing the fabric vigorously. The basement sink glugs when I pull out the plug. I wring out the sweatshirt and hold it up. I sigh at the deep orange-brown tidemark circling the shoulder. As it is I'm going to have to stitch up the ripped seam. My sewing isn't up to much, so either way she's going to be cross that I ruined her favourite top. It's the one she always lounges around in, the one she cries at soppy black-and-white films in while hugging a box of chocolates, the one she's had since she was about sixteen. She didn't know I took it. Cecelia will not be pleased.

'You should have put that in to soak straight away,' Jan says. I turn around, suppressing my shock. She's standing with her hands on her hips, scowling at my rather useless attempts at hand washing. 'Blood?' she asks.

'Yes,' I say nervously. I fumble with the sweatshirt, trying to fold it so the stain is hidden. 'I'll probably just throw it away,' I add, trying to indicate how unimportant it is.

'Nonsense,' she continues. 'Here, let me see.'

She reaches for the dripping fabric but I recoil, holding it to my chest. 'Really, it's fine. It's ancient. It's for the bin.' Then I make the mistake of chucking it in the basement rubbish bin and, of course, Jan lunges for it. I know she's only trying to be helpful.

'What you need is to soak it in some hydrogen peroxide.' She slaps the sweatshirt back into the sink and rummages in the cupboard beneath. 'I swear there's some in here.' A moment later she stands up beaming and holding a black plastic bottle. She shakes it. 'Should be enough,' and she douses it onto the sweatshirt along with some water.

'Thanks, Jan,' I say through gritted teeth. 'I'll sort it now. I'll rinse it out in a few minutes.'

'Oh no, love. Best leave it for a few hours. Did you have an accident?' She hooks up the bloodied shoulder with her little finger.

'Yes . . . yes, I did,' I say. 'I fell off my bike.'

'You must have a nasty cut,' she says, but I brush it off, claiming it's just a graze. 'Some graze,' she says incredulously, looking at the top then back at me again. 'Looks more like murder.' Then, before I can reply or protest, she's heading back up the steps. 'See you next week,' she calls out.

I don't say that, if all goes to plan, she most certainly won't.

I decide to take Jan's advice and leave the top to soak. No one's home to question the gory-looking garment and Jan seemed to believe me when I told her about falling off my bike. Bloodying a sweatshirt is pretty high up on my list of idiotic things not to do while I'm in this house. Drawing unnecessary attention to myself is not on my agenda. I really can't afford for

Claudia to become suspicious about me. I certainly wouldn't want anyone with bloody clothes looking after my children.

My children, I think, and then Cecelia is back in my head again, yelling at me for ruining her favourite slouchy top and not being able to give her a baby.

I'm relieved that Claudia went into work this morning. Judging by her pale colour and proximity to her due date, I was convinced she wouldn't. While she doesn't complain much about the effort it takes to move around the house or climb the stairs or even bend down to pick something up, I can see the frustration and exhaustion written on her face. Having seen Cecelia again so soon after I promised myself I wouldn't (so much for my self-imposed contact ban of at least a month since our separation), I'm even more convinced that me not getting pregnant naturally was a blessing in disguise. Cecelia doesn't see it that way, of course.

I take the opportunity of an empty house to sneak back into James's study. This time I'll make certain that the photos are off my camera and safely uploaded. I'm sure Claudia is suspicious, that she was probing through my things. I don't miss the irony of this as I turn the key to the study door.

'Right,' I say, still not having much of an idea what it is I'm looking for. 'Where to begin today?'

I bite my lip and look around James's inner sanctum. I wonder if he senses, from all the way under the sea, that I'm in his domain. When he

323

gets home, will his nose twitch and his eyes dart around the room, picking up any vague scent I might have left, or will he spot misplaced items? The carpet is a deep red colour and plush underfoot. I must be careful not to leave footprints in the nap when I leave. If Claudia comes in, which I know she does from time to time, she'll be sure to notice.

I pull on the drawer of an antique wooden filing cabinet but, as I suspected, it's locked. Last time I was in here I covered the contents of the metal cabinet, thinking that the fireproof one would contain the more interesting documents. While some of the papers I photographed might prove useful, I'm certain what I need is yet to be found. There is money in this family, I am sure of that, and I'm certain it came from the Sheehan side. But I need proof, so much proof, and I need it fast. I have to think of my future.

In a flash, I locate the key to the wooden filing cabinet. It's tucked beneath a rather dry-looking pot plant on the windowsill. I ease open the top drawer with no idea what I'll find inside, if anything, but if I'm to do this properly, if I'm to succeed — *oh God, let me for once have some luck!* — then it has to be in here. I need that elusive *thing*, the proof, the deal-sealer. Someone like me doesn't get many opportunities like this. If I think about it, it's all being handed to me on a plate. That's why I'm so nervous, I realise, as I pull out the first file. If I mess up, if I don't come away with exactly what I want, if I get caught before I'm finished, then I'm going to have a lot of explaining to do to the police.

I spread out the contents of the first file on James's desk. It's a load of statements — some kind of investment fund — ranging from 1996 to 2008. I carefully photograph each one. It takes me twenty minutes. I sigh and stare at the crammed cabinet. What is this really going to achieve? *A better life for you,* says the voice inside my head that torments me with the rights and wrongs of what I'm doing. It hasn't shut up from the moment I answered Claudia's advert.

Professional working parents seek experienced, kind, loving nanny to look after four-year-old twin boys and soon-to-be-born baby girl. Own room and bathroom in beautiful family home in Edgbaston. Light domestic chores but no cleaning. Use of car and weekends off. Must have formal training and exemplary references. Immediate start.

How perfect, I remember thinking when I first saw the advert. What an absolutely uncanny, sent-from-the-heavens, amazingly-timed opportunity, and it had landed in front of me almost as if I'd been hand-picked for the job. Again, I laugh at the irony. It's not as if I really want to do what I'm doing. In fact, I have little choice — no choice — in the matter. There are some things in life that you just have to get on with, and I came to realise this the day I moved out of Cecelia's flat, which happened to be the same day I moved in here. Out of one fire pit and right into another.

Still, I console myself, at least I'm doing

something worthwhile and avoiding the cutting edge of Cecelia's cruel tongue when I can't provide her with what she so desperately wants.

I stuff the file back in its slot and pull out another. 'Life Insurance', the label reads. I raise my eyebrows. *Useful*, I think. *Hope they have plenty.*

Half an hour later and I'm waiting for the kettle to boil, just as if it's any old tea break in any old job. I stare out of the kitchen window and down the well-kept garden. The trees are gnarled and winter-craggy against the dull, low sky and the grass is a greeny-grey smudge of summer's forgotten fun. I suddenly feel very alone, very scared and very like giving up. I touch the phone in my pocket — my line to everything safe and familiar, my line to Cecelia. I wonder if she is thinking the same, tracing a finger over the keys of her phone that could so easily tap out a message to me. What is she thinking at this precise moment? Does she even realise that I'm doing all this for her? Does she hate me? Will she ever want to see me again? The thought that she won't makes me go cold inside. It also makes me return to the study and begin searching through files again. I must surely be close to something useful by now.

The file marked 'Gardening' surprises me. It's the same drab shade of beige as the rest of the folders in the cabinet but a lot thicker, more stuffed full of papers than the others. So much so that it takes a good pull to remove it from its file hanger. When it comes out, I see that its contents have nothing to do with gardening at all. If I was expecting to read about the latest in ride-on mower technology in sales brochures gathered at the garden centre, or tree-lopping services and block-paving quotes, then I couldn't have been more wrong. The Gardening file contains yet another file, a tattier one, that is simply labelled 'Trust'.

My heart races behind my ribs. My ears strain to hear the sounds of anyone coming home — the noise of a car drawing into the drive, the slam of the door, someone's key in the lock. In the distance I hear the rise and fall of a siren scream as it races to a far-off emergency, and in my head I hear the sound of my own breath as it forces its way in and out of my lungs.

I open the folder and take out the first document. I speed-read it and then take a photograph. I do the same with the rest of the contents. It takes me an hour and a half to complete the task. Even when everything is put back neatly in its place, when the study is locked and I'm back in my room, my heart doesn't stop its ridiculous dance in my chest. I can't stop thinking about what it means. But, mostly, I can't stop thinking about Cecelia.

33

Grace was staring at the carpet and picking her thumbnail. Her foot rubbed back and forth until Lorraine told her to stop. She took no notice and continued more vigorously until she was kicking the leg of the coffee table with her toes and banging the base of the sofa with her heel. Her cheeks grew red and her bottom lip began a virtually undetectable quiver, bringing her to the edge of tears.

'Well, how kind of you to call in,' Lorraine said sourly. She hadn't meant to take that tone but her hopes of Grace returning for good had been crushed after her daughter rang the doorbell — *rang the doorbell!* — and announced she'd just popped back to get a couple of things.

'Darling . . . ' Adam began.

Grace said nothing. They had coaxed her into the living room and got her to sit down. But the sigh, the tightly folded arms, the pout and the sharp stare at the ceiling did more than suggest that she would rather be anywhere else.

'Stop kicking, Grace, you'll hurt your foot,' Lorraine said, probably too harshly.

Grace finally straightened and sat still.

'Your mother's right,' Adam added pointlessly. 'Grace, you have to talk to us. How can we help you if you won't even speak about it?'

'I don't need your help,' Grace said, still

staring at the carpet. 'There's nothing to talk about.'

'Is that boy pressuring you?' Lorraine asked anxiously.

'That boy,' Grace replied, 'has a name, you know. And no, Matt is not pressuring me. We both want to get married. We love each other.'

'But what about university? What about getting a good job, having a decent life? You're just a kid still.' Lorraine had a sudden vision of her daughter, seventeen, pregnant and living in a council high-rise on the dole. Matt was nowhere to be seen, of course.

'We understand how you feel,' Adam said.

'Well, I don't, actually,' Lorraine interrupted.

Grace took a deep breath. 'I'm very aware that neither of you understand,' she said quietly. 'That's why I've left home, to get away from you both. If I have to leave school and get a job to support myself, then I will do it. Matt and I are serious about getting married. His mum's being brilliant.'

Lorrained flinched in pain. 'You wanted to be a scientist,' she said weakly.

'We're looking at wedding venues at the weekend,' Grace said, as if she hadn't even heard her mother.

'And you were thinking of a gap year in the States.'

Grace slowly looked up at her mother, shaking her head, as if the last seventeen years had all been a hazy dream and none of this was true. '*You* wanted me to be a scientist,' she corrected. 'When you weren't busy fighting with Dad, that is.'

Lorraine felt a slight wave of madness sweep through her. 'Fine. Leave school. Go and live with another family — a better one, no doubt. Get married and have a dozen kids before you're eighteen and work nights in a supermarket.' She sensed she'd got her attention. 'As of this moment, you're free, Grace. Just think, no more Mum and Dad nagging at you, no more homework, no more ground rules. You're on your own, my love, and you needn't think you can come running back to us when you have no money.'

'Dad doesn't nag,' Grace stated calmly. 'But you do.'

'Jesus!' Lorraine put her hands to her face.

Adam shifted uncomfortably on the sofa. 'Ray, don't.'

'I'm not finished yet — '

'It's OK, Grace,' Adam said. 'If you've thought about this long and hard and it's really what you want . . . ' He trailed off unconvincingly. 'We just don't want you to rush into anything.'

'You're still a *kid*,' Lorraine said in a final attempt to change her daughter's mind. 'You can't possibly get married. You have absolutely no idea what it means.'

'At least I'll have someone who loves me,' Grace responded, so quietly Lorraine thought she'd misheard. 'Because neither of you two do.'

'Oh darling, that's just not true and you know it.' Adam leant towards her, taking her hands. 'How can you say such a thing? Your mum and I both love you very much.'

She replied with a slow shake of her head, as if even that hurt too much. A single tear left her eye.

'Of *course* we love you,' Lorraine reiterated, shocked to the core by what Grace had said. 'Why on earth would you think we didn't?'

'Because you don't even love each other,' was Grace's meek reply.

It made Adam recoil. A quick glance snagged between him and Lorraine.

'Yes, we most certainly do,' he said indignantly.

His duplicity was obvious, Lorraine thought. How could they have been so naive to think that their problems, swept conveniently into a dark corner of their minds, had not affected their daughters?

'Stella thinks the same,' Grace added, beginning the foot-tapping again. 'You're always arguing and whispering and fighting about stuff. You think we don't hear but we do. Stella cries at night sometimes.'

'Of course Dad and I love each other, darling,' Lorraine said, noticing Adam's head drop a little. 'We have a lot of stress at work and maybe we bring it home, which is wrong, but we do . . . love each other.' Across the cushions, she took Adam's hand, forcing her fingers into his.

The one and only time they'd seen a marriage counsellor had ended similarly, when the woman had asked Lorraine to touch Adam, to see how it made her feel. At the time, she could have answered that without moving a muscle: *sick*.

'Touch?' she'd asked incredulously. A sharp pinch or a sly kick was what she'd felt like giving him, but instead she'd gone along with it. She'd reluctantly held Adam's hand.

'How does it *feel?*' the therapist had asked.

'Warm?' Lorraine had suggested.

'Warm,' the therapist had replied. 'That's good. Perhaps it feels as if he's alive, as if he's like you, as if his veins are filled with emotion and love.'

'Oh for fuck's sake,' Lorraine remembered saying. She'd whipped her hand away. 'He's warm all right. Warm-blooded and male and he can't keep it in his pants.' Now, sitting opposite Grace, Lorraine could almost hear the exasperated sigh Adam had let out during the counselling session. 'It wasn't like that,' he'd said, yet again defending his behaviour.

The meeting had been drawing to a close, and Lorraine was furious. The stupid therapist was obviously on Adam's side — perhaps she was also an Other Woman and her priorities were different to hers. Either way, she wasn't about to be patronised and ridiculed by a stranger. And neither was she going to pay to hold her husband's hand after he'd admitted to a one-night stand. She'd already agreed to rein in her feelings and keep things together for the children, though as things stood she hadn't been entirely sure how long that would last.

Lorraine felt Adam's fingers close on hers. 'All we're trying to do is help you see the sensible path, Grace. Getting married at your age would be a disaster. This time last week we were chatting about university.'

Grace stood up, smoothing down her top. Lorraine noticed how clean and well ironed it looked. Matt's mother clearly had too much time on her hands. 'Mum, Dad, my mind's made up. I'm leaving school and getting married. I hope you'll come to our wedding.' She turned and calmly left the room.

★   ★   ★

'I thought that went well,' Adam said sarcastically. They'd retreated to the kitchen, having sat in stunned silence following Grace's departure once she'd collected her things. Matt had been waiting outside in his car. Neither of them had known what to do or say.

Lorraine sighed and dialled into her messages. She raised a finger at Adam to get his attention. She listened, then tucked her phone back into her trouser pocket. 'It was Carla Davis's doctor at the hospital finally following up. He's been unreachable all day so I left a message with his secretary. I must have missed his call while we were talking to Grace.'

'Go on.' Adam filled the kettle.

'Apparently, Carla's kidneys had been badly damaged by her long-term drug use. She was advised at the start of her pregnancy that carrying her baby full term could quite possibly lead to her own death either before or after the baby's birth.'

Lorraine paused to absorb this conflict-ridden dilemma. How was someone so ill-equipped

333

emotionally as Carla supposed to make a life-changing decision like that?

'Put simply, she was risking her own life by carrying the baby full term. She was advised to have an early termination and, initially, she agreed. Then she changed her mind. Dr Farrow wasn't Carla's doctor at the time, but her records show that she was made to think very seriously about the health implications of continuing with the pregnancy. It was literally a life-and-death decision.'

Adam frowned. 'The health implications of this pregnancy weren't so good for her anyway, as it turned out,' he said rather humourlessly.

'So why did she change her mind? Did someone talk her round against medical advice?'

'Maybe her social workers can throw some light on it,' Adam said after a moment's pause. 'Carla might have confided in them.'

'You think we should talk to them again?'

Adam was already nodding. He glanced at his watch.

'You're not serious?' Lorraine said grimly. She was exhausted. 'Tonight?'

'I think we should. There's something I want to . . . ' He hesitated. 'It's probably nothing.'

'But their offices will be closed . . . ' Lorraine trailed off, knowing better than to question Adam when he had one of his gut feelings. In the past, things he'd noticed and kept to himself had, once or twice, turned into major leads. He might have made a serious error of judgement in their personal life, but this was work, this was him doing his job, and he was good at it

334

— infuriatingly so at times. She would go along with him, see what transpired. After all, he was in charge.

He reached for his car keys. 'I'm going to pay that social worker another home visit, which'll give us an excuse to find out about this Heather Paige woman, see where she fits in.' They'd already called round earlier in the day to follow up on Cecelia's story but the house had been empty. 'Coming?'

Lorraine reluctantly trailed him to the front door. She called out to Stella that they'd be back in an hour and received a vague grumble in reply. She and Adam exchanged glances at the bottom of the stairs before Adam took her by the hand and led her out to his car.

As she fastened her seatbelt, her fingers still tingling from the contact, Lorraine realised that was the second time she'd touched her husband's hand that day.

34

The house was unlit at the front and the driveway was darker than the surrounding street, almost as if the property was trying to shrink back and appear inconspicuous — that's what Lorraine thought, anyway, as they crunched across the gravel to the impressive entrance for the second time that day.

'I hope she doesn't mind,' Lorraine said. 'She's not far off having her baby. She might want an early night.' She took a moment to study each curtained window. There was actually a faint glow that she'd not noticed at first glance coming from a ground-floor room. Someone was still up.

Adam gave her a look that instructed her to switch from concerned woman back to detective. He rapped loudly on the door.

A moment later, Claudia Morgan-Brown opened the door. She looked shocked to see them.

'Everything's fine,' Lorraine began with a comforting smile, remembering her previous anxiety. 'We're very sorry to disturb you during the evening but there are some further questions we'd like to ask you about Carla Davis.'

'Oh,' she said quietly. 'Of course.' She stepped aside and beckoned them in. She looked tired, Lorraine thought as they followed her into the sitting room. 'Please, sit down.' The television was on quietly and Claudia flicked it off with the remote control. 'I must have dozed off.'

'We'll be as quick as we can.' Lorraine gave Adam a pained look but he failed to notice. She didn't see why the visit couldn't have waited until tomorrow. She doubted they'd learn anything case-changing.

'Can I get you some tea?' Claudia asked, still standing. She pulled back her thick hair into a temporary ponytail before allowing it to fall around her shoulders again. She was pretty, Lorraine thought, for a woman who was clearly very tired.

Lorraine smiled. 'No, we're fine, thanks.' She glanced around the room and noticed a few forgotten toys by the window — some Lego, a couple of plastic trucks, a picture book lying open. She assumed Claudia's sons were already in bed. She wondered where the nanny was.

'We wanted to ask if you, or anyone in your department, knew anything about Carla's health problems,' Adam said.

Claudia frowned and thought. She sat down and drummed her fingers on the side of her neck. 'She wasn't in the best of health, as I recall,' she said. 'The drugs had already taken their toll on her body, even at her young age. But as I said before, it wasn't me who was in charge of the case when Carla's unborn baby first came onto our radar.'

'But you met with Carla?'

'Oh yes,' Claudia replied. 'I told you that. I encountered her on a number of occasions.'

337

'Were you aware just how serious her health problems were?'

Claudia frowned. 'No, I didn't know about any specific issues apart from her addictions.'

'So you weren't aware of her poor kidney function?'

Claudia's eyes grew large and she bit on her bottom lip. When she released it, blood flushed beneath the skin. 'No. What was wrong with her kidneys?'

'Because of her prolonged drug use, Carla was advised that continuing her pregnancy could likely cause her death either before the baby was born or soon after. Her kidneys just weren't up to the job.' That was as medically detailed as Adam was able to be, given that neither of them knew the specifics of the condition.

'So that's why she was originally booked in for a termination?' Claudia seemed surprised.

'Exactly,' Adam said. 'Although for some reason Carla later changed her mind. We wondered if you had any idea why she might have made such a life-threatening decision.'

Claudia hung her head. After a few moments, she cupped her face in her hands. Lorraine saw the small quiver in her arms as they supported the weight of her head — the weight of guilt, she wondered?

'What is it, love?' Lorraine was aware of Adam's foot tapping against the leg of the coffee table and it made her think of Grace.

'It was me,' Claudia whispered without hesitation. She let out a couple of pathetic sobs before lifting her face to them. It was spread with blame and her cheeks were burning red. 'But I swear I had no idea how serious her health problems were. I thought I was doing the right thing.'

'Calm down,' Adam said rather coldly. 'No one's accusing you. Just take it steady and tell us what happened.'

Lorraine sensed Adam's disappointment. That it was simply a professional worker who had, rightly or wrongly, advised Carla to keep her baby wasn't of any great significance. It wasn't going to provide the lead he'd been hoping for or, indeed, a link to the Sally-Ann case.

Claudia gulped for air. Lorraine wasn't sure that pursuing this was in her best interests, given the circumstances. She watched the woman's frown grow deeper as she tracked back over events.

'Carla had an appointment with Tina about six months ago but Tina was off sick so I met with Carla instead. I went to her flat.'

'Go on,' Lorraine urged. She was hungry and could feel her stomach gurgling beneath her winter coat. She wanted to get home to Stella.

'I'd not seen her for quite a while. She'd been in and out of foster homes with us for years. Anyway, she'd only just found out that she was pregnant. My job was to assess her mental state, her living conditions, her drug habits, that kind of thing, so we could decide what to do about her baby. She told me she was really trying to get clean but was finding it hard. She was drinking heavily too. Nothing much was right in Carla's life. Except . . . '

Claudia looked up at Lorraine. It was a shared moment of understanding.

'Except the baby,' Lorraine finished.

Claudia nodded. 'I could see the flash of hope when she talked about it. She showed me a pair of tiny pink socks she'd bought from the market.' Claudia let out a half laugh, half sigh. 'She said she only bought ten fags that day instead of twenty so she could get the little socks. I saw something change in her when she talked about the baby and that's why I was really shocked when she told me she was going to terminate. She said she just wanted someone to love her back. It really chimed with me.'

It chimed with Lorraine, too. She swallowed down the lump in her throat, refusing to look at Adam, given the conversation they'd just had with Grace. 'So you discussed going ahead with the pregnancy.'

'Yes,' Claudia said frankly. 'But I swear I wasn't aware of any medical contraindications. Carla never mentioned anything was wrong with her. I would have told her to see her doctor again. Anyway, my advice wasn't to keep the baby. That would have been wrong, given her overall circumstances and her drug dependencies. She was barely capable of looking after herself, let alone another life. Chances were I'd only have to take the baby from her when it was born anyway.'

Adam was making notes but Lorraine was just listening, thinking about poor Carla and her dead baby.

'But given that you knew of her long-standing

drug problems, didn't you assume she might have some underlying medical complications?' Adam asked.

The shocked and hurt look on Claudia's face reflected exactly what Lorraine was thinking. She glared at her husband for being so insensitive, but he ignored her.

'In my job, Detective, it's never safe to assume anything. But I'm not a doctor and there was nothing on her file about a medical condition. It simply stated that she was booked to have a termination. If she didn't follow through with that, then it was my duty to protect her unborn baby. The possibility of her pregnancy actually *killing* her never occurred to me. All I saw was a desperate young woman with a tiny fleck of hope in her eye. I wanted her to consider all her options, and that included keeping the baby.'

Claudia stood up and stretched out her back. She pulled a pained face. 'Carla promised me she'd get off drugs, go to the rehab centre, stop drinking and even cut down on her smoking. She promised not to see the wrong people, and we even spent time cleaning up her flat. That's not in my job description, but I saw such optimism, such possibility, something perfect growing within her, I admit a big part of me wanted her to cancel the termination. Is that so wrong?'

'No,' Lorraine agreed almost immediately. 'It's not.'

'What are your views on abortion, Mrs Morgan-Brown?' Adam asked. 'I'm sorry if that sounds insensitive, under the circumstances.'

'I don't mind you asking,' Claudia said

pensively while spreading her hands across her baby. Lorraine swore it had visibly grown in size the last couple of days. 'Being pregnant means the world. I've always dreamed of being a mother.' The smile fell away. 'Thing is, I never anticipated all the sadness it would bring. But, here I am. Twin step-sons and a little girl on the way.'

'Sadness?' Lorraine asked.

'Unfortunately, this isn't my first pregnancy. My previous partner and I tried many times for a baby and . . .'

'It's OK, love. No need to elaborate.' Lorraine was sorry she'd asked.

'No, it's relevant. I've had many miscarriages and stillbirths. No one knows why. So this pregnancy is incredibly precious to me. When I hear about abortions, I try not to be judgemental, but it was more than that with Carla. I somehow felt she needed to have that baby, even with the risk of it being taken away.' Claudia exchanged looks with each of them, gave them a moment to understand what she was saying. 'You don't think my personal feelings somehow clouded Carla's judgement, do you?' Her voice was suddenly anxious and guilt-ridden.

'You were only trying to help,' Lorraine said.

Claudia was nodding thoughtfully. She sat back down again, still obviously agitated. She chewed nervously on a nail. 'There's something else that might be relevant.' Claudia stood up again and paced about. 'Oh, but I don't know. It's probably nothing, and James would say I'm being utterly paranoid.'

'It's those 'probably nothings' that often help us the most,' Lorraine pointed out.

'Well, OK, but this is confidential, right?'

'That all depends,' Adam was quick to say.

'It's just that if I tell you and I'm wrong, I don't want her to know I said anything. It would make things very uncomfortable for me.' Claudia's voice was suddenly low and she glanced at the closed door several times.

'We'll do our best,' Adam said unconvincingly.

'It's my nanny, Zoe. I think you met her briefly the first time you called round,' Claudia said directly to Lorraine. 'Well, I had reason to be . . . to be looking for something in her room the other day. I know that doesn't sound right but trust me, I'm glad I went in there. To get to the point, I was looking at pictures on Zoe's camera. Yes, yes, I know I shouldn't have been . . . ' Another moment of guilt. 'Anyway, I'm glad I did. There was a photograph of . . . ' Claudia hesitated again, struggling to get it out. It finally came through a deep sigh. 'There was a photograph of Carla Davis's case file on Zoe's camera.'

She seemed relieved to have told them yet suddenly even more nervous. 'It had all Carla's personal details on such as her address, age, date of birth, GP, and her basic issues. It's obviously confidential information. I feel absolutely terrible that this has happened. It's completely my fault for bringing the file home. I thought I'd kept the file locked up in the study the whole time, but I must have been mistaken. I have absolutely no

343

idea why Zoe would want Carla's details.'

'Is she here now?' Adam asked.

Claudia pulled a pained face. 'She's gone out but could be back any time.' She glanced at the door again. 'Look, it sounds crazy, but I don't really want to stir things with her. I mean . . . ' She was becoming distressed. 'Perhaps I was mistaken. I only glimpsed the photograph quickly. I zoomed in but the camera screen was so small. I could have misread it, I suppose.'

'We'll need to speak to her, you understand?' Lorraine said.

'I really don't want Zoe upset by this because if she leaves, I'm stuffed. James is away and . . . and I'm going to need the help.'

'There are other nannies,' Lorraine said kindly. 'But surely if there's an innocent reason for the photograph, then Zoe won't leave you. She'll be happy to explain.'

Claudia thought for a moment. 'I suppose you're right. It's just that being on my own, I feel rather vulnerable.'

'We understand,' Lorraine finished. 'We'll come back another time to speak to Zoe.'

'And it's probably best if you don't mention this to her in the meantime,' Adam added.

'One last thing,' Lorraine said.

Claudia raised her eyebrows. 'Yes, anything.'

'Does the name Heather Paige mean anything to you?'

She pulled a puzzled face, flicking her eyes to the ceiling for a second in thought. 'Sorry, no. Why?'

'So no one called Heather Paige has ever been

344

to this house either recently or in the past?' Adam said in a more accusatory tone than Lorraine would have liked.

'Definitely not,' Claudia said.

'Well, thanks for everything,' Lorraine said, standing up. 'We're so sorry for having taken up your time.'

'No problem,' Claudia replied. She followed them to the door and shook hands with them as they left.

35

I watch them leave, although they don't know it. I am peering out between the thick hallway curtains in the dark, tracking the red tail lights of their unmarked car as they drive off down the street. When they are out of sight, I go back to the sitting room and drop down onto the sofa. I pinch myself hard on the arm for being so stupid.

Why did I have to go and tell them about Zoe and the photographs? She'll find out everything now and be furious I was in her room. She'll be mortified that I don't trust her, she'll be paranoid about the future, and no doubt by tea-time tomorrow she'll have packed her bags and left.

And where does that leave me?

Not a good start to a trusting relationship. If James was here, he'd tell me to ask her immediately if she'd been in the study, clear the air, be open from the outset. He wouldn't like all these secrets.

I'm certain there must be a rational explanation, and it suddenly occurs to me that perhaps Zoe picked up our camera by mistake. It was lying about after the aquarium trip and they are very similar models. Perhaps the photographs were already on there and it was James who took the pictures, though I have no idea why he would want to. Apart from the one I zoomed in on, I

346

have no idea what the other photographs were, although I could see that they also appeared to be documents. That scenario, although unlikely, wouldn't seem quite so sinister. But when I go to check if our camera is in the kitchen drawer where I usually keep it, it is right there where I left it. I check through the pictures in case Zoe had put it back after realising her mistake, but there are no images of paperwork.

'Oh James,' I say, returning to the sitting room. 'What should I do?'

What should I do? I must have asked him those words a thousand times since we've been together. I think the first time he heard them was when I admitted my love for him. We were sitting by the canal, holding hands and excavating thoughts from the depths of each other's eyes. To onlookers, we must have appeared like a pair of lovesick teenagers, but it wasn't long before James had to go back to sea and I wanted to know if we had a future. It all seemed very wrong, so soon after Elizabeth.

'What should I do?' I took a sip of my drink. I pulled my cardigan around my shoulders as a shiver dug into my body. It was a warm night but I knew that the rest of my life rested on the answer to that question.

'What should *you* do?' he'd replied incredulously. 'It's not you, Claudia, it's *us*. I know you feel responsible. I know you're holding back for my sake.' He squeezed my fingers. I felt safe.

I bowed my head. 'People will talk,' I said.

'Stuff other people,' James replied. 'They know nothing about how we feel.'

347

'It's so soon,' I reiterated. I'd said it a thousand times already.

'Elizabeth would want me to be happy,' James said. 'She was remarkable like that.'

'I'm sad I never got to meet her,' I said, but then realised that if I had, James and I wouldn't be talking about living together. Was it selfish to feel glad that she'd died? We'd been seeing each other for several months by then. By seeing, I mean on a level far greater than me helping him secure the boys' welfare. James was doing a fine job caring for the twins. In fact, I believe that between immersing himself in looking after his sons and our burgeoning relationship, the babies and I carried him through the early stages of his grief.

'It just seems too soon,' I insisted. 'People *will* talk, whether we like it or not, James. They'll say I'm some kind of vulture, moving in to take Elizabeth's place.' I wanted to weep with frustration but I held it back. After everything that I'd been through, after pretty much giving up hope of ever meeting anyone else after breaking up with Martin — we'd been together eleven years after all — I never thought I'd find love again, let alone have a family.

'I don't care,' James told me. He pulled me close and felt my shivers. 'Hey,' he said gently, 'don't be scared.' That's when he took me by the shoulders and held me at arm's length. My left cheek had a single stray tear that I cursed for escaping, for betraying my feelings. 'I want you to move in with me and the boys, Claudia. I

348

want that more than anything else in the world. Say you will.'

Inside the privacy of my head, my answer snapped out immediately: *Yes!* But I knew better than that so I put on my thoughtful face, tried to quash the smile that wanted to erupt. This was the start of a new life. Finally, after all the heartbreak and emotional turmoil I'd suffered with Martin, I was being offered another chance at happiness. I'd never thought it would happen. 'That's utterly crazy,' I said with a laugh. James laughed, too. In fact, he'd laughed in the days immediately after learning of Elizabeth's passing, and I couldn't quite understand. Now, knowing him as I do, I realise it was his way of coping. A person can only take so much stress before their minds naturally divert them as close as possible to normality. It's self-protection and, to a certain extent, I was doing exactly the same thing. We were both on the rebound, both hopelessly lost and needy, though trying to be terribly sensible and grown up about it.

'Crazy, yes. But I've fallen in love with you, Claudia. I want to marry you. I want you to be a mother to Oscar and Noah.'

I only heard the words *I want you to be a mother*. It was the nearest he ever got to a proposal. The actual wedding seemed to flow as naturally as me cooking supper or taking care of the boys without him ever actually asking again.

How many times had I tried to be someone's mother? How many times had I failed?

Suddenly, I wasn't a failure any more. I ignored the shrieks of doubt in my head; indeed,

I ignored the cautious warnings of family and friends when they raised eyebrows and made comments about the dubious timing of my relationship with James. *He's just lost his wife, Claudia ... Do you really want to take on someone else's children? ... His money's come from his dead wife ...* I had no idea of the extent of what Elizabeth left him or her family fortunes; I'm still uncertain about James's private affairs. But the comments and warnings came thick and fast from do-gooders uncomfortable with my new-found happiness.

For us, it was simple. He was hurting. I was hurting. Together, we were mended. It never once occurred to me that James was using me as a surrogate mother or a convenient live-in nanny and housekeeper to heal his broken life. And if this had crossed my mind, I would have dismissed it immediately. I loved James and I loved his sons. I wanted to be their mother. I wanted to be James's wife. He'd promised me a baby of my own and I trusted him to give me that. To begin with I didn't dare mention all my miscarriages and stillbirths. I wanted that to be a part of my past, not my future. I'd concluded it was all Martin's fault and nothing to do with my body. Even when the doctors told me they doubted I'd ever be able to have children, I refused to give up hope.

'Damn and bugger,' I say just as Zoe comes home. She's singing to herself.

'Did I hear someone cursing?' she says jovially, poking her head round the sitting-room door.

She catches me sucking my finger. 'I'm

completely useless,' I tell her, glancing up casually. I wave the blouse about.

'I'm so sorry, I meant to do that for you.' Zoe blushes a little and comes in, gently taking the garment from me. The tiny button dangles from the knotted cotton. She doesn't know that I wasn't swearing about the blouse or, indeed, my pricked finger. I was swearing because of my stupidity in mentioning Zoe to the police before I'd spoken to her myself.

She sits down next to me. 'How are you feeling?' she asks.

I look intently at her face. There's nothing to betray any underhandedness, and nothing, either, to give away my anxiety.

'Zoe, sit down. There's something I need to ask you.'

'Oh, OK,' she says obligingly. 'What's up?' There's a little line of doubt in her voice, but nothing that reflects what I'm about to bring up.

'When I was looking for that book up in the attic, Zoe, I couldn't help noticing that there was blood on one of your sweatshirts.' I pause. Now she knows I was in her room.

'Oh that,' she says with the beginnings of an embarrassed smile.

'I wasn't snooping, I promise,' I add. 'I thought the book might still be in your wardrobe.' I had indeed once stored some of my university papers and books in that wardrobe. 'But I forgot that I'd moved some of them into the basement before you arrived. I spotted the sweatshirt and was wondering if you'd hurt yourself.' I can't possibly mention the photos or

351

the pregnancy test kit now as well.

'Yes, I did hurt myself,' Zoe says automatically. She holds her shoulder. 'I fell off my bike. But I'm OK,' she adds, probably because my face is adopting a disbelieving expression. 'I was dashing down to the shops to get some milk and my brakes failed. Don't worry, the boys were at school. It stopped bleeding eventually. More of a broad surface graze than anything, but because I carried on to the shop, it made a right mess of my sweatshirt.'

I stare at her. It sounds entirely plausible except I can't help wondering why she didn't mention it to me.

'I would have told you but didn't want you to have any more worries,' she says as if she's read my mind. She reaches out and taps my arm. 'Or for you to think that I'm a clumsy idiot as well as a bad driver.'

I can see her point.

'Do you want to see the graze?' She makes to unzip her top and wriggle out of the sleeve.

'Oh, no, really. You don't have to do that.' I feel stupid now. 'I'm sorry for asking.'

'Claudia' — she pauses while staring into my eyes — 'I would have asked too if I'd seen my nanny's top covered in blood.' She laughs, probably more than is warranted, and begins to unpick the mess I've made of sewing on the button.

36

Moving in with Cecelia two years ago wasn't an easy decision to make. Neither was moving out. Now I've left, I'm worried what will become of her. I feel utterly responsible for her well-being yet every sane cell in my body screams at me never to go back, that she is poison, that as long as I'm with her I'll be weighed down as heavy as the crazy thoughts that inhabit her mind.

She's always battled with her health — body as well as mind; *mostly* mind — and I'm sympathetic as far as I can be. But Cecelia isn't like other women. No one apart from me understands her, gets her irrational fears or anxious fits that can take place any time of day or night. I was the one who trailed her around the darkened high street in the dead of night when she went Christmas shopping in July. It was me who picked her up from hospital and held ice against her cut feet after she'd walked ten miles barefoot searching for a baby that didn't exist. No one except me knows what she's been through; no one but me understands her need to be loved a certain way — a way that only a real mother can, she once said.

It's for this reason that Cecelia refuses to adopt — not that she'd be allowed to anyway. Despite her innate desire to reproduce, she truly believes she's always been infertile — even before her operation. She says her hips are too narrow and nothing would want to grow inside her anyway. She says God made her barren as the desert. Sometimes, I'm inclined to agree.

So, one way or another, it's fallen to me to get her a baby. I admit, it started off as me humouring her, to keep her agitated thoughts passive and her imagination sated. But as she began to believe what I was telling her — that somehow, one day I would get her a child — she behaved, worked and functioned in a semi-normal way. It was, I concluded, all about keeping the hope alive.

Cecelia demanded that we co-parent the baby. I thought about it. I had doubts as to whether either of us was ready to mother a child but, because it soothed Cecelia, because I was trying to hold down a demanding job while looking after her needs, I allowed her to believe I would do it.

She had always been determined and, frighteningly, for me, she was furiously planning and getting it all worked out. I would continue to be the breadwinner while she looked after the child. She would continue to make her jewellery but in a scaled-down way. She wanted me to get pregnant from a sperm donor. That's where the plan fell apart, really. I didn't conceive.

I can't say I tried my hardest: unbeknown to her, I flushed the samples down the toilet without even trying. After the sperm bank didn't work, we supposedly tried seven times with sperm given to us by a good friend. After that she made me try a couple of other willing friends, and then when that failed Cecelia

354

announced she wanted me to hook up with a man in person — any good-looking chap would do, she said — and I remember laughing so hard it made me feel sick. 'Hook up?' I asked. 'You make it sound like a lab experiment or in-flight refuelling.' I was shaking my head all the while, worried she would actually want to witness the act. There was no way I was doing it. Stringing Cecelia along with botched inseminations was one thing, but ending up pregnant by a random man was quite another. Still, I had to keep the hope inside her alive. It was pretty much the same as keeping *her* alive, even though I was beginning to feel Cecelia's madness might be contagious. Work was becoming harder and harder for me alongside keeping Cecelia's demands at bay. Deep down, I knew I had to get away but had no idea it would be nearly another year before I finally did.

It was a Christmas party that so very nearly got Cecelia what she wanted. It was almost classic, along the lines of a photocopier fumble or water-cooler tryst except we had full-blown unprotected sex in a hotel room. All the while I was thinking of Cecelia, pretending I was doing it for her. Really, it was because I couldn't admit to *wanting* to do it with a man I didn't know. After taking care of Cecelia and being part of her crazy world, and holding down a job, the notion of actually enjoying myself was rather foreign. But it was Christmas, after all, and my short hair came tumbling down. It was the glint of his wedding ring under the bedside lamp while he pulled on his socks that sent me running to the chemist to buy the morning-after pill the next day.

As I sat with the pill's empty foil packet in my hands, waiting for the chemicals to work their magic, I mulled over the night before. He'd wanted my number.

'But you're married,' I'd reminded him. I tried to imagine his wife.

His answer was a shrug as he buttoned up his shirt. He was good-looking and fit, intelligent too, but I couldn't imagine why he'd done this. When he was ready to leave, he took me by the shoulders. 'Yes, I am,' he said, with the first glimmer of regret. 'But I want to see you again.'

Perhaps he thought that's what I wanted to hear and he had no intention of ever really calling.

'Well you're not going to,' I told him.

In the end, he concurred easily. 'You're right.'

I wished him a merry Christmas and left, praying I wouldn't see him again.

I actually told Cecelia about my encounter — a kind of twisted Christmas present to keep her going until my next period, although I didn't mention the pill I'd taken. She was overjoyed with what I'd done. Never mind the taste of guilt I'd been left with for shagging some woman's husband.

But then a week later, Cecelia went into one of her unfathomable and petulant fits of moodiness. She refused to get out of bed, wash, eat or talk except when she screamed at me. I had no idea why. It was just what she did from time to time. It lasted at least the next three weeks, and

356

by the end of January I'd had enough. I told her I was going to leave.

'If you do, I'll kill myself,' she announced, and I knew she would, so I stayed.

I was desperate with worry for Cecelia yet felt the weight of our turbulent lives together pressing down on my shoulders. I was at a loss what to do. We muddled along for most of the rest of the year and things seemed to get better. But come November when the leaves turned and the wind whipped up, so did Cecelia's mood once again. She catapulted herself into a particularly high-functioning manic state and worked tirelessly on pieces for a London show. Her jewellery was selling well and, at the time, she was making more money than me.

Then she found another willing donor. Cecelia wanted to try for a baby again. After all, that's what I'd always promised her. This time I did it properly, for her sake — for my conscience's sake. I thought it might make things better even though I prayed it would fail. But her mood got worse. Things could have been good for us but she continued to hiss and spit and growl at me just for being alive, as if I was the cause of her illness. My days became more and more miserable and I was hauled in front of my boss several times for performance issues.

So when I learnt of the job with Claudia and James, I decided it would be a fresh start for us both, and I finally left Cecelia. If it turned out I was pregnant, I'd do the right thing and go back to her. If I wasn't, then I swore to myself it would be over.

Deep in my heart, in the place where it hurt the most, I knew I didn't mean it, that I would never really leave her. But then wasn't I being petulant too? I'm ashamed to say it, but the day I walked out of our flat, I was filled with hate for her.

★ ★ ★

So here I am, out to impress my boss, thinking of my future and welfare for once, but all I see are final warnings and last chances. Cecelia flashes through my mind, her hair blowing wildly; her laugh, spilling out through a demented toothy grin, jangles between my ears. If I'm honest, everything seems bland and empty without her — a vague reverberation of lives once shared echoing around the edges of a dream that fizzled out for what, a nameless baby? I can't blame Cecelia for everything that doesn't go my way, but feeling so responsible for her has taken its toll. Inexplicably, I still want to look after her.

I take the long way back from the shops. It gives me time to think about what Claudia told me this morning: that the police came calling again last night. Why didn't she tell me when I was sewing on her button? She seemed more concerned with confessing to snooping in my room, even though she says she was just looking for a book. I'm not stupid. And what if she found my camera and saw the photographs? I don't think any amount of explaining-away would prevent her from sacking me on the spot. As it was, I don't think she believed me when I told her I fell off my bike. I should have been more careful than to leave a bloodstained top lying about.

'What did they want exactly?' I asked earlier as I made the boys' breakfast. Each twin stuck an ear close to the cereal when I told them to count the pops. It kept them amused as I chopped up some fruit and asked their mother about the detectives. 'It was rather inconsiderate of them to come calling so late.'

Claudia looked embarrassed. 'They asked questions about my work,' she said, plausibly.

I arrive back and unlock the front door, ready to get on with everything I need to do. Immediately, I freeze. There are low voices coming from somewhere inside the house. Unfamiliar male voices. Cautiously, I peer out of the front door again, down the drive and beyond into the street. It looks tempting, safe, full of freedom and the rest of my life if I choose to run. I'm about to turn, make a dash, when two well-dressed men appear in the hallway. One of them is clutching a stack of papers and they look as surprised to see me as I am to see them.

'Who are you?' I'm shaking, pulsing with adrenalin. They might not be intruders. They could be friends of Claudia.

'We were about to ask you the same thing,' the tall blond one says.

'Are you family friends? I wasn't expecting anyone.' I take a step sideways, trying to see what they've been up to. This doesn't feel right. Judging by the files they are holding, they've been in James's study. My heart pounds as I edge forward, rounding the corner to see what they've done. I gasp when I get a view of the study door. The lock has been jimmied open. The wood is splintered. 'Oh my God,' I say, taking several steps back, 'you've broken in!'

The fearful look on my face tempers the cocky attitude of the men and the shorter one holds up his free hand in defence. 'Don't be alarmed,' he says. 'We're Elizabeth's brothers. We've come to collect some of her things.' His expression is cold and devoid of emotion.

'But you've broken in,' I say, trying to buy a moment to think. This is not good. My job will be on the line for sure. 'I'm really sorry about your sister. I never met her, but . . . ' I'm frowning. I'm rubbing my forehead. They broke the lock on James's door. Every bit of me screams out to call the police . . . except I can't. 'Look, should I phone Claudia to let her know you're here? I'm her nanny.'

The two men seem more at ease when I mention who I am. *Just the dumb nanny*. 'We're leaving now so no need to bother her,' the blond one says with a nasty grin. 'Nice to meet you. And sorry about the door.' They stride briskly out of the house.

'But . . . ' I say, holding out my arms helplessly as they pass. I'm certain they shouldn't be taking all those documents, and when I realise the implications, I make a dash for the downstairs toilet. I throw up. Then I set to work cleaning up the mess they've made.

360

37

'Thanks for attending at short notice,' Adam said to the team of detectives working on the investigation. Some were chatting, some were perched on the edge of desks, while a couple leant against the wall. Everyone wanted to get on. Lorraine was jabbing buttons on her phone, working her way through the school's options menu. Adam scowled at her but she didn't care. He could update her later. She stepped out into the corridor, but the reception wavered so she darted out of a side door to the small area of concrete where the smokers went. She could hardly hear the headmaster's secretary when she finally came on the line.

'But it's important,' she said in response to being told that he was busy for the next few days. 'I need to speak to him urgently about my daughter.' Lorraine sighed heavily. 'Yes, Grace Scott.' There was a pause, and Lorraine thought she heard the woman cover the phone and speak in a low voice. 'Thank you, I appreciate that,' she said finally and hung up with an appointment at nine-forty the next morning. She texted the details to Grace in the hope she would come along too.

'Get a move on,' Adam said, catching up with Lorraine in the corridor. 'We're going back to St Hilda's Road. I'm not convinced we can't find our Miss Paige.'

'You seem in a good mood,' Lorraine said sourly, feeling the exact opposite.

'You'd know why, if you'd been in the briefing,' he said, quickening his pace.

Adam jangled his car keys inside his pocket as they entered the underground car park.

'Put me out of my misery then,' she said, knowing he enjoyed keeping her waiting.

It wasn't until they'd pulled up outside the big Georgian house in Edgbaston, wipers arcing furiously across the windscreen, smudging the sleet that was now falling, that Adam divulged what had lent the urgency to his driving. Lorraine knew better than to press him. He was punishing her for putting their personal life — their daughter's welfare — before work. She'd never change that ethic and didn't think, if really pushed, he would either. The acknowledgement of that was strangely comforting, that between them, somehow, they were still a team.

'There's a DNA match between the Sally-Ann and Carla samples,' he said perfunctorily. 'It's the same person for both cases and confirmed female. Carla was talking sense.' Adam wrenched on the handbrake and hitched up his collar in readiness for the grim weather.

'Jesus Christ, why didn't you say before?' Lorraine's voice squeaked in disbelief and anger.

'Because you were on the phone.'

'I was sorting out an appointment with Grace's headmaster,' Lorraine snapped back. 'Someone has to convince her to stay on at school.'

'Not on police time,' Adam retorted. 'And she

362

doesn't want to stay at school.'

'There *is* no other time,' Lorraine was quick to say. 'All our bloody time is police time, whether I'm cooking dinner, taking Stella to ballet, or fucking well trying to take a piss. Do not ever, ever, make me feel guilty for looking after my family, Adam. Just because you . . . you feel able to . . . ' Lorraine checked herself with a particularly weak-sounding and feminine *oh* before diving out of the car headfirst into the full-blown snow that was now falling. Everything she'd just said was not how she felt in the slightest.

Within moments, they were back in the car. Apart from the cleaning lady, there was no one home, and she'd confirmed that there wasn't a Heather Paige living at the address. Lorraine complained to Adam that they'd wasted their time, that Claudia had already told them no one by that name lived there.

'The only other person is the nanny,' the cleaner had said, leaning on the upright hose of the vacuum that she'd dragged to the door. 'But she's out too. Gone to help out with the nativity play at school.' She'd seemed happy to divulge almost anything at the flash of their ID.

'Is it worth going to see Zoe Harper?' Lorraine asked Adam as she buckled up. 'She might know where we can find Heather Paige. Perhaps Heather was visiting Zoe and that's what Cecilia saw when she followed her.'

She snapped down the sun visor and looked in the mirror, wiping water off her face with a tissue. She brushed snowflakes off her shoulders.

Adam was already searching for the primary school address from the name the cleaner had readily told them and, moments later, they were on the way.

Millpond Heath Primary School was a newly built, low-level school on the edge of a quickly whitening park. The secure grounds were surrounded by trees on one side and a number of pleasant semi-detached houses curving down the quiet road in an understated arc of middle-class existence on the other. The tarmac playground was already painted with a layer of overnight frost, and the snow was quick to settle on top. The festive Christmas card effect was somehow spoilt by the erratic trails of small slushy footprints zig-zagging between the various buildings that made up the school, as if the ground had been roughly tacked on to the earth by a careless seamstress. Stop-start music emanated from one part of the school and Lorraine scanned the rows of steamed-up windows hoping it was the nativity play rehearsals, which would lead them to Zoe Harper without too much fuss.

As they walked across the playground to the entrance marked Reception/All Visitors, Lorraine felt overly conspicuous in her dark tweed jacket, yet somehow not as misplaced as Adam appeared in his long black overcoat as it swept behind him. Neither of them looked as if they were there on school business.

'Detective Inspectors Scott and Fisher,' Adam said gruffly to the school receptionist. She was young and immediately became nervous in their presence. No one liked to see the police in a school, not unless they'd come to give a to talk to the youngsters on road safety or community crime prevention, and that didn't fall within their remit.

'Oh,' the receptionist said, her fingers still poised over the keyboard.

'We're here to talk to a woman who's helping out here today. Her name's Zoe Harper.'

'Oh,' she said again. This time she managed to take a visitors' book off the shelf on the open glass window that separated her from the school foyer. She scanned down the list of names signed in for the day's date and eventually looked up. 'Yes, she's in class 1B doing donkey stuffing,' the young woman said, taking off a pair of glasses. Her eyes suddenly appeared much smaller. She said 'donkey stuffing' as if it was a known activity, and the detectives should respect its importance and not interrupt her.

'Where would we find class 1B?' Lorraine asked.

'Oh.' It seemed everything was preceded by this single syllable. 'Across the playground and over to the art and music block. Go in the main door and it's down the corridor and second on the left. You'll need to sign in and take this swipe pass.'

'Thank you,' Lorraine said, doing as she was instructed. A minute later they were walking down an empty corridor to the smell of powder paint and the sound of 'Oh Little Town of Bethlehem' ringing out of a classroom.

'Does it take you back?' Lorraine asked,

peering in through the glass square in the door. About thirty children sat cross-legged on the floor. Some held tambourines while others dangled triangles. One or two children were picking their noses or biting their nails, staring out of the window or, now, at the strange face that had appeared at their classroom door. A dark-haired teacher struck up on the piano again, nodding her head at the disinterested bunch of children in her care.

Lorraine and Adam walked on and arrived at class 1B. Through the window in the door, the room looked empty at first until Lorraine spotted a group of three women crouched in a corner wrestling a grotesque-looking creature with four gangly legs sticking in the air.

As soon as they went in the women turned, and Lorraine immediately recognised one of them to be the nanny she'd spoken to briefly at the St Hilda's Road address. She coloured scarlet at the sight of them.

'Sorry to interrupt your festive activities, ladies,' Adam boomed more enthusiastically than was necessary, glaring at the nanny.

He's over-compensating for something, Lorraine thought, although she had no idea what. It was a voice he usually reserved for raids or serious situations that demanded instant clarity and understanding. Three women manhandling a . . . *oh God, what was it?* . . . was hardly cause for an approach like that.

'We're Detective Inspectors Fisher and Scott,' Lorraine said, putting her name first for a change. She flashed her ID. 'Miss Harper?' she

366

said to the youngest of the women. 'So sorry to bother you when you're clearly . . . ' Lorraine glanced at the mess on the floor and the reams of fake donkey skin and hoof that lay in a road-accident-style arrangement at their feet. 'We just want to have a quick word with you if we could.'

Zoe Harper straightened up. She was ankle deep in foam stuffing. Clumps of the fibres were clinging on to the baggy grey cardigan she wore over skinny black jeans. She brushed off her hands, which were daubed with brown paint, no doubt from painting the creature's cardboard head that lay gawping up at the snowflake-bedecked ceiling. 'I know, horrid, isn't it?' she said with a cheerful laugh. Rather over-zealous, too, Lorraine thought. 'The kids are going to have nightmares for ever.' The other two women laughed.

'Is there somewhere we could talk privately? We have one or two quick questions to ask you.'

Lorraine stared hard at Zoe Harper. What was it about her that stirred her curiosity? Was it the cropped blonde hair, jagged at the edges and darker at the roots, or the vibrant blue eyes that flicked about nervously between her and Adam; or was it the slight yet muscular body, or the practical lace-up worker boots that looked like something a man would wear rather than the nanny of a well-to-do family? No, it was something else. Something caught in the periphery of her consciousness, yet it was screaming out a warning to her. She still had no idea what it was.

'You can go in the staff room,' one of the other women suggested, clearly trying not to sound interested in what was going on. Lorraine assumed her to be a teacher. 'It'll be quiet until the bell rings in fifteen minutes,' she added.

Zoe Harper tentatively led the way to the empty room, and they sat in low chairs around a coffee table piled with Rich Tea biscuits and custard creams. Half a dozen dirty coffee cups littered the table along with copies of the *Daily Mail* and *heat* magazine.

'You were at the house the other day, weren't you?' Zoe said to Lorraine while picking at her short fingernails.

'I was indeed.'

'My colleague here was talking to your employer about someone she's been working with. Someone who was brutally attacked, actually.' Adam's voice was still booming and inappropriate. Lorraine had no idea what had got into him.

Zoe coloured raspberry again and stared at her feet as if she'd rather be anywhere else than there, talking to them.

'We wondered if you know anyone called Heather Paige,' Lorraine said. 'We would like to talk to her and have reason to believe she's been at your employer's address.'

Zoe looked up, finding some confidence from somewhere. 'Sorry, never heard of her.'

'Heather Paige's partner gave us the address so we're pretty certain she's been there. Can you think very hard if there have been any visitors in the last few days?'

'Her partner?' A small frown formed then disappeared just as quickly. 'Not while I've been there,' Zoe replied. 'Only Jan, the cleaner, and Claudia's friend Pip, plus a couple of deliveries, the plumber and . . . ' She was about to say something else but stopped. 'Sorry I can't help you more than that.'

'Do you know anyone called Cecelia Paige?' Lorraine asked.

Zoe pulled a surprised face. 'Nope. Sorry.' Then the raspberry again.

'Not a very good liar, are you, Miss Harper?' Lorraine said wearily.

'I don't think you're in a position to judge that,' Zoe snapped back at them both.

'Your ring,' Lorraine continued, noticing the flash of it as Zoe brought her hand to her face. She flicked at an errant tuft of hair. At the mention of it, Zoe tucked her hand back on her lap. 'It's very unusual.'

'It was a present,' she said.

'Who from?' Lorraine asked.

Zoe shrugged. 'A friend.'

'It must have been a very special friend to buy a present like that for you. Those are expensive.'

'Look, I don't know, I'm afraid,' Zoe said. 'Was that all you wanted to ask me? I should be helping with the donkey.'

'Do you know anyone called Carla Davis?' Lorraine asked.

'We should go,' Adam said quietly. He was fidgeting.

What the hell was wrong with him? Lorraine wondered.

369

'Sorry, no,' Zoe said.

'Or Sally-Ann Frith?'

This was going nowhere, although she, and supposedly Adam, could tell that Zoe Harper was hiding something. Or perhaps it was just what Claudia Morgan-Brown had said about her nanny and the dead girl's file that was influencing their thoughts. She tried to remain impartial, but it was hard, no thanks to Adam's weird behaviour. She decided that was unsettling her more than anything.

'No, sorry. I'd tell you if I did.'

'So maybe you'd like to explain why you had a photograph of Carla Davis's confidential details on your camera?' Lorraine said. She wondered if Adam was actually going to bring any of this up. As far as she could tell, all he wanted to do was leave.

Zoe pulled a face. 'I have no idea,' she said convincingly. 'I've certainly never taken pictures of any file. Last thing I remember photographing was when I took the twins to the park. I thought I'd shoot some video for their mum to watch. It's what nannies do.'

'We're going to need to take the camera in for a look, I'm afraid,' Lorraine stated sympathetically.

Zoe shrugged. 'Fine. It's in my room at the Morgan-Browns' house. Help yourselves.'

'Adam?' Lorraine hoped a prompt might get him to ask something expedient.

'Are you sure you didn't photograph Carla Davis's personal information?' he said uselessly.

'I am certain, DI Scott,' Zoe said. 'Why would I do something like that? I'm a nanny.'

'No one implied you were anything else,' Adam said thoughtfully.

★ ★ ★

'How did she know your name?' Lorraine asked. She hugged her jacket around her and pulled her scarf up over her ears, determined not to let Adam know she was freezing. The last thing she wanted was him offering her his overcoat. Not that there was much chance he'd do that. Any last remnants of chivalry had long been gobbled up by the marriage-eating monster.

'Because you told it to her, stupid.' Adam gulped his coffee greedily.

'No. I told her *both* our names. She assumed which was which.' Lorraine took Adam's paper cup and chucked it into a bin as they walked past. 'Don't know what's got into you, Adam Scott. You know you can't take caffeine.'

'Then it must have been a lucky guess.'

'I suppose,' Lorraine said, though she didn't believe that for one minute. There was something more astute about Zoe Harper than that, as if she'd been interviewing the pair of them, not the other way around.

They'd wasted no time in flicking through the pictures on the camera that Zoe had willingly handed over when they took her back to the house on St Hilda's Road to fetch it. As she'd already told them, there was nothing more incriminating on it than a few pictures of the twins in a ball pit, and a badly shot video of a sibling fight taking place on the swings.

'Forensics can still take a look,' Lorraine had said, bagging the item. 'They might dig up something.'

Adam had agreed.

'Hurry up, I'm freezing,' Lorraine said. She could tell Adam was deep in thought about something, she just wished he'd do it in the car with the heater on. 'By the way, about that ring Zoe was wearing. I recognised it.'

He glanced sideways at her as they strode along the pavement. 'It looked a bit tasteless if you ask me.'

'I wasn't asking you what you thought of it. It's incredibly similar to the ones Cecelia Paige makes. Unmistakably so, in fact. I saw lots of her work when I went to her flat. It was like a magpie's nest or Aladdin's cave. Stuffed full of . . . crap, basically, apart from this amazing jewellery that she makes. She might seem a bit unhinged but she's really talented.'

'So you think Zoe does know Cecelia then?'

'I'm certain of it.' Lorraine got into the car. She'd never felt so cold.

'Me too,' Adam said, getting in the driver's side. Lorraine wondered why he sounded so dejected about the revelation.

'Which means?' Lorraine said, wanting Adam to offer up his thoughts first. When he didn't, she continued, 'If you ask me, Zoe Harper's not quite who she says she is.' Lorraine pulled off her gloves and took out her phone. She was going to get some checks done. 'And if you asked me again, I'd put my money on Zoe Harper being Heather Paige.'

38

Every time I lost a pregnancy, a little part of me died too. I don't think Martin ever understood this, or my friends, or the obstetricians and the nurses who picked up the immediate pieces of my life. Three times I've given birth to a stillborn foetus, and I've pretty much given up counting the number of times that a tiny life has dribbled into my underwear.

All in all, it's made me feel like an unworthy shell of a woman over the years, a freak incapable of carrying a live baby full term; and, after so much internal anguish and pain, I came to the conclusion that it was a conspiracy, an unwritten warning emblazoned on my soul to all potential sons and daughters: stay away from this woman. She is not a good mother.

I was in Debenhams. I'd gone to get a few items for the twins and a dress for me. James and I had been invited to a christening, and I had nothing suitable to wear. The thought of spending a morning in church while everyone cooed over someone else's baby was abhorrent, but James and the father had been friends since their schooldays so I knew I would have to go. I tried not to be affected by other people's good fortune and their perfect families, but the plain fact was, jealousy stuck in my craw like a bowlful of mud shoved down my throat.

I found new sweaters and trainers for the boys

no problem. They were at playgroup for the morning so I'd taken the opportunity to dash out to the shops. Besides, it was part distraction therapy. The day before, my period had come. Once again, I wasn't going to be a mother. I was a couple of weeks late and my breathless hope had been shattered. Something deep inside me told me it was more than my regular monthly cycle, that I had indeed conceived James's baby before he'd gone off on a short mission, and now it had spontaneously aborted, I'd not be able to welcome him home with a tiny pair of baby bootees placed on his pillow as I'd planned.

It was holding on to this thought that sent me to the baby department of the store. As I wove between the displays of prams and cots, car seats and clothes, I was confronted by every stage of a baby's early life — a place I'd never been to except in my dreams. It was a kind of punishment, I suppose.

'Can I help you, madam?' the assistant asked.

'Oh, I'm just browsing, thanks.' Stupidly, my hand went straight to my flat stomach as if there really was a baby growing in there.

The assistant smiled and I could tell she was considering asking when I was due, but the shop floor was busy. 'Let me know if I can help,' she said before heading off to offer her services to a young couple who, to be honest, didn't look as if they could afford anything from this store.

I went dizzy among the soft sleep-suits hanging from tiny hangers on the display racks. The edges of the little plush clothes feathered into unreality, just the same as my vision and

374

sense of self blended into the noisy world around me. There I was, out to buy a christening dress to wear to another family's celebration, and I'd ended up in the baby department trailing my shaking hands over equipment I would most likely never need to own. All I could think of was how unfair it was; how, if I could only have the chance, I'd be the best mother that ever lived. Instead, I spent my days taking babies and children away from unfit parents. The irony made me laugh out loud.

'Oh, sorry,' I said. I'd ploughed straight into the woman from the couple I'd spotted before. I'd been watching them through my slightly teary eyes as they coveted everything from a white cot to a pram that doubled as a car seat. The woman was clinging on to a small fluffy lamb with a red sale price tag. It was probably the cheapest thing for sale.

'Watch it,' the man said. He was scruffy and belligerent and reminded me of the fathers I dealt with in my job. 'She's pregnant, you know.'

'It's all right,' the young woman said. She was pale, almost to the point of appearing grey. She didn't look very well at all.

'I'm so sorry,' I repeated. 'Are you all right?'

The woman nodded and the man scowled and they went on their way. I wanted to tell them that I was pregnant too, compare due dates and talk about the benefits of econappies and breast versus bottle, but I felt too empty to do much more than fumble my way through a rack of tiny dresses in Easter shades of yellow and pink. Everything went blurry again and I was just about to succumb to the tears, make a dash for the toilets or disappear into the lift when I heard a heart-stopping shriek. I glanced around but couldn't initially make out where it was coming from.

Then I saw the woman I'd just bumped into flailing her arms about her head. My first thought was that I must have really hurt her, perhaps caused a spontaneous miscarriage. I suddenly felt contagious as panic gripped my body. I could barely breathe as I tentatively walked, wide-eyed, towards the couple. The man was trying to pin down the woman's increasingly wild arm movements without much luck. Her eyes bulged as if she was possessed by a demon while her hands lashed out for whatever was within reach.

'Madam, please, let me help you,' the shop assistant said.

The young woman completely ignored her pleas to calm down and spiralled into further frenzy as she swiped down displays of toys and baby-feeding equipment. An entire zoo of fluffy animals went flying alongside the clatter of melamine plates and plastic bottles. She ripped clothes off their stands and sent them into a jumble of unborn chaos and shoved prams wheeling down the wooden aisles, narrowly missing the gathering spectators who were eager to see the woman who had flipped.

I knew I had to do something. I felt as if it was all my fault.

I went up to her, not caring if I received a swipe. 'Please, calm down. You're going to hurt yourself or the baby.'

She stopped momentarily when I said the word 'baby'.

'I don't want the sodding baby,' she spat out and then continued with her flailing until two security guards managed to restrain her. I was still beside her and dropped with her to the floor when her knees buckled. Her arms were pinned behind her back.

'Be careful, she's pregnant,' I told the guards. They slackened their grip. Tears streamed down the woman's face as she sobbed and hiccuped her way through the remains of the outburst. 'It's going to be OK, just breathe calmly if you can.' I showed her how to cup her hands over her face as her ribs forced air in and out of her lungs as if the world was running out of oxygen. It couldn't be good for her baby.

Eventually, her state levelled and it finally seemed as if she was listening to me. The crowd dispersed thanks to the shop assistants, while the woman's partner was stroking her head and holding her hand. She didn't seem to know where she was.

'Is there somewhere she can sit for a while?' I asked the assistant, who willingly took us to a back room while her colleagues began to clear up the mess. Between us, the man and I got her sitting down and sipping on a glass of water. The colour was finally returning to her cheeks.

'I don't want this baby,' she said through trembling lips. 'I'm scared.'

An icy flood powered through me but I kept the welling dam under control. She knew nothing about me, our lives were entirely separate, yet she would never know how hard she had just pinched the deepest nerve in my heart.

'I'm Claudia,' I told her gently. She wasn't thinking straight. Of course she wanted her baby. 'I can help you. There's no need to be scared.' At this she seemed to relax. 'Your body is undergoing amazing changes right now and believe me, it can do crazy things to how you feel.' I gave her a reassuring smile.

Her hands shook as she sipped the water. 'You're pregnant too?' she whispered.

'Yes,' I said, nodding. It just seemed the right thing to say, under the circumstances. I wanted to win her trust, to keep her calm and, most importantly, to prevent her from doing something she would regret for the rest of her life. 'So I know exactly how you feel.'

'I feel so sick all the time and my mind plays tricks on me. I don't know which way up I am these days and I can hardly keep awake yet I never sleep at night. I'm not even three months gone so heaven knows what I'll be like at the end.' She let out another stream of sobs. 'If I even get to the end.'

'You're a beautiful pregnant woman and you're going to have a happy, healthy baby,' I told her. 'Every baby brings its own love into the world with it. These feelings won't last long.' I looked at her partner. The shop assistant had left us alone. 'You'll feel so much better soon, probably by this time next week. Probably by tonight, even,' I said with a small smile. I had to give her hope.

'I'm booked in for a termination,' she whispered to me. I saw the shame in her eyes but didn't want her to know how I felt. I willed myself to hang on, to keep control of my feelings. It wasn't her fault I'd had such rotten luck.

'That's a big decision,' I said.

She immediately nodded. 'I don't know what to do.'

'No one can tell you that,' I said. 'But you have another human growing inside you. You must cherish that life as you would your own.' I saw the flash of light zip between her teary eyes as if a particularly painful realisation had just woken her up.

The young couple held each other in a vice-like grip. The woman snuffled helplessly, and he rocked her gently as if she were a baby herself. I thought about taking their names, about passing on their details to their Social Services department, to at least let them know of the woman's emotional state, but I realised that it would most likely be my department, if they were local as their accents suggested, and that I would end up dealing with it. In the end, I decided to let it drop.

'I feel better now, thank you,' the woman said, standing up. She steadied herself on me, the nearest thing to her, as she wobbled to her feet.

'Will you be OK?' I asked.

'We'll be fine,' the man said, rather too gruffly, I thought, seeing as I'd given up my shopping time to help them.

I felt my eyes prickle with tears as the woman made to leave. It felt wrong. 'Take care then,' I said, reaching out for her hand. We exchanged a brief squeeze of fingers. 'Are you sure you're going to be OK?' I repeated in what I suppose was desperation. I didn't want her to leave. I was worried that she'd change her mind and go ahead with the termination. But really, what business was it of mine?

She nodded. 'Thanks for your help,' she said with a smile, and then they were gone.

I left the back room of the store and wandered about the nursery department in a daze. If I couldn't have a baby of my own, then I couldn't see a life ahead for myself. The tears came. Then I thought of James and the boys and things didn't seem quite so hopeless. I was being self-indulgent and selfish.

I left the shop without a dress and headed for the car park. It was only as I slumped in the driver's seat that I realised I'd left my shopping bags containing the boys' clothes in the store room. I didn't care. I just wanted to go home.

As I drove up to the ticket barrier, all I could hear were the midwife's words last time it had happened.

Do you want to see your baby, love?

I'd declined with a vigorous shake of my head, preferring instead to dissolve into a self-absorbed mess of pity that refused help of any kind.

I sobbed as I wound down the window and inserted my ticket. I happened to look across at the beaten-up old car in the lane next to me. Loud music and voices attracted my attention. It was the couple I'd met in the shop. They were arguing. The man glared at me and roared away as soon as their barrier lifted up.

I pulled myself together and blew my nose. When my barrier opened, I ended up behind the other car on the spiral ramp. As we emerged into the spring sunlight, I squinted and drove behind them for a couple of streets. I watched, dismayed, as they went across a set of lights on orange. My foot twitched over the accelerator as all I could think about were regrets and babies and the fact that I would never be a real mother.

39

There was something about Zoe and Heather and Cecelia that made Lorraine uneasy. She couldn't put her finger on it exactly, but the thought wouldn't leave her alone. However, when Adam reported that Heather Paige hadn't flagged anywhere on the system, she forgot about it temporarily and concentrated on her wayward daughter.

'She didn't arrive at school,' Lorraine said, trying to remain calm despite the surging feeling of panic. She went over again and again what the secretary had said when she'd phoned.

'Hardly surprising, given that she's just announced she's leaving.' Adam got out of the car.

'I don't know how you can be so casual about it,' Lorraine said. 'She's not thinking straight. She's obviously miserable. And now it would appear she's gone missing.' She got out of the car too, slammed the door, and marched up the steps and into the dismal grey building. She never normally noticed the grim architecture that was home to CID, but today the uninspiring concrete, the aluminium windows, the depressing monotony of the front facade, shouted out to her like a beacon of lost hope.

Adam caught up with her. He grabbed her by the arm.

'We all know what this is really about,' he said.

His breath froze in the air between them. He released her when he saw he was hurting her.

'I have no idea what you're talking about. It seems pretty black and white to me.' Lorraine continued up the steps but tripped on the last one. Her hands went out to the concrete and her bag fell off her shoulder, spilling the contents around Adam's feet. She stayed there for a moment, prone on the slick surface. A pain bloomed in her right knee, causing her to wince as she stood up. Adam was already picking up her belongings and sheepishly placing them back inside her bag, staring at the items as if he'd always wondered what was in there.

'Here,' he said, holding out a hand. 'I'm sorry.'

There was a pause. Lorraine wasn't sure what he was apologising for.

'I don't see how we can go from Zoe Harper to our errant daughter to the mountain of mess that is our marriage, ending with a vague apology, all within two minutes.' She hugged her coat around her. The palm of her right hand stung.

Adam flapped his hands at his side, a gesture that had always annoyed Lorraine. It made him seem like a small boy. 'Lorraine . . . ' He sighed and guided her away from the door of the building, which seemed like the entrance to a hive with their colleagues coming and going around them. He drew in a breath and began again as if it was his last and only chance. 'Lorraine . . . this thing between us, I don't want it any more. Every time you speak to me, whatever you say, it hurts like a punch in the

383

guts.' He turned his face away for a moment.

Lorraine felt a familiar sinking feeling in her stomach. Was this it? Was this where it would all begin or end, on the steps of police HQ? She'd envisaged the showdown happening somewhere else, probably their living room, their bedroom, the kitchen, the garden — anywhere except in public, and at work, of all places. A pair of colleagues dashed past, raising their hands in greeting.

'I don't think — '

'I do,' Adam said sternly. 'I think all the time. What happened consumes every single one of my waking hours. Correction: it consumes *all* of my hours, waking and sleeping. How can I explain to you what happened when I don't understand it myself? It's been nearly a year now, and I don't know how to move forward. I did something stupid, you know that, I know that, but how I explain or rationalise it to you or myself, that's the problem.'

Adam was turning around in semicircles. His frown was deeper than ever, his shoulders more hunched than Lorraine had seen them in a long time. Of course, she could keep him in this limbo-land of misery, suspend his agony for as long as she wished, but was that what she really wanted?

'Let's go inside,' Lorraine said. 'I'll try calling Grace again.' She needed to control this conversation, where and when it happened, and it couldn't continue here in full view of their colleagues.

Adam followed her as she went inside. He was

384

contrite, that was for certain, but, inexplicably, she preferred it when he put up a fight, when he denied his misdemeanours, when he acted as if nothing had happened. It was a familiar comfort blanket of lies, and at least it made her feel that he perhaps hadn't done anything so awful after all.

Alone in the lift, Adam forked his arms around Lorraine in a tight V-shape. His face was close and his jaw was clenched. 'The truth is I made a mistake. It was one night. I was drunk. She was drunk. We had sex. I have not seen her since.'

Lorraine felt sick, and it wasn't from the lurch of the lift as it drew to a halt at their floor. It was his closeness, his breath on her face.

The doors slid open and Adam stood back as they were faced with several people in the lobby. Lorraine headed for her office, and was about to shut the door when she noticed Adam's arm reaching round to stop it closing.

'I refuse to discuss it here, Adam. We have two murder investigations and a daughter who is trashing her life. Why on earth would you think I want to talk about our situation now?'

Lorraine slumped down in her chair and started up her computer. She dialled Grace's number.

'Still no reply,' she said, putting her phone on the desk.

'Are you worried?' Adam asked.

'Of course I'm bloody worried,' Lorraine said. 'Our daughter hasn't arrived at school. She's moved out. She's intent on marrying Matt, and she's not answering her phone. But I know one thing.'

Adam raised his eyebrows hopefully.

'Unlike her father, she's not an idiot.' She took a breath, raised her head and looked at her husband properly for what felt like the first time in a year. 'OK then. I want to know what happened. All of it.' Lorraine dug her nails into her palms. 'Until you tell me, this isn't going to go away, is it?'

Adam remained perfectly still. She had no idea what he was going to say or how she would feel when he said it. It could be the end of everything, or it could be the beginning of an understanding that she hadn't reckoned ever getting to grips with. Either way, it was a process she knew she had to go through. She just hadn't expected it to be now, today, in her office. *Damn him*.

'It was last December.' Adam's voice was dry and rasping. 'You were ill, but you told me to go to the Christmas party without you, knowing how much I hate those events.'

Lorraine withheld her anger. Had she really told him to go? She couldn't remember. She'd been poorly, she knew that much. Flu had swept through her and her three-day fever had caused her mind to operate on a tenuous thread of unreality. She waited for Adam to continue.

'I got there late. It was an inter-department gathering and the venue was heaving. A jam-packed bar isn't my idea of fun.' He shrugged, a passive indicator that none of this had really bothered him. Lorraine knew he could hold his own as well as anyone at a party.

'There were a couple of people I recognised so I chatted with them for a while. I guess I'd had too much to drink even by then.' They both knew that he wasn't good with alcohol. He rarely drank.

'I saw her standing on the other side of the room. I knew she was staring at me. Eventually she came up and introduced herself — '

'Stop! I do *not* want to know her name.'

He nodded. 'She said she'd seen me before although I didn't recognise her. We chatted. We got drunk together. We did a stupid thing.'

'And that would be?'

'We went to a hotel across the road. She paid for the room, in case you were wondering.'

'I wasn't.'

'It happened. I dressed. I left.'

Lorraine knew what he was doing. Those short, clipped, monosyllabic sentences were typical of Adam when he was trying to portray the bare minimum while not being accused of withholding information. It was pretty much like questioning a suspect, although in this case Lorraine was certain of his guilt.

'OK,' she said quietly. 'I could ask things such as 'Was she good?' or 'Did you get her number?' but I won't.' She hated it that her voice was shaking. 'But the thing I really want to know, Adam, is *why?*'

There was a predictable silence in the office; the kind of silence that was big enough to fill the space that had grown between them since this had started nearly a year ago.

'In all honesty, I have no idea. I wasn't thinking. She was attractive. She was there. Had I not been drunk, things would have been different.' Normally, Lorraine knew, Adam would be acting out his feelings by rubbing his face or ruffling his hair or even fiddling with his cuff button. But he wasn't doing any of these things. He just stood, limply, as if every part of him had surrendered to his situation.

Lorraine shook her head, exhausted by the magnitude of it all. 'I guess I was hoping that you'd say something more tangible, like it was because of me or the girls or because your home life sucked. But that it was purely down to your bad judgement makes me worry, Adam. It makes me worry a lot. It makes me think this could happen again.' She lifted her hands, but then dropped them into her lap. 'And for the record, I don't believe that you haven't seen her since.'

'I —'

Adam was halted by the bleep of Lorraine's phone. She lunged for it. 'It's Grace.' She read the few words and closed her eyes. 'She's OK but she doesn't want to see us.'

Adam sighed. 'I can understand why. We've done nothing but pressure her since this began.'

'Pressure? You think asking our daughter to see sense is pressuring her?'

Adam raised his eyebrows, making Lorraine stop and think.

With reluctant fingers, she tapped out a reply: *We're here when you need us.*

★ ★ ★

388

As far as Lorraine could see, the text from Grace had come as a welcome interruption for Adam. He'd told her the basics, given her enough of a picture of what had happened that night to ease some of the mystery that she'd embellished to outlandish proportions over the previous year. For the time being, though, there were other issues to deal with, not least the complex web of relationships between the characters in the Sally-Ann case.

With investigations in full swing and their team working round the clock, Lorraine and Adam had decided to go home for a couple of hours given that they both had an afternoon off. They'd travelled home separately, however, and Adam had already changed into his running gear by the time Lorraine had taken off her coat and turned up the central heating. She was making a cup of tea when the doorbell rang. Thinking it might be Grace, she went to answer it.

Matt stood shaking on the top step, jangling his car keys and glancing nervously down the street. As soon as Lorraine opened the door, he began babbling some kind of apology.

'Matt,' Lorraine said, putting her hand up to stop the flow. 'You'd better come in.'

He followed Lorraine into the kitchen. Adam looked stunned to see him, but somehow Matt kept his composure, albeit shakily.

'Is Grace OK?' Lorraine said, suddenly concerned.

Matt nodded solemnly. 'She's fine. I mean, you know, OKish.' He let out a sigh. 'I don't know what she's told you about everything but — '

'You don't know?' Adam barked, standing up from tying his trainer laces. 'That's a bit rich, seeing as you're responsible for our daughter leaving home and school.'

Matt looked despondent. Lorraine gripped Adam's arm in order to silence him.

'It's not exactly like that,' Matt continued. 'Grace is a bit confused.'

'Damn right she is,' Adam said, pulling away and taking a step towards Matt with his fists clenched. Lorraine came between them.

'I know she's planning on leaving anyway, but Grace didn't go to school today,' Lorraine said. 'And we have no idea where she is.'

Matt raised his hands in defence. 'She was with me,' he confessed. 'We were talking and stuff.' He bowed his head. 'Look, that's why I'm here. There's something important I have to tell you.'

40

The house telephone stops ringing just before I grab it. As I skid to a halt on the hall tiles, I realise my whole body is tingling. My nervousness is fuelled entirely by thought. This scares me. It's like a volcano eruption that I have no control over, or an illness that can't be cured. I pick up the receiver to make sure that the caller isn't hanging on, waiting for me. Almost immediately my mobile phone begins to ring. I run around searching for it and finally find it in my bag in the kitchen.

'Hello?' I say before I have even pressed the answer button. There is something unusually urgent about this afternoon, something oppressive and final, as if my time here is nearly up when I really don't want it to be; a make-or-break span of existence that I simply hadn't expected to end so soon.

'Hello?' I say again. 'Who's there?' All I can hear is the convulsive breathing of an unidentified caller. It's as if all the air in the kitchen is being sucked in and out of the phone. 'Who is this?' I'm about to hang up when I hear a woman's voice.

'Please help me,' she says, and I know in an instant it's Pip. My heart skittles inside my chest. I know why she is calling. My hand drops limply down to my side as I take it in, as I decide what it means. When I bring the phone back to my ear, the frantic breathing continues. I can almost feel the squeeze of her hand on mine as her body tears her apart, as her womb prepares to empty.

'Pip?' I ask, even though I know perfectly well it's her. 'Are you OK?'

There is a long pause. Eventually she speaks. 'The baby's coming.' More panting followed by controlled breaths now, as if just speaking to me has somehow calmed her down.

'Did you just ring the land line?' I ask stupidly.

'Yes, yes,' she says, during a plateau between contractions. 'I'm so sorry to bother you. I didn't know who else to call. I left a message.'

I haven't had a chance to listen to it but I like it that she contacted me, that in the mess of her body's contortions, she turned to me for help.

'Will you come over?' she asks. I can almost see the grimace of pain on her face. 'I really need you to help me. This baby will be here very soon and I can't get hold of anyone. Clive must be in a meeting.'

The shock of what she's just told me jolts me out of inaction. Even before we have finished the call, I am shoving on my shoes and grabbing my coat. 'I'm on my way, Pip. Just hang on.'

I keep her on the line, hunting everywhere for my car keys, but they're nowhere to be found. I decide to take James's car, then remember it's at the garage being serviced. I pull at my hair in frustration but try not to let Pip hear my anxiety. 'Please, you mustn't give birth without me. I want to be there. I promise I will be there soon.' Then I ask her if she has called for an ambulance, and when she tells me she hasn't, I give her very specific instructions. I pray that she will do as she's told.

The freezing air takes my breath away, but not so much that I can't think straight. Without transport I am left with only the bicycle. I drag it out from behind the side gate and swing my leg over the saddle. When I first begin to pedal, I am slipping all over the place on the icy road. A car hoots as I swerve between parked vehicles and I regain my balance just in time to miss clipping the side of a van.

It's not far to Pip's house — or at least it's never seemed that way when I've driven — but now, powering myself, I might as well be trying to get to the other side of the moon. The sky is overcast and low, bearing down on me like the weight of my mission. This is a culmination, an eclipse, a perfect opportunity that I can't afford to miss. I chant this over and over in my head as my legs cycle round and round, getting me closer to where I need to be.

Pip's street is a perfect middle-class haven. Everything about it is comfortable, reassuring, safe and serene. Last time I visited her at home I was bringing the twins to play with Lilly. It almost seems like a dreamscape now, part of another life, as I pedal frantically onwards to help her. *Dear God, don't let her have given birth without me.*

'Watch out!' a man yells from his car window as he reverses out of his drive. I swerve and narrowly miss the back end of his car.

At the head of the cul-de-sac I screech to a halt on the gravel of Pip's drive. I let the bicycle fall to the ground and charge up to her front door. I jab the bell with my finger several times as well as rapping the knocker.

Pip answers the door quicker than I expect and, at first glance, she appears perfectly normal, smiling when she first sets eyes on me. But the smile quickly falls away as she drops into the abyss of another contraction. I replace it with one of my own smiles and look at her, relieved, exhausted, happy that this is finally going to happen. She is still very pregnant. I shove her roughly into the hallway and slam the front door.

'I'm sorry, Pip,' I say. 'I never intended for this.'

She is horrified and unable to speak. She clutches at her abdomen and leans against the wall while pulling a face, the like of which I have never seen before. Her forehead crinkles, and her mouth contorts, exposing her teeth in a smile of agony. Then her eyes roll back and she seems to be in a different place for the next minute or two, not even able to care about my forceful entry into her house.

I go to her and tentatively stroke her shoulder, feeling a sudden pang of guilt. I expect her to flinch away, but she doesn't even seem to know I'm here. When I put a hand on her stomach, it feels as hard as rock. Her muscles are clamping around the baby, making me wonder how it will survive such trauma.

'I really think you should sit down, Pip. I'm worried you will fall.'

For a moment she ignores me, but then it is as if someone has flicked a switch and the old Pip returns. She stares at me, wondering if I am the person she knows.

'Pip, I want you to sit on the sofa.' My voice is commanding and mean, something she has never heard from me before, but I have a job to do and nothing will stand in my way. She opens her mouth to speak and my finger automatically presses against her lips, silencing her. She doesn't pull away from my touch. 'Just relax. We don't want anything to happen to baby, do we?'

'I . . . I don't understand. What the hell is going on? I want Clive.' Her lips wet my finger as she speaks.

It occurs to me that he might be on his way. 'Did you speak to him? Did you get through to him? Tell me!' I glance at my watch. I don't have long.

Pip shakes her head. 'I left him a message, that's all.'

'Did you call anyone else?' I place a hand on the shiny white mantelpiece to steady myself. The dizziness comes in waves, escalating my need.

'Just the hospital ward,' Pip says after a moment's hesitation.

'The ambulance?' I told her not to. I told her to wait for me.

Pip is shaking her head, fearful of what I might do if she admits to calling for help. Once again her body is consumed by a contraction. It has only been a couple of minutes since the last one.

I get down on my knees in front of her and take her hands in mine. 'Oh, Pip. Breathe through it. Focus on me, focus on my eyes.' I don't want her to give birth yet. In an out-of-body way, she seems to connect with me and our minds lock in a contraction-surviving battle. 'We can do this together, Pip,' I tell her, but she doesn't seem to hear me. A growl emanates from her lungs and all I can do is watch and suffer my own mental agony as the clamping of her body passes through her.

When it has subsided, I go to the kitchen to get supplies. On my return, I see that she has disobeyed me and has her phone in her shaking hands. I take a swipe and send it skidding across the floor. 'Stupid bitch! Don't you trust me? Don't you think I know what I'm doing?'

Pip stares at the phone lying on the floor. Oddly, she stays perfectly calm, and turns to me, offering me one of her motherly smiles. 'Of course I trust you,' she says.

Another quick glance at the phone from her makes me stamp on it with my boot, smashing the screen into a map of jagged shards.

'I'm so sorry,' she says. 'I didn't mean to upset you.'

I offer up the tea towel I have wetted with water. 'Let me cool your face,' I say. She allows me to dab it across her head.

'Thank you,' she says. 'That's very thoughtful.' Her shoulders are shaking.

In my right hand I am holding the kitchen knife. When I bring it out from behind my back, Pip screams. I have no idea if it's from fear or another contraction.

41

I decide, seeing as I'm home, that I should probably put on a load of washing. The mundaneness of the simple action keeps me occupied during this interminable period of waiting. I sort through the garments, which have got into a muddle in the utility room — a dirty tangle of everyone's clothes. I put my laundry in the machine but it's only half full, so I grab some other items of a similar colour and I'm about to shove them in too when I notice the blood.

I shake open the fabric and identify a stain of red where there really shouldn't be one. I don't understand, and neither do I want to touch it. Half of me believes this can't really be what I think it is, that there is bound to be some rational explanation, while the other half of me knows exactly what it means. I stare at it for a few more moments and decide not to put it in to wash. Instead, I bundle the yellow garment inside a pillow case and hide it at the bottom of the laundry basket.

'Surely not,' I say to myself as I go up from the basement.

I am alone in the house so checking all the cupboards is easy, although at first I don't see what it is I am looking for. It takes some not very careful rummaging and dislodging of items, which will probably give away my nosing about, to finally confirm my suspicions.

I go into the kitchen, still puzzling over what I have found. It doesn't make any sense at all. The light is flashing on the telephone base, indicating a message has been left. I've not been back long. I press the button and at first I think it's a hoax caller but somewhere, in all the panting and demented breathing, is a woman's desperate voice.

'Are you there? Anyone? Help me . . . please?'

'It's Pip,' I say, sounding almost as breathless as her message. *Perhaps she's gone into labour. In that case, why isn't she in hospital? And why didn't she call her midwife or Clive? I hope nothing is wrong.*

I phone her back immediately just to check everything is OK, but when I dial her number it goes straight to her voicemail. I'm puzzled, but suddenly realise the time. I have to fetch James's car from the garage, after which I should probably drive over to Pip's to check everything is all right.

Twenty minutes later I find the car only needed a tail-light bulb and a handbrake adjustment. Still distracted, I pay the bill and the mechanic hands over the MOT certificate. I can't get Pip's pitiful message out of my head. It's stuck there right along with the contents of the cupboard and the bloodied garment. My mind is suddenly made up. It's only a short drive to her house. Besides, she might be grateful for someone to fetch Lilly from school.

Ten minutes later and I'm pulling onto Pip's drive. Her car is parked in front of the garage as usual but there is also a familiar bicycle lying discarded on the tarmac. My heart stutters at the sight of it. I stare at it intently as I walk past, wondering what it means, half expecting the front wheel to start turning and squeaking. I shrug it off but swear I see the flash of someone's face dart away from the front window as I approach the door. I didn't see who it was.

I ring the doorbell and wait. No one answers. I peer in through the bay window but the living room is dark and empty. As my eyes scan around the room, I notice several cups on the floor, one smashed, and a broken phone lying beside the fireplace.

That's odd, I think. Pip is always ridiculously tidy.

I ring the bell again and rap on the letterbox. Then I open the flap and call through, singing out her name, hoping that if she is upstairs she will hear me. I don't want to panic her but can't help it that my voice increases in urgency.

'Pip, Pip, are you there?'

I put my ear to the hole and listen for a reply. Nothing comes, not even the clattering claws or the squeaky yap of her little Jack Russell dog. I wonder if she has gone for a walk to help her labour along, if indeed she is in labour, or perhaps she has been whisked away already by an ambulance. But I swear I saw someone in her living room.

I go down the path at the side of the house, thankful the gate isn't locked. I half expect Jingles to come skittering up to greet me but the dog isn't outside either. Pip's garden is a neat square of winter green and pruned shrubs with a couple of brightly coloured balls strewn about the grass. A plastic pedal car is badly parked on the patio outside the kitchen door. I push it away with my foot and cup my hand against the glass. This time the person inside doesn't have a chance to dart out of the way.

As she turns to face me, her expression crumples into something I don't recognise — an emotion that I have never seen on anyone before — but then, in an instant, she is herself again, back to the person I know, composed and in control. I want to sigh with relief because Pip has help already, but then something inside me prevents this from happening. To begin with, I can't figure out what it is, why I am not feeling grateful on Pip's behalf that assistance and comfort has arrived. Only when she has unlocked the back door and has coaxed me inside do I realise why my heart is racing and my fists are balled into tense knots. By then, it is too late.

Zoe.

Claudia.

The greeting is fake and punctuated by tense nods of our heads. I try to remain calm. My mind is racing ahead of my mouth and I know what I want to say, ought to say, but I don't. I'm still not sure what this all means.

'Where is Pip? Is she OK?' I take a step forward into the kitchen, trying to see through into the living room. She takes a couple of steps back but is still blocking my way. 'Did she go to the hospital?'

She is shaking her head at everything I say.

Her hands rise up helplessly and push through her hair. Then they drop down by her sides again.

'Her baby,' she says pitifully, and I'm not sure if those two words are filled with sadness or joy or despair or something else I haven't yet picked up on.

'What about her baby?' I say. 'Has she had it? You have to tell me what's going on.' I'm conscious of my voice rising in panic as I try to get past her in order to check the rest of the house, but she darts in front of me.

'No, no, stop it! You don't know what you are doing.' She's crying now. Snot bubbles at her nose and her cheeks are scarlet.

A piercing howl suddenly fills the house and a loud bang from upstairs makes the ceiling light judder.

She turns and charges into the hallway, taking the stairs two at a time. I come up behind her but she easily beats me to the bathroom at the top of the stairs and slams the door closed. I hear the lock slide across at the same time another gut-wrenching moan spills out.

She's got Pip in there.

I lunge against the door with my shoulder but it won't open. 'For God's sake, let me in! What are you doing?' I don't get a reply, but I hear Pip scream. She yells my name twice and then there's a slapping sound followed by silence.

I thump on the door and try hurling my weight at it several more times but it's holding fast. I stop, try to think calmly for a moment about what is going on, but it's too much, too big, to take in. I pace the landing, listening to fresh wails from Pip as her labour marches on.

'Listen to me!' I scream. 'Can you hear me in there? Please, just let me know you can hear me!'

There is an interminable silence, but finally I hear a very weak, 'Yes.' Then another soul-gripping noise from Pip as her contraction peaks and eventually subsides.

Over the gentle panting and pitiful sobbing, I try to talk sense through the door. I'm still not certain what she is doing. 'Pip is having a baby,' I say, wanting to kick myself for stating the obvious. 'She needs to be in hospital so she can be taken care of. Surely you want the best for her and her baby, don't you? Pip is a friend. Why do you want to hurt her? Can you hear me in there?'

She doesn't reply. Then I hear the gush of running water, as if someone's filling the bath. It's followed by a clattering sound, perhaps something metal being dropped. I can't be certain.

'No, no! Dear God, please, no! Help me!' The half screams, half pleas don't sound like Pip any more.

My phone falls from my shaking hands as I attempt to call for help. I pick it up and dial 999 first, giving details as clearly as I can. Then I call the other number, the one I never thought I would have to use, and calmly give an update. I admit that I have failed comprehensively and will face the consequences, but the screams coming from the bathroom — way more than labour pains now — send me and the entire weight of my life crashing against the door once again. I have to get Pip out of there.

I feel the wood give a little and go further back down the landing. I charge at it again, hurling my hips and shoulder at it with all my might. I hear the wood splintering followed by more screams and banging and I'm lunging at the door like a madwoman. Whatever else I have messed up, I can't let anything happen to Pip.

Suddenly the door bursts open and I fall into the bathroom, stumbling and banging my cheek on the edge of the basin. I am not prepared for what I see, even though my mind has been wrestling with crazy thoughts from the moment I saw Claudia standing in Pip's kitchen wearing tight-waisted jeans that even I would struggle to get on.

'Claudia,' I say. I am so angry that my voice shakes. 'No one is going to hurt you if you stay calm. I want you to put the knife down on the floor.'

The bathroom is small and airless and already stinks of death. I haven't dared look at Pip yet but I am aware that she is lying supine in the bath. I hear her shallow, desperate breaths and know she is still alive. I must not take my eyes off Claudia or the knife that she is clutching above Pip's naked belly.

'You must listen to me very, very carefully, Claudia.'

She turns and stares directly at me. Her right arm is outstretched, and her fist grips the wooden handle of the kitchen knife. How can this be the same woman who interviewed me to

403

be her nanny just a short time ago, or the mother who tucks her twin sons into bed at night with the same love as if they were her natural offspring? Something is missing from Claudia's eyes as she stares back at me. It's as if her irises have been bleached and her soul scraped clean of any compassion. I am uncertain if she is evil or ill.

'Help is on the way, Claudia. If you do as I say now, then we can sort this out. I know you don't want to hurt Pip or her baby.'

'It's not fucking fair,' Claudia says in a voice I don't recognise. 'I just want her baby.' Her arm is shaking violently and tears are rolling down her cheeks. She turns rigidly to stare down at Pip, who is clutching the side of the bath and weeping. There is a pink tinge to the few inches of water in the bath and I'm worried that she's been wounded.

I recall the contents of the keepsake box in Claudia's wardrobe — a desperate stash of pitiful memories and lost hope. 'I know it's not fair,' I begin. 'But it's not fair to hurt Pip either, is it?'

'I need her baby,' Claudia says, kneeling down at the side of the bath. 'I *have* to get it.' I can see the lines of muscle tension in her face. 'The baby is coming and I must get it out safely.' She sounds eerily calm as she places her left hand on Pip's belly, rubbing her palm over the dome.

I take a step forward, but she swings around so the knife is pointing directly at me. I back off, and her attention returns to Pip.

'I want you to tell me when you're between contractions,' she says in a changed voice, as if

404

she is a midwife and has the situation under control. 'I will have baby out of you in no time.' The knife is still fixed in her right hand, her knuckles white from the grip.

Pip can't speak. She lies on her back in the bath, trying to control the pain that sweeps through her every couple of minutes, consuming her even more than the fear. For a brief moment she stares up at me, imploring me to help her. From behind Claudia, I nod slowly and mouth *It's OK*, hoping she will understand.

Then I hear it, noises coming from the street below. I pray help has arrived. I wait for Claudia to react but she is too preoccupied with feeling along the muscle striations on Pip's abdomen to notice anything. I don't know which way to turn. If I leave her alone and go downstairs, Claudia could sink the blade into Pip in a second. On the other hand, I can't risk any knocking on the door because a sudden threat could have exactly the same result.

'Why don't you wait a moment, Claudia,' I say. 'Take it slowly. There's no rush and you want to get it right, don't you?' It's the only thing I can think of. I'm not trained for this sort of thing. 'Shall we make Pip a nice cup of tea?'

Slowly, Claudia looks up at me. The knife tip is resting on Pip's pale skin. Pip is shaking as another contraction takes hold. I stand in the doorway, praying I have distracted her enough to postpone the ghastly procedure. I could make a lunge for her, grab the knife, wrestle her to the floor and smash her head against the side of the toilet, but if I get it wrong or she overpowers me then it's over.

I hear another noise. It's definitely coming from beyond the front door. There are people outside the house. It must be the police.

Claudia's head whips round.

'How about it? Pip looks as if she could do with a biscuit, too,' I say with a dredged-up laugh trying to cover the noise downstairs.

To my utter disbelief, Claudia is nodding, frowning a little, as if the horror of what she is doing is gradually dawning on her. She stares at her own hands, at the glint of the knife in her right fist, at half-naked Pip lying helpless and wheezing in pain as the contraction finally wanes. She shuffles on her knees and grips the edge of the bath with both hands. The knife knocks against the plastic as she stands up, still frowning, thinking, seeming almost remorseful. 'A cup of tea, yes,' she says, and a wayward smile is set free on her face. She stares into the mirror as if she is gazing into infinity, not at herself. The knife is loose in her hand, dangling down her thigh.

'That's right,' I reply. 'We can talk about your baby.' I glance at Pip who is in a moment of lucidity despite her shaking, despite the froth of spit in the corners of her mouth. 'Come on, Claudia, let's — '

But the sudden banging on the front door changes everything. Claudia loses her moment of sanity, drops heavily to her knees and presses the tightly gripped knife against Pip's skin again. 'You think I'm stupid, that I can't do it, but I've been practising,' she says determinedly. 'I'll get it right this time.' Licking her lips, she tilts her head sideways, studying the area of skin below Pip's navel.

I am braced in the doorway. The banging downstairs is more insistent now, and a paramedic is yelling through the letterbox. But I'm certain Claudia will strike if I go down to open the door. I can only pray the police will batter their way in. As long as I'm up here, there's a chance I can stop her.

'I should have cut this way, see?' Claudia says, drawing a line horizontally across Pip's lower belly with the point of the blade. Pip lets out a little sob and grabs the side of the bath. With one deft movement, Claudia has her head slammed back. I hear the dull crack as her skull connects with the tap. 'There are no shortcuts, you see,' she says, looking up at me with a fistful of Pip's hair, while pressing the knife against her skin.

The line of blood doesn't emerge immediately, but then I see the bead of red seeping out from the surface cut. Claudia concentrates on it, as if it's whetted her appetite to continue. I am in no doubt she will go through with this now so, as the front door smashes open, I finally make my move on Claudia, lunging at her with all my strength.

For a second, I feel nothing.

Then I hear Pip screaming. I hear the roar of the officers as they charge up the stairs. I hear Claudia's grunt as she sinks the knife into my shoulder. I hear my own breathing, rasping in and out, as something slowly registers in my brain; that something is not right.

Then I feel the hands on me, yanking me back so that my head whip-lashes against someone's thigh. I feel a moment of doubt as the officer sizes me up, deciding whether to haul me to my feet and cuff me or rescue me, and I feel the beginnings of pain as the first stab of agony winds its way to my brain.

'Drop your weapon!' the second officer screams. His cheeks are scarlet from effort and spit flies from his mouth. I see the hard lines of muscle in his arms as he gets a grip of Claudia's wrists and virtually ties them in knots behind her back. I see the look of shock and despair sweep across Claudia's face as she realises that she has failed; that it's over.

'I'm bleeding,' I say quietly. I stare at my fingers, not even aware that I had touched the wound on my shoulder. The officer who is restraining me slackens off a little and helps me to my feet. 'It's OK,' I tell him. I automatically reach for my back pocket but the pain in my shoulder prevents me from retrieving my ID. 'I'm a police officer. This woman needs immediate medical help.'

Then I'm shoved aside as the first officer manhandles Claudia out onto the landing. The knife is lying on the bathroom floor, a bead of red on its tip. I leave it exactly where it is while the officers take her into a bedroom.

Meantime, a paramedic and I attend to Pip, helping her out of the bath in a dripping mess of water and blood. Surprisingly, she composes herself and focuses her eyes on mine as the next contraction comes. She grips on to me, wincing and groaning and breathing through it in a controlled way just as she has been taught. Another paramedic comes and between us, amid the chaotic scene going on around us, we get Pip lying on her bed and much more comfortable. The second paramedic grabs her bag, lays out some equipment, and begins a speedy assessment.

'There's no time to get you to hospital, love,' she says. 'I don't think baby will be very long coming.' She stares at the ceiling as her gloved hand confirms the late stage of Pip's labour. The other paramedic takes her blood pressure and attends to the minor wound on her stomach, while I retreat from the bedroom. Pip is in safe hands. A portable ultrasound machine hisses the comforting swishing sound of new life as I go down the stairs clutching my shoulder.

'You need to get that sorted,' the detective in the hallway says.

I freeze on the bottom step. He is glaring at me. His partner is beside him. She frowns at me as I clamp my hand to my wound. Our eyes lock momentarily, each sizing up the other.

'Yes, sir,' I say. This time the fingers of my good hand manage to delve into my pocket and retrieve my ID. Habit forces me to flash it at them. 'Undercover, in case you hadn't already figured that one out,' I say, predominantly for DI Fisher's benefit. She is looking more incredulous than anything else.

Something inside me wants to send out a delirious and inappropriate grin but it just won't form on my face. After this, I doubt I'll be working anywhere ever again. I reckon it was my last chance to make a good impression and I blew it. I'll be sorting files in the basement from now on.

'Adam?' I hear DI Fisher say as I retreat to the living room. I feel dizzy and need to sit down. I swing the door shut behind me. I don't want to hear him telling her or her figuring it out. I just want to sleep, but it seems I am not allowed. Another paramedic is beside me, snipping at my clothing to expose the knife wound on my shoulder.

'Nasty, but you'll live,' he says, sucking in air through gritted teeth.

'No doubt,' I reply. 'Anyway, not all that mess is stab wound. I fell off my bike the other day.'

I hear more screams coming from upstairs, but this time they are different. They are not screams of fear.

The paramedic cleans me up and puts on a dressing. I thank him. We both pause, tilting our ears to the door. I smile. 'Hear that? There are two cries now,' I say, swallowing the lump in my throat. Pip's screams of pain have turned into emotional sobs of joy, while the second cry is much softer, much newer, and only just audible from downstairs.

I imagine the baby snuggling against its mother. I feel utter relief at its safe arrival and wonder if it's a boy or a girl.

I decide not to see Pip now but to wait and visit her in a day or two when she's recovered. Already several neighbours have called round, no doubt alerted by the police cars and ambulance arriving. I see that one of them has had the good sense to fetch Lilly from school. Then, when Clive finally arrives home, anxious, flustered, and desperate to see his wife and new baby, I make a quiet exit. For me, it's the right thing to do. The detectives won't be pleased that I left without making a formal statement, but I need to go home.

It's only when I step out into the street that I realise I have absolutely no idea where home is.

42

When they arrived, the driveway at the end of the cul-de-sac was already cluttered with police cars and an ambulance. Half a dozen neighbours had come outside and were drawing close as if the house was a giant magnet, pulling them towards the drama in the usually quiet street.

'Looks as if we missed all the action,' Adam said, unclicking his seatbelt.

Lorraine yanked on the handbrake and they got out of the car, striding up the drive.

The call had come just after Matt had left, as they were trying to absorb what he'd told them about Grace. Adam had briefed Lorraine on the way with the little information he had so far been given, and they'd spent the speedy journey trying to fit the irregular-shaped pieces of the investigation together. An unfamiliar police officer met them in the doorway and brought them up to date.

'Sir, ma'am, we're not sure if it was a domestic situation yet or what. There's a pregnant woman with minor injuries upstairs. We can't move her, she's in advanced labour.' The officer was panting as if he had just been involved in a scuffle. 'It seems as though one woman went psycho, had a knife, was about to wreak all kinds of mayhem. I'm thinking she was disturbed by a friend or something because there's another female in there who was handling the situation

412

before we arrived. Not taken any statements yet but things are currently under control with no fatalities or serious injuries.'

'Good. Thank you,' Adam said dismissively.

They went into the property and took stock of what was going on. There were far too many people in there for Lorraine's liking. She was at Adam's side when a woman came down the stairs clutching at her shoulder. She stopped on the bottom step.

It was that nanny, Zoe whatever-her-name-was. There was blood on her clothing. Lorraine stared at her, and for a moment, their eyes locked. There was something about her, as if she was carrying a deep pain, and not just from the wound. And then Adam spoke.

'You need to get that sorted,' he said in that ridiculous manner again.

'Yes, sir,' she replied in a voice that was the same yet subtly different to when Lorraine had encountered her before. She was more authoritative now, as if she had shrugged off a false layer. She reached into her pocket and pulled out her police ID. 'Undercover, in case you hadn't already figured that one out.' It was directed mainly at Lorraine, although her glance whipped to Adam. There was a certain getting-one-over tone to her voice.

Lorraine felt a tightening in her throat, looked over at Adam, and read his staunch poker face as a direct response — some kind of subtext perhaps — as if he'd known about Zoe all along, as if they'd shared a secret.

'Adam?' Lorraine said, as Zoe retreated to the

living room. A paramedic followed her in, closing the door behind him. 'What the hell's going on?'

'Your guess is as good as mine,' he said, without looking her in the eye. 'But my first thought is that we've got ourselves another amateur Caesarean.'

'No, Adam. *Her.* That woman. The nanny. You seem to . . . to know her all of a sudden.' If she'd not been married to him for so long, she probably wouldn't have picked up on it. Sometimes she thought she knew him better than he knew himself. 'What undercover work is she doing?'

Adam positioned his hands on his hips, and Lorraine watched his eyes track around the comings and goings in the hallway. 'I have absolutely no idea,' he said unconvincingly.

'But you do know her. I can tell.' Lorraine was certain of this. What she really wanted to know is why he hadn't told her when they'd encountered her before.

Adam shrugged. 'You're right. I do know her.' Then he hurried up the stairs to join the two officers on the landing.

Lorraine waited a moment before following him, and then there was no chance to question her husband further because they were taken into a bedroom where the suspect had been detained. The shock of seeing Claudia Morgan-Brown handcuffed and being led by two officers from the bedroom blew everything else clean out of her mind.

★ ★ ★

414

For all of thirty seconds, Lorraine felt broody. She stared at the tiny mite bundled up in a white blanket and nestled safely in its mother's arms. Its scrunched-up face peered out like a turtle's head poking out of its shell, seeming to sense its mother was close, while its perfect little mouth lifted sideways at the slightest brush of her clothing or finger.

'Boy or girl?' Lorraine asked. She felt like a clumsy intruder in this most personal of moments. Judging by the way he was hovering by the door, she guessed Adam felt the same.

'Another little girl,' the man sitting beside the bed said. 'I'm Clive,' he added shakily. 'I don't know whether to celebrate or what. I get a dozen messages telling me the baby is on the way, then when I get here I find out that my wife has almost been killed. It doesn't make sense.'

'Clive . . . ' the woman said.

Lorraine thought she looked drunk on her new baby. Either that or she was still in shock from the trauma. Lorraine remembered the sweet relief and aftermath of giving birth so well yet, oddly, it was a memory rarely called upon during the chaotic years of bringing up children. She suddenly felt guilty, as if she had discovered a dozen new photograph albums that she'd never bothered to look at.

The woman continued. 'I can't think about that right now, Clive, or I'll lose it for certain. Let's just focus on . . . ' She hesitated, staring down at her baby. 'What will we call her?' she asked with a smile.

'Bloody lucky,' Clive said.

415

Lorraine had been thinking exactly the same thing.

★ ★ ★

She drove home alone. She was exhausted and emotionally drained. Adam had gone with the arresting officers to the station, and as she pulled up outside their house, he phoned with the news. Claudia Morgan-Brown had just confessed to the attacks on Sally-Ann Frith and Carla Davis. She would be formally interviewed tomorrow.

For a few moments, Lorraine sat quite still in the car. The world went on around her — traffic cruising slowly down the road, a mother pushing a pram with a giggling toddler trotting along at her side, a man on a bicycle stopping to talk to his mate, the road sweeper pushing his yellow humming machine — and all this regular activity somehow made her feel safe, perhaps only a grasp away from normal life.

Once the engine was cut, the heated air in the car cooled quickly. She got out and went inside, hating the thought of coming back to an empty house. Stella had been picked up by Kate's mum, and Grace . . .

Oh, Grace, Lorraine thought with a sorrowful clench in her heart.

Gone was the laughter and happy banter of her daughters as she came home weary from a day's work, and lost were the fond jibes from Adam as they good-humouredly bickered their way through the evening in a flurry of hasty meals, catch-up, wine and, finally, exhaustion

416

and sleep. She already missed the chaos of their normal family evenings. Instead, all she had to look forward to now were morose thoughts of how she'd let Grace down, of being a neglectful mother to both her girls, of having lost the love of her life, and, worst of all, of having lost her trust in Adam.

How could things ever be the same again?

She dumped her coat over the banister rail, chucked her keys on the hall table, and headed for the kitchen.

She stopped in the doorway. Grace was sitting at the table. Her school books were spread out in front of her.

Grace looked up slowly. Her eyes were heavy from lack of sleep, sadness, remorse.

'Hello, Mum,' she said.

'Love,' Lorraine replied, stepping forward. 'You're home.' She shouldn't have made the comment, she realised instantly. It sounded way too contrived.

Grace shrugged, fiddling with the page of a chemistry text book. 'Yeah,' was all she managed in reply.

Lorraine dumped her saggy leather handbag onto a kitchen chair. Had Matt finally managed to talk some sense into her or had she come back of her own accord?

'Not that you care,' Grace added, breaking the awkward silence. She shoved a couple of books across the table and leant back in her chair.

Lorraine could now see that she'd definitely been crying. No, not crying, exactly. That implied a mundane, everyday type of sadness that could be blown out into a tissue. This was more than that — a full-on sobbing, an expulsion from deep within her soul. The puffy red eyes and rivers of mascara that reached down to her jaw told a heart-breaking story.

'Of course I bloody care, you silly girl.' Lorraine sat down beside her. 'I've done nothing else since the moment you were born.'

'Then why are you and Dad always arguing? Why can't you just be normal like other parents?'

Lorraine drew breath, wanting to jump in when Grace hesitated, but she bit her tongue.

'Stella and I feel . . . we feel so forgotten and left out. In the evenings, you spend more time talking about bloody work instead of asking how we're feeling. Have you even noticed that Stella got her ear pierced again?'

Lorraine just gave a little shake of her head. It hurt so much.

Grace stood up and went to the kitchen sink. She poured herself a glass of water and spun round to face her mother square on. 'You're so wrapped up in your own world. All you do is work, drink, and snipe at Dad. What's he ever done to you, Mum? Jesus, you never even fucking smile any more. And then when there is a bit of drama, you still manage to carry on as if nothing has happened. I left *home*, I was about to quit *school*, Mum, get *married*, and you didn't even care.' Grace's voice was strained with frustration.

Lorraine felt a welcome release inside as she noticed Grace use the past tense.

'You really think I don't care?' She felt an unstable quiver between her words.

'I don't see how you can. You came round to Matt's house to take me home but you just *left* me there. You never really wanted me back. You were glad I'd gone and — '

'Enough!' Lorraine said, standing up again.

Grace's eyes widened.

'You have absolutely no idea what you're talking about. You and Stella are my life. I would literally lay down mine for you. But I also have a job to do, a very stressful and demanding one.' She took a couple of paces towards Grace, who remained firmly fixed against the sink. A deep breath focused her. 'And you're right about Dad and I having some issues at the moment.'

There. She'd said it. How would she reply if Grace asked what those issues were?

'But nothing compares with your and Stella's happiness. And I'm so very sorry if you feel I've been neglectful of that.' Lorraine came closer and took Grace's hands lightly in hers. 'Do you know how it feels to have one of the people you love most in the world reject you in one swift blow, to have them walk out of your life with barely a backward glance?'

There was a moment when neither of them spoke, and then Grace burst into tears.

'Oh, darling, my sweetheart, come here.' Lorraine tucked her daughter inside her arms and pulled her close. She let her sob onto her shoulder for as long as she needed, rocking gently back and forth until most of the sadness and despair had come out.

419

'I do know, Mum,' Grace said, sniffing and reaching for a tissue. 'I know exactly how that feels. And I did it to you and Dad. I'm so sorry.' Her words were punctuated by hiccups and sniffs.

Lorraine frowned. 'Matt?' she asked, pretending not to know.

Grace nodded and blew her nose. 'He dumped me this afternoon.'

'I'm so sorry to hear that,' Lorraine said. And she genuinely was sorry for Grace that their relationship had ended, although, given time, she reckoned they would be able to remain friends. And Matt had hoped the same, when he'd come round earlier to tell them about it.

'Grace had been falling behind with her schoolwork for a while, Mrs Fisher . . . *Detective*,' he'd added coyly. 'She'd been copying homework off friends and bluffing with teachers for ages. It was getting bad. Our relationship was really distracting for her. She said that . . . well, she said that she hated school and wanted to leave, that there was no point carrying on because she'd got so far behind with everything. I didn't realise that us going out together had put such pressure on her. I don't want to be responsible for ruining her life. I think there's still time for her to catch up.'

'I had no idea,' Lorraine had replied, shocked that she'd not noticed any of this. 'I always thought she was on top of her schoolwork.'

'Well she's not,' Matt had said, shaking his head. 'Then she told me that she wanted to get married and . . . and, oh God.' He covered his

420

face. 'I should have said something sooner but I thought I was doing the right thing. I suppose I was flattered. By going along with her, I thought I was making it better for her. My mum's so easy-going, she doesn't mind who I have to stay at the house, and we didn't exactly tell her about the getting married or leaving school bit.'

'Go on, Matt.' Lorraine had sensed Adam's impatience as he stood behind her.

'It kicked off a couple of weeks ago. Grace announced that she was going to leave school, and if we couldn't live together and get married, then she was going to . . . she was going to, well, run away for good.'

Lorraine had taken a deep breath. 'Matt, you've done exactly the right thing by telling us. Where is she now?'

'At my house. Packing. If you must know, I've just ended our relationship. I told her to go home and go back to school.'

Frantic with worry, Lorraine had left a message on Grace's voicemail, telling her to call immediately, that everything was going to be fine, that they loved her and she must come home.

And here she was now, shaking in her mother's arms, fitting snugly inside the fold of her embrace. At first, Lorraine thought she was crying again, but when she gently tilted her daughter's head back, she saw that Grace was actually laughing.

'What's so funny?'

'You. Us. This.' She wiped her nose again and tossed the tissue into the bin. 'Our family. We're a bunch of freaks, right?' A nasal, snotty laugh again.

'Definitely freaks. Freaking freaks,' Lorraine added.

'The freakiest freaks ever.'

'Who's a freak?'

They both turned. Stella was standing in the kitchen doorway with Adam looming behind her.

'All of us,' Grace told her younger sister, and they both burst out laughing. 'Especially you.'

Lorraine glanced at Adam. His relief came in the form of a warm look above Stella and Grace's heads as the sisters embraced.

Missed you, freak, they heard Stella mumble.

I was hardly gone came Grace's reply.

Adam sidestepped round them and came over to Lorraine. 'What a day,' he said quietly in her ear. The feel of his breath on her neck made her shiver. She felt his leg against hers. It felt better. More *right* somehow. As if she'd only been an inch away from happiness all along.

★   ★   ★

'So that's that then. Grace is home. She's going back to school. Drama over.' Lorraine let out a huge sigh, one she felt she had been holding for most of her life, as she walked into the study.

It was late, and the girls had been in bed for an hour. On the way up, Lorraine had peeked into each of their bedrooms — a habit she used to indulge every night when they were younger. Now, as teens, she daren't invade their privacy even when asleep. But this was different — the *start* of things being different.

'It certainly is,' Adam said, and the look he gave her as he peered up from his computer screen spoke way more than the words actually meant. His face began to form a half smile, but it dropped away as he remembered she was most likely still mad as hell at him.

Lorraine sat down on the wooden chair the other side of the desk. The study was a box room with a sloping ceiling and also doubled as a laundry-sorting room, occasional homework room when the kitchen was too noisy for the girls, and a bedroom with a fold-out futon, where Adam had been sleeping recently.

'Good,' she said, dragging the conversation out. Inside, she still felt the residue of anger and resentment. Her exterior probably just looked worn out. 'I'm just glad we got her back.'

'Me too.' Adam stood and came round to the other side of the desk. He stared down at Lorraine. She felt as if he expected her to rise and mould herself within the curve of his arms, when what she really wanted to do was jerk her knee up hard between his legs.

'I know it was Zoe, or should I say Heather Paige.' She thanked God that her voice held out, crisp and determined. She was going to continue but, to her surprise, Adam was already nodding. It wasn't a particularly vehement action, and it wasn't contrite either. It was just a plain nod indicating that she was correct.

He folded his arms against his body. 'To out her would have had serious repercussions. I knew she was a DC and that she'd done some undercover work. She was working on a fraud case. It was an unfortunate coincidence. Karma biting my arse, I suppose, but I had to keep quiet. What happened at the Christmas party was bad enough, let alone jeopardising both of our careers by blowing her cover.'

'My heart bleeds for you . . . '

'Don't start with the clichés.'

'Clichés, Adam? Your behaviour is the only cliché around here. Do you know how I feel right now, knowing that you shared a secret in my company? I don't expect you to reveal that she was an officer, but telling me that you'd fucked her would have been the decent thing to do.'

Lorraine spotted the nearly full glass of red wine on the desk. 'Do you mind?' she said, reaching for it.

Adam nodded and watched as she gulped half of it down. They were only inches apart, and she let all the emotions rush through her. She was sick of fighting them, sick of *having* them.

'I could kick you out, you know. Tell Grace and Stella what you did.'

Adam nodded. He seemed braced for anything.

'I could go it alone with the girls. We'd be fine.'

For a moment, Lorraine held this situation in her head. She didn't like the feel of it, not if she was honest. Grace and Stella needed their dad, however much of a jerk he had been. She drank more wine. And if she was completely honest, she needed him too.

Adam remained silent.

'Whatever happens between us, there must be no more lies,' she stated. 'I can't take it, and the girls don't deserve it.'

Then, before he could reply, she found herself reaching for his hand. She was desperate to touch him. She noticed how tense he felt, and found herself thinking of everything she loved about him — his passion for sport and fitness, the way he encouraged their daughters to join teams and how he stood pitch-side, cheering them on in all weathers.

The way she'd caught him looking at her over the years, as if she was as integral to his life as his own heartbeat. The way he played music way too loud in the car, and fell asleep in the cinema. The way he bought terrible gifts for her birthday and always wore his baggy grey sweater with the hole under the arm when he had a Sunday off. The way he'd taken up golf last year then promptly given up, or the way he insisted on wearing brightly coloured socks in court.

Ridiculous, tiny things that, when added together, were bigger than life itself.

The way he just was . . . just Adam.

Lorraine shut her eyes. Everything tumbled through her mind, out of control and unbearable yet joyous, beautiful, and innate. The warmth, safety, passion, familiarity, love, worries, hopes and needs of her family flooded her thoughts. She couldn't give up on him. This family had been her life's work.

Putting down her wine, she drew him closer. She would try. She would try her hardest to forget, and every day when she woke up, she would promise to see the man she married, the man she loved and adored, instead of the man Adam had briefly messed with in a fit of bad judgement.

'Stella needs new school shoes,' she whispered against his neck as she brought her face up to his. He felt warm and familiar.

'And the gutters need clearing out,' Adam replied, allowing his hands to slide onto her hips.

'There's nothing for breakfast either,' Lorraine stated as her mouth brushed across to his.

The kiss was unsure and gentle at first, apologetic yet forgiving. Then, through the meeting of their lips, a mash of searching hands and winding limbs, Lorraine thought she heard him mumble something about being sorry, about loving her always, but after that she didn't really recall much else.

43

'It's you again,' he says, glancing up from the pile of work on his desk. The teacher grimaces at me before scowling at the twins. Between them they have made a Lego tower taller than themselves. Noah stands on a small chair beside it, holding the top steady while the whole structure bends in the middle.

'This is the last time you'll see me, I promise.'

At the sound of my voice, the boys both look up. 'Hooray!' Oscar sings out. 'Zoe's here!' Noah jumps off the chair and they both run over to me. The tower comes crashing down.

'Get your lunchboxes, lads. We're going home.' I've already gathered their coats from the hooks outside the after-school club. Both boys are hugging my legs and I have to prise them off in order to get them ready. 'This one is yours, right?' I say to Noah, knowing full well it isn't. He laughs and play-punches me. For some reason, I want to cry.

'Is Mummy home yet?' Noah asks. His hand is hot and slightly sticky as it nestles in mine as we walk along the pavement. To be honest, I don't want to let go.

'No, she's not.' I have absolutely no idea what to say. I never expected to feel this way about them when I took the job. *Get in, get the information, get out.* That was the basic brief. Mess up, and I knew I'd barely have a job any more, let alone anything undercover ever again. As it stands, making tea and shining the boss's shoes would seem like a lucky escape.

'Is Daddy home yet?' Oscar says, echoing his brother. I give his hand a squeeze.

'Stupid,' Noah jibes. He worms his way between Oscar and me, trying to prise Oscar's fingers out of mine. Gently, I ease him back to my other side.

'He's not home either, I'm afraid. But you know what? I don't think it will be long before he returns.'

I've already had a word with my boss and he's contacting the relevant people. I pray they can get in touch with James. Even though the boys were too young to remember last time they lost their mother, I don't think they should have to face this mess without their father.

'Anyone fancy sweets on the way home?' I get the response I was expecting and we stop off at the newsagent on the way back. It takes a good ten minutes for the twins to fill a little paper bag with pink shrimps, raspberry chews and sherbet flying saucers. It takes their mind off what I tell them on the remainder of the walk.

'So has Mummy gone away like Daddy?' Oscar asks when I've finished explaining.

I expect Noah to come back with his usual cutting sibling remark but he remains thoughtful and silent, sucking on a sweet, as we approach the front door.

'Yes. Mummy will be away for a little while. She did something naughty.' I screw up my eyes as I unlock the door and let them in. For me, the rest of the day will be packing up and reporting back. But first, I need to make a phone call.

'But you'll be our mummy now, won't you, Zoe?' Oscar says, as if he's got it all worked out.

I crouch down beside them as they untie their shoelaces and stuff their feet into their slippers. The bags of sweets are scrunched up in their palms as they struggle to take off their coats.

'No, I won't be able to look after you any more.' There's no point in lying to them. 'I'm really sorry. I have liked being your nanny though.' That's the truth. I found myself caring more than I ever thought possible — even getting up in the night to check on them when I heard noises. I hadn't meant to give Oscar nightmares and make him think there was a monster in his room.

I study each boy's face in turn and my heart shrinks a little as their cheeks flush. Oscar bursts into tears.

'Baby,' Noah says meanly, but I know he's feeling the same.

'Am not!'

That's when I know they will be OK. They have each other; they are two halves of a whole. And with that, they dash off to the sitting room and squabble over the remote control.

I know exactly how they feel.

* * *

The jimmied study door is still wide open. Elizabeth's brothers' unwelcome intrusion makes sense now, since I spoke with my boss

429

after leaving Pip's house. I didn't know where else to go so I drove the car here first and then walked straight to the park. I sat on a bench, shell-shocked by the afternoon's events. I dialled the number and told him what had happened. He revealed to me that the Sheehan brothers would have been searching for the same papers as me.

'You did well, Heather,' he said, as if it was never a given I would succeed. I allowed myself to enjoy the praise. 'I know your work was curtailed, but several of the documents you sent through were key. The Jersey fraud squad has a solid case now, thanks to you.'

I'd figured this assignment was my last chance to impress. Cecelia's demands had taken their toll on my career over the years. Fake sick days from me coupled with regular phone calls and crazed visits from her to the station made it almost impossible to do my work properly. She needed looking after and there was no one else to help. Sisters, just like twin brothers, have to stick together. I'd promised Mum that much before she died, leaving the world in her own fit of unreality and delusion eighteen months ago, and I'd whispered the same into Dad's coffin before they shut the lid when I was a teenager. It was just Sissy and me now.

So I was baffled why they picked me for this particular undercover job. The hopeless maverick with a less-than-average track record was hardly top choice for a major fraud assignment. Perhaps I just looked more like a nanny than anyone else in the department.

'Surely you've had experience with kids?' the chief had said after he'd initially briefed me. He was almost telling me I had.

'No,' was my honest reply.

It had all happened very quickly once they decided I was the one. Zoe Harper was created out of nothing by a team dedicated to producing rock-solid backgrounds for undercover cops. As a relative newbie, I'd heard stories of course but never once thought I'd bag anything like this so early in my career.

I spent the next five days with my head buried in reports and fact sheets and discovered that my new CV contained details I didn't even know about the real me. I studied books on childcare, including the Montessori method, and researched all the places I was supposed to have been with my previous families. It was a whirlwind submersion in someone else's life, all to get evidence of an otherwise inaccessible accounting paper trail.

It was, to be honest, just what I needed because Cecelia was driving herself, and me, utterly mad.

'You ride a bicycle, by the way,' they'd told me.

'I do?' I hadn't done that in a long while.

'And you keep in touch with several of your previous charges.' He'd handed me a bunch of letters, all opened and slightly creased, with childlike handwriting on the front, to an address I didn't recognise. 'It's where you lived for a while,' he'd said as I ran my finger over the unfamiliar village name. 'Items such as this will

431

be packed with your general possessions. They will be ready for collection twenty-four hours before you move in. Don't even think of taking anything else with you. Assuming you get the job, that is,' he'd added with a grimace that I took to be threatening. I was right. 'And you'd *better* get the job,' he'd finished. 'The costs if you don't are innumerable. We're working with the Securities Exchange Commission in Washington on this one and don't want to look like a bunch of fools. It's a tiny part of the whole investigation but you're in at ground level and have a chance to help make a bit of history.'

I'd swallowed, listening intently, feeling absolutely terrified.

'Hundreds of trust funds in offshore centres around the world have been stuffed with funds that have, let's say, a less than healthy provenance. Top that with the trusts being illegally managed — enter our Jersey connection — and you've touched the tip of a very large worldwide money-laundering scam.'

He'd gone on to tell me that 228 million dollars had been moved to various offshore accounts around the world from the United States a year ago in the aftermath of a pump-and-dump scam. Following an internet-manufactured frenzy, share prices for Chencorp, a new company boasting an overi-nflated contract with China to supply educational materials, sky-rocketed and left the major shareholders filthy rich.

'The *pump*,' he'd announced.

I didn't really know what he meant and kind of glazed over, just wanting to get on with what I had to do, but then he told me that a share price crash had naturally followed the massive sale of stock — the *dump* — and the genuine investors — 'Your average Joe like me and you' — lost all their money.

I thought about this. I was starting to understand, and I really felt for the 'average Joes' my boss was referring to. Things like that weren't fair, especially when he told me that the perpetrators got off with a non-custodial sentence and a minuscule payback in comparison to what they made.

'The thing is, they're key philanthropic figures, Heather,' he'd said when I grumbled on about capitalists. 'They make regular donations to many major research facilities, medical institutions, the space programme, education — you name it. It's just how the world works. The best we can do is make it as hard as possible for them. And to do that, I need little old you in this house in rainy Birmingham looking after those kids.'

I was up for the challenge.

It turned out the Sheehan brothers were only a very small part of the criminal activity, and without the paperwork I discovered they might have got off on a technicality. My boss assured me that with the evidence I'd provided in the form of letters, printed emails and statements, there was no way they could claim they didn't know the provenance of the money they were laundering on behalf of their clients.

They were bang to rights and would go to trial in the spring.

Elizabeth Sheehan hadn't known anything about her brothers' activities. Her legal work had been at the opposite end of the social spectrum. And having got to know him a little before he'd left, it was a shame that James hadn't come out quite so clean. His involvement with the brothers was now a matter for the Navy after it was discovered he'd conveniently 'inherited' illegal trust funds in Elizabeth's name. There would be a full Naval inquiry and no doubt a dismissal from service.

'If in doubt, photograph everything,' my boss had said, and it stuck in my mind. 'Nearly everything,' he laughed at the end of our phone call. He told me he'd already destroyed the images of the irrelevant social work files I'd taken to be on the safe side. I'd been instructed, over the course of several weeks, to copy everything I could get my hands on, from the contents of filing cabinets to messy papers in the kitchen drawer. I was simply following my brief and, by all accounts, had given them exactly what they needed.

However, I'd never expected to feel so dreadful at the prospect of leaving the household just as Claudia was due to give birth. It felt as if I was well and truly doing the dirty on her. 'We'll feed you a plausible reason to leave,' my boss had told me, but, of course, a reason was never needed.

Right now, I'm feeling stunned, empty, bereft

and certainly very low at the prospect of what I know I have to do.

While the boys are watching television, I make the phone call I have been dreading. They will need a short-notice foster home, and I asked my boss to allow me to deal with this myself. I take a deep breath and make the call to Social Services.

★　★　★

'I'm home,' I sing out tentatively. It feels odd saying it. The flat smells of strawberries and coffee. Cecelia is sunk into the couch with four boxes of the ripe red fruit arranged around her. She grins up at me. It feels as if I've never been away.

'Heather,' she says sweetly, almost convincing me everything's normal. I pray she's having a good day. There are things we need to discuss.

'Sissy,' I say, launching straight in. 'I've been thinking. Things are going to get better around here.' I stand with winter steaming off me. I remove my jacket.

She doesn't react. Rather, she puts the biggest strawberry I've ever seen into her mouth. She looks dreamy and unreal.

Look after your sister, Heather, Mum had said. *She's going to need you for the rest of her life. Promise me you'll take care of her no matter what.*

'Look, I don't know if I nearly lost my job because of you or kept it because of you.' It's the start of what I have to tell her, things that I've just decided on the walk home but that I've been thinking about for ages. 'I want to look after you, Sissy, honestly I do, but things are going to have to change. *You're* going to have to change.' I have her attention. 'I'm a police officer and it's a really tough job. I need your help.'

Her eyes don't divulge whether she's known this all along and just forgotten it, or if it's the shock of the century. Either way, she keeps perfectly still.

'We have to agree on some things.'

Cecelia doesn't have a clue about my undercover work and I don't intend to tell her. She remembers that as a geeky eighteen-year-old I joined the force in a fit of panic. I had no idea what to do with my life. I was the clunky average-achiever at school whereas Cecelia was always the arty, creative and fanciful one. She had to be the centre of attention but, unbeknown to her, I was in the background keeping the bullies at bay. Her own secret security guard. It's always been my job to look after her.

These days, in her more lucid moments, she gets angry and defiant when I shrug and tell her I'm in between jobs, that I've left the force and I work in a bar, that I'm a cleaner or a door-to-door salesman. It explains my erratic hours, my sometimes odd clothing, and it's often loosely the truth depending on the case, but the spoilt side of Sissy still comes thrashing out. She senses when I'm being shifty and she feels threatened. As far as she is concerned, I am alive solely to look after her. And mostly I do.

But in the last year or two, her grasp of reality has loosened and her focus has shifted from obsessing about my work to wanting a baby. The doctor said it might be all the changes of medication she's had. They can't seem to find the right one.

'I've been thinking long and hard about stuff.' I sit down beside her. The sofa groans beneath us. 'About us, Sissy.'

'Strawberry?' she says, holding one out. 'I want to make edible jewellery.' She holds the fruit against my neck.

'For a start, we're going to move into a new flat.' It will be a blessed relief to get out of this tiny place.

Cecelia lowers her hand and stares at the strawberry before licking it. It's as if she hasn't heard me or digested the implications.

'We can have a good old clear-out,' I say. 'Get somewhere better, somewhere with more room for you to make your jewellery.' She's at her best when she's creating. More volatile and unpredictable, certainly, but somehow she seems more alive. I prefer her that way; the way she was meant to be.

Cecelia's got a streak of your mother running through her, Dad told me once. *When we're dead and buried, you'll have your work cut out with that one.* He'd laughed and lit a cigarette, and died a few months later. Responsibility passed down the line. It sometimes seems as if our childhood happened to someone else.

Cecelia laughs and pops the strawberry in her mouth. When she bites, juice dribbles out from between her lips. 'Where will we move to?' she says incredulously. 'We never move.'

'Exactly,' I say. 'So it's about time we did.'

I watch her scan the contents of the flat, mentally packing it all up, making sure I don't chuck out her much-prized clutter.

'I've got a bit of money saved up,' I tell her. 'I can use it as a deposit. And I might be up for a promotion soon.' She barely reacts to my good news, but that's just Sissy. My boss sent me an email telling me to see him next week. He wants me to apply for an internal vacancy.

'We could have a party,' she suggests. 'And a cat. And maybe I could get a little shop again.'

I sigh. I'd better get on with what I really want to say before she overthinks my plan. 'You know those little twin boys I told you about?' I curl my fingers into my palms, hoping she'll take my lead. Cecelia tries to appear disinterested but nods all the same. Apart from anything, I want someone to know the twins' fate so it isn't consigned solely to my thoughts. 'They're going to a foster home.' After that, I don't know what will become of them. It depends on their father's fate. 'And talking of children . . . of babies . . . ' I stumble.

She's not listening to me.

'Cecelia,' I say, taking both her hands in mine. Her heavy eyes try to focus. 'We've got to get one thing straight. You're not going to have a baby. Do you understand me?'

The blank look gives nothing away.

'I know you get these ideas in your head and it all seems exciting and wonderful, but believe me, you're better off concentrating on your designs. Put all your energy into that, will you?'

'I see,' she says flatly. I can see the beginnings of an outburst swelling from her feet up. She jams her knees together and locks her arms in a defiant embrace around her body. Then the deep breath in comes, sucking up the entire room, followed by the flushed cheeks, the clenched jaw and the sharpening of her stare. Followed by nothing. The calm before the storm. I know it so well.

'I'm serious, Sissy. I'm run ragged after what you've put me through. I thought I was doing the right thing by trying to indulge your demands, but it got way out of hand. I was as much to blame as you, to be honest, and I should have said a firm no from the start.'

There. It's out. I was lured into a dark corner of Cecelia's mind and got caught up in the torrent of her desire. There's no way she could look after a baby, despite me believing it could be just what she needed, and there was no way I wanted to be pregnant either. I would have had to give up work and take care of the poor little thing myself. That was never in my life's plan.

'I want to put it all behind us, Sissy, and pretend it never happened. I'm not proud of what I did, but I'll hear no more about babies, right?' I take her by the shoulders and force her to look at me.

'You have no idea how much I want a baby,' she whispers in a voice that throws me. For the first time in ages, Cecelia sounds . . . normal, sincere, as if her thoughts have come from somewhere sane. 'I have *always* wanted a baby.'

'Oh, you poor thing,' I say, and I can't help

but think of Claudia for a moment.

'Ever since I was a little girl, I've had this huge desire to take care of a baby. To love it, to feed it, to keep it warm and watch it grow up.' There's a pause. A still moment of memory. 'I had this doll,' she continues, with tears in her eyes. 'And I prayed it would come to life. I did all kinds of magic to make it real, but it just stayed a cold lump of plastic.'

'Sissy,' I say. 'I had no idea.' To think, we went through an entire childhood without me knowing this.

'Perhaps it was because Mum never really, truly loved us.'

It is the most plausible thing ever to have come out of Cecelia's mouth. 'I . . . I don't know if that's true. I'm sure she loved us in her own way.' In my head there's a woman, existing, interacting, taking care of her children, going through the motions of life; but as for love, I can't say if she truly cared. Perhaps I was too busy watching out for Sissy to notice. As Sissy says, having something to love goes a long way towards filling the void that not being loved leaves behind.

'Anyway, I know you're right,' she continues, sounding less morose now.

'You do?'

'I know I can't have a baby,' she says quietly. 'I'm utterly sad about it, though.' There's a pathetic finality to it, as if her life had always been written up as childless from the moment of her own conception. 'To be honest, I probably wouldn't have been a very good mother,' she adds resignedly. 'And, Heather?' Her face remains disturbingly calm, as if all those years of agony, desire and longing were nothing more than a miscarried dream gone wrong in her unfathomable head.

'Yes, Sissy?' I say. Her hands are warm in mine, slightly sticky from the fruit.

'I'm sorry. Really, I am.'

And then her head is resting on my shoulder, right where it belongs.

Epilogue

RECORD OF INTERVIEW
Person Interviewed: MORGAN-BROWN, Claudia
Place of Interview: Police HQ, WMP, Birmingham
Date of Interview: 28/11/12
Time Commenced: 10:18 **Time Concluded:** 11:14
Duration: 56 minutes (inc. break)
Tape/Image Reference Number: 11/BH4/03561
Interviewing Officer(s): DI 1093 Adam
Scott, DI 2841
Lorraine Fisher
Other Persons Present: DC 8932 P. Ainsley

DI Scott: This interview is being tape-recorded and may be used in evidence if this case is brought to trial. The interview is taking place at Birmingham Police Headquarters and the time is currently eighteen minutes past ten a.m. on the twenty-eighth of November two thousand and twelve. I am Detective Inspector Adam Scott and also present are Detective Inspector Lorraine Fisher and Detective Constable Patrick Ainsley.

We are here to interview you about the offences for which you have been arrested. Can you state your name, please?

CMB: Claudia Morgan-Brown.

DI Scott:	And your date of birth?
CMB:	Fourteenth of April nineteen seventy-two.
DI Scott:	And please will you confirm, for the tape, that there are no other persons present in the room except those already mentioned?
CMB:	Yes, I can confirm that.
DI Scott:	Before we begin, I must remind you that you have the right to free independent legal advice, but you have elected not to have this. This is an ongoing right, and if you change your mind, please let me know and I can stop the interview so you can do this. I will now caution you that you do not have to say anything, but it may harm your defence if you do not mention when questioned something which you later rely on in court. Anything you do say may be used in evidence. At the end of the interview I'll explain to you what happens to the interview tapes.
	Do you know why you've been arrested and brought here today?
CMB:	Yes.
DI Scott:	Please speak loudly for the tape. Did you attack and kill Sally-Ann Frith and her unborn baby on or around the fourteenth of November two thousand and twelve?
CMB:	Yes. But I didn't mean for them to die.
DI Fisher:	Will you explain what you mean by that?

CMB:	After I'd got her baby out, I was going to call an ambulance. I wanted her to be OK. But she put up a fight and made the operation harder. She caused her own death.
DI Fisher:	You believe that it was Sally-Ann's fault she died?
CMB:	Yes.
DI Fisher:	How do you feel about their deaths?
DI Scott:	For the benefit of the tape, Mrs Morgan-Brown has just shrugged.
CMB:	It made things harder. I was running out of time.

Inaudible due to someone exhaling.

DI Scott:	What do you mean by that?
CMB:	A fake pregnancy can't last for ever. I needed a baby by my due date. When it didn't go to plan, I panicked and just left them.
DI Fisher:	Will you tell us why you . . . you wanted to take Sally-Ann's baby?

Long pause.

CMB:	Because all of mine died. Sally-Ann didn't want hers. I wouldn't have done it otherwise. I saw her in the department store. She went crazy, yelling out she didn't want her baby. I'm a social worker, Detective. I know a good mother from a bad one.

444

Another pause.

DI Scott: For the tape, the accused is nodding.

CMB: Look, I tried to help her. She was smashing up the shop and I calmed her down. Afterwards, I followed her home. I was sick with worry about her baby and I felt it my duty to check up on her. Over the next few months, I tracked her to college, to the shops, to her hospital appointments. It was easy to work in around my job. I'm always visiting unfit mothers. I was overjoyed when I saw her growing in size. She'd taken my advice.

DI Fisher: For the tape, Claudia Morgan-Brown is drinking water. She is standing up.

DI Scott: Sit down and continue, please.

CMB: Sally-Ann never knew I was watching her, although I spoke to her in passing a couple of times. Once, when I touched her tummy in the college canteen, she told me she was having a little girl. She didn't recognise me.

DI Fisher coughs.

DI Scott: How did you fake your own pregnancy?

DI Fisher: For the tape, the accused is grinning and shaking her head.

CMB: I'd never have believed it possible. And that's the truth. She told me that unless they see you totally naked, no one will ever know.

445

DI Scott:	Who told you?
CMB:	The woman from the internet who makes the suits. She was right, too. With my medical history, James wasn't allowed to touch me, so that was easy. He works away most of the time.
DI Fisher:	Describe the suit, please.
CMB:	It was made especially for me. It fitted like a glove. I had to go and get measured. She told me she sells quite a few, that some women like to feel pregnant all the time. They enjoy the fuss made of them. But for me, it was actually real. I was finally pregnant and I wasn't going to miscarry. As time went on, I pumped it up with gel like the instructions said. There were weights inside that moved when I did. When the kicks came, they were realistic. You'd never think it, would you?
DI Fisher:	No.
DI Scott:	Did you wear the suit when you murdered Sally-Ann?
CMB:	No. It was cumbersome. I didn't murder her. She died in the operation.
DI Fisher:	Please describe the . . . the operation. Tell us how you did it.
CMB:	I went to Sally-Ann's flat. She seemed rather nervous at first but I talked her into letting me inside. We chatted about babies and stuff. She eventually relaxed.
DI Scott:	Will you remain seated, please? For the

	benefit of the tape, Mrs Morgan-Brown keeps standing up.
CMB:	Sorry. *Inaudible*. It was funny. She told me she was going to have a Caesarean in a few days' time. I'd been lucky.

A pause.

	I told her that I could do the operation for her now. I locked the door to her flat and took the key. I said it would save her having to go to hospital. She thought I was joking at first. It would be easier, I told her, if she got in the bath, but she didn't want to. She told me to leave. I got a kitchen knife from the drawer. I did my best to make it easy for her but all she did was scream. Should I carry on?
DI Scott:	Yes.
CMB:	The thing is, she wouldn't keep still. I was way stronger than her, but not strong enough to hold her down as well as do the procedure. And I didn't want to hurt the baby. She was going to be mine. I had no choice but to knock Sally-Ann out. It was no worse than an anaesthetic.
DI Fisher:	And how did you knock her out?
CMB:	I found a hammer in the cupboard under the sink. She tried to escape again. She was making it really hard.
DI Scott:	What did you do with the hammer?

447

CMB:	I hit her on the head with it.
DI Scott:	Where were you when you hit her with the hammer?
CMB:	In the bathroom. I'd dragged her in there.
DI Scott:	Do you think she was being unreasonable by not wanting you to cut her baby out of her?

A long pause.

CMB:	Yes.
DI Scott:	What happened after you hit her?
CMB:	She fell down. It took two blows.
DI Fisher:	Did you think she was unconscious or dead?
CMB:	Unconscious. I could see her breathing. I had to consider my baby.
DI Scott:	Describe what happened next.
CMB:	May I have more water please?
DI Fisher:	For the tape, DC Ainsley is pouring water. Continue.
CMB:	I got her into the bath. It was hard. She was heavy. I cut her clothes off. Then I cut into her. Have you ever cut human flesh, Detective?
DI Scott:	We'll ask the questions. Please continue.

DI Fisher coughs and clears her throat.

CMB:	It's surprisingly easy. And I had to be mindful of my baby inside. I sang a lullaby, in case she could hear me. I

	made an incision. Going this way.
DI Fisher:	For the tape, Mrs Morgan-Brown is indicating a vertical line from her chest to her lower abdomen.
CMB:	I know it's not technically correct but it was going to make for the biggest opening. Then something awful happened.

A pause.

	She woke up. She was staring at me, half out of it, and then she saw what I was doing. She suddenly went mad and was screaming and thrashing about.
DI Scott:	Did she say anything?
CMB:	She begged me to stop. It was hard to understand her. Then she just made heaving noises. Her womb went into a sort of spasm.
DI Scott:	Could you see the baby?
CMB:	Yes, just about.
DI Scott:	What happened then?
CMB:	I hit her and she passed out again. Then I half pulled out the baby. I tried to cut the cord but it was difficult. Most of it was still inside, deep and buried, and her muscles were really tight . . . as if she didn't want to let go.
DI Fisher:	Was the baby alive?
CMB:	Yes. I felt it moving in my hands. Its legs and bottom came out first. And then I saw it. It was an awful shock.
DI Scott:	Saw what?

A long pause.

CMB: That it was a fucking boy. I was having a girl.

DI Scott: We'll take a short break. Pause the tape.

The tape is stopped for eighteen minutes. PC McMAHON enters the room and DC AINSLEY remains. DIs SCOTT and FISHER exit the room.

DI Scott: The interview with Claudia Morgan-Brown is resuming at ten fifty-eight a.m. The same persons as before are present.

Mrs Morgan-Brown, did you attack Carla Davis with the purpose of removing her baby from her womb?

CMB: Yes I did.

DI Fisher: Why?

CMB: Because she didn't want her baby either.

DI Scott: Did you also knock her out?

CMB: No. She didn't struggle.

DI Fisher: Why not, if she knew you were going to harm her?

CMB: Because I gave her drugs.

DI Fisher: What kind of drugs?

CMB: Ketamine. A large dose. It was easy to get. I deal with people who take drugs all the time, and Carla was always after something. She took it of her own free will.

DI Scott: Then what happened?

CMB:	She was on the sofa. I made her comfortable while the drugs worked. I'd brought a knife with me. This time I would get my baby and I would call an ambulance and Carla would be fine after the operation. But . . .

A long pause.

DI Scott:	For the tape, the suspect has just banged her face on the table three times. She now has blood on her lip.
CMB:	I'd known Carla a long time. I should have realised.
DI Fisher:	What do you mean by that?
CMB:	She'd obviously had lots of boyfriends, not just the one I'd seen hanging around. I never thought . . . when I cut into Carla and first saw the baby girl, my heart sank. She was beautiful and sweet and I wanted nothing more than to have her as my daughter.

A pause.

	But James could never have been her father. The baby wasn't white. I felt utterly despondent and ready to give up.
DI Fisher:	But you didn't give up, did you?
CMB:	No. No, I didn't.
DI Scott:	Was it your intention to remove Pip Pearce's baby from her womb yesterday?

CMB: Not until she called me. She asked for my help, Detective. What was I supposed to do?

A pause. DIs Scott and Fisher confer inaudibly.

DI Scott: So to recap, you're confessing to the murders of Sally-Ann Frith and her unborn baby, the attempted murder of Carla Davis and the murder of her unborn baby, and you were intending to inflict serious bodily harm on Pip Pearce?

A pause.

CMB: Yes.
DI Scott: Have you anything further to add?

CMB sighs heavily.

CMB: Would you like me to tell you about the others?

We do hope that you have enjoyed reading this large print book.

Did you know that all of our titles are available for purchase?

We publish a wide range of high quality large print books including:
Romances, Mysteries, Classics
General Fiction
Non Fiction and Westerns

Special interest titles available in large print are:
The Little Oxford Dictionary
Music Book
Song Book
Hymn Book
Service Book

Also available from us courtesy of Oxford University Press:
Young Readers' Dictionary
(large print edition)
Young Readers' Thesaurus
(large print edition)

For further information or a free brochure, please contact us at:
Ulverscroft Large Print Books Ltd.,
The Green, Bradgate Road, Anstey,
Leicester, LE7 7FU, England.
Tel: (00 44) 0116 236 4325
Fax: (00 44) 0116 234 0205

POPPET

Mo Hayder

The mentally ill patients in Beechway Secure Unit are highly suggestible. A hallucination can spread like a virus. When unexplained power cuts lead to a series of horrifying incidents, fear spreads from the inmates to the staff. Amidst the growing hysteria, AJ, a senior psychiatric nurse, is desperate to protect his charges. Detective Inspector Jack Caffrey is looking for the corpse of a missing woman. He knows all too well how it feels to fail to find a loved one's body. When AJ seek Caffrey's help in investigating the trouble at Beechway, each man must face a bitter truth in his own life — before staring pure evil in the eye . . .